CW00482581

**Central Bedfordshire Libraries**

# Read & Recommend Book

We hope that you enjoy this book from one of the authors who will be appearing at Ampliterary 2023 on Sat 10 June at Parkside Community Hall, Ampthill.

Please pass it on to someone else once you have finished reading it.

For more information about AmpLiterary and to buy tickets: https://bit.ly/3L7v2DZ

Central Bedfordshire Council Libraries proud sponsors of

# THROTTLED

A B MORGAN

This edition produced in Great Britain in 2021

by Hobeck Books Limited, Unit 14, Sugnall Business Centre, Sugnall, Stafford, Staffordshire, ST21 6NF

www.hobeck.net

Copyright © A B Morgan 2021

This book is entirely a work of fiction. The names, characters and incidents portrayed in this novel are the work of the author's imagination. Any resemblance to actual persons (living or dead), events or localities is entirely coincidental.

A B Morgan has asserted her right under the Copyright, Design and Patents Act 1988 to be identified as the author of this work.

All rights reserved. No parts of this book may be used or reproduced by any means, graphic, electronic, or mechanical, including photocopying, recording, taping or by any information storage retrieval system without the written permission of the copyright holder.

A CIP catalogue for this book is available from the British Library.

ISBN 978-1-913-793-31-9 (pbk)

ISBN 978-1-913-793-30-2 (ebook)

Cover design by Jayne Mapp Design

Printed and bound in Great Britain

❀ Created with Vellum

## ARE YOU A THRILLER SEEKER?

Hobeck Books is an independent publisher of crime, thrillers and suspense fiction and we have one aim – to bring you the books you want to read.

For more details about our books, our authors and our plans, plus the chance to download free novellas, sign up for our newsletter at **www.hobeck.net**.

You can also find us on Twitter **@hobeckbooks** or on Facebook **www.facebook.com/hobeckbooks10**.

*To The Bearded Wonder who, after all these years, still has the power to make me laugh, give me confidence, and sing along with me – no matter how naff the tune sometimes.*

# A FATAL FIND

*A*fter banging loudly and ringing the bell, Sarah resorted to shouting through the letter box. 'Scott? Scott, are you in there?' There was still no answer, which wasn't unusual. Neither was the fact that he'd ignored her calls and text messages for the last hour. She hesitated at the door, because although she had a spare key for emergencies, she would never normally let herself into Scott's flat. It was an unwritten rule of their relationship. That would all change once they were living under the same roof, but for now they kept to their agreement to allow for personal space and treat each other's home with respect by knocking and being invited in.

When there was no sign of him inside, it was easy enough to predict where he'd be instead: at the back of the block of flats, in the garage, taping up boxes and labelling them, ready to move in with her as planned.

What Sarah had to say to him was churning over in her head. She'd rehearsed every line, every nuance. As she trotted down the rear stairway and across the car park, she went over it one more time.

'Scott, I want no more arguing about this. I've thought about what you said, and I don't think it's fair to make me choose between you and my own son. You were right about Ryan needing professional help. You were right that he would act on his threats. But, no matter how old he is, I'm his mother and I must do what's in his best interests. You can't move in until he's back on his feet and has a job to go to.'

It was unapologetic, assertive, and wouldn't give Scott time to argue before she'd said what she had to say. His reaction would inevitably be emotionally painful, but this had to be done, she was losing sleep.

Scott's pickup truck was in the parking bay for flat five, confirming her hunch. He was here and, although she couldn't hear any obvious noises coming from within the garage, she was steeling herself for what was ahead. With a determined stare at the partially open roller shutter, jawline set firm, she swore under her breath: 'Don't let the bugger grind you down, Sarah.' Once again it was time to stand up for her son, her only son. The son who had descended into madness in a matter of weeks. This was the worst moment for Scott to make himself unavailable. It was the day she had been dreading, so where was he when she needed him?

She dipped under the doorway and allowed her eyes to adjust. The scream never reached her throat. The rush of adrenalin spiked the moment she spied him slumped on the workshop floor and her strangled words came out in short bursts. 'Scott! Oh my God! What happened?'

At first she thought he'd had a dreadful accident, tripped and knocked himself out. With a motorbike on the hydraulic steel ramp, he'd been working from a low stool, which had been knocked off its legs. So, too, had Scott. To the left of the stool, he sprawled in a widening stain of his own blood, the spiral airline from the compressor caught around one ankle.

Down on her haunches beside him, Sarah held one hand to the jagged wound above and behind his right ear, the other probing in vain for a pulse in his neck. She cast around, seeking to make sense of the scene.

Toppled against a leg of the workbench was a compact fire extinguisher, blood and hair visible on the rim at the base. She grabbed at it and pulled it towards her, then let it drop with a loud clang. Reaching again for Scott's body, feeling the blood viscous on her hands, she knelt next to him, a cold shiver coursing from chest to feet. She fumbled for the phone in her pocket but didn't press a single key to call for help. 'Christ, Ryan… what have you done?' she moaned.

Time seemed to decelerate as she scrabbled to her feet and blundered away from Scott's lifeless form, aiming for the shutter to close it from the inside; to hide the sickening mess, to buy more time. But it was too late. The shadow of a rounded frame appeared in the open doorway as someone heaved up the roller shutter with a rattle. Sarah was beaten to it. Gasping, she stumbled backwards as Colin McIlhenny, Scott's neighbour from flat number six, was revealed.

'Shit! Stay with him, I'm calling an ambulance,' Colin blurted out, his voice faltering. 'Don't move him. His neck might be broken.'

What Colin had seen was Sarah running for the door. How he'd interpreted her actions was entirely different from the truth. He'd most likely assumed she was looking for help until she said, 'It's too late. He's dead.' And followed this up by laughing. Laughing of all things.

The nervous habit of a shy child, she'd never grown out

of the terrible and embarrassing giggle reflex when faced with bad news. If someone told her, through sobs and tears, that their precious pet cat or dog was dead, she would laugh. Lost your job? You could bet your life good old Sarah Holden would find it funny. She'd offended so many friends that way.

Colin's wary eyes never left hers as he replied to his phone. 'Police. A death... Don't rightly know. There's blood everywhere.' He paused briefly to listen to instructions. 'Aye, I do that... his name is Scott Fletcher. The garages at the back of Primrose Court, Bakers Lane, Bosworth Bishops.' His demeanour shifted from unsure towards decidedly uncomfortable when he explained that Sarah was at the scene of the crime with the body of her boyfriend and might need medical attention for shock. 'She looks dreadful,' he said, not making any move to comfort her. 'She's got blood all over her hands.'

At this precise moment Colin was joined by his plump and perky wife Trina. She bobbed up from behind him and clutched his arm when she saw Sarah standing by Scott's body. 'Holy shit,' Trina exclaimed, tilting her head to look up at Colin. 'Is he dead?'

He nodded. 'The police are on the way. They said not to touch anything. That we must all stay right where we are.' There was a move on his part to make his tone of voice reassuring. Whether it was for Trina's benefit or hers, Sarah couldn't say, but being asked to remain "where they were" was most definitely intended for her ears specifically. Plainly, Colin and Trina thought she'd killed Scott, and, what's more, she didn't blame them for thinking that way, especially when another nervous titter escaped her lips, unbidden. With her legs refusing to hold her up, Sarah sank to the floor, holding out her hands out in front of her, staring at them blankly.

'Oh, I say,' said Trina. 'Did she find out about the wife?'

## 2

## NO PLACE LIKE HOME

*R*yan sat on the side of the bed. Even with a visitor present, he wasn't permitted to close the door to his room. He was being watched the whole time: in his bedroom, in the bathroom, everywhere he went. Before Bez had turned up, he had been subjected to blood tests, tasteless food and a string of questions while doctors and the nursing staff on Caister Ward dutifully filled in reams of paperwork. When this was done, he was handed a couple of leaflets explaining his rights under The Mental Health Act and left to fret about his fate. Bez was hiding something from him, Ryan could tell by the way his friend was fiddling with the plastic cup in his sweaty hands.

'So, you're locked up, like?' Bez said, his Bosworth burr making him sound even more of a yokel than he looked.

'Yes, mate. My GP, who I hardly ever see, a posh nob of a psychiatrist and some scrawny-arsed social worker with a weird job title, read me my rights and told me I'm banged up for a month to see how mad I am.'

'And because you twatted one of 'em.'

'That may have had something to do with it,' Ryan conceded.

'It's lucky you—' The look of relief on Bez's face when a male nurse knocked on the open door was unmistakable. Clearly he couldn't wait to get out of this place. Neither could Ryan.

'Sorry to break up the party, lads, but your solicitor is here, Ryan.'

'I didn't know I had one,' he replied.

'Your friend should come back another time. He was lucky I was in a generous mood today.' The imposing staff nurse, who went by the name of Wayne, held the edge of the door and shooed Bez out. 'You can come back any evening after six, visiting finishes at nine. And next time, leave your cigarettes and lighter in your vehicle. Follow the signs and one of the other nurses will let you out.'

Bez turned back and gave Ryan a cock-eyed smile, pulling at the peak of his tatty baseball cap. 'See ya, mate. I'll come back to visit soon. After work, like.'

'Yeah, see you around. I'll be out in the next day or so, as soon as Mum comes to her senses. They can't keep me here; I've got an appointment with Juicy Julie's giant baps. She can't get enough of me.' Ryan tried to keep the panic from his voice by putting on a ballsy front but, from the way his friend reacted, he didn't think Bez had fallen for it. Before turning and slinking away down the shiny corridor in his filthy overalls, Bez glanced at Wayne who was shaking his head, lips pressed tight together.

The truth was that Ryan wouldn't be going home any day soon.

Although he didn't agree, the staff at the unit had assessed him as a high risk of violence to others. It was written on a report Wayne had asked him to sign. 'Look,'

Ryan had said, arguing the point, 'anyone in their right mind would have done what I did. If people don't want to get decked, then they shouldn't have carted me off to the madhouse acting on the lies and sick twisted fantasies of my mother's psychopathic lover.'

Wayne sympathised, but said he couldn't alter the facts. 'You did slot Dr Taylor on the conk – made it bleed all over the shop. It isn't broken. Lucky, I'd say.'

'They should have listened to what I was trying to tell them,' Ryan asserted, curling his lip. 'My mum believes Scott Fletcher's lies and the nutter-police believed her. There are plenty of people who believe me... even Bez, and he's as thick as shit.'

But there was no changing what he had done, how he had behaved and the conclusion to which the doctors had come: Ryan Holden was suffering from a mental illness warranting his admission to hospital for psychiatric assessment. He couldn't get out without help.

'How come I've got a solicitor so soon?' Ryan asked Wayne, who hooked a finger, beckoning for him to follow.

'You must be special,' the nurse said as they marched in step along the ward corridor. 'I've never known anyone else have a visit from their legal rep on the day they were admitted, let alone at this time of the evening. Someone must be keen to help you.'

The hard knot in Ryan's guts eased. His mum had relented, it was the only explanation. There was no way she would be able to live with the guilt of having him sectioned. Maybe she'd finally seen through Scott-the-psycho's lies, he reasoned.

Wayne led him to a stuffy side room, a low table and three chairs the only furniture. 'Mrs. Morris, this is Ryan Holden.' A woman Ryan judged to be of a similar age to his mother stood up to shake his hand. She was tall with broad shoulders, dressed in an anonymous-looking black trouser suit and wore tortoiseshell glasses that made her large green eyes seem even rounder. Her greying light brown hair was swept up into a loose bun held in place by what looked like a plastic clamp that matched the frame of her glasses.

Mrs Morris stared at him for a moment or two and the corners of her mouth twitched with the hint of a smile. Older women often reacted like that when they first met him, their impure thoughts giving them away before they even knew it themselves. Ryan smiled in return, flashing his film-star teeth, allowing the smile to reach his eyes. Women loved his eyes; glacier blue, enhanced by dark lashes, he used them to great effect.

'Pleased to meet you, Ryan. My name is Monica Morris and I've been asked to speak to you on instructions from your grandmother. You can, of course, decide to choose another person or law firm to represent your interests and appeal against your section.'

'Good old Gran, I knew she wouldn't stand for this nonsense. So, tell me my mother is going to get me discharged. She can do that, right?'

Monica directed him to sit and asked Wayne to stay in the room because she had something to say that Ryan potentially wouldn't react well to.

He was sure he knew what was coming. 'I get it. She doesn't want me to live at home anymore. She'll get me off the section if I stop banging on about Scott.' He threw himself into a chair, stretched his arms up and interlocked his fingers behind his head. 'But she'll have to listen to me eventually. The bloke isn't who he says he is. He's a con artist. He's no more Scott Fletcher than I'm Kylie Minogue.'

Ryan straightened his back, releasing his fingers. 'Did she find him?'

Monica Morris adjusted the glasses on her nose, changed her mind, took them off and cleaned the lenses. 'What do you mean?' she asked, and she glanced at Wayne for his reaction and so did Ryan, who saw Wayne shake his head at her just like he'd done to Bez minutes earlier. Ryan's arms fell back into his lap, feeling unaccountably heavy.

'Is Mum still looking for the bastard? Is that why she hasn't shown her face yet?' It was his turn to shake his head. 'She should have found him by now.' When he looked from Monica to Wayne, their faces both wore the same expression of caution. 'What?' he asked, opening his hands wide, inviting an explanation.

Monica sighed loudly. 'Your mother isn't here, Ryan, and she won't be coming.' She held up her hand to stem any interruption from him. 'She's at the police station.'

'Good. Finally.'

'Actually, it isn't good. The police were called to the scene of a serious crime and she's helping them with their inquiries.'

From Ryan's perspective, this was a fine piece of news. After the tension of the day, he let out a whoop, rejoicing in the possibilities, startling his audience. 'You're talking about Scott aren't you? Is Mum okay?'

Mrs Morris's reply was non-committal. 'She's unharmed.'

'*He's* not looking so good though, right? How long until she can get me out of here?'

'Ryan, you may be having some trouble understanding what's going on right now,' Monica said.

And she was right.

## 3

## NOT ON SARAH'S BUCKET LIST

*T*here was a sour smell in the cell, which Sarah imagined was caused by the sweat of fear, and other unspeakable bodily fluids left by drunkards and druggies. The police force had been part of her life. She had been married to it until her husband's death. In spite of his career as a senior ranking officer, she'd never seen the inside of a police cell, other than on the television, and had never expected to. Besides which, being arrested by the police wasn't in her life plan, nor on any bucket list. Not that she had made either such list; it would be tempting fate.

The shock of being arrested and cautioned at the scene hadn't abated and her stomach remained unreliable throughout the ensuing hours in custody. Knees to chin, she hugged herself for what seemed like hours, tasting her own panic, the metallic taint of Scott's blood on her hands even though she had scrubbed them until they were raw. Numbed by the seriousness of her rash decision to take the blame for his death, her mind faltered and stuttered, preventing her from rational thought.

She stretched out and got to her feet. Fierce and contradictory feelings were vying for Sarah's attention as she began to walk back and forth in the police cell, waiting to be questioned formally. Her head was bowed, her chest tight; every now and then a child-like whimper would escape her lips.

At the garages of Primrose Court, she'd told the officers on scene that she'd hated Scott enough to kill him, which wasn't the case. There were plenty of occasions when she'd been annoyed by him, irritated, hurt maybe, but she had never been angry enough to physically attack anyone. And yet she now had to sway the judicial system into believing that she had carried out the most terrible of crimes.

Her breathing quickened and she touched the place at her neck where her St Christopher pendant should have been, somehow she felt more vulnerable without it. Her turbulent thoughts raced on. The police would ask her about Scott, how they'd met, what he was like, why she had assaulted him, why she'd wanted him dead. They would ask because of what she'd told them: 'I did it. I killed him.'

\* \* \*

She cast her mind back to those early days of butterflies and first-date nerves; feelings she'd never thought she would experience again after Jim's death. The memories played like a film in her mind. After years of avoiding relationships out of loyalty and love for the man she'd married, Sarah had fallen for Scott Fletcher within a matter of weeks. On the day of the big first date she was "bricking it", as her son Ryan would say, a bag of nerves. She very nearly backed out. Only her better nature and the cajoling of her friend Carol had prevented her from standing him up. They had agreed to meet at the crazy golf course and arrived in separate cars. Carol had advised her it would be safer that way and had also made sure Sarah took her mobile phone with her.

The date had gone so well that any initial misgivings were quickly eroded, as was her guilt about seeing another man. She told herself that Jim would have understood and actively encouraged her to find happiness and companion-ship. A silver fox, Scott Fletcher was the same age as Jim would have been, had he still been alive, and the two men would have had shared interests.

The final push towards commitment came when her own mother-in-law Maggie Holden told her to let go of the past. 'It will drag you down and make you a miserable widow instead of a merry one,' she had said firmly. When Maggie finally met Scott, the two of them seemed immedi-ately at ease together and all the pieces for a happy new life seemed to be beginning to fit together, apart from one: Ryan. He never took to Scott, which was not an insur-mountable problem. After all, her adult son had his own life to lead. As did Sarah.

The first sign of trouble came with a phone call from Ryan eight weeks before Scott ended up dead on his garage floor. Eight long weeks of escalating tension and looking out for eggshells to avoid.

Scott was helping Sarah to decorate the hall stairs and landing and put the finishing touches to the gloss on the skirting boards. When she ended the call with her son, she sat down on a step with a heavy sigh. 'That was Ryan.' An unnecessary statement, as it was perfectly obvious she'd been talking to her son. She was well within earshot of Scott and the content of the call was not difficult for him to guess at.

'So… he and the long-suffering, if slightly dim, Sienna have parted ways and he wants to come home for a week or two to get over his broken heart. Is that about the size of it?' Scott had said, wiping his paintbrush on a cloth before carefully placing it into a jar of white spirit. 'Does he know this house is going on the market?' He peeled latex gloves from his hands. 'Only I didn't hear you set him a deadline for leaving again.'

The criticism was thinly veiled and well-deserved. Sarah had failed to make specific provisos because she couldn't bring herself to be that heartless. At best she'd been vaguely discouraging. 'I told him ages ago you and I were planning to move in together. He knows I've wanted to downsize ever since he moved in with Sienna.'

Scott raised an eyebrow at her. 'He's not stupid, that boy of yours. I'm sure he'll find somewhere to live soon enough. Nobody his age wants to hang around with a couple of boring old farts like us, now do they?'

'Well, he's been stupid this time,' Sarah said, rubbing at her forehead, feeling the blob of paint she knew was there as it spread under her fingertips. Clumsy and careless were her middle names and she never was the best with decorating, often painting herself as well as the walls. 'You're not going to believe what he's done now.'

'Try me.' Scott tipped his head towards the kitchen. 'Cuppa? I've got a feeling we're going to require one. By the look on your face, I'd say this news isn't going to fit in with our plans for a bright and peaceful future together, is it?'

Sarah couldn't deny it and the tension rose in her. Ryan and Scott had clashed on first meeting, and things hadn't improved since. Although there wasn't any overt animosity between them, she'd soon twigged that they both put on a good act for her benefit. They tolerated each other when in her presence, said all the right things, but it was the looks each gave the other that more accurately reflected their true feelings.

'I suspect there's more to the story than he's telling me,' Sarah said. 'Apparently, Sienna's father is furious.'

'That'll be awkward in the office,' Scott said, pouring boiling water into two mugs. With his back turned to her, Sarah felt somewhat braver than if he'd been looking into her eyes when she spoke.

'He won't have to worry about any embarrassment at the office because Laurence has sacked him. Out, gone, finished, here's what we owe you... goodbye.'

Scott gave a half-laugh. 'No way? You can't sack someone that easily.'

'That's what I told Ryan, but seemingly someone had it in for him. A jealous colleague made up a story that Laurence believed. Ryan said he would explain it when he got here.'

From the way his body stiffened and the veins in his neck stood out, Sarah could tell Scott was barely holding back his irritation. 'I'll make myself scarce then, shall I? Give you two some time together?'

'Look, Scott, I—'

He shook his head, passing her a mug of tea. 'Come on now, Sarah. It's no big deal. I go back on site visits for the next three weeks at least, so he'll have plenty of time and space for job hunting without me being in the way.' Smoothing his silvery hair, Scott threw her a winning smile. 'If we are to have any chance of moving on together, on our own terms, you'll need to stand your ground. You deserve a life of your own. He can't keep running home to Mummy. How many more times will he cock up his privileged life and ask for your help?'

Who was she to argue? Ryan had wanted for nothing. She'd spoilt him, her mother was as bad, and her mother-in-law Maggie was worse.

'Jim would never have wanted his son to be pampered,' Scott continued. 'He'd want him to be a man. Stand up for himself and be independent. Be more like his cousin.' It was gently delivered and well-meaning. Sarah couldn't argue back because Scott was right on all counts and she knew it. She stayed silent.

'Ryan is twenty-seven years old. He had a good job, a roof over his head, a loving relationship – and it sounds like he's screwed it all up. I can't wait to find out how that little lot was blown right out of the water. Although, thinking about it, you might want to call Sienna and find out how bad the situation is in reality. For all you know he might be panicking over nothing.'

Sarah relaxed with the relief of a more palatable explanation for Ryan's sorrowful request to come home. 'It never crossed my mind, but you're right, he and Sienna could have had a nasty spat and fallen out over something trivial. These things happen. Let's see what he has to say before we all get in a tizzy.'

Scott took a sip of steaming coffee and shook his head. 'You know deep down what he's like; anything for an easy life. He'll sob for a day or two, mope about, then pick himself up. You'll feed him, indulge him and so will the grandmothers, and then he'll piss off again. Me? I'm just the man who loves you, who'll be with you forever. Whereas he'll disappear in a cloud of ingratitude when he's found someone else to shag.' Scott exhaled noisily. 'I don't suppose our plans mean that much to him.'

'Now that's not fair,' Sarah said, injecting a firmer tone

into her voice. 'I'll hear him out and then we can have a grown-up discussion.'

Scott scoffed at the very idea and she knew what he was thinking: to do that, Ryan would have to grow up.

And that was where it had started to go horribly wrong.

* * *

*F*reeing herself from thoughts of the past, Sarah touched the cell door, willing her solicitor to come. She felt dreadfully cold and shivery. 'Oh, Jim, what have I done?' she asked, her eyes turned to the ceiling. To heaven.

Exhausted, she lay down on the bare mattress once more and let the tears flow as she curled tighter into a foetal position. 'Jim, can you hear me? Talk to me,' she wailed. Hiding her face as best she could from the camera mounted in the far corner of the room, she sought guidance from her dead husband; the man she'd loved and cherished through richer but never poorer, through sickness and in health, the man who had been her rock until the day he and his motorcycle parted company. Like many accidents, his untimely death could not have been predicted. He wasn't supposed to be on the road that day, he'd volunteered to fill in for the Chief Superintendent and was making his way to headquarters for a meeting and had chosen to travel by motorbike. An accomplished rider, he had years of experience riding motorcycles, it was his passion, but all it had taken was one speeding lorry to end his life. The driver was never found. 'Damn it, Jim. Just answer me for once,' Sarah begged, sobs choking her. 'I need you to tell me what to do.'

During custody processing, a female police officer had produced a tee-shirt and some jogging bottoms to replace the clothes they had taken away for forensic examination; with so much of Scott's blood on her, Sarah made the job easy for them. For her, going through the motions of giving a DNA sample and fingerprints was surreal; something akin to being the subject of a documentary, rather than watching it on a screen while sitting on a sofa making critical comment. And although it passed by as if she were inside a strange unfocussed tunnel, she noticed the furtive glances cast her way by older officers and guessed they knew about Jim. The ignominy only served to worsen her desperation.

The police had the good grace to let her know about Ryan after she'd pleaded with them to check her mobile phone for messages and to call the social worker. The custody sergeant said Ryan was somewhere called the Marsworth Unit. She'd never heard of the place, but then why would she?

The reality of the situation became more stark when she was allowed to call Maggie. 'She's my mother-in law,' Sarah told the custody sergeant. 'She'll know a solicitor.' Maggie Holden was pragmatic and could handle the stress far better than almost any of Sarah's blood relatives.

It never occurred to her to phone her own mother, and she flirted with the idea of calling her brother Chris for less than five seconds. Predicting the reaction of his cow of a wife to hearing of Sarah's predicament put her off alto-gether. She shuddered at the very thought.

Being elderly, Maggie's balance wasn't good, and she used a walking frame most of the time, so when the phone was answered and Sarah realised there were two pieces of shocking news to impart, she made sure her mother-in-law was sitting down. Hearing about Scott's violent death would be bad enough but finding out her beloved and only grandson was sectioned in a psychiatric unit would be worse. It wouldn't take her long to work out that both of those disasters were down to one person, Sarah Holden, the golden daughter-in-law who could do no wrong: until now.

She heard Maggie catch her breath and start to weep. 'Oh, God, I knew this would end badly,' she gasped. 'I'll send my solicitor. Don't say anything until he gets there. His name is Bernard Kershaw.'

'Can you ask him to let Ryan know where I am?'

'You tell him that yourself. He'll take your instructions. You can trust Bernard.' Maggie never once asked her whether she was guilty of the crime, for which Sarah was grateful. Any explanations would be overheard, and with two police officers at her side Sarah couldn't risk incriminating her own son. She didn't want Maggie to ask because that wisest of matriarchs would know she was lying to protect Ryan and it would kill her if she learned what her grandson had done. Two deaths for the price of one.

'I'll make sure Ryan is cared for,' Maggie said, her voice sounding strangely detached.

'Maggie… are you alright?'

'Not really, dear. You are all I have left. You and Ryan. I'll do what I can.'

## 4

## BAGSHOT & LAKER

'Come in, Monica. Good of you to agree to such an early start.' Bernard Kershaw produced a beaming smile, which distracted the eye slightly from the prominence of his ears. 'Make yourself comfortable. Fiona is on her way, bringing breakfast muffins or suchlike with her.' He hung his suit jacket on a coat stand before lowering his ample frame onto an impressive antique chair. Monica took up position on the opposite side of his leather-topped desk.

'What would we all do without Fiona?' Monica said. 'You'd be lost without that woman. She's far more than a secretary.'

'True. But don't tell her I said so.' Bernard dragged a notepad and pen within range and looked up as the brass handle of his office door turned. 'Right on cue, here's Peddyr. Try not to encourage him this time – I know how you two love to spar, but we must get our thinking caps on. This is a rum old do, Monica. Bloody rum indeed. And I'm a little rusty when it comes to serious criminal cases.'

With a well-cut suit hiding his muscular frame, Peddyr

Quirk could easily be mistaken for a partner in the firm of Bagshot & Laker but wasn't. On the other hand, Bernard Kershaw had worked many years for the privilege. Despite his reputation for dogged determination and hard work, he wouldn't have been the successful lawyer he was without the backing of his old friend Peddyr Quirk. 'I see Connie's had the clippers out again,' said Bernard, with a wink to Monica, who grinned at the severe haircut.

The comment was met with a wry smile. 'At least I've still got most of my hair,' Peddyr retorted as the two men shook hands. 'Before I forget, thanks for giving me a free pass this morning. Saved me from another trip to DIY hell. Connie is on full throttle at the moment, redecorating two bedrooms.'

Having met Peddyr's wife Connie several times, Monica could appreciate his need for a calm sanctuary on occasion. As devoted to his wife as he was, she was a whirlwind of brains and vitality; a force of nature who often left Monica feeling exhausted after time spent in her company. 'This better be worth it, Grasshopper,' Peddyr said to her with a smirk. He pronounced this as "glasshopper" in homage to the old 1970s TV series. Monica remembered it well. Grasshopper was the willing acolyte of the Kung Fu Master, so the pet name Peddyr had bestowed on her fitted perfectly. As the recipient of Bernard's mentorship over the preceding six years, she was his Grasshopper.

The law was Monica's second career. She'd crossed over from mental health nursing and retrained, adding a law degree to her list of qualifications. Bright and cheery to boot, she was a real asset to the law firm. She had learnt much from Peddyr Quirk about enquiry work and over time had developed a soft spot for the private investigator often used by Bagshot & Laker.

From observation of him she knew that once you got past the brash exterior and the dry wit, there was a rare creature to be found beneath. A man of integrity, who took pride in getting to the truth of the matter, if occasionally by unconventional means. Peddyr Quirk was a safe pair of hands.

'Pedd, old bean,' Bernard began. 'There's leg work to be done.'

Peddyr pulled out a chair, tugged at the knees of his trousers and sat down adjacent to Monica. He stared directly at Bernard. 'Is there indeed? Then you're out of luck, I'm afraid. Thanks to you, my leg hasn't worked right for well over twelve months, and my donkey's not available either, before you ask.' He leant back and cocked an eyebrow. 'What's the skeet?'

'Yes,' Monica chipped in. 'Any update from the custody suite?' She hoisted her voluminous handbag onto her lap and unzipped it, leafing through the contents to find her smartphone and ensure it was muted.

'In a nutshell, Sarah Holden, a widow of fifty-three, is currently putting herself in the frame for the killing of her boyfriend Scott Fletcher, though as yet the police haven't charged her. I happen to agree with their cautious approach – something here doesn't smell right. So it comes down to their investigation.' Bernard picked up his pen and fiddled with it as he spoke. 'Her story fits neatly, her DNA and prints will be everywhere, she had a motive of sorts and at a push could have carried out the assault in the way she described...'

'But?' Peddyr asked.

Bernard Kershaw chose his words carefully. 'It's as if she is deliberately incriminating herself. She insists she and Fletcher had a blazing row and that she lost control.

However, she is woolly over certain significant facts as to the cause of death; and by that I mean she had no idea that, as well as a head injury and strangulation, an air compressor had been used to lethal effect. The line of questioning was rather too obvious on that point. Then there's the glaring issue of her son.' He pursed his lips for a second. 'Sarah's son Ryan Holden was seen in the vicinity of Primrose Court flats approximately an hour before his mother arrived there. An eyewitness described him as behaving oddly, lurking around the garages.'

Peddyr frowned at his ruddy-faced friend. 'Hold up, we're talking about the widow of Jim Holden, are we?'

'We are. I thought I mentioned that to you on the phone when I called you into action late last night.'

'You didn't. The incident was reported in the news, but no names were mentioned, not even by you. And I didn't know the son was involved in this as well.'

'Do you know the family then?' Monica asked, intrigued by Peddyr's reaction.

'I knew Jim Holden, mostly through a mutual love of motorbikes. I often saw him at the bike club. He helped out sometimes, giving lectures on maintenance now and again. We were never stationed together but our career paths crossed several times. He was killed in a hit and run, fifteen years ago now. The boy must be in his late twenties. Cor, how time flies.' Peddyr rubbed at his forehead, smoothing out a frown. 'Young Ryan, was he a regular lurker at Primrose Court?'

Catching his eye, Monica nodded. 'Quite right, Pedd. We should explain the background to you a little better. Ryan Holden was sectioned under the Mental Health Act at about the time his mother was being arrested by the police. While subject to paranoia, it would be safe to surmise that his behaviour might have appeared suspicious.' She switched her gaze from Peddyr back to Bernard. 'So, if Sarah didn't kill anyone… then you're saying Ryan Holden killed Scott Fletcher? If that is so, then less than sixty minutes after dispatching Fletcher he was visited at home by an approved assessor and two doctors who judged it necessary to admit him to hospital under the Act.' She paused to let this timetable sink in and then addressed Peddyr. 'By the way, Pedd, the assessment didn't go well. Ryan punched the GP on the nose and launched a flying kick at the accompanying police officer who reacted too slowly to prevent the assault in the first place.'

Peddyr looked puzzled. 'I must say, Jim Holden never struck me as a man prone to violence, but it seems his lad has the potential to batter the life out of his new daddy. Interesting.'

Peering at Bernard, Monica asked, 'is this perhaps a classic case of a mother taking the blame for her child's actions?' Giving her own question more thought, she flicked her eyes upwards. 'Blimey, I thought the blood on Ryan's shirt was from the GP. Maybe it wasn't… When I spoke with him last night, Ryan intimated that he was *expecting* his mother to find Scott. Did he mean he was expecting her to find him alive or find him dead?'

'Jeepers, Monica, you've come on in leaps and bounds,' Peddyr chimed in, giving her an approving nod. 'We'll make an investigator out of you yet, Grasshopper.'

'Pedd, if you don't mind,' Bernard huffed impatiently. 'Monica is a Legal Executive and a Mental Health Accredited Practitioner with Bagshot & Laker. As a well-respected law firm in Bosworth Bishops we should be nurturing her career, not encouraging her to go gallivanting around with the likes of you.'

Peddyr shrugged. 'Point taken... Got out of bed the wrong side this morning, did we?'

With a brief sigh, Bernard got underway again. 'Where were we? Oh, yes... Did Ryan expect his mother to find Fletcher dead or alive?' He placed his elbows on the walnut desk and interlinked his fingers. 'Only Ryan can answer that one. And if you allow me to expand on this without interruption, I'll explain,' he said, shooting Peddyr a warning look. Monica pretended to be distracted by the hem of her tunic top but was in fact disguising a smirk.

The solicitor cleared his throat. 'The chronology of events was covered during initial police questioning yesterday evening,' he continued, his mellow tones punctuated by the occasional pause. 'We are told Sarah left the house shortly before eleven o'clock yesterday morning. If he hadn't lost his job and moved back in with her, it would have been a different matter, but it seems she didn't want to be present during Ryan's assessment. The social worker called her to confirm Ryan was at home and to let Sarah know to leave the house. She needed an excuse not to be there.'

This made sense to Monica. No parent undertook such a life-changing step as arranging for their child to be sectioned unless there was a serious problem. 'Not being there at the time can preserve a relationship,' she explained.

'Seems reasonable to me,' Peddyr concurred. He was picking at a fingernail on one hand with the thumbnail of the other. Something he did when concentrating, Monica noticed.

'I understand Sarah Holden and Scott Fletcher argued about Ryan on more than one occasion,' Bernard said, scribbling something onto the pad of paper at his side. 'Fletcher wanted Ryan to move out of the family home, so he could move in permanently and oversee the sale of the property. During police interview, Sarah said she was angry with him for forcing her to choose between them. Before the assessors arrived at the house, she told Ryan she was going to look for Fletcher, to end the relationship.'

'Perhaps she was,' Monica suggested. 'It must have put a heck of a strain on them, bearing in mind what Ryan has been saying about Fletcher.'

'Which is?' Peddyr asked, tilting his head.

'According to Ryan, Scott Fletcher was a devious fraudster out to diddle his mother. There's no proof of that but it is what the lad believes.'

'In which case, I would have thought *Ryan* far more likely to assault him,' Peddyr concluded. 'If anything, he would surely have tried to prevent his mother from facing a screaming argument when she confronted Fletcher. Unless Ryan knew he was already dead.'

'Dead men do no harm,' Bernard said, nodding his agreement. 'He wouldn't stop her going if he knew she was in no peril.' With an unexpected bark he turned on Peddyr. 'And will you stop treating this place like a doss house! Pick your bloody fingernails in your own time, you thoughtless oaf.'

Taken aback, Monica stared aghast at Bernard. His normally unflappable self seemed to have been temporarily replaced by the irritability of a hungry bear emerging from hibernation. 'Woah... steady on,' she said. 'He always does this when he's thinking.'

'I am here, you know,' Peddyr cut in. 'There's no need to talk about me as if I've left the room.'

'That's just where you'll be going if you don't buckle down and pay attention!'

At this jibe from Bernard, Peddyr rose sedately from his

seat and Monica feared what would happen next as he placed his knuckles on the desk, rocked forward and locked eyes with Bernard. She needn't have worried.

'Life is too fucking short to spend it with a woman who despises you. Don't take it out on me, or anyone else who loves you dearly. Divorce Dreary and do it soon. Do I make myself clear?'

"Dreary" wasn't the real name of Bernard's wife, but it did describe her perfectly, bringing Monica up short. Poor old Bernard, she thought. Too old fashioned to bring an end to his unhappy marriage, he suffered the painful pretence of contentment with weary resignation on the whole. However, given his foul mood of late, she guessed that a fulfilling retirement was not to be for Bernard. Perhaps his plan to ease into it, by cherry-picking which clients he would take on, didn't provide enough time away from the humdrum of his domestic situation. It was no wonder he'd accepted this tricky case in preference to spending more empty hours at home.

Subtlety wasn't Peddyr's style but after he'd so precisely identified the source of Bernard's ill temper, he made clear it was out of friendship, and not meant to belittle his respected pal. Taking this on the chin, Bernard apologised, adding a request that Peddyr should refrain from future discussion of private matters in the workplace.

'Fair enough,' he agreed. 'How about we meet in the Queen's Arse when you've finished down the cop shop this evening and have a manly chat?'

'I thought you two were banned from the Queen's Arms,' Monica piped up, giving the pub its correct name.

'Not by the landlord, we're not,' Peddyr said reprovingly.

'If I remember rightly,' Monica countered, 'Connie frowns upon you drinking together on a school night. She tells me your leg injury was a result of a drunken accident involving the two of you, a takeaway curry and a road sign, which you tripped over while trying to walk home with your eyes closed. Bernie landed on top, I gather.'

An unspoken exchange between the two men was confirmation of the accuracy of her statement. 'Why not speak with Connie?' Peddyr suggested to Bernard.

'I agree,' Monica added. 'Seek the wisdom of the organ grinder, not the monkey.'

Head in his hands, Bernard Kershaw groaned loudly as he appeared to battle with exasperation. 'Yes, yes, I'll consider it. Ask Connie if I could call by this evening, legal priorities permitting, there's a good chap. Now can we please move on from my personal life?'

'Did you want her monkey there too or am I not good enough company for you now?' Peddyr asked, his lopsided smile deepening life's creases at his temples.

\* \* \*

*T*he awkwardness of the moment when Bernard Kershaw's professional and private life collided, soon passed and, much to Peddyr's relief, discussions at Bagshot & Laker swiftly returned to the killing of Scott Fletcher. Not being much of an agony aunt, death was a safer subject than emotional drama and besides he owed it to the Holden family to do what he could.

'But if it *wasn't* Ryan who killed him, then why would Sarah lose it and batter the life out of the man she planned to split up with?' Monica stated. 'Rather a drastic step, don't you think? And not a very feminine thing to do. Historically we prefer poisoning our victims.' She referred back to her short but stressful meeting with Ryan Holden the previous evening and agreed with Bernard's concern about Sarah's confession. 'There was no love lost between Ryan Holden and Scott Fletcher, Ryan hated the man, but when I told him about his mother he appeared genuinely shocked. Read into that what you will.'

Each time he was tasked to work with Monica, Peddyr was struck by her ability to assess people's characters without taking them at face value. His wife was gifted in the same way. 'Was he shocked because of the killing? Or the fact that his mother was being interviewed by police under caution?' he asked.

'Good question,' Monica replied, doffing an invisible cap in response.

'Unless Ryan is so deranged he has no recollection of the event,' Bernard chipped in, aiming his thoughts at Monica. 'He is, after all, incarcerated in a mental hospital. What was his condition when you saw him, apart from the odd blood splatter?'

'Unclear,' she replied, absentmindedly fingering a piece of fluff from her trousers. She glanced up. 'There was no real chance to make a proper assessment yesterday, but first impressions were conflicting. Ryan Holden is a handsome young devil, and he knows it. On the outside he's attractive to look at but with an arrogance about him that I didn't take to. There was nothing obviously psychotic in his presentation, but his mood was incongruous, if only briefly. The cocky bugger seemed thrilled at the prospect of his mother assaulting Scott Fletcher. He actually approved.' She screwed up her eyes at the memory.

'Mind you, he soon stopped talking when he discovered his mother wasn't coming to rescue him. Poor sod. I suspect he's been an overindulged, fatherless, only child who can generally persuade his mummy to do whatever he wants.

Anyway, to answer your question more specifically: the working diagnosis detailed in notes from the admitting doctor suggests a delusional misidentification disorder. Young Ryan is adamant that Scott Fletcher is not who he says he is. I mean… was.'

The two men looked at her askance.

'Imposter syndrome,' Monica explained, 'Sometimes known as Capgras Delusion. Very rare, but incredibly hard to treat. That is the working diagnosis he's been labelled with but… let's just say, I'm not persuaded.'

Peddyr was well aware she spoke with authority on the subject.

The phone on Bernard's desk buzzed. 'With any luck this will be Fiona announcing the arrival of breakfast,' he said, picking up the phone. His spare hand moved to his midriff, and he patted the curve of his shirt, flicking at his tie. 'Splendid. Hang on, I'll check.' He looked across at Monica. 'Tea, no sugar?'

'She never forgets. Yes, please.'

While they waited for the door to open and breakfast to be delivered by Bernard's secretary, they mulled over their plans. 'I'll be in touch with custody and speak to whoever I can – see where things stand for Sarah,' Bernard said. 'The clock is ticking, and I fully expect them to haul me back in any minute now to put her through more questioning. Her possible motive and opportunity raise the chances of a charge being brought, even if she didn't commit the crime.'

'While you do that, I'll see how Ryan is holding up,' Monica said. 'And I'll try to complete a thorough assessment. It's only fair. From my time with him yesterday evening, I'm cynical about his working diagnosis; it's too convenient.' She fiddled with an earring. 'What if he's using us? What if he and Sarah conspired to kill Scott Fletcher for some reason?'

Bernard gifted her a tolerant smile. 'You've been around psychopaths too long for your own good, Monica. Stick to the job in hand and be careful what you let on to young Master Holden. Keep your questions relevant to his detention in hospital.'

In reply, Monica shot him a long-suffering look. 'Don't panic, boss. I'll reserve judgement until I've sussed him out. If he's rational, competent and lucid and he divulges anything that puts him in the frame for Scott Fletcher's murder, then I'll be in touch with the SIO. DCI Mshana, is it?'

'No such luck,' Bernard said, rising from his seat as the brass door handle to his office moved with a squeak. He rushed to help open the door. 'Webster,' he said, wagging a finger at Peddyr as Fiona McFarland waddled across the floor and deposited a large tea tray onto his desk. 'No swearing in front of Fiona,' he admonished, seeing the letter F forming on Peddyr's lips.

Obeying without question, Peddyr held himself in check. Nobody wanted to cause offence to Fiona, who was always so fragrant and polite and Scottish. 'I'm working on some new expletives,' he said. 'Marshall, Hannah and kid chaos are coming for Christmas. Hence Connie's mad panic to decorate. I've been told not to swear in the presence of the child. Some bloody hope.'

'I think Mrs Quirk may have a difficult job on her hands,' Fiona said with a teasing lilt. 'You don't seem to have mastered the art as yet.' A smile remained in place on Peddyr's face while Fiona poured the tea and asked about his grandson. 'How old is wee Euan now? It must be his first birthday soon.'

'It was two weeks ago, Fiona. Connie and I made a flying visit to Glasgow for jelly and ice cream. We shall have our hands full come Christmas,' he replied, stretching out for the drink offered to him. 'We hope to have both of our boys home for a plate full of turkey this year. Connie is at warp factor nine even though September has barely begun. Cheers,' he said, raising the cup to his lips.

Only when Fiona had left the office did Monica succumb to a micro rant about DI Webster being in charge of the investigation. 'He's a prize pillock.'

'Very mild by your usual standards, Monica. One mention of the magnificent example of high standard policing that is DI Webster, and you normally turn the air blue. Lost your touch?' Bernard asked.

'Actually, my head is crammed with a fine selection of profanities, thank you very much, Bernie,' Monica replied. 'But in my last review you advised me to reduce my habit of peppering sentences with fruity language. Or words to that effect. And if Pedd needs support to give up swearing, it's only right I try to set an example.'

'She's right though,' Peddyr added. 'The man's a knob.' DI Webster was, in his view, a first-rate arse and a second-rate detective, and the one person from the county force both he and Monica dreaded having to deal with, although for different reasons.

Bernard shook his head in despair at their efforts. 'Pillock is a swearword, as is knob.' He dipped his head, catching Monica's eye over the rim of his teacup. 'There's no fooling me. I think you secretly hold a torch for Duncan Webster.'

'Mr Halitosis? Piss off. And before you have a go at me, piss is not an expletive – it's an excretion.' Monica grinned at Bernard and took a second bite of the cheese muffin in her hand, gracefully acknowledging the round of applause from her boss.

'Like him or not, I have some bad news for you both. DI Webster is acting up for DCI Mshana in her absence and is so far proving to be more unbearable than usual.'

In unison, a number of choice words were muttered by Monica and Peddyr whose humour evaporated at the thought of what Sarah Holden might be facing.

'If Acting DCI Webster is as slapdash as we suspect he might be,' Bernard continued, 'then Sarah Holden could find herself charged with murder.'

'And if she didn't do it,' Monica parried, 'her son could be off to a secure unit on a Home Office Order before you can say blunt-force trauma.'

Bernard rattled his cup back into its saucer. He couldn't tolerate use of mugs. *Fine bone china was invented to pay respect to the tea*, he would say if anyone questioned him. *And little fingers come into their own. It's what they were designed for.*

Rushing, Monica brushed the front of her blouse and stood as if to leave. 'Thanks, Bernie. I'll get what I can from Ryan about his movements and about Scott Fletcher, if it can be relied upon. Peddyr can come with. I'll see you at the Marsworth Unit, Pedd. Meet me in reception. Time is pressing.'

'What am I? Your lackey? Try asking nicely and I might consider it.'

'If you want to get into a psychiatric unit to question a possible suspect you need a good reason to be there, Pedd. You are not my lackey, but you will have to bluff your way through by pretending to be a mature trainee solicitor.'

Oh, how the tables turn, thought Peddyr, smiling inwardly at the chance of a direct insight into Ryan Holden's state of mind. Secretly, he was delighted by the prospect. 'How much do we know about the victim from the interviews yesterday evening?' he asked of Bernard.

The solicitor shook his head vigorously. 'Not nearly enough, which is why we need to carry out a thorough investigation of our own.'

Making her way to the door, bag tucked under her arm, Monica halted. 'And who, pray, will be paying the fee for you and your costly investigator?' She threw a smile at Peddyr who answered for Bernard.

'The same person who instructed Bernie. Sarah Holden's mother-in-law, and she's a very wealthy lady. Physically frail but as sharp as a tack up top.' He tapped a forefinger to his temple. 'Remember, her son and I were in the same line of work and she'll want this case to have a proper conclusion. They never did find the vehicle that knocked Jim Holden from his motorbike.'

## 5

## LIMBO

*T*here was no way of knowing what the precise time was, but morning announced itself with a grey light and pigeons debating among themselves. Sarah sat up on the mattress and threw back the blanket from her legs. The borrowed clothing was functional and made for a sorry sight as did she, with hair bedraggled, skin ashen, dried dribble on one cheek, and salt from tears at the outside corner of each eye. Everything was so degrading. Sitting on the mattress in a lonely cell, Sarah listened to the sounds around her, gathering herself to use the toilet again. The security camera in the ceiling made it hard to be reassured of any privacy and dignity. 'But as a suspected killer I don't deserve any, do I, Jim?' she said aloud.

She was no killer, she knew that, but the question at the front of her mind was about Ryan. Was he so deluded he could despatch Scott, not in cold but in hot blood? Hot, thick, suspicious, paranoid blood? Coming to terms with being the mother of a killer was almost worse than admitting to a crime she hadn't carried out. Shamefully, she would soon be exposed as the mother who should have acted sooner to get help for her son. Caught in a personal hell, it felt as if she were trapped between a raging forest fire and a bottomless canyon. There was to be no happy ending for her.

As far as she was concerned, it was imperative the police believed she had killed Scott in a momentary aberration, a flash of rage and loss of control. If they didn't buy the story, then they would immediately realise who had actually carried out the killing and she would lose her son to the prison system, or worse, to suicide. These were the thoughts hammering around in her head, the fears and terrors of a mother for her son.

Ryan was in the best place to get help, she told herself. At least being sectioned in hospital would keep him safe. The police couldn't question him until the doctors said so.

Sarah's thoughts about her son were hard to formulate, partly because of the unrelenting stress of her situation but also due to the pressure on her bladder. With little choice other than to brave the metal toilet in the corner or wet herself, she went for it. In the corner of the cell she pulled down the baggy joggers and her knickers; the ones that didn't match her bra, the ones she'd been wearing for nearly a whole day and night. She prayed Bernard Kershaw would soon secure her release on bail. The likelihood of remand prison filled her with a deep dread, but ultimately she was prepared to accept her fate. Make the maternal sacrifice.

During questioning by detectives the day before, Sarah had used every ounce of energy she had to make her story sound plausible. There wasn't much fabrication involved, apart from the description of the assault on Scott.

'A quick recap for the benefit of clarity,' the detective in charge had said, leaning back in his seat and unravelling an antacid tablet from a small pack before popping it into his mouth. He crunched at the tablet for a few agonising moments. 'At 09.52 you receive a text from Scott Fletcher which says, and I quote, "Has he gone yet?" To which you take great offence. Believing that he's referring to your son, infuriated at his disregard for Ryan's mental illness, you decide to confront Mr Fletcher.'

'That's correct,' Sarah stated, trying not to look up and left. She'd read somewhere that's what you do if you're telling a lie. Or was it up and right? She stared at the detective's shirt collar instead of his eyes because she'd also read that keeping direct eye contact for too long was a sign of deliberate deceit or in some cases lust, although that was the last thing on her mind currently.

Bernard Kershaw, Maggie's trusted solicitor, met her before the first interview. A man in his late fifties, perhaps early sixties, she estimated. He looked well fed and watered, and was blessed with enormous ears and a kindly disposition. "Public school background", "topflight university", "illustrious career" were some of the reassurances given to her by Maggie when describing Mr Kershaw. He certainly had a plum wedged in his mouth and wore an expensive suit and tie, she noticed. But Sarah wasn't put off by these indications of his establishment credentials and, in spite of the conflicts and panic in her head, she warmed to him. Unfortunately, this only added to her shame at having to lie. Most of what he said reached her in a jumble of words and, although she wanted to understand, she couldn't concentrate. Nothing was going into her brain and staying there. Giving in to her inadequacies, she could only drift with the flow.

'Answer the questions put to you, as you see fit. Keep to the facts, don't embellish. I'll deal with any points of law and ensure you are interviewed in line with PACE,' her solicitor instructed her.

Sarah stared at him blankly. Although she knew this stood for the Police and Criminal Evidence Act, and she knew there was a time limit to how long the police could hold her for before they were required to charge or release her, she was a blank when it came to the finer details. She didn't have the presence of mind to ask for clarification.

After years of reassuring bemused clients, Bernard Kershaw picked up on her ignorance. 'The Police and Criminal Evidence Act is a huge piece of legislation. Let me worry about that,' he said. 'You listen carefully, and if you're not sure of anything, ask me. The reply "no comment" should be avoided unless there is absolutely no alternative.'

During the interview, Sarah didn't want her statement to appear too glib but stuck to the facts where they applied and fudged the rest. Acting DCI Webster helped her along.

'With no reply when you visit the flat where Scott Fletcher resides, you go to the garages where you find Mr Fletcher working on his motorbike. You approached Mr Fletcher from behind.'

'Yes.'

'And you say you were so incensed by the words in his text in reference to your son, that you picked up a nearby fire extinguisher and swung it forcefully at Mr Fletcher's head?'

'That's right.'

'And he didn't hear you approach?'

'No, he was putting air in the tyres. It was noisy.' So convincing was this statement, Sarah almost believed her own words until Detective Duncan Webster asked at what point she'd turned off the compressor. This was a stumbling block. The compressor wasn't running when she found

Scott, so she guessed Ryan had turned it off before leaving, which meant his prints could be on the extinguisher and the switch.

'Did you turn off the compressor at the wall or at the switch on the compressor itself?' the detective asked, not waiting for a reply to his last question.

'Er, I don't remember. It was all such a blur once I realised what a terrible thing I'd done.' Pressing her hands to her cheeks, Sarah gasped and let out a sob. 'I can't believe what's happened,' she added, and really meant it.

She could only hope Ryan had worn gloves. Would he have had the presence of mind to take some with him? There would be no need for him to wear any in the recent mild weather, so unless he'd taken latex ones from the kitchen first aid kit he was unlikely to have had a pair on him. She had seen him come striding up the driveway on his return home that fateful morning but had already spent so long panicking about where he was and when he'd be home, that she wasn't focussing on anything else. The mental health team was due, and he'd gone out some time before half-past nine. She had become so wound up about the doctors and social workers who would soon be arriving that her memory wouldn't let her be certain whether her son had taken his bicycle or if he had left the house on foot.

'So you can't be sure,' the female detective asked as if it were a statement. Her name was Helen Forstall, a detective sergeant, and Sarah became unsettled by the negative way she phrased the question. 'Did you plan to have a discussion with Mr Fletcher or was it your intention at that time to kill him?'

'I wasn't thinking straight. I was angry… vengeful.'

The female detective looked steadily at Sarah. 'Can you say whether you planned to kill him or not?'

'No, I didn't want to kill him, it just happened.' A large crater seemed to open up and yawn in front of Sarah as she spoke. Murder required forethought. She would be charged with murder, she realised, if she confessed to any plan to kill Scott. Manslaughter was vastly preferable to that. It was quite a shock to acknowledge the enormity of the hole she was in. Such a shock that it resulted in laughter. Inappropriate, nervous laughter.

The claustrophobic room was filled with the sounds of her incongruous mirth and it was some time before the two police detectives, eyes wide, glanced at each other and tried to restore some order to the interview .

Composing herself with a gentle cough, DS Forstall asked, 'What can you tell us about the morning leading up to the assault on Mr Fletcher?'

Once she had gone through the events of the morning, not mentioning the hour Ryan had gone missing, Sarah answered a few generalised questions about her relationship with Scott. After which she was returned to the cell.

Bernard Kershaw explained how preliminary inquiries were often undertaken to gather the basics, and that a wider investigation team would be extremely busy working overnight to pull together evidence. In serious cases, if they needed more time to question a suspect, an extension was sought. 'All part of the provisions under PACE,' he told her. 'With a serious crime such as this, you could be held for a total of ninety-six hours but I'm hopeful it won't come to that.'

\* \* \*

*T*he tone of Mr Kershaw's voice had been warning enough. The police would soon be asking her more questions, trying to catch her out like they had about the compressor. If Sarah was going to pull this off, she realised she had to be better at predicting what questions would be asked. 'Any more slip-ups, Jim, and they'll know I'm not guilty.'

Sarah's thoughts turned back to her arrest. Colin and Trina, Scott's neighbours, thought she'd whacked Scott and killed him, she could tell by the way they'd looked at her while they all waited for the police to arrive. This had her wondering about how Jim would have viewed the scene. 'The detectives would have spoken to them too, and no doubt Trina will be revelling in the notoriety,' she said, sharing with her husband's ghost what she thought he ought to know.

Through no fault of their own, Colin and Trina were not gifted with a high level of intellect, and Sarah could easily imagine how excitable Trina would become when she babbled about what had happened, to all her friends and neighbours. *Do you know, Jim, you could be right. Their lack of knowledge may help my cause.* She smiled, a weak and pitiful expression. Her dead husband hadn't really spoken to her. These were her own thoughts, and it was actually a blessed relief when Jim failed to answer her appeals to him. If he did ever strike up a full-blown conversation with her, she knew she would willingly cave in to the madness, because just to hear his voice would bring her untold comfort. She wanted to believe that although he was out of reach, he had heard her all the same and was here with her.

'Come on, God,' she pleaded. 'I know you have him. Please let him come to the phone. I need to speak to my

Jim.' She sighed forcefully. 'Bonkers it may be to talk aloud to God and a man long since dead, but give me a break, one of you.' In a state of anguish and fearsome uncertainty, it soothed her to challenge the great unknown. It proved she hadn't submitted entirely to fate.

Lying once more on the discoloured blue mattress in her cell, she visualised the headline: *Sarah Holden, mild-mannered property manager at Craven & Tilbury, murders her lover. Police are baffled.* Thanks to Trina's loose tongue and the local news reporters, who'd appeared out of bushes shortly before the police arrested Sarah, the gossip would be all over Bosworth Bishops and beyond by now. The pubs would be buzzing with the scandal of the copper's widow who turned on her lover. The next thing, people would be asking if she'd sent her own son round the twist.

Whatever was happening outside the walls of the police station that morning was well beyond her control. The only thing Sarah could do was to stick to her story. Mentally she prepared herself. Before too long her solicitor would be back and the questioning by detectives would begin again.

## 6

## RYAN'S NEW REALITY

*R*emaining for any length of time in Marsworth Psychiatric Unit wasn't going to be easy for Ryan. His room was minimal in both size and content, like a stripped down version of an economy Travelodge pod. The building itself was single-story and Ryan's window over-looked a courtyard surrounded by other parts of the hospital unit, giving a panoramic view of more windows, brick walls and two sets of double doors.

After spending a while staring at the bare walls, doing sit ups, press ups and then reading the information leaflets about his detention, the boxy bedroom became decidedly oppressive. With no distractions to occupy him in the long hours of his first night, Ryan braved wandering the corri-dors of Caister Ward, keeping away from the other patients. They creeped him out.

The communal rooms gave no privacy to those within. Surrounded by toughened glass, the patients were on full view, being constantly observed, as was he. There was a television in the dayroom, which was empty save for one sleeping occupant who, curled into a chair, was snoring loudly. Everyone else was queuing for night-time medication; their daily dose of sleeping pills.

Under surveillance from the healthcare assistant assigned to keep him within view, Ryan entered the dayroom quietly and sat in front of the TV screen, gazing in wide-eyed disbelief at the headlines on a local news programme. A woman's arrest was being announced and given the location of the crime scene and the glimpses of the neighbours being interviewed by the press, it was obvious that the wanker Scott Fletcher was dead, which was a good thing. He deserved to die. He was the reason Ryan was locked up in the loony-bin. He was the reason his mother had been pushed to the edge.

One problem: from what he could gather, she was the most likely person to have killed Psycho Scott, which would explain why she had been notable by her absence. It would also account for the strange facial expressions he'd observed on the nurses whenever he referred to his mother. The thought of what she might have done made Ryan feel sick to his stomach. Without her he would be stuck in the nuthouse for the foreseeable. Without his mother to undo what she'd done, he would have to rely on Mrs Monica Morris whom he'd only just met. His grandmother would have to step in. She could pay someone to get him out. He had to get out. There was nothing wrong with him.

There was one other chance of proving his sanity; if the police did their jobs properly they'd soon find out that "Scott Fletcher" didn't really exist, Ryan thought. He had tried his hardest to get his mother to believe him, but she had fallen for the lies her boyfriend told her. Over and over again. However, once he had been shown as the imposter he was, Ryan knew they would have to let him go. He wasn't mad, he was right.

The nurse in the corridor gave Ryan a quizzical look when he sang out, 'Would the real Scott Fletcher please stand up?' He allowed a mocking smile to form as he made his way back to his room. He'd seen all he needed. Whatever his mother had done, it wouldn't be long before he could prove his sanity and leave this place.

*  *  *

*W*hen he was woken the next morning by the sound of guttural screaming coming from a nearby room, a terrifying new reality slapped Ryan in the face. Locked up in one of the strangest places he'd ever spent the night, he fought to stay in control of his breathing as the nightmare continued. The recollection of doors banging at all hours, not loudly, just noisily enough to make him jump, seeped into his conscious mind. What with that, the shock of his mother killing a man, the sound of shoes on polished floors, and the guard outside his door, he'd barely slept for more than a couple of hours. The fog clouding his ability to think refused to lift.

He hauled himself out of the narrow bed – one with a bedwetter's mattress on it barely covered by a thin sheet and inadequate duvet – and followed directions to the dining room only to find that breakfast was horrendous. The food was tasteless crap and the whole experience of meeting the mindless patients brought him up sharp. He looked in their faces to see not one glimmer of friendly recognition for a newcomer. Broken blokes with no hope were what he was confronted with, and as a result breakfast was shovelled down his neck as fast as he could manage without choking.

'Can I have my phone back?' he asked one of the staff. 'Need to speak to my solicitor, I have to get out of here.' That was the first of a series of questions and all the answers he received were wrong. No, he couldn't have his phone. No, he couldn't go out. No, he couldn't call his solicitor, she was coming later. He would have to wait.

Even when the answer was yes, it was still wrong. Yes, he had to take the medication if he didn't want to end up being forced into taking it. Yes, he had to speak to another bloody doctor. Yes, he really was sectioned. Yes, someone could bring clothes and toiletries in for him, but he would have to wait.

Wait, they said. Wait for the doctor. Wait for Bez to visit. Wait for permission to use his phone which had no charger. Wait, to find out what happened to his mum. Wait to find out what she did to Psycho Scott. Wait for Mrs Monica Morris.

According to a lady calling herself a Mental Health Act administrator, Ryan had agreed to representation from Mrs Morris and to a further meeting this morning. News to him, but he wasn't complaining. When he found out his mother wasn't coming to the unit and wasn't getting him off his section, he'd switched off from what Mrs Morris was saying. Now he needed her to tell him his options.

After breakfast, his volcanic eruption was one to be proud of, even though he said it himself. The rest of the inmates may have lacked spark and decent personal hygiene standards, but when Ryan was handed a towel and some cheapskate hotel freebies in the shape of shower gel, he lost it. 'Look, mate, this is nice of you but where's the deodorant? And how the fuck am I supposed to have a shave without a razor?'

Lack of clean clothes was yet another source of frustration. 'No, I don't have anyone bringing me in my necessities, as you call them, because you lot won't let me use my phone! My mum can't visit because she's in the nick for killing a psycho. I told everyone he was a fucking phoney but only Bez and Dexter listened, and I can't talk to them now because you knobsters won't let me!' At this point he lobbed the shower gel at a male nurse – a wiry man by the name of Joran who was joined by several other "nurse blokes" as Ryan referred to them, and a female nurse he thought looked like a bloke. With no preamble he was bundled into his room for a stern talking to. After that he had been left to cool off and persuaded to "dial it back" before he ended up on a dose of something zombifying. He was still sulking when Mrs Morris appeared.

## 7

# THE INSIDE STORY

*M*ost hospitals have a similar odour, a set of expected norms such as bustling corridors with trolleys being wheeled up and down them, and a reverential level of noise. There is the same sense of anxiety when you step through any door into an A&E department, and uncertainty as you navigate through labyrinthine passages to find a particular clinic where clusters of patients wait in anticipation of being called. A psychiatric unit has its own undeniable air of tension too, but for very different reasons.

Peddyr wasn't experiencing a mental health unit for the first time in his life but he'd never been to this particular one and even with Monica by his side he found it disconcerting. He had no authority here, he was a visitor, a passive on-looker. Braced for action, he prepared to check exits, clock CCTV cameras, and scan faces to pick up on the fragile peace maintained by staff trained to expect agitation, hostility and aggression from patients.

'Caister Ward today, Ruby. We are here to see Ryan

Holden. We're expected.' Monica smiled broadly in greeting at the West Indian lady barricaded behind a Perspex screen at the main reception desk. She was required to sign them in and seemed to know Monica quite well. She scanned Peddyr, batting long false lashes.

'He's a bit old for a learner, isn't he?' Ruby might have looked West Indian, but she certainly didn't sound it. Her accent was one more commonly found in Basildon, not Bosworth Bishops. Her comment about his age amused Peddyr but discretion being the better part of valour, he avoided a verbal reply. Instead he played it safe with a brief grin of acknowledgement.

'The Mental Health Act department have been asked to make the patient notes available for scrutiny,' Monica informed him as they trotted up a short flight of stairs and waited to be let through a system of locked doors. Standing side by side as they waited to be let through, she was straight faced and sombre, in confident work mode.

'They have a whole department for one act of parliament?' he questioned.

Her whispered aside was barbed. 'Jesus, Pedd. A trainee solicitor would have some idea how the system works. Try to keep stupid questions to a minimum, there's a good chap. Best you confine yourself to making notes and watching carefully.'

\* \* \*

*I*n the unfamiliar surroundings Peddyr continued to be on alert and yet Monica seemed entirely at home. 'I used to be a staff nurse on an acute ward years ago. It wasn't anything like this. We weren't allowed to lock the doors in those days, only secure units had that privilege.'

Having read through the case notes and perused the section paperwork, they followed a staff member down a glossy corridor, shoes squeaking on the vinyl flooring. The feedback on Ryan Holden wasn't encouraging. He'd had an agitated night and reacted badly to seeing the late headline news on the ward television. 'It plays to itself most of the time,' the staff nurse told them. 'He just happened to be passing by the dayroom.'

'How did he take it?' Peddyr asked, pleased to have chance to employ his own skills.

'Remarkably well. He seemed more upset when he realised that Mummy wouldn't be coming to get him out of here anytime soon. Ryan is all bluff. He puts on a brave front and tries to act like he's one of the lads, but he's just a scared young man hiding his expensive education by swearing and dropping his aitches. He spoke properly enough this morning when he went off on one about not having any fresh clothes and no wash kit.' He slowed as they approached Ryan's room.

Through the gap in the open door, Peddyr could see a muscular young man sprawled across an unmade bed, wearing jeans but no shirt.

Monica was straight to it. Her voice floated down the corridor as she approached. 'Morning, Ryan. Find yourself a shirt and let's go for a chat somewhere more amenable. We have use of a private room.'

Ryan sat upright and a flash of a pitying smile hinted at his opinion of Monica. Muscular with a strong jaw, Ryan Holden had a shock of wavy chestnut hair tied back in a ponytail, but his striking ice-blue eyes and strong jawline reminded Peddyr of the lad's father. Jim Holden was a man he had met with several times in the course of his latter career in the police service and was someone he chatted to on occasion at the motorbike club. In all that time it never struck him as particularly unusual that he and Jim had lived in the same town, both worked in law enforcement but never bonded as real friends; they mixed in different company outside of the job and had contrasting characters. Jim had come across as a nice enough bloke when they did meet, but too serious, too straight. Chief Superintendent material through and through.

Staring at Ryan Holden, it saddened Peddyr to recall the events surrounding Jim's tragic death. As part of the investigation into the incident, Peddyr had been asked for his opinion of Superintendent Holden's motorcycle riding abilities and professionalism, as if it were some sort of reference. The official line was that Jim had been on his way to an important strategy meeting at HQ because this was what his wife told everyone. There was such a meeting, but Jim had not been expected. He was not on the list of attendees invited to that meeting. Taking this into consideration, Peddyr argued that if Jim Holden had intended to represent the Chief Super, he would not have chosen to travel there on a motorcycle because he would have been expected to wear full uniform. With his protests ignored, his services were suddenly no longer required, and he was not called as a witness when an internal enquiry followed.

The whisper from the investigation team was that the vehicle responsible hadn't attempted to brake, there were no skid marks. Several people in the street at the time mentioned a white van, but the country was full of them zooming about making deliveries, so it wasn't exactly helpful information. With no reliable witnesses and only a few flakes of white paint to go on, the inquiry petered out and the case was never solved. To Peddyr, the whole investigation stank of carpet sweepings and fish. It wasn't what a loyal officer deserved, and he said so to the top brass.

His protests were quashed, and he was sternly reprimanded.

The funeral was a dignified affair which Peddyr attended along with dozens of other retired and serving officers to pay his respects. Sitting in on the coroner's inquest, some months later, he had the unpleasant experience of witnessing Sarah Holden as she sat bereft on hearing the details of her husband's death. The verdict brought with it no peace of mind. Nobody was ever found to take the blame for Jim's death. Verdict: Open. And for as long it remained that way, there was never any closure for the family or for Peddyr.

He had seen Sarah in town over the ensuing years. He recognised her but she wouldn't have known who he was. What a pickle the family were in now, he realised. Sarah was in a police cell; her son was sectioned and, from the looks of it, one of them had killed a man.

'This is Peddyr. He's a trainee solicitor,' Monica said to Ryan, forcing Peddyr out of his reverie. 'You don't mind if he tags along, do you? It's the only way he can learn the ropes of the Mental Health Act and I can't leave him outside unattended.'

Hiding the grin that threatened to surface, Peddyr noted how well Monica made use of the leading question. Ryan wouldn't disagree because he had been skilfully manoeuvred into compliance. He shook Peddyr's hand with a firm grip and made direct eye contact, which was more than any other patient had done since their arrival on the ward.

'You're a bit old for a trainee, aren't you?' he asked.

'Change of career. Mid-life crisis,' Peddyr replied.

'What from?'

'Security consultant.'

'Right. Only you look like a copper. My old man was a copper.'

'Was he now...'

The conversation faded out, Ryan rapidly losing interest. Monica suggested they should take a walk around the building. 'What's happening with my mother?' the young man enquired, shoving his hands into his pockets. As they followed a wide corridor past a series of side rooms and offices, Peddyr admired the skill with which Monica put her client more at ease. Reassuring him completely was never going to be achievable, not in a place such as Caister Ward and not under such trying circumstances.

'We'll discuss your mother somewhere more private. How was your first night here?' she asked.

Ryan forced a harsh laugh. 'How do you think? I've hardly slept a wink. This place is as scary as fuck,' he said. 'Don't these manky geezers give you the creeps?' His eyes followed a dishevelled man as he stumbled past swearing under his breath. The man looked at Ryan like he'd offended him by simply being there. 'There are some right nut jobs in here.'

A female healthcare assistant by the name of Janelle unlocked a door to a windowless side room to allow them in. 'I'll be outside if you need me,' she said as she took a seat in the corridor. 'He's under level three obs.'

'Which is?' Peddyr asked.

'Within sight at all times. So don't take your eyes off him,' Janelle responded, flatly.

Her lack of social skills annoyed Peddyr, who'd been expecting more empathy and psycho-babble, not prison warder mentality. Still, it explained the open bedroom door.

Monica continued the conversation with Ryan. 'Most

people are here because they need to be. Many, if not all, because they're mentally unwell and need care. Anyway, you were asking about your mother.'

'Was I? Oh, yeah… If she's still locked up then I'm not going to get out of here today, am I?' His voice caught. He tugged at the collar of his shirt; a crumpled fitted shirt, blood on the sleeve, which he'd rolled up to hide the stain and made a bad job of. 'For now, all I want is a shower, some clean clothes, two brushes – one for my hair, one for my teeth – and to have a shave. Then I'd feel less like a tramp.'

Monica gave him an understanding smile. 'We can help to arrange that.'

'You can? That would be great,' Ryan said. Straight to the practicalities, clearly Monica was going up in his estimation. 'I want to call Bez or someone… but all the numbers are in my phone,' he said.

'And you're lost without it?'

'Too right I am. The arseholes here won't give it back.'

'Who would you phone first, if they did?' Peddyr asked.

'Depends. Mum if she's out of the nick yet. Or Bez, if she's not. Or Dexter, my cousin.' Ryan faced him square on. 'Is Mum out yet?'

Monica shook her head. 'Sorry, we don't have the latest update. The last I heard, police were due to question her again in the next hour or so.' She was so matter of fact that Ryan's rising annoyance never amounted to anything more than a vague huff. 'Apart from your mum, who has a key and can get into the house?' she asked.

'Scott has one. Had one,' he corrected. 'Granny Holden has a set, but she can't walk very well… And my set was taken by the Gestapo in here.'

'Nobody else?'

'Not that I know of.' He sighed, giving more thought to the question of accessing clean clothes. 'Bez is at work, so is Dexter, and I can't stand being like this all day. Must be against my human rights and all that.'

Monica tipped her head to one side, glancing across at Peddyr. 'What about other family members?'

'You must be kidding! Granny Glenda lives in an old people's home and barely knows what day of the week it is. Uncle Chris lives miles away with Aunty Hilary who has a resting bitch-face to be proud of because she's a bitch. Anyway, unless she was supervised, Mum would never allow her anywhere near Derwent Drive even if they did come back here.'

It was becoming obvious that Ryan lacked trust in people, but for good reason he was responding well to Monica and to Peddyr; they were useful to him, they were on his side.

'If you give me permission, I could collect some clothes for you,' Peddyr offered. 'You give me a list, I'll follow it to the letter, and I'll have fresh clothes here for you by this afternoon.' He paused, allowing Ryan to think this option through before adding, 'and I'll make sure the property is secure into the bargain. Put your mind at rest.'

If Ryan was as paranoid as the doctors were saying, this was unlikely to work as a proposal. Nevertheless it was worth a shot. Peddyr would be going to the home address at some point in his investigation and the sooner the better.

'I'll think about it,' Ryan conceded. 'I'll need to tell you where everything is, and even though I'll give you the code for the alarm, you'll have to knock on Carol's door before you let yourself in. She's a nosy old cow and she'll think you're up to no good.'

'Carol?'

'Our neighbour. She's at number thirteen. She and Mum are best mates. She'll be in a right state over this.' Stopping mid-thought, Ryan turned from Peddyr to ask Monica a burning question. 'How did he die?' he asked. 'Scott Fletcher, how did she kill him?'

'Sorry, Ryan, I don't have those details to give you. But —' She held her hand up to stop him from interjecting, which he was about to do. His mouth was open, ready for action. 'Before you criticise me for being unhelpful,' she continued, 'I can let your mother know how you are, if you wish. In the meantime, you can help yourself by giving me as much information as possible about how you ended up in here. The legal process requires me to act on your behalf, and because you want to appeal your section, we effectively started yesterday when you instructed me, so you need to give me every detail you can.'

'What, now?'

'Got anything better to do?'

'Where am I supposed to start?'

## 8

## A PAINFUL TRUTH

*B*ernard Kershaw had been called back to the police station. Sarah Holden was to be interviewed again and he wondered how long it would be before she realised that her story wasn't ringing true; not with him and not with the police. When he met up with her beforehand, she appeared slightly more alert than the previous evening when he'd left her trembling and petrified at the thought of being locked up overnight. 'Sarah, how are you doing?'

'A bit better now I've been given some clean underwear,' she replied, looking embarrassed and running her fingers through her tangled hair.

He replied with a sympathetic nod. 'Indeed, this process is very degrading for someone such as yourself. But let's see if we can't get you released today.' He ruffled some papers and sat down next to her. 'Now then, you told the police that you had argued with Scott Fletcher and assaulted him in a moment of anger. Yesterday, I advised you not to answer anything in such a way as to incriminate yourself.

You declined the suggestion of a written statement.' He cleared his throat. 'In my opinion the investigation will be focussing on your relationship with Fletcher and on the details of the assault on him. Be prepared for some tough questioning. And again, I beg you, avoid any use of "no comment" as your response; it's a double-edged sword that can make you appear guilty if overused.'

She leant forward. 'How is Ryan? Have you heard anything?'

'Nothing to tell you I'm afraid, but he's in a safe place and receiving care.'

'What about Maggie? She's a tough old thing but God knows what state she'll be in. Oh, and work. Did you call them, and did you speak with Carol? Is the house locked up?'

With Sarah Holden worrying about everyone and everything, except for her own predicament, this was going to be an arduous day and Bernard could only hope Peddyr and Monica were having more luck with Ryan than he was having with the young man's mother. She continued to implicate herself and yet he was certain she wasn't being truthful.

The situation was not helped by DI Webster's habit of keeping suspects and solicitors waiting before commencing an interview, ramping up the pressure and forcing them to succumb to foul coffee and floor pacing. Now he had been made Acting DCI he was pushing the boundaries even further and applying brinkmanship. The clock was ticking on how long Sarah could be held in custody and it wasn't a sensible move on Webster's part to waste precious minutes. Then again it could work in Sarah's favour.

The instant coffee on offer was something Bernard usually avoided, but after a sleepless night he needed a hit of caffeine, no matter how cheap and nasty. It had barely kicked in when the interview finally started.

'Remind us, when did you first meet Scott Fletcher?' Webster shifted his chair closer to the interview table and Bernard tried not to recoil. In his opinion the man's breath smelt less palatable than the cell in which Sarah had spent the night. Involuntarily, he rocked back in his chair. His client did much the same, unable to disguise a grimace of disgust as the detective continued to puff out his inquiries.

The interview room soon contained a heady mixture of oral miasmas and nervous sweat. The air became even more toxic when it was enhanced by the faint aroma of stale cigarette smoke emanating from the clothing of DS Forstall. As before, Duncan Webster was choosing to lead by example rather than leave questioning to his team. DS Helen Forstall looked close to exhaustion, ramping up the likelihood of sleep-deprivation-induced interrogation methods.

The fine tremor in Sarah Holden's fingers was becoming harder for her to hide and seemed to be getting worse, so a grilling was something she could do without. 'I thought we went through this yesterday evening?' she asked, angling a sideways look at her solicitor. In sharp contrast to her unkempt appearance, Bernard was wearing his usual tailored suit and crisp white shirt, red braces on show as he reached for a pen from inside his jacket.

'There are one or two details we'd like to clear up,' Webster continued.

'Are you planning to charge my client, Acting DCI Webster? Mrs Holden has answered your inquiries at length, under caution, and has been cooperative through-out. The least she can expect is an expedient conclusion to this business and I'm unclear why you need details of her relationship in any more depth.'

The detective ignored Bernard and produced a photograph. 'Do you recognise this man?'

'Yes, that's Scott on the left.'

'And do you know the lady on the right of the picture?' he asked.

'No, but it looks like his wife Stephanie. Scott let me see me a couple of photos from years ago. They're separated. I've never met her.' In the photo, the woman and Scott were standing moulded together, arms around each other's waist, grinning at the person behind the camera. They were posed against Scott Fletcher's truck. A shiny new pick-up.

'Do you have an address for her?' DS Forstall asked, her voice gravelly from her substantial smoking habit.

Bernard was keeping a close eye on how Sarah answered each question, and he noted the length of time she took to study the photograph, dejection appearing in her face as she ran the tip of her forefinger across the numbers and letters showing the licence plate to be a recent one. The truck could not have been more than six months old. She was clearly thrown.

'Me? No, why would I have her address? I know she lives in Lutterworth, but I couldn't tell you where. She works as a hairdresser.'

'You've never seen her with Mr Fletcher at his flat?' the DS enquired.

'She's never been there, not to my knowledge.'

The questions were coming in rapid succession and Sarah replied without hesitation. She wasn't lying now, Bernard realised.

'And you said that Scott Fletcher, the man in this photograph, worked for EDF as a performance engineer at their base in Barnswell. He had a roving brief across all the nuclear power sites which took him away overnight sometimes for weeks at a time, according to the answers you gave yesterday,' Webster said.

'Yes, that's right.'

'Met any of his work colleagues? Socialise with any of them?' Webster went on. The two detectives were using a quick-fire strategy, trying to trip her up and so far it was failing.

'No...' Sarah's voice faded and wavered as her thinking became intense. 'We bumped into one chap. A funeral director who knew him. Thanked him for fixing a refrigerated unit in their mortuary. Scott said he'd done it as a favour for an old friend, but I couldn't tell you his name.' She went on to explain that she and Scott had been on a romantic trip and taken a walk along the river in Dovedale one weekend. 'The bloke seemed chatty and clearly knew Scott well enough, it was all "mate" this and "mate" that,' she said, uncertainty crossing her face as if an uncomfortable thought had occurred.

'What about other friends and acquaintances? Did you meet anyone who knew Scott well?' Another question from the DS.

'As I explained before, he was at junior school with my husband Jim. There's a school photograph with them both in it.'

'The junior school on Kentish Road, here in Bosworth.'

'Yes.'

'Are you in touch with any more of your husband's old friends? Specifically, do you know anyone else who was at school with your husband?'

'Quite a few, yes. His mate Tim, our best man. There's

also Jim's friend Nick. They were both at Kentish Road Junior School with him and with Scott.'

'And they remembered Scott Fletcher from those days even though he left the area after that time?'

'Tim and his wife met Scott and me for a drink a few months back. They had quite a chat about the school and the teachers.' The explanation came rattling out of her mouth but appeared to be a way of justifying Scott's presence in her life and was a little too exaggerated for Bernard's liking. He noticed the way her eyes moved from left to right and her shoulders became increasingly hunched as she retreated into herself, lying once more.

'Actually,' Sarah went on, causing him more concern about the veracity of her answers. 'Tim and Barbara manufactured an excuse to meet us – me and Scott – because my son Ryan had been on the phone to them, hounding them to sound him out. It was all part of Ryan's paranoia. Like I said yesterday, he's got a serious mental illness.'

This opened the door to another line of questioning from Acting DCI Webster.

'It must have been extremely irritating when Ryan started sticking his nose into your relationship.'

'It was to start with, until I began to understand he was ill, but it took some explaining to Tim and Barbara. Once they saw the evidence, they were brilliant and couldn't have been more apologetic.' Sarah didn't sound as confident as her words were designed to be. She was clearly floundering. 'You can ask Tim,' she suggested.

There was a crushing pause in proceedings while Webster rifled through his paperwork, chewed another indigestion tablet and left Bernard to wonder where the questions were going next.

'We have been speaking to a number of your friends and

relatives in the course of our inquiries, Mrs Holden. My officers have also taken statements from residents at Primrose Court. As you can only be held initially for twenty-four hours I must be satisfied that the evidence stacks up, either to charge or to release you.' He gave Bernard a sickly grin before directing his next question to Sarah. 'Were you aware that your son was seen in the vicinity of Primrose Court yesterday?'

The silence was telling, and as Sarah became shockingly pale Bernard thought she was going to be physically sick. It had happened to him during questioning of a previous client some years before, an event he prayed would not be repeated now.

'He was at home,' she eventually mumbled, barely looking up from her hands that were gripped together. 'And when I was at Primrose Court, Ryan was being assessed under the Mental Health Act from about eleven o'clock.'

'So you're saying, at the time you killed Scott Fletcher, your son was being interviewed by doctors?'

'I told you this yesterday.'

'And you are sure he never left number fifteen Derwent Drive earlier that morning?'

'He was in his room. Ryan was becoming quite paranoid and didn't like to go out.'

Bernard knew then that his client had fallen foul of the police trap. She had lied.

'We beg to differ, Mrs Holden. Your son was often seen at those flats in recent weeks. He sometimes made use of a pushbike and was seen on foot at Primrose Court by witnesses yesterday.' The ensuing tidal wave of questions about Ryan didn't come. Unexpectedly, Acting DCI Webster changed tack completely.

'Explain to me what you did with the compressed air gun, Mrs Holden.'

She didn't move her head, but when Sarah answered, Bernard distinctly saw DS Helen Forstall swivel her eyes to her senior officer, who didn't let up with his barrage of questions.

'Sorry?'

'The compressor in the garage, how did you use it to kill Scott Fletcher? You omitted that detail in your statement yesterday. Perhaps you can enlighten us?'

Sarah Holden looked at Bernard Kershaw and her eyes gave her away. 'No comment,' she said, jumping straight in instead of seeking his advice. However, this mistake on her part could be the turning point for an effective defence, Bernard realised. Just like the day previously, under questioning she couldn't answer because she didn't know what they meant. And that was because she hadn't killed Scott Fletcher.

'Come along now, Mrs Holden. As your solicitor has said, you've been cooperative to this point. You practically made a full confession, and yet you decline to answer this one specific question. It makes no sense unless you are trying to protect someone...' He closed the file in front of him. 'Mrs Holden, I'm going to ask you if you wish to amend your statement.'

Bernard had seen this coming. 'I'd like to speak to my client in confidence,' he said. 'Can you give me a few minutes?'

With those words, Sarah sat upright, eyes beseeching the detectives to listen to her. 'No, you don't understand. I must have blacked out...'

Bernard put a finger to his lips; her efforts to prove her own guilt were complicating matters. The two detectives left the interview room, giving Sarah time to gather herself before Bernard told his client that she had fooled nobody.

'It is my duty to advise you that perverting the course of justice is taken extremely seriously by the law. It is apparent to me that you want police to charge you with the unlawful killing of Scott Fletcher, but it's as plain as the nose on my well-worn face that you are not the person who committed the crime. The police have given you another chance here. A chance to amend your statement and to tell the truth. I strongly advise you to do so.'

## 9

## DIVIDE AND CONQUER

*R*yan Holden had resigned himself to replying to Monica's questions. Peddyr could tell this by the throw-away protests; the ones teenagers always produced when they didn't want to lose face. 'Yeah, whatever... If it makes you happy, I'll say what happened. I'll answer your stupid questions.' Before doing so he made arrangements with Peddyr to collect clothes and a wash kit from his room at number fifteen Derwent Drive. A quid pro quo, allowing Ryan a small victory.

The plan was to divide and conquer. Monica would continue her assessment and Peddyr would begin his own investigation, firstly with Ryan, then by introducing himself to Carol Brightman, the Holdens' neighbour living at number thirteen Derwent Drive. He had Ryan's permission to enter the house and couldn't wait to get back out into the real world and away from the confines of Caister Ward. But although he'd be more than happy to leave Monica to her job while he got on with his straightaway, he couldn't. He needed to hear what the lad had to say. With an understanding look, Monica persuaded Peddyr to contain his impatience long enough to listen to the beginning of Ryan's story.

'So, the house on Derwent Drive was where you and your mum lived before you moved out to live with your girlfriend?' Monica asked. She covered the basics first to see how well he was concentrating. It was an easy way of checking whether the facts in the file were correct and if Ryan could be relied upon to give a straight answer to a statement about his age, his family members, his relevant medical history. Peddyr would have done something very similar.

Once satisfied, Monica widened her inquiries. 'What's an intelligent independent man, such as yourself, doing living with his mum? Or is that an insensitive question?' Having had time to read the file, both she and Peddyr knew the answer, but they wanted his version, not the one given by his mother to the social worker.

'I split up with my girlfriend.'

'Right… well, you won't be the first… but why go back to your mother's?' Peddyr asked. 'Bit of a backward step isn't it?' It was a well-considered dig at Ryan Holden's ego, which was clearly larger than average. Peddyr and Monica had fallen into a mild version of good cop, bad cop, without even trying. 'Couldn't you have rented somewhere or moved in with your mate Bez?'

Ryan shifted in his seat. He barely raised his head. 'I lost my job.'

'Oh, right, so when you told Monica you worked in sales and marketing, that's firmly in the past tense is it? Sounds like a bad week. What did you do to get your P45?'

'What do you care?'

Monica shook her head at him. 'This isn't about caring.

The questions we are asking are to help us understand what was going on for you, why your path in life landed you in here.'

In the back of his mind, Peddyr was toying with a number of possible scenarios. On occasion, some misguided individuals needing to hide from the law, would manipulate their admission to a psychiatric facility. He and Monica had discussed such a possibility at length while poring over the case notes. According to her, some malingerers would make a half-hearted suicide attempt, behave irrationally or concoct auditory hallucinations so as to feign illness. An illness of convenience did not often succeed however. On experiencing the reality of a stay in an acute unit, most would-be malingerers made a rapid and miraculous recovery. Generally, they had psychopathic tendencies.

So far Ryan Holden hadn't come across as massaging the system to meet his needs. He wanted out and there was no playacting of symptoms that Peddyr could discern. Then again, he wasn't the expert so would have to rely on Monica's invaluable knowledge and expertise.

On the surface, it looked as if Ryan had fallen foul of the system and of his mother's belief that he was paranoid. He certainly didn't look or act paranoid.

Peddyr jotted down some notes about Ryan's boss being his girlfriend's father, about Agri Solutions the company he worked for, and how a complaint had been made against him for indecent and improper behaviour. 'Let's have the gory details then, fella,' he said, not allowing Ryan to skirt the issue. 'Who did you get caught shafting?' The question had the desired effect and Ryan's jaw dropped open so widely his back teeth were exposed.

'Oh, my days,' the younger man said, with an embarrassed laugh. 'Are you allowed to talk to me like that?' He looked across at Monica who merely shrugged.

'It saves a lot of time,' she said, sitting back to listen.

Peddyr took his cue and probed again. 'So, although you had a girlfriend, whom you lived with, you were having a bit of how's-your-father with someone else. Or have I misunderstood the meaning of indecent and improper behaviour? Immediate dismissal on the grounds of gross misconduct would have to be memorable. A man of your age and good looks...'

Given a chance to boast about his sexual magnetism, Ryan was soon spewing out lurid details of his regular "sexathons" with a young lady he unashamedly referred to as Juicy Julie. Ryan had worked in sales and marketing for Agri Solutions who specialised in drone technology to help improve crop yields, among other applications. Having good reason to visit many farming businesses, he had expanded his portfolio by servicing a number of females in the course of his travels; Juicy Julie being one of his favourites. Their hay bale romps came to an abrupt end when Julie's father caught them at it.

'I didn't think farmers still used pitchforks,' Monica replied in response to the lurid story as Ryan stood up. 'And I really don't need to see the evidence,' she exclaimed, fanning herself with a file.

Taking the hint, he tucked the end of his leather belt back in its loop and sat down again. 'Well, he did, and it hurt like fuck. Old Roger Chambers said I was a prick and deserved to feel what that was like. He went turbo. Don't know how he missed my arse the second time.'

The rest of the tale was predictable enough. Mr Chambers, who ran a large estate farm, contacted Agri Solutions and was put straight through to Laurence Griffiths. Ryan was sacked on the spot and ordered to confess all to Sienna Griffiths, his unsuspecting girlfriend.

'I stayed with Bez for two nights while I worked on Mum.'

'His place too small for you, was it?'

'Too small, too smelly, too crowded. He lives with three other blokes in a rented house. It's like a squat. And there was no spare room, nowhere to store my stuff.'

'What sort of stuff?'

Peddyr could have written the list himself; oversized TV, laptop, DVDs and a vinyl music collection, a guitar that Ryan one day hoped to play in a band. Gym equipment also featured. However, he hadn't expected to hear the words "climbing gear".

'As in rock-climbing?' Monica asked, angling forward.

Making his hands into claws, Ryan had the temerity to wink at her. 'Fingers of steel, core strength Spiderman would kill for, and great legs.' He placed his palms on his thighs and virtually dared her to make a comment. She resisted, as Peddyr knew she would; ego-feeding wasn't what she was here for.

Ryan's being a rock climber would explain the clean living; no smoking, no drugs, alcohol rarely, he'd said. Cycling, running, gym membership... all these fitted with his desire to look good, to be admired. It helped to make sense of why he was so appalled at not having a shave or a shower or his finery to change into. The outer layer. The protective shell.

'Can I get this straight?' Monica said, adjusting her posture. 'You phone your mother, give her the sob story and negotiate a return home while you look for a job and somewhere to stay. The problem with your mental health arises when you move in. Talk me through it from the day you rock up on your mother's doorstep.'

'I don't have a mental health problem. I never did.'

'That aside, tell us what happened when you got back home.'

'Bez gave me a lift in his van. We made a couple of trips, filled a spare room with my gear, and I took back possession of my old bedroom. Simple as that.'

'Really?' Peddyr queried. 'Your notes say that when you rang to ask your mother to have you back at home, you were in a state of distress, crying and insisting you had been a victim of a plot against you at work. You told your mum another employee at Agri Solutions had made up the whole story about you and Julie Chambers. This man pretended to be her father. You swore none of it was true.'

After making this statement, Peddyr found himself on the receiving end of a fierce scowl. 'Yeah, well, she and Scotty-Boy were tight. I knew she'd never let me stay unless I… you know… gave her something to really worry about.'

## 10

## SARAH TELLS THE TRUTH

*W*hile Sarah had thought she was protecting Ryan, she didn't feel any guilt about lying, just a desperate need to shield him from prison, to save him from ruining his life. But now... now, she was in the wrong whichever way she played it. She had committed an actual offence by admitting to a crime she didn't carry out, a serious one.

'My client wishes to amend her statement,' Bernard Kershaw said.

The truth was much easier to manage. Sarah didn't waver, just trotted out the facts. She hadn't used a fire extinguisher to kill Scott Fletcher; she had found him already dead on the garage floor and had assumed her son was the culprit because of his mental illness, for which he was now sectioned. Ryan had in fact left her house early that morning and hadn't returned home until shortly before ten-thirty or thereabouts.

Once they had established the chronology to their satisfaction, the Forstall and Webster Show began again in earnest. Questions were delivered slowly as if their suspect were a simpleton, an untrustworthy miscreant who had plummeted in everyone's estimation, including her own.

'And which version do you expect us to believe, Mrs Holden?' Acting DCI Webster asked. He folded his arms and sniffed audibly. 'Your fingerprints are on the fire extinguisher; you were at the scene. You didn't deny killing Scott Fletcher – quite the opposite. Now, all of a sudden, when you realise you could be charged with murder, you change your story to implicate your son – the one you say you are trying to protect.'

Just when Sarah thought she couldn't feel any worse, she did. Saliva flooded her mouth and the sensation of overwhelming nausea returned.

'We didn't find anyone else's prints, apart from those of a Mr Colin McIlhenny who, as you know, witnessed you at the scene, laughing because you had killed your lover. Your cheating lover.'

Bernard Kershaw stiffened in the chair next to his client's. 'Now come on, Inspector Webster, that is supposition on your part.'

'Is it?' Intransigent, Webster had his face set in a sneer. 'Our investigations continue, Mr Kershaw. And for the purposes of the recording, my rank is currently that of Acting Detective Chief Inspector.' He emphasised the word "Chief" with boastful pride.

Sarah turned to Bernard Kershaw imploring him with her eyes to explain. 'I don't know what he means,' she said with a whimper.

'Did you have any concerns that Scott Fletcher was cheating on you with another woman?' the detective continued.

'No, why should I?' she answered, taken aback by the question.

'Shall we talk about your son?' Webster drawled, delighting in his power to switch topics and derail his suspect. 'You said Ryan was displaying signs of mental illness before moving back to live with you at number fifteen Derwent Drive. Can you explain what you mean by this?'

She heard the question but wasn't present enough to answer it. Were the police trying to fool her? She couldn't let it ride. 'Why would you say Scott was cheating on me?' she asked.

'So you did know.' Helen Forstall had pounced on another opportunity to catch their suspect out.

'He wasn't. Not as far as I know,' Sarah replied, looking from one detective to the other, seeking a glimmer of understanding from either of them.

'But then again, you're not very keen for us to get to the truth, are you? You identified the woman in this photograph as someone by the name of Stephanie.' Helen Forstall slid the photograph shown earlier back towards Sarah, prodding at the face of the woman standing too close to Scott to be anything other than on intimate terms with him. He was leaning against his new truck; the one purchased since he and Sarah had been seeing each other. 'You said she was Scott's ex-wife. Sorry, let me correct myself. You said they were separated, soon to be divorced. So when was this taken?'

'Why ask me?'

Webster twitched impatiently. 'Because you know it was taken very recently. We found this on a phone belonging to the man you knew as Scott Fletcher. One of his two phones.

He lived in a flat rented through Craven & Tilbury, the letting agents where you work.'

'What question exactly are you asking my client here?' Bernard Kershaw demanded. 'You have made a series of statements. Is there a question you require an answer to, *Acting* Detective Chief Inspector Webster?'

There was a momentary pause as the detective narrowed his eyes at the implied criticism. 'Mrs Holden, when did you find out that Scott Fletcher had no intention of divorcing his wife?' Duncan Webster's expression was now stern.

'I didn't. He told me the financial settlement was being finalised, that it was by mutual agreement and not acrimonious.' The words of Sarah's reply were swallowed up as she collapsed in on herself, knowing that even though Ryan was sick in the head, he might have been right about Scott not being the man he said he was.

'I put it to you, Mrs Holden that you discovered within the last...' the detective checked the clock on the wall '... twenty hours that Scott Fletcher was still very much married and had no intention of getting a divorce. He was stringing you along, prepared to commit bigamy. He led a double life, juggling two relationships.' He placed his hands flat on the table between him and Sarah and inclined his head. 'And you killed the man you knew as Scott Fletcher in revenge for his heartless deception of you. He broke your heart and broke your son. Scott Fletcher made Ryan out to be mentally ill, didn't he? To get him out of the way because he was too close to seeing the truth. You fell for Fletcher's stories until you let yourself into his flat yesterday and discovered the painful truth. You saw this picture, didn't you?'

'No. I didn't see anything suspicious.'

'How do you think Ryan feels? His mother doesn't believe him. She shops him to the authorities and has him locked up. She betrayed her only child in favour of a love-cheat.'

The sound-proofing dulled Sarah's shocked response to this attack. 'Oh, God,' was all she could come up with.

Nobody spoke for several seconds while Sarah sat with her head bowed, shaking. 'Ryan was already paranoid about a workmate. It's why he lost his job. He lost everything – his home, his girlfriend. He said Scott wasn't using his real name. You don't understand...' She could not look more guilty. First she had confessed, then she had told the truth. A truth which made her appear as if she were blaming her son. Which she was.

\* \* \*

*I*n the first two days of his return to Derwent Drive, Sarah wasn't certain Ryan was being truthful with her about his need to move back home. So many times he had pulled the wool over her naive eyes and used her affection for him to his own ends. She couldn't be sure, so following Scott's directive she called Sienna, Ryan's girlfriend. Something she had delayed doing from an underlying fear of being proved right about Ryan having some sort of mental breakdown.

Sienna had sobbed down the phone, bless her heart, but her words struck a chord. 'There's something wrong with him, Sarah. He's been behaving so weird. Checking up on me, asking me where I am all the time, making sure I am where I say I am. He's never been so possessive before. He said someone was out to get him. To discredit him, to split us up. And now they've done it. He must be in a fearful state: tell him to ring me. Please, Sarah. I want to talk to him, but he says it's too dangerous. You have to help him.'

What a blow it was to hear her say such things. Sarah could only conclude that Ryan's paranoia was much worse than he'd let on.

* * *

'*A*nd after he moved in, how did he seem around Scott Fletcher?' DS Helen Forstall was speaking again. Sarah hadn't been paying proper attention. She shook herself.

'He and Scott stayed out of each other's way as much as possible.'

'Why was that, Mrs Holden?'

Describing the change in atmosphere in her house when Ryan moved back in was almost impossible. 'If Scott was around, he locked himself in his room, coming out for meals and drinks,' she told them. But what she didn't mention was that the loss of his job did not seem to concern her son. In fact, he revelled in his freedom. Exercise became his salvation; he went out for runs every day, covering miles and miles through the streets around Bosworth Bishops. 'By the second week at home he'd found his old bike in the shed and put on new tyres with the help of his cousin Dexter. Ryan isn't as mechanically gifted as his dad used to be.'

'Didn't he have a car?'

'He could have used mine if I wasn't at work. He lost the use of his company car when he lost his job,' Sarah explained, pushing away the guilt she felt at not buying her son what he had asked for. Instead, she had used the money to purchase Scott's new truck. He was going to repay her, so she made Ryan wait. Something he found hard to comprehend. 'Sometimes he went out with Bez on a Friday as usual, but he isn't a big drinker so often drove a group of mates in Bez's van between pubs and bars, preferring to avoid a hangover.'

Sarah reflected on these testing times. While Scott had been working away, Ryan had settled into a routine of "job hunting" and after that there had been constant excuses for failing the interviews he attended. There was always a reason: they stared at him funny, he didn't trust the bloke who carried out the interview, they gave off bad Karma. He *was* paranoid.

'Mrs Holden, could you answer the question, please?'

Sarah's mind repeatedly wandered off and she knew she must appear evasive. 'Sorry, I forgot. What was your question?' She had been asked about her future plans. 'As I said before, Scott and I were going to move in together.'

'Buying a home together?'

'Yes.'

'In joint names? Using the proceeds from the sale of your home. I see.' DS Helen Forstall put her pen to her lips briefly. 'And Scott Fletcher's contribution was to come from...?'

The words were out of her mouth before Sarah cottoned on to what she'd done. 'I'm not sure. He said it was from the divorce. Plus he had a good job of course.'

Webster smiled like a crocodile. 'The divorce he wasn't going through with,' he said.

Unwittingly, she'd given them confirmation of another motive. A broken heart, a broken son, and being the victim of an attempt to defraud. Sarah shrank into her seat. What a fool she had been, a gullible, trusting fool.

'Sarah Jane Holden, your detention is being extended for a further twelve hours. During this time our investigation will continue while we interview further witnesses and examine the available evidence. If a further period of detention in custody is required, application will be made to the court…'

Sarah began to laugh.

## 11

## CAR KARAOKE

*I*t had been nearly a year since Peddyr had cause to visit Derwent Drive where Gabriella Dixon had once lived. She had been a client of P. Q. Investigations and the puzzling case was one he would never forget. While reminiscing about the disappearance of Gabby Dixon, the first few bars of a familiar tune rang out inside the car and he found himself singing along to the radio as he drove past number six, admiring what the new owners had done with the place. Opposite Gabby's old house was a bungalow that hadn't changed from how he remembered it looking for years. The property was an eyesore in many respects and didn't fit in with the middle-class gentility that surrounded it. When it came to it, neither did its owner, a certain Kenny Eversholt.

There were motorbikes outside the bungalow, as before; at least fifteen at the last count, though by the looks of things at least one was missing. The rest were under their black-and-silver covers, rotting where they stood. The whole place had the air of abandonment about it; weeds growing through cracks in the tarmac, peeling paint, no curtains at the windows. Through the large front window the lounge, contents could be easily seen and were a reflection of the peculiar man the neighbourhood so flagrantly ignored whenever he showed up there; he was an infrequent visitor, preferring to live elsewhere. Like the windows, the walls of the large front room were unadorned and the only furniture to be seen came in the form of Dexion shelving. On the metal shelves were several bulky packages wrapped in black plastic. Gabby Dixon had once joked about the place being reminiscent of a murder scene from a police drama. Peddyr smiled at the recollection as he drove past.

He eased on until he reached number fifteen and pulled into the kerb, checking for signs of movement, for a police presence or members of the press. Local TV news had broadcast from outside the house early that morning, making much of Sarah's status as the widow of a police officer. For all that initial fuss, the street now seemed a picture of suburban calm once more as media attention focussed on Scott Fletcher's garage at the rear of Primrose Court. Camera crews loved the sight of a white tent and forensic activity.

In his peripheral vision Peddyr caught the vague outline of a woman he assumed to be Carol Brightman at the bay window of the Edwardian semi next door to where the Holdens lived. He didn't rush and allowed the car to idle while he listened to the final bars of a once favourite song; his Connie track, as he called it. Only then did he open the car door. Tapping his suit jacket pockets before pulling it on, he double-checked for the letter of permission from

Ryan Holden and the attached list of items he was to collect. All present and correct.

By the time he was halfway up the drive, Carol, a woman of a similar age to himself, had arrived at the front door, dressed in a flowing swirl of colours and carrying a couple of artists' paintbrushes in one hand. Her mass of butter-cream-blonde ringlets formed a mane about her shoulders, curls wafting in the breeze.

His preconceptions were shattered. Expecting an older lady, all permed hair and blue rinse with a pot plant on every windowsill, he had to readjust the settings on how to approach her. Ryan had described her as old and nosy but then, being young and self-centred, he would.

'Don't you guys communicate with each other?' she drawled, in a diluted American accent. 'If you spent more time contacting the station and less time on car karaoke you may have saved yourself a journey, detective. I gave my statement yesterday evening when your bobbies called by.'

What with door-to-door inquiries and press intrusion, the woman would be sick of answering questions, Peddyr realised. He would have to watch how he tackled her. 'Mrs Brightman, you'll be pleased to hear I'm not a member of the local constabulary.' He avoided denying he was a detective because that wouldn't have been strictly correct. 'I'm here on behalf of the legal team representing Ryan James Holden. He has given me permission to collect some personal items from his home address and advised that I should speak with you first.' He held up the set of house keys handed over to him on Caister Ward and jiggled them gently. 'Any idea which one of these fits the front door?'

Carol Brightman's frostiness melted instantly. She shot a look at the house next door before inviting him inside.

'You'll have seen the news about Ryan's mother. How much more can that family take? The cops were in the street last night, knocking on doors, taking statements. It's been hell. I hardly slept and I'm on a deadline. I'm only surprised they haven't got a warrant to search Sarah's place.'

'They will, soon enough,' Peddyr replied. In awe, he looked around him at the decor. It was as loud as the colours in the dress the woman wore. 'An artist, that much is obvious. But what are you on a deadline for?' he asked, handing her the paperwork confirming his details.

'I illustrate children's books among other things,' she said, in an offhand way. Looking closer at the letter he had given her, she started. 'Your name is Peedwire?' she enquired, screwing up her nose. 'What sort of name is that?'

He'd heard many variations of his name, mostly Paddy or Peter, but nobody had ever called him Peedwire before. He laughed softly. 'It's pronounced Ped-er, and it's a Celtic name. I'm Manx.'

'Oh, I get it. From Manchester.'

He laughed again. 'No. I'm originally from the Isle of Man but like you, Mrs Brightman, my accent has faded over the years.'

Carol put down her paintbrushes not seeming to care that she'd splattered luminous pink droplets onto the hall table and the morning's post. She clapped her hands together. 'Now, tell me how I can help,' she said. 'And we can chat as we go. I need to find out how Ryan is coping, so I can phone Maggie Holden and put her mind at rest, poor sausage. I don't suppose you know how Sarah is. Can I take her some clothes and personal stuff? Have they charged her? Is she going to be released soon?'

Gushing questions and information, Carol Brightman

whisked Peddyr through a gate in the fence dividing the two properties. Touching him as often as she could get away with, she ushered him into the front entrance of number fifteen and punched a five-digit code into the keypad for the alarm. 'I reset it when I heard the news about Sarah being arrested,' she said. 'She is always so careful to make sure the place is secure. Jim was a stickler for locks and alarms.'

The internal design and feel of the place could not have been in greater contrast to Carol's home, which was full of warm vibrant colours, psychedelic fabric wall hangings, reflective surfaces and polished floorboards. Sarah Holden had chosen muted colours, pale cream carpets, gentle greens and golds to bring out the warm browns of the Edwardian antiques placed to complement the more modern furnishings.

Following Carol's example, Peddyr slipped off his shoes, silently congratulating himself on wearing a pair of matching socks, ones without holes in at that. 'While she's at the police station for questioning you can't visit, you can't take Sarah anything. The custody rules are really strict. But before this place is swarming with police looking for more evidence, let's see if we can help Ryan.'

'Yes, how is he? Bouncing off the walls yet? Does he know about Sarah?' As Carol led him down the hallway, Peddyr answered her as succinctly as he could without disclosing too much.

'Did he tell you he only moved home a few weeks back?' Carol said. With Peddyr close behind, she trotted upstairs to a landing and headed for a door to her right, into a room overlooking the rear of the property. 'Keeps it neat, don't he? The kid had so much clutter most of it is in one of the other bedrooms.'

Peddyr removed the list from his pocket again and approached a mirrored sliding door to a vast fitted wardrobe. 'Where do I start?' he asked. Examining the rows of clothes on hangers in defined sections, he stepped back, placing hands on hips. Ryan Holden clearly had a pronounced need for order in his surroundings because from left to right were a series of jackets both smart and casual, followed by a section for trousers and jeans, one for suits, and next to them hung shirts of all types. Neatly folded tee-shirts, shorts and vests, were on shelves to one side. Socks and underpants Peddyr found in a set of drawers integrated into the wardrobe.

When it came to identifying the correct toiletries, he asked for help. 'See if you can find this shaving balm, can you, Carol? There's so much smelly stuff here I can't see the Paco Rabanne from the Tommy Hilfiger. Mind you, it will be wasted where he's staying.' Hand laid flat over the top of an open bottle he tipped the contents, releasing a small amount of liquid. Replacing the bottle on the shelf he then rubbed his palms together and sniffed hard. 'Very nice. I think I'll ask my wife to buy me some for Christmas,' he said, twisting the lid back on. 'Any idea where we could find a suitcase or a holdall?'

He'd spied a large sports bag, but it was already filled with clothing, trainers, water bottle, cycle helmet and cycling shoes. Expensive stuff and all cared for and packed away with precision. Next to it lay kettle bells and a weighted vest.

'I'll take another look,' Carol replied as she busied herself placing items onto Ryan's large bed, ready to be packed. 'What a terrible thing to happen,' she said. 'The boy was making his way in life, then wham, he loses the plot and the men in white suits cart him off over the cuckoo's nest.'

Taking in the tidy bedroom once more, Peddyr found it hard to comprehend that a person could descend into psychosis but remain so fastidious. This room belonged to someone who cared how they looked, a person who imposed structure on his life. A place for everything and everything in its place, as Benjamin Franklin once said. 'How did his mum know he was becoming so mentally unwell she had to have him sectioned?' he asked, turning the conversation to his advantage. 'Couldn't she have found another way to get help for the lad?'

Taking up a relaxed pose on the side of Ryan's bed, Carol let out a long sigh through her nose. 'I was thinking about that when the police were bundling the kid into the squad car yesterday. What a mess. So badly handled.'

Carol Brightman was the sort who spoke with her hands. She emphasised her words with a flap or a flick of an invisible baton. Always animated, rather like Connie. 'They rock up here, Ryan refuses to let them in but agrees to talk to them on the front driveway. I watched the whole thing. There was plenty of shouting about Scott.' She hesitated and glanced across at Peddyr who lounged against a wall, arms folded, eyeing up the table where a laptop lay.

'Ryan told me all about Scott Fletcher, so I'm up with the general gist of things,' he confirmed, still toying with the idea of taking the laptop, then dismissing the idea as a risky plan.

'Well, then it turns nasty. Ryan lashes out at one of the men. It was the worst thing he could have done, but he's adamant that Scott Fletcher is up to no good. What you Brits call "a wrong 'un".'

'And was he? In your opinion, was Scott Fletcher out to cause harm?'

She re-crossed her legs, adjusting the layers of bright

material in her dress, flashing her shapely limbs in his direction. 'I didn't think so, but I didn't know him well enough to say one way or the other with any accuracy. We chatted about life, the weather, his new truck... Sarah certainly didn't have any worries about him. She was besotted with the man and he was a catch. A real Richard Gere.' She emphasised this statement with a flutter of her eyelids. 'He and Ryan just didn't gel. It created friction. I guess the creeping paranoia became worse because of it.'

Pushing himself from the wall, Peddyr swivelled round to look out of the window. 'How did you and Sarah know it was paranoia on display and not genuine concerns or a jealous son trying to elbow out a man destined to become his stepfather?'

From what Carol told him, Ryan was seen a number of times at the flats in Primrose Court where Scott lived. 'Sarah had complaints from a couple of the other residents. She works for the management company who rent the flats out,' Carol explained. 'They said Ryan was spying on them, and he never denied it. He was watching Scott come and go, keeping an eye on who visited his flat, where he went. Scott said he even had calls at work. Not to him directly, but questions about him being asked by a man who refused to leave a name. He constantly guarded his mobile phone because Ryan had taken it once and was caught trying to unlock the PIN. The boy even went to the police station, can you believe that? Each evening he spent hours online trying to trace information on Scott's private life. And worst of all, he badgered old friends of his father, demanding they help expose Scott as a fraud. It was just endless.'

'When did this behaviour start?' Peddyr asked, casting an eye over a series of sheds, garages and a workshop arranged around a courtyard to the back and side of the house. They were in good repair, padlocked and secure, with a motion sensor light above the doors and Peddyr spotted wiring that would indicate an alarm of some sort. Jim Holden really had been security conscious.

'Sarah reckons the paranoia began when he worked for Agri Solutions and was the reason he lost his job. She's too soft sometimes because I'm pretty certain he deserved the sack. That boy can't keep his thing in his pants, if you get my drift. The problems really began when Dexter came over to make an inventory of furniture and other crap Sarah wanted to sell. She was getting ready to move house.'

'I did see the sign outside,' Peddyr said.

'There, and I thought you were too busy singing in your car to notice.' She got to her feet and began placing items in a small suitcase she'd found in the wardrobe. It didn't escape Peddyr's notice that she angled herself to display her cleavage to full advantage. 'What was it you were belting out and head-banging to anyway?'

Peddyr cringed. He was hoping she wouldn't bring up his car-warbling again. 'It was *Hong Kong Garden* by Siouxsie and the Banshees if you must know, and I wasn't head banging.' When he was flirting with Connie, some time before they were married, he used to sing 'Hong Kong, darling' to her without realising he had the wrong lyrics and hadn't understood the meaning of the song at all. It became a standing joke and a firm favourite in their singa-long repertoire.

He changed the subject rapidly, embarrassed that his unguarded moment of pleasant reminiscence had been harshly judged. 'Dexter is Ryan's cousin, Sarah's nephew, am I right? So, he is Dexter Booth. Where can I find him?' Ryan had mentioned his cousin but the hospital records had no details about him. He was someone Peddyr needed to talk with, as was Maggie Holden.

'Listen, Carol, before we go, can I take a look at the spare room where Ryan keeps his other stuff? He said he had some multivitamins he wanted me to pack for him.'

## NOT SO CLEAN

*W*hen Peddyr had returned to the Marsworth Unit having completed a successful visit to Derwent Drive, Monica was waiting for him in the main reception area. It was as good a place as any to have a quiet chat, so they sat huddled together in a corner. 'You've just missed some of your old mates,' she said.

'Oh?' At first he didn't understand the reference.

'A couple of Bosworth's finest have been to collect Ryan Holden's shoes and clothing. He's either as naked as a jaybird or is now suffering the embarrassment of wearing borrowed hospital clothes or at best a surgical gown.'

'In which case,' Peddyr replied with a smirk, 'let's make him wait a little longer. I have a few things I want to run past you.' He shared with her his impression of Ryan from what he saw of his bedroom and from what Carol Brightman had said to him. 'If I'd known she was going to be flirtatious I'd have taken Connie with me,' he told her. 'Don't worry, I coped. Carol may have been full on, but she was a source of valuable information, confirming Ryan's version of events regarding his sectioning, and the timeline for that morning. She doesn't think of herself as a nosy neighbour, but she doesn't miss a bloody trick,' he said with a rueful grin.

Monica looked drained. She flapped an A5 spiral-bound notebook at him. 'Good observations. What you said about his neat and obsessively tidy bedroom is very telling. I don't think Ryan Holden is paranoid at all, and what's more I didn't get the impression he was lying to me.' She angled her head, widening her eyes. 'The cocky little bumalo is selfish, has an inflated sense of entitlement, a skewed view of his place in the world, narcissistic traits and a Casanova complex.'

'Is there such a thing? And what the heck is a bumalo?'

Monica grinned. 'I've been researching replacements for swear words,' she said, wafting her phone in the air. 'A bumalo is a type of tropical fish. It's dried and becomes Bombay Duck. There's one for the pub quiz.'

With a thumbs up, Peddyr approved the new strategy for reducing his use of common expletives. 'Nice. The best I've managed is Shih Tzu and Bulldog, but Connie thought I was being unfair to dogs.' He gave a bashful grin. 'And the Casanova Complex? True or false?'

'Some psychologists think it actually exists as a clinical condition, but I was using the term as the best way of describing Ryan's behaviour towards women. Apart from loving himself and spending on clothes, it's the biggest vice I can find in him.'

She sat back in her chair and glanced across at Ruby the vibrant receptionist who was dealing with an irate visitor, one who had not taken kindly to being refused entry to the ward until official visiting hours. Peddyr was watching the goings-on with interest, wondering why people found it hard to comply with simple regulations. The visiting times were displayed quite clearly. He heard Monica muttering under her breath.

'No chance, mate. You won't get past Ruby-Rottweiler today or any other day.'

He grinned, appreciating just how formidable Ruby could be. Returning to their previous conversation about Ryan's vices, or lack thereof, Peddyr said, 'When he assured us he didn't do drugs, didn't drink, didn't smoke... I got an earworm.' He poked a finger into one ear and waggled it. '"Don't drink, don't smoke. What do you do?" Remember that one from *Top of the Pops*?'

'Thank Christ. I thought it was just me,' she chuckled, tapping her sternum. 'But of course Ryan isn't squeaky clean, his appetite for sex could be his addiction. It gets him into trouble, it's toxic for the women, it feeds his need to be adored. Having said that, we all do something unhelpful, wasteful or self-destructive. I may have to call for the winebulance tonight just to see me through,' she confessed.

As he often did, Peddyr explored his thinking aloud. Mostly he did this with Connie to hear her valued opinion, but Monica had inside knowledge in this instance, and she could help him understand the anomalies he had noticed in Ryan. 'You are not alone. Connie likes a game of Mah-jong or poker, for money I hasten to add. I spend cash I can't afford on too many motorbikes and a penchant for beer. Bernie is a glutton. Which all very well because we fit the profile for our generation, for our gang of mates, but Ryan Holden isn't like his friends. He isn't even like his father. So who does he take after? Or is he a product of some psychological claptrap that I don't get?'

To help him out, Monica told Peddyr about her evaluation of Ryan Holden's mental state and he was impressed at the involved nature of the assessment.

'So, there's a difference between types of delusional thoughts?' he queried, trying to get up to speed on what this could imply.

'Yes, in the same way as there are different types of delusions affecting the senses; visual, tactile, auditory, gustatory and olfactory, to be precise.' She tapped at her head a couple of times. 'Ryan denied any type of thought insertion – ideas being put into his head from another source. This is different to being influenced by a debate, or by what a friend tells you. More like special messages that only he could interpret. He found it as strange as you do to be asked if his thoughts were being sucked out of his head, or if he had times when thoughts were so muddled they made no sense. His memory is spot on, he's orientated to time, place and person. And yet…' she trailed off, scrubbing a hand over one side of her face.

'What?' The frustration showing in her every move was not the result of her assessment of Ryan Holden's mental state. It was obvious to Peddyr that she was comfortable with these findings. Her annoyance stemmed from elsewhere. 'A bigger problem?' he asked, as he leaned against the back of the chair, crossing an ankle over a knee.

Monica gave him a grateful smile. 'I've just had a confrontation with Ryan's consultant psychiatrist. God alone knows where they dredged him up from. Some Victorian asylum judging by his outdated knowledge and appalling people skills. Casanova Complex meets God Complex and I tried to referee. Bad plan.' She left Peddyr for a moment to pour two plastic cups of cold water from a nearby fountain. Regaining her composure, she expanded on the dilemma.

'Dr Ashok Chowdhury is of the opinion that Ryan Holden has a fixed delusional disorder. As it says in the notes we read earlier, he has diagnosed Capgras Syndrome and is thrilled to have a subject on which to write an academic paper. Narcissist A meets Narcissist B and one of them holds all the power and control; the one who seeks kudos among his peers in psychiatry. The one who decides Ryan's continued detention. What an utter wankapin. And before you ask, it's a type of lotus.'

It wasn't unlike Monica to swear, disguised or not, but use of such language in this context was a warning sign. She was up for a fight.

'Over to me then,' Peddyr said, sitting upright again. 'I may have something for you to work with. Ryan Holden is more than a fitness fanatic. He has a home gym in the spare room, a multi-gym and free weights, and a full-length mirror. A chin-up bar in a doorway.

Monica pursed her lips briefly. 'Doesn't surprise me.'

'He also has an enormous stash of supplements and muscle building compounds on shelves. He asked me to bring some back with his clothes. Take a look.' Peddyr handed her a glass jar labelled as "Skulpta-Bulk". 'For extreme sports and bodybuilding, according to the label.' He gave a self-satisfied grin. 'There was loads more of this muck.' He referred to his notepad. 'Fat Stripper, Testo plus, and tablets called Vasculators. Would you believe they're only available on the internet?'

Shaking the bottle, Monica returned his smile. 'You may be the oldest trainee solicitor in town, but by crikey you know your stuff when it comes to cracking puzzles. Here is Ryan's vice. He *does* do drugs, ones laughingly called natural. Dietary products like whey protein and creatine, and supplements which most likely contain testosterone and steroids.'

'I can see what it's supposed to do to your body, but what does it do to your head? Enough to make you paranoid?' Peddyr asked.

With a quick twist of her wrist Monica read the label on the jar in her hand. 'Most of these labels are inaccurate,' she said, scanning the minuscule writing. 'If he's taking these and they contain steroids it could explain the quick temper. Potentially they could be a cause of irrational thinking. One thing's for certain, they are not good for you. Too much of this crap and the liver packs up, and your willy shrinks, never to be seen again.'

Peddyr felt reassured about his suspicions. Ryan Holden was not squeaky clean. 'That boy is looking increasingly guilty of harming Scott Fletcher. If he was rational, then what he alleged about Fletcher may well be correct. There's the motive. He had the time to commit the crime that morning. He had the strength. In the meantime the police have his mother in custody and Ryan is agreeing with them, acting as if he thinks she killed Fletcher.' He stood. 'Right, if I can pass scrutiny from Ruby-Rottweiler on reception, I'd better take these bags to the lad or he'll think I've forgotten him.'

## 13

## INGRATITUDE

When they had arrived no more than an hour earlier to bag up Ryan's remaining clothing as part of the murder investigation, the police had allowed him to keep his underpants. However, Joran had insisted Ryan wore more than a pair of boxer shorts while he waited for his own clothes to arrive, and made it clear this was non-negotiable. The items of clothing provided were so appalling Ryan refused to put them on at first. 'I wouldn't be seen dead wearing those,' he had said. He didn't win the argument and couldn't wait to take off the musty-smelling baggy tracksuit pants and oversized sweatshirt on loan to him. So it was fortunate that Mr Quirk had arrived when he did. The indignity of being stripped of his only possessions rapidly evaporated when fresh clothes and footwear arrived. His own clothes from home, neatly packed. 'Escape from Carol without getting groped, Peter?' he asked.

'I stand before you in one piece.'

Until then Ryan hadn't taken much notice of Mrs Morris's assistant. Now he deigned to give him the once over. The bloke was almost as tall as him and sturdy. He had the sort of eyes that let you know he was watching you, interested rather than critical. The way his mouth turned up at the corners, ready to smile at short notice, made him appear reliable and friendly. Apart from furrows on his brow, there were laughter lines creasing his face, most of them around the eyes. Summing him up, Ryan decided he was physically strong but mentally weedy; a mug. Easily fooled because he was eager to please. 'So, Mr Security Consultant, is my mother's home as you left it?'

'All the doors and windows are tightly shut and locked. Your neighbour Carol is one of the best guards I've come across in my time and she is keeping an eye on the place. However, it won't be long before the police trot along and rummage through the drawers.'

Ryan buttoned up the flies on a pair of jeans. 'Tell them, if they go through my stuff they'll find the evidence about Scott Fletcher on my laptop. I kept a diary, like a blog I was going to post when I found out his real name. I was so close. The police have to follow the information I've saved, it's not hard. Even an average copper could manage it.' Resigned that his mother could not secure his early release from hospital, Ryan was pushing hard at the only door to freedom.

'The trouble is, once the police take your laptop as evidence it will disappear for months while they investigate.'

This was something Ryan had not considered. He just needed to get his hands on the laptop, and he would publish what he had. The stink created in the media would be enough to get his section papers torn in two. 'Shit. I need that little tosser of a consultant to see the proof I'm not mad. Can you go back and get it for me, Peter?'

The man shook his head. 'You can't keep it here. If I bring it in to the unit, the staff won't let you have it back until you're discharged.' There was a long pause while Quirk appeared to think deeply. 'And if I smuggle it in pretending it's mine, it will be confiscated if they see you using it.' He flicked his eyes towards the corridor and the member of staff sitting there pretending not to be listening to the conversation.

Ryan sat down, tight-lipped, on the side of his bed. This man was right. Staff nurses Wayne and Joran had taken every single item out of the bags Mr Quirk had brought in. They had confiscated Ryan's razor, telling him he would have to request it when he needed a shave and be closely monitored while using it. He wasn't allowed to keep his supplements. The one consolation was being permitted the snacks, fruit and biscuits Carol had packed for him. 'Eat the pies now. You can't keep them in your room,' he was told by Wayne.

As he chomped on a homemade mini quiche, not offering any to the man who had gone out of his way to bring his clothes and wash kit, Ryan tried again. 'I tell you what, Peter, Mrs Morris would be impressed if you found proof of my sanity. It would save her a job.' The man so willing to prove his worth would surely fall for this, Ryan realised. He was so incredibly malleable. Ryan loved people-pleasers like Peter Quirk. 'You really could help her,' he added, with his most winning smile.

There was a momentary pause while this proposal was considered, with some low humming accompanying the thoughtful expression on Mr Quirk's face. 'I suppose it wouldn't do any harm if I were to collect your laptop, take it back to our offices, print off the information and, if useful enough, Mrs Morris could present that to your doctors as proof.'

Mr Peter Quirk was obviously an idiot. Ryan knew he wasn't supposed to do things like that. 'Could you? It would be brilliant, and I'd be able to get out of here and be there for my mum.'

Sounding sincere was easy enough; so was exploiting the ancient trainee solicitor to whom he willingly gave the passwords and usernames required to access his blog site. Naive and pliable, that's how Peter Quirk came across. A man who would keep his word. 'Hold on to my set of house keys for as long as you like. I may need one or two other things from my room. Wayne says there's a gym here I can use if I behave myself. Right now, the Nazi bastards won't even let me go for a run unless its round and round the courtyard.' He flicked a thumb towards the window.

'There are shorts and some trainers in your bag. I'm sure you'll get to the gym soon enough.' Mr Quirk paused. 'I'll be off then,' he said.

Ryan pulled on a tight fitting tee-shirt, admiring himself, flexing his pecs. Glancing over his shoulder as his visitor left the room, he acknowledged the efforts made on his behalf with a brief, 'Cheers for this, Pete,' and began unpacking, placing the rest of his clothes neatly within the slim doorless wardrobe. All he had to do now was to keep himself occupied and wait for his discharge in the next couple of days. Meanwhile, he would amuse himself by flirting with the only attractive female in the place, a young occupational therapist by the name of Tiffany.

## 14

## OPEN YOUR EARS

*L*unch had been a wishful thought, so when Peddyr reached home that evening, he sniffed the air almost as soon as he'd opened the back door to the flat. He and Connie had lived there since well before setting up P. Q. Investigations on his retirement from consultancy work. An ex-policeman had a limited shelf-life when it came to high-profile security contracts and the physical demands they entailed. Besides, he had made a promise to Connie and, as good as his word, when son number two left home, they distracted themselves from their empty nest with a new adventure. One less fraught with danger and derring-do and notably fewer trips abroad; some because of their sensitive nature, never to be discussed before, during, or after the event.

'I'm home,' he shouted, lifting his head to sample the air once more. 'Tell me spag bol is on the menu? All I can smell is fresh paint.' Above the sound of Abba coming from a Bluetooth speaker in one of the spare bedrooms, the reply was cheery.

'Is that you, Lao Gong?'

Peddyr didn't acknowledge her affectionate Mandarin greeting of him as "husband", instead he headed to the kitchen in search of emergency rations. He was standing at the fridge with the door wide open when Connie buzzed into the room wearing paint-dappled dungarees and a bright polka dot headscarf to protect her sleek bob. Holding a paint kettle in one hand and a brush in the other, she paused, stretched up on tiptoe to kiss his cheek then passed by, aiming for a compact utility area.

'I'll be right with you. Just got to clean my brushes,' she said. 'Dinner is in the oven. Can you last ten minutes?' With a chunk of cheese in his mouth, Peddyr couldn't reply with more than a shake of his head and a strangled hum through his nose. As the door to the fridge swung gently closed he turned his attention to the kitchen table and sighed.

'I'll lay the table, shall I? I take it you've been decorating all day.'

'Not the whole time,' his wife replied, throwing her comments over one shoulder as she worked the paintbrushes clean, her slender hands in vinyl gloves. 'I started the background searches as soon as you called. I know it was all over the national news, but as usual they never mention a name, just that a woman has been arrested. I never for one minute imagined it would be Sarah Holden. What an appalling situation. She must have had good reason to behave like that. I can't quite take it all in, she's usually so serene.'

Peddyr too was wrestling with his conscience. Tragedy had struck the Holden family for a second time. As soon as Bernie had confirmed Sarah Holden was the client he was so determined to defend, Peddyr had vowed to do what he could in support of Jim's family.

Two table mats laid opposite each other, cutlery in one fist, Peddyr was on automatic pilot. Salivating at the thought of a filling meal, he placed condiments in the centre of the table. He was never disappointed with anything Connie cooked because his wife was a dab hand at turning simple ingredients into dishes any chef would be proud of. True to her Hong Kong roots she was also lightning with a wok, a knife, and a chopping board. Fortunately, she loved him and had never raised a kitchen utensil in anger.

'Bernie doesn't think she did it,' he told Connie when she emerged from the utility room to throw her gloves into the swing bin.

Her delicate frame stiffened. 'That's not what the media are saying,' she blurted out, regarding him closely. 'Today, BBC Valley Radio said a woman in her fifties had been arrested at the scene and police were expecting to charge her.' She trotted across the kitchen and stood directly in front of him, resting her hands on his upper arms. 'Jim Holden is haunting you, isn't he?' she asked, staring up at him, sympathetically. 'Reparation is the word you are looking for,' she said. 'I know you too well. I see it in your eyes, I hear it in your voice. You think an injustice was done when police closed his hit-and-run case, and you want to go on a personal crusade to right that wrong.'

He released a pent up sigh. 'There are times, Lao Po, when I wish you wouldn't read my mind. However, this isn't one of them. It's going to be tough and I'm determined not to be fobbed off by bureaucracy. You have hit the proverbial nail on the head, Wifey. I'm still firmly of the opinion that the investigation into Jim's accident never went far enough.'

Seated at the table, beef stroganoff piled into a nest of rice, Peddyr could concentrate on nothing else until his hunger was satisfied. 'Mighty. That's better, my guts were eating themselves, I was starving.' He brushed off the doubtful glance from Connie. 'Really... Ask Monica if you don't believe me. We were so bloody long at the hospital, I thought I'd never see daylight again.'

Lively eyes never missing a thing, his wife was straight in with her interrogation. 'Which hospital? Why were you and Monica speaking to Sarah's son anyway? Does this have anything to do with the killing? I thought you and Bernie were taking on her case. Is Bernie still coming here this evening?'

Pretending he was caught in a wind tunnel, because that's what it felt like, Peddyr threw himself backwards. 'Hold the bleedin' phone, woman. One question at a time.'

In truth he'd forgotten about the arrangement made earlier with Bernard Kershaw, and resentment at having his evening disrupted bubbled to the surface. 'Bollocks. I suppose he'll be blathering on for hours about Dreary and how marriage is sacrosanct. Make him see sense, will you? He's turned into a proper grouch. He even had a pop at Monica. Actually, when she's around he's worse than grouchy.'

'Only because he's in love with her,' Connie piped up. She lifted a glass of water to her smiling lips and winked at him. 'Or hadn't you worked that out, Mister Investigator?'

Speechless, Peddyr froze and several seconds passed as he thought about this revelation. 'Bugger... Is he really? I must be overtired or something. I completely missed the clues on that one. Bloody hell...' he said, blinking down at the last few grains of rice on his plate.

Connie had him in her sights and there was no escape. 'Yes, you've had a long and tiring day and for that reason alone I haven't nagged about your swearing this evening.

Bloody, bugger and bollocks, have put in an appearance and I'm waiting for the obligatory bastard, which is bound to slip out soon enough.'

She cleared his plate and carried on with her insightful lecture while loading the dishwasher. 'Bernie is wrestling with his conscience. He and Deidre have held a delicate truce for decades; each leading their own lives, filling time with work, bringing up children, rugby, golf, the Rotary Club, and the like. But faced with the hideous reality of a retirement spent with someone whose company you find intolerable... well, is it any wonder he was back in the office within a fortnight of his last case?'

Connie Quirk was not only a good cook, but she was also talented with languages and an extraordinary observer of life. Rarely was she wrong. If she was, she admitted to it. When the call arrived at Bagshot & Laker from Maggie Holden, Sarah's case should have been directed to the criminal law hotshot in the firm. However, flexing his senior partner muscles, Bernie had agreed to take it on, not merely as a favour to the family but as a means of escape. To return to a place where he was needed and admired.

Peddyr had worked that out without much effort, but he had completely missed Bernie's infatuation with Monica. 'I think you should speak with him in private about that tonight,' he suggested to Connie. 'He's already said he'd like to talk to you about the situation at home but he'll never open up about Monica if I'm there.' And so it was agreed. In return, Peddyr had to share the events of his day by chatting with Connie in the time between finishing a bowl of ice cream and when he knew the doorbell would ring at precisely eight o'clock. Bernard was a stickler for punctuality.

'I'll head to my office and take a look at what you've found for me,' Peddyr said. 'Anything on Ryan's friend Bez?'

'The reports are on the shared computer drive, Lao Gong. Seek and ye shall find,' Connie replied with a patient laugh as she wiped down a kitchen work surface. 'I told you that not ten minutes ago.'

'Sorry, I must have been listening with my husband ears on.' Like many a married man, Peddyr had developed selective hearing to tune out anything resembling nagging. It didn't always work. 'Did you have time to check out Ryan's cousin? His name has cropped up a couple of times today.' The wet dishcloth hit him slowly but squarely on the left cheek.

## 15

## THE CHAIR THAT EATS YOU

*U*nusually, Bernard Kershaw had been late to see
Connie, and Peddyr was already ensconced in his
office when the doorbell rang. The room was his haven. A
gift from his wife, Peddyr's office had been 'specially deco-
rated for him, in secret, while he and Connie were away
from home undertaking their first-ever case. He looked up
from the computer screen to remind himself of her efforts.

In her quest for a special present to celebrate their new
venture, Connie had imagined a stereotypical film-noir-
cum-Sam-Spade theme and this had been realised with help
from a young student designer in return for six language
lessons in basic Cantonese. Ever careful with money,
Connie had trawled junk shops and car boot sales to gather
the necessary items of furniture and she had done a brilliant
job. The door was part-glazed in acid-etched signage
announcing that the heart of P. Q. Investigations lay within.

Inspecting the pictures on the walls, he acknowledged
the familiar faces. Peter Falk as Columbo, Raymond Burr as
Ironside, and Humphrey Bogart as Sam Spade himself

gazed back at him. Knowing her husband's love for British detective stories, Connie had dedicated a whole section of one wall to studio portraits of classic characters old and new: Sherlock, Poirot, Morse, Frost. It was pure unadulterated cheese, and Peddyr loved it. In recent years he'd been contracted to act as a consultant on one or two well-known TV detective series and, as mementos, several signed photos took pride of place in reception behind Connie's welcoming desk. They nestled among the cacti and succulents she was so proud of not killing.

Having spent most of the day driving back and forth between Bosworth Bishops and the Marsworth Unit, Peddyr was making out a list of people he wanted to speak to next, but before he could decide, his office door opened, preceded by a gentle knock. Connie entered carrying a plate of doorstop sandwiches followed by a frazzled Bernard with a glass of milk in his hand.

'You have good reason for breaking the golden rule, I take it?' Peddyr asked. For as long as his office had been fully functional, the house rule was a simple one: the office is for work only. He raised a frowning query, staring at the plate of sandwiches. 'More food?'

'These are for Bernie, not for you, greedy guts,' Connie admonished. 'He's been at the cop shop all day.'

With one sentence it was made plain this was no social visit.

'As a suspect in an indictable offence, Sarah Holden is being held for a further twelve hours on the Chief Super's say so, and they've applied to court for an extension on top of that.' Making the mistake of heading for the most comfortable seat in the room, Bernard handed Connie the glass and sank deep into a leather armchair. Despite his height and full frame it seemed to envelop him. He immediately sought help. 'How am I supposed to get back out again?'

'Never mind that for now,' Connie said, moving an occasional table within his reach. She placed the glass of milk down beside him and passed over a paper serviette and the sandwiches. 'You relax and we'll pull you out when it's time to leave.' Trying not to laugh, she gave him an apologetic smile. 'The springs went some time ago.'

Steering the conversation back to business, Peddyr asked if Sarah Holden was the only suspect in the eyes of the police. He listened with his investigator's ears finally tuned in to Bernard's account of the questioning at the police station and to his concerns about his client.

'The thing is, Pedd, she didn't kill the fellow. I know it deep in my enormous gut and slightly balding head. Regrettably, the police have a different view. Webster wants a result, and he wants it pronto. At any time this evening, he could have charged her and dragged out the investigation with her on remand, but he's out to make an impression. He thinks he has the guilty party bang to rights and he's going to prove it in record time.'

Connie's face fell at the mention of the detective in charge of the case. 'You never said it was Whiffy-Breath-Webster who was questioning Sarah Holden, Pedd. Oh, that poor woman.'

'Sorry, love. Didn't want to put you off your DIY mission.'

Bernard picked up a thick sandwich packed with cheese and pickle, giving it a loving look as it neared his lips. 'Anyway, Pedd, how did you and Monica get on with young Ryan?' he asked, before taking his first bite. He then signalled for Connie to stay in the room and to sit with them. 'I need you in on this Connie. I'm afraid the decorating will have to wait if we are to see justice done.'

Having brought Bernard and Connie up to date with Monica's findings and her pending showdown at the tribunal hearing due in the next fortnight, Peddyr explained to them what he had found so far on Ryan's laptop. After that he made a series of proposals.

'We need to split up,' he said. 'Connie, you go to see Maggie Holden. Grandmother to grandmother, find out everything about her relationships with Ryan and Sarah, and most importantly what the financial situation is. Scott Fletcher was up to something and it must involve money. Bernie, get some sleep but keep us informed of new developments and dig out anything discreditable about Scott Fletcher from the police. They know he's not legit. I am going to speak to a lout called Bez who drives a van, and then to meet up with Dexter Booth who I'm told works at Tottering's auction house.'

Connie looked shocked. 'Tonight?'

'I'm meeting Bez tonight because Ryan assured me he'll be at home now. I've been advised not to wear any decent clothes and not to sit down. The place is a filthy pit by all accounts. Dexter I'm meeting tomorrow, probably at his place of work. He's not expecting me because it's better if I go in cold, like I did with Carol Brightman. After that, Lao Po, we are going to delve headlong into Scott Fletcher's private life and cross reference it with Ryan's findings.'

He got up from behind his desk and sat on one corner of it, stretching his back. 'If Ryan was right and Fletcher was leading a double life, let's find out for ourselves who we are dealing with. We haven't got long. And somewhere along the line, I'm hoping that the niggle in the back of my mind will turn into a fully-fledged theory.'

The timescale was very tight indeed and Peddyr explained to his wife why they had to work so quickly. 'Duncan Webster needs bringing down to size. He's more interested in arse-licking the top brass than he is in carrying out a thorough investigation.' Bernard and Peddyr were competitive by nature and this challenge was one neither of them was prepared to lose.

'If Scott Fletcher was *not* killed by Sarah Holden, he could have been killed by her son,' Peddyr said. 'But if he was not killed by Ryan Holden and the police are not looking for anyone else, then it's down to us to find an alternative culprit.' He placed one hand flat on the desk. 'I'm telling you: Ryan is either the best liar I've come across or he's innocent of any murder.'

'And I'm telling you, his mother is completely innocent as well as the worst liar I've ever represented,' Bernard said, resting his empty tumbler back on the table. 'Now, you two, take one arm each and pull at them like Billy-O. Failing that, call the fire brigade. I can neither drive nor sleep in a bed whilst wearing an old chair.'

Leaving the flat, Peddyr accompanied Bernie to his car. It was only a short drive to the other side of the park where he lived and in normal circumstances Bernie would have walked and stayed for a glass of wine or two, but the clock was ticking for Sarah Holden and both men strongly suspected a rat was running loose and undetected. So far.

## 16

## JIM HOLDEN'S GHOST

*I*n the airless cell, Sarah was alone again with her thoughts and memories, some of them crushed by the recent painful revelations about Scott. She tried to push his treachery from her mind, preferring to believe the police were wrong in their assertions, but that photograph of him with another woman kept flashing to the front of her mind, robbing her of emotional strength. What if the police were right?

In an effort to see what he might have hidden from her when they were together, she rewound to the moment she and Scott first met. What had she missed? Had she been so blinded by infatuation that obvious signs were overlooked?

Staring into space, she sat on the unforgiving mattress, blocking out the noises around her. She asked herself an important question, a defining question. Why had she never believed Ryan about Scott being a con artist of some sort?

And the answer? Because she hadn't wanted to doubt Scott and because she thought Ryan was paranoid. Her son's behaviour had led her to that conclusion. It was irrational, compulsive, obsessive and destructive.

\* \* \*

*T*he first time Sarah had met Scott Fletcher face-to-face was when he had walked into Craven & Tilbury Letting Agents' office. His story had been a typical one of separation, pending divorce, needing to settle somewhere he was familiar with. 'Holden… I went to school with a boy called Holden. Are you related to Jimmy Holden, by any chance?' he'd asked her over the phone. After that, conversation had become more relaxed as they had found common ground. 'Sorry to hear about Jim. What a shock for you. Perhaps I shouldn't have mentioned I knew him.'

'No, I don't mind at all,' Sarah had replied on hearing the embarrassment in Scott's voice. 'Talking about him keeps his memory alive.'

'I never knew him as an adult. We left the area when I was ten. Are his parents still around?'

By the time she shook hands with Scott Fletcher they had already built up a picture of each other's lives. Or so she had thought at the time. However, she hadn't been expecting to see such a handsome man giving her a captivating smile. Mr Scott Fletcher seemed to reel her in with his steel-grey eyes as he had taken her hand and hypnotised her with his voice. Her friend Carol would have called him "distractingly hot".

Scott Fletcher had wanted to see the flat at Primrose Court, but to do so he was required to produce relevant identification. The days of unscheduled viewings were long gone, and thanks to Jim, Sarah took her personal safety very seriously.

Copies of Scott Fletcher's driving licence and ID from his job with EDF Energy were produced. Sarah was satisfied and her visit with him was duly logged onto the computer system and shared with office colleagues. Her whereabouts would be known, the CCTV at the entrance to Primrose Court would provide additional security. Like any other day in her job she had no real reason to feel unsafe.

'He liked the flat, Jim,' she said aloud, once again seeking guidance from the one man in her life she had always trusted. 'We checked references, bank statements… he even produced a letter from his solicitor about divorce proceedings. The police must have it wrong.'

Again that photograph of Scott with Stephanie popped into her mind's eye. Where had it been taken and when? Another memory jolted her. Something Trina McIlhenny had said while standing in the doorway of Scott's garage. *'Oh, did she find out about the wife?'* She had said it in such a way that Sarah knew there was something in the police's line of questioning. They had asked if Stephanie had been to his flat. Sarah had no idea. Had she – and if so, when and why?

Sarah realised she needed to get a message to Bernard Kershaw; she wanted to know more about Stephanie Fletcher.

## 17

## THE SMELL OF GUILT

*P*eddyr made the most of a pleasant late-summer evening and walked a mile via footpaths and cut-throughs to where Bez resided, a cul-de-sac in a rundown housing estate. He spied the tatty white LDV diesel van parked at the kerbside, noting the rust coming through the door sills, the Macdonald's wrappers and other detritus taking up space atop the dashboard. Annoyed, he sucked air through his clenched teeth. It irked him when vehicles weren't cared for. This was a work horse, a tool of Bez's trade and yet it was neglected, as was the outside of the house where its owner lived.

Steeling himself for the odours he was about to face, Peddyr approached the door. The doorbell wasn't working, so he poked at the letterbox and rapped his knuckles on the frosted glass until a shadowy outline appeared. Predictably they were wearing a baseball cap, indoors, back to front. After a quick scan as the door opened, Peddyr found nothing to surprise him: a man in his late twenties wearing grubby combat trousers, topped off with an equally unhygienic tee-shirt with a faded logo on it. To Peddyr's dismay the man had come to the door in flip-flops. Ordinarily this wouldn't have attracted his attention, but the feet on display were blackened with filth between the toes and under the nails. 'I'm looking for Bez. I phoned earlier,' he said, not wasting time on civil introductions.

'That's me.'

Bez was exactly how Wayne the staff nurse at the Marsworth Unit had described him; And Carol hadn't pulled her punches, saying he was a "dim little scruff-bag". Ryan's so-called best friend was his polar opposite in every way. In one hand he held a burning cigarette, the rest of his dirty fingers were wrapped around a can of lager. He invited Peddyr to enter by saying grudgingly, 'You'd best come on in then.'

Bosworth Bishops nestled in the Cotswolds and Bez's accent reflected this more obviously than most people his age. He didn't seem to care about his clothing or the way he sounded. Given the funk of body odour that trailed him, Peddyr judged that Bez also didn't much care for water and soap.

A long day behind him already, Peddyr repeated his reasons for being there, with no frills attached. 'As I said on the phone, I'm working with the legal team representing your friend Ryan Holden in his appeal against being sectioned. We are required to collect relevant information to build a picture of Ryan's mental state and how it could have deteriorated. On top of this, we're looking to identify his support networks in the community in anticipation of his discharge from hospital.' The two men stood in the hall-way, a television blasting out from a room behind them. 'Are we alright to talk here?'

'We could go in the kitchen, like,' Bez said, paddling

round on the sticky carpet. He headed to a compact kitchen strewn with unwashed pots, pans and crockery. The pedal bin overflowed with takeaway packaging and the whole room reeked of rotting food. However, with the door closed it was marginally quieter than the hallway had been.

'What do you want to know?' Bez asked, dragging a wooden chair away from a cluttered table, one obviously never used for eating meals on; it would have been an impossibility without calling in contract cleaners beforehand.

To avoid leaning against any surface, Peddyr remained on his feet, poised uncomfortably near the back door. 'Did you notice Ryan becoming paranoid at all?'

'Don't be bloody daft. He's never been paranoid in his life, and I should know. I done enough weed in my time to send any bugger round the bend. Went to Amsterdam once, nearly never made it back 'cos I thought every fucker I saw was out to get me.' Bez poked at the edge of one nostril before examining the findings and wiping it down a trouser leg.

'If you don't mind me asking, how come you and Ryan are mates?' Peddyr asked, trying to mask his disgust. 'You're chalk and cheese. What are his other mates like?'

'He don't have a big group of mates, just me and a few others. We go out, he drives, pulls the skirt, gives 'em one in my van, like… or anywhere he can find. He does the driving while we get bladdered. He's more of a loner. Used to spend a lot of time with his Uncle Chris until they moved to Wales. He's tight with Dexter though. That's his cousin, like.'

'And what's *he* like?' Peddyr wished he hadn't made use of the word "like" because it was clearly Bez's favourite and already overused. 'Does Dexter go out drinking with you all?'

The reaction was telling. 'Dexter Booth? Are you kidding? He wouldn't be seen dead with a bunch of trades. All my mates are plumbers, tilers, toshers, sparks... that sort of thing, like.' Tipping his head back as far as he could, Bez took a long last slug from the can in his hand and dragged on the remaining millimetres of his cigarette before putting one inside the other with a short-lived fizz. 'Now then... Chris Booth, Dexter's dad, used to be Mr Smooth back in the day, a real lady's man. To be fair, I think he still plays away from home, which is why his wife is so pissed off all the time. Know what I mean?'

Peddyr knew exactly what was meant and at the mention of the name Chris Booth he sharpened his questions. He had never met the man but knew more than most about his background. 'And Dexter takes after his old man which is why Ryan likes to dress well and chat up the girls. Is that it?'

'Sort of,' Bez said, frowning. 'Ryan would love to be just like his Uncle Chris, and he sure as heck would like a wife as pretty as Dexter's. Of course, *he's* Mr Family Man these days with a babby on the way. You see, Dexter is the man Ryan was supposed to be.'

'I don't get you?' The cigarette smoke was irritating Peddyr's throat and his eyes were stinging with it, but he was gaining some interesting insights and ignored the discomfort.

'Ryan's dad was fuzz, top brass, like. He was a man's man and an honest family man, like Dexter is. Jim Holden was the sort of bloke who could turn his hand to anything, like. If the lawnmower broke, he'd fix it himself. That sort of thing, sort of like.' Bez was progressing in his vocabulary, Peddyr realised. He'd added "sort of" to "like".

'And Ryan?'

''E can't fix nothing. All 'e wants to do is make himself look good and smell nice for the ladies. 'E had a good car for work but lost that with his job when 'e got caught screwing Juicy Julie, like. It's his body they love. Cycles miles, goes to the gym, and took up rock climbing to prove how macho 'e can be. It's sort of for effect.'

For all his lack of eloquence, Bez was quite astute when it came to analysing Ryan. 'I'm not daft. I know 'e hangs around with me 'cos I've got a van and me and the boys are no threat to him, no competition, like. I'm useful when he wants something fixin' or mendin'. Keeps his mum happy too. She has loads of money tied up in that house of theirs and when his gran dies Ryan will cop the bloody lot in 'er savings account. Keeps them both sweet.'

'But he wouldn't get everything if his mother married again,' Peddyr said. 'Scott Fletcher was about to ruin his long-term plans for a life of idle luxury.'

Bez nodded along, twisting his baseball cap to face the front. 'That's about the size of it. Ryan couldn't let it lie. 'E was fucking beside himself. 'E hated that bloke. But it were Dexter what put him onto Scott, like. 'E's the smart one.'

The police hadn't been to see Bez, neither had they shown more than a passing interest in Ryan other than to note his presence at Primrose Court on the morning Scott Fletcher had been killed and take his clothes for forensics way later than they should have been. Peddyr vacillated about whether Ryan Holden had killed Scott Fletcher, and whether he was of sound mind at the time of the crime. Maybe he was simply a good liar, a very adept one. Then again, maybe he was innocent.

These doubts continued to grate as Peddyr walked home again.

\* \* \*

*A* hot shower and a thorough scrub later, he slid into bed beside Connie with the intention of reading his book for a while. He could tell by her breathing she was still awake, and it wasn't long before curiosity got the better of her.

'Well?' She rolled over and sat up.

'I'll tell you how it went if you tell me what Bernie said to you in the kitchen while you were making those sandwiches.' The game was on. 'You go first.'

'No, you go first, Lao Gong,' she replied. 'Yours is work, my information is personal.'

Once he had reprised the story of his visit to Bez's unsavoury home, he picked up his book again, as if preparing to read. 'So, as Monica thought, Ryan Holden is only out for number one. Classic narcissist. Whether he has the guts to kill anyone is another matter but I'm pretty sure he is involved somehow, if not the actual perpetrator.'

Connie tapped him on the shoulder. 'Do you want to hear about my chat with Bernie, or not?'

Teasing her, he said, 'No, it can wait, Lao Po. Besides it might alter my working relationship with Monica. She's very good at her job, that woman. After seeing her doing her stuff today, I wish we had used her last year in Gabriella Dixon's case. Still, I'll know for next time.' He aimed his nose back at the page he was reading.

'So you don't want to hear that Bernie is barely functioning because he can't stop thinking about Monica? Or that he has no idea whether the feeling is mutual, or that he's actually losing weight and has taken up exercise?'

'No, and I don't need to know,' Peddyr replied, deadpan.

'Right. Then I won't tell you.'

'Good.'

Connie lay back down again and snuggled under the light duvet. This lasted all of five minutes and Peddyr had barely picked up the story where he'd left off the previous night, when she abruptly sat up again. '*Macmillan and Wife*,' she said.

'What?' Peddyr placed the open book into his lap.

'Rock Hudson and…' She paused, frowning. 'Oh, dear. Who played the wife? The one who used to wear baseball shirts in bed.' When there was no answer from Peddyr, she shrugged. 'Never mind. The point is, they are missing from your investigator wall. I must find them.'

'Do what you like, just leave me in peace and go to sleep.'

'I can't. I keep thinking about Bernie telling Deidre he wants a divorce.'

Finally she had divulged the real reason for her fidgeting and frequent interruptions. The news baffled Peddyr. 'You managed to persuade him to divorce Dreary in the time it took to make a sandwich?' Straight talking was his default response when a diplomatic approach was required, but Connie was generally more tactful.

'Well, it was either that or play a round of golf with the man, and he hates losing, so I saved him the embarrassment. He may have all the gear but his skill at Thwack Bugger is about as good as yours.'

She hadn't caused offence. Peddyr was painfully aware how poor he was when it came to hitting a golf ball with a club in a specific direction, hence the name he gave the game. *Thwack… bugger* was the soundtrack to his sorry efforts at mastering golf. The reason he never took up the game seriously.

'And it saves me from The Phwah-Phwahs,' his wife added, raising her eyes to the ceiling for a second.

Formal gatherings and the occasional brief visit to the golf club were the only occasions Connie and Peddyr spent in the company of Bernard's wife. She was bitter and over-bearing, spending as little time as possible talking with her husband, preferring the company of the pompous and boastful couples who were to be found dining out at private clubs and overpriced restaurants.

These objectionable people were referred to collectively by the Quirks as The Phwah-Phwahs, mimicking the superior, self-important tone of their voices. 'I can't abide The Phwah-Phwahs,' Connie said emphatically, sticking out her tongue.

Deidre Kershaw likewise held the Quirks in low esteem. They were not good enough for her family and she made that plain enough with a pained smile and deliberately bland conversation whenever she was forced to socialise with them. It was her firm belief that Peddyr in particular was to blame for her husband spending too much time at the rugby club, being rowdy and uncivilised. Peddyr was the one who dragged the infinitely more respectable Bernard to the pub and forced him into socially embarrassing situations. In her opinion, Peddyr was common and uncouth. Because of him, her husband refused to climb the social ladder, for which Deidre increasingly despised both men.

'I wish you hadn't told me that,' Peddyr announced. Then, picking up his book again, he said, 'Now we'll have to take sides.'

Connie gave a gentle chortle of contentment.

\* \* \*

*I*n the morning, Peddyr headed out for an early-morning dip at the Bosworth Lido. The air was fresh at that time of day, but he wouldn't be the only mad fool going for a swim in the outdoors, there was a regular crowd. Luckily, he had built up a good relationship with the couple who ran the facility, Ted and Doreen Impey. They were stalwarts of the place and flexible enough to allow him use of the pool after closing, if he knocked at their door for the key. 'Just don't drown,' was the only stipulation. Since his knee had suffered as a result of Bernie Kershaw landing on top of him with a bag of curry, his days of jogging round the park had been put on hold, but swimming was still there to save the day and he much preferred the outdoor pool to using the larger indoor facility during the winter months. Bosworth Leisure Centre was too far to walk as well as being impersonal and over-chlorinated. The lido was the opposite in every way.

'Missed you yesterday, Peddyr,' Ted Impey said, waving him through.

Pushing the turnstile, dutifully flashing his season ticket, Peddyr replied with a smile. 'Had a bloody breakfast meeting, would you believe? How's the water temperature today?'

Ted didn't have time to answer before another customer arrived. A familiar figure in unfamiliar clothes presented himself at the lido kiosk. 'Don't mind if I join you, old bean? Your wife thinks it's high time I made this part of my regular fitness regime.'

Peddyr's response escaped as a loud 'Pah!' as he inwardly cursed Connie for her eagerness to be helpful, thereby ruining her husband's morning routine. As much as he appreciated Bernie's company and friendship, the pool was Peddyr's mental escape zone. The chilly water magically restored him. It would never work if Bernie was going to start counting how many lengths they had achieved. 'Fancy that,' he said, recovering his composure and silently chiding himself for being ungracious. Bernie needed friends right now. 'What does the rest of your fitness regime consist of, may I ask?'

Bernie screwed up his face as he handed payment to Ted in return for a paper ticket. 'I'm foregoing golf. Taking up swimming and Tai Chi instead.' He looked around at the unfamiliar layout of the lido. 'Where do we change?'

Smiling, Peddyr led him to the wooden cubicles that were so cold and draughty in the early mornings. Poor old Bernie, out of his depth in love and lidos, he thought with a guilty trace of *schadenfreude*.

## DEXTER

*A*ccording to everyone Peddyr had spoken to, Dexter Booth held an important position at Tottering's Auction House. Not quite up there with Bonham's, Sotheby's and Christie's, Tottering's had a reputation for dealing in quality furniture and specialised in motor vehicles of all types. Peddyr was hoping to catch an auction in full swing and, from the anonymity of a crowd, watch Dexter wield a gavel.

He checked the website before leaving home and decided to take one of his motorbikes for a spin, while Connie made use of the car on a mission for him, reasoning that it would be easier for parking and for slipping through traffic jams. Connie gave the bikes stupid names, but Peddyr wasn't into personifying his machines. He rode the Triumph or the Kawasaki or the CCM. When he took his wife out on the red BMW, she rode pillion on "Rosie"; the yellow Enfield Continental GT she called "Daffodil". Typical Connie.

Today, Tottering's was holding an auction of militaria.

Flicking through the brochure, there was an advert for a specialist sale planned for October that caught Peddyr's eye. 'I wouldn't mind going to that,' he muttered. Tottering's were to be present at the International Classic Motorcycle event, selling everything from rare bikes to a set of Barry Sheene's leathers. Peddyr took a photograph of the advertisement with his phone in case he forgot the date or lost the brochure.

'Excuse me but is Dexter Booth running the sale today?' he asked one of the assistants registering bidders. She laughed in response. 'He likes to think so.' Her eyes swept the room. 'There he is on the rostrum, holding out a bottle of water to the lady in the pinstripe suit and pink tie. She's today's auctioneer. You'll like Jennie, she's funny and she really knows her stuff.'

Peddyr thanked her and melted into the throng of eager bidders.

Tall and striking, smartly dressed and clean-shaven, Dexter Booth bore a passing resemblance to Ryan Holden, although he was a slighter figure. He wore his neatly cut, thick coal-black hair swept back from his face. Together with three other men of varying ages, he took up position to one side of the room. As the auction participants settled into an excited hubbub, the auctioneer began her introduction and Dexter reached for the item at his feet which he held aloft for potential bidders to see.

'First in your catalogues, we have this fine example of World War One trench art,' the auctioneer informed the room.

Caught up in the excitement, it was several minutes before Peddyr could bring himself to slide away and speak to other members of Tottering's staff. He found an administration office and introduced himself as a potential customer making discreet early inquiries before taking the plunge and committing to sell precious items by auction. 'Can you explain to me how the commission charges work?' he asked. The woman dealing with his enquiry was trying her best to be helpful, but he could see from her level of distraction that he had chosen an inconvenient time to speak to her.

'It's all in the leaflet,' she said, flicking her eyes from him to the pamphlet in his hands and down to her computer screen. 'Or on the website,' she continued, rapidly. 'You can set up an account there too.'

'So, I'd need a valuation. Does Dexter Booth cover oriental art?' he asked.

'Dexter? No, he is one of our valuers but not of fine art. He's working on the operational side today. Lots of blarney and running around. He knows everything about this place, he started here with a part time job when he was still at school.' She gave a sympathetic smile as something crossed her mind. 'By rights he shouldn't even be here today. Family problems.' She sighed loudly. 'I don't know how the poor man is keeping so calm.'

With a sudden flurry of activity and a call from a colleague for assistance, she abandoned him.

It was plain Peddyr would not have chance to speak to Dexter at work, it had been an ill-conceived plan, so he rang Connie and instead arranged to meet her at Maggie Holden's home address.

\* \* \*

*W*hen Bernie had told him Maggie Holden had moved to a bungalow because of her mobility problems, he had been expecting something much more compact. What he saw was a world away from his image of an old person's bungalow, it was more of a single-story ranch house, complete with fountain and veranda. Of Texan proportions, Maggie Holden's property was situated well back from the road, beyond a sweeping driveway and carefully manicured lawns.

He parked his bike next to Connie's car, leaving his crash helmet and jacket outside. They were the disadvantage to travelling by motorcycle, as were his leathers and boots which creaked as he walked to the ornate porch.

The door was open before he had chance to use the brass bell pull, and he was greeted by a willowy unassuming woman with inquisitive eyes and a soft voice. The housekeeper, he assumed, although later he discovered she was a live-in companion and carer; evidently the word "housekeeper" was nowadays seen as demeaning. 'Do come in, Mr Quirk. Your wife is here, and Mrs Holden is expecting you.'

Apologising for his attire, Peddyr was shown into the extensive gardens at the rear of the house where he spotted Connie nattering to an elderly, immaculately dressed lady at a round teak table on the terrace shaded by a wide sun umbrella. Chiffon and pearls on subtle display, Maggie Holden was a gracious old-style hostess, not only in the way she dressed but in the way she held herself and spoke. She put on no airs and graces, immediately insisting that Peddyr should not be at all embarrassed about wearing the correct clothing for riding a motorbike.

'Your wife tells me you once worked with James,' she said, delicately shaking hands with him. 'I'm so glad to see you still take an interest in motorcycles.'

Peddyr felt a tug of embarrassment. How could he have been so thoughtless? James Holden had been killed while riding a damned bike and Peddyr had just rolled up her driveway on one. What an insensitive berk, he thought to himself. 'Needs must, Mrs Holden. My wife wanted the car this morning and I had several places to be. And she's right, I did come across James a few times over the years. We were on a number of training courses together, but he was a highflyer. I was more of a plodder.' He had decided against making a big issue of Jim's death. This wasn't the time. 'Did Connie tell you why we are here?'

'Yes, she did, and please call me Maggie. There's no need for formality.' She looked up at her companion. 'Flora dear, would you mind arranging for some refreshments? Tea, coffee or perhaps a soft drink?' she asked, touching manicured fingertips to Connie's hand.

Orders placed with the accommodating Flora, the talk turned to Sarah and Ryan. 'Your wife and I have been talking about Sarah. I love her like a daughter, you know. She's so kind and worries about everyone else apart from herself. She would never, ever deliberately harm another person.' Maggie clasped her bony hands together, holding them to her chest. 'I've been kept up to date by Bernard Kershaw – such an impressive man,' she went on. 'He believes Sarah to be innocent, and I agree with him. She will be acting as she is to protect Ryan. That boy has her wrapped tightly around his little finger and I'm ashamed to say I too have overindulged him.' Her rheumy eyes turned to Peddyr. 'You don't think *he* killed Scott Fletcher, do you?'

Peddyr took a deep breath. The question had been unexpectedly frank. 'I think he had a good enough motive, and he was seen at the flats at around the time Scott Fletcher met a sticky end, but when I saw him, he appeared to have no inkling of how Scott had been killed. Unfortunately, it seems he thinks Sarah did the dreadful deed.'

Maggie pulled her cashmere shawl tighter around her

shoulders. 'What a muddle. They must each think the other one did it.' She paused for a short while before continuing. 'Ryan was envious of Scott, you know. The very thought of another man getting his mother's attention would be hard enough, but once Scott had married Sarah, Ryan's ability to exploit the women in his life would be curtailed. Scott saw right through him.'

Connie had remained unusually quiet, but now she spoke. 'Who does Ryan take after with his ability to charm women?'

'Not my James. He was so tongue tied when he met anyone of the opposite sex he always sounded like a first class nincompoop.' This made Connie laugh. 'I think Ryan's personality comes courtesy of the Booths,' Maggie explained. 'Sarah's side of the family. Her brother Chris can be a smooth one when his wife allows him to be. Get him on his own and he's very witty. It's how they met, you know.'

'Who?' Connie enquired.

'My James met Sarah through Chris Booth. He and Chris knocked about together as youngsters. Those boys would spend hours fine-tuning their motorbikes. They were friends for years through the motorcycle club. Although they didn't attend the same school, it didn't seem to matter when it came to evenings, weekends and holidays. When they got to a certain age, Chris would chat up the girls and James would benefit too. Sarah was Chris Booth's irritating little sister, until James came to appreciate the lovely person who had been under his nose all that time.'

Maggie picked up her cup and took a small sip before explaining how her son had gone on to join the police while Chris had flitted from job to job as a mechanic of sorts, eventually setting up his own import-export business.

'Always to do with motorbikes. I understand he's still obsessed with anything mechanical.'

'Do you see much of him these days?' Peddyr asked.

Maggie released a rueful sigh. 'Very rarely. He and his wife moved to Pendine in Wales. I think someone said he had retired early. Their son Dexter is a pleasure to talk to, but the daughter Celia is rather acerbic, like her mother. I try to avoid her at family get-togethers.'

'So, Ryan's cousin Dexter... is he a charmer too?' Connie asked, carefully teasing out the information they needed from Maggie. 'He and Ryan are quite close, we understand.'

'They look like they could be brothers, but are very different characters,' Maggie said, inclining her head. 'Dexter is a couple of years older than Ryan, and when James died, young Dexter tried to become Ryan's role model, like an older brother to him. To some extent he managed this. He and Chris showed my grandson how to dress impeccably and chat to the girls.' She heaved a deep sigh. 'But Ryan only does what Ryan wants to do. I wish he'd chosen to be more like James, but I'm grateful to Dexter for what he tried to do. He's a good boy.'

The drinks arrived, ice jangling in tall glass tumblers, bringing a halt to the conversation as Flora joined them at the table.

'We were talking about Dexter and how helpful he's been to Sarah and Ryan these past years. Nice boy.'

Flora nodded in agreement. 'He's a lovely young man and he's done so well for himself. Let's hope Ryan listens to common sense. Once he's back on his feet and better, I'm sure Dexter will help him.'

'If Sarah goes to prison, I suppose he'll have to put a hold on the items due to go to auction,' Maggie said, a sorrowful expression clouding her face.

Peddyr took his cue here. 'I'm hoping to see Dexter later today. He wants to help in any way he can. I left him a phone message and he's replied via text to say he'll meet me. Work have given him some time off. Is there anything you want me to pass on?'

Connie sipped at her glass of cucumber water, catching Peddyr's eye with a meaningful look. He tried to read it but failed, returning her glance with a puzzled frown. Replacing her tumbler on the table, Connie asked, 'Did Sarah need to sell furniture for financial reasons?'

Maggie tittered, as did Flora. 'Goodness, no, dear. My James left her very well accounted for, and she's always worked; part time hours but even when Ryan was tiny she went to work, made her own money, kept her independence. It's what I admire about her.' Maggie seemed to lose the thread of the conversation, requiring Flora to remind her of the question about why Sarah was selling possessions at auction.

'She was getting rid of items that were unlikely to fit in a smaller house because she had her eye on a cottage, which would mean ridding herself of the larger pieces. As for the contents of the loft and garages, it was to be a mammoth task. Without Scott and Dexter's help she would never have managed.

'Ryan hasn't got a practical bone in his body. Having said that, he did help Dexter to make the list of items for auction. Not much of a contribution, but as some of the items belonged to him or were left to him in James's will, it was only right he took part.'

'Was Scott Fletcher present at the time the list for auction was being made?' Peddyr enquired.

'Oh, no, dear, that would have been inappropriate,' Maggie said, with a shake of her neat silver curls and pearl earrings. 'This was a personal family matter. He knew better than to make waves. He and Ryan were at logger-heads by then, with my grandson accusing him of being some sort of imposter. I knew it would end in tears.'

This was an astounding understatement to Peddyr's mind. More than tears had been shed.

## 19

# WHO WAS HE?

*C*onnie had been industrious since their return from seeing Maggie Holden. Her familiarity with genealogy sites, online registers, social media and local records was a considerable boon to P. Q. Investigations. So much so, Peddyr referred to her as "the brains of the outfit". Equally tenacious as her husband, her intellect outstripped his at times like these. The information she had gleaned from Ryan's laptop had been meticulously cross-referenced by her and the resultant notes revealed much about Scott Fletcher. 'Ryan Holden was on to something,' she announced, marching across the kitchen while pulling on a lightweight cardigan. 'Do you know how many Scott Fletchers there are on social media in the UK alone?'

'I know there's at least one actor, a tennis player, a golfer and a couple of entrepreneurs,' Peddyr replied. 'I quickly had a look myself.'

'So did Ryan by the looks of things, and a whole lot more besides…' She referred to the sheet of paper clutched in her hand. 'Ryan Holden has been spying on the flats at

Primrose Court, keeping a note of dates and times when Scott Fletcher was at home. He contacted EDF Energy on a number of occasions too. Then having struggled to extricate employment records to his satisfaction, he did some very detailed searches to find out about the private life of Scott Fletcher.'

'Worth the trouble of lifting the laptop then?'

'Most definitely. He was horribly close to the truth and his blog is not the ramblings of a madman, I can safely say that much.' Connie grinned eagerly. 'Did you know that Stephanie Fletcher, the wife of Scott Fletcher who works for EDF Energy, is not a hairdresser from Lutterworth? We know this because the Scott Fletcher who works at EDF is not a married man… Never has been.'

Halfway through zipping up his jacket, Peddyr raised his head. 'What?' He was gearing up to meet Dexter Booth at his home address and was taking the bike for another spin. Connie needed the car again. She had arranged to meet Colin and Trina McIlhenny in response to an urgent request from Bernie who had spent the vast majority of the morning at the police station, keeping P. Q. Investigations abreast of developments whenever he could. 'Well, who is the woman in that photo Webster reportedly produced during his questioning?' Peddyr demanded to know.

'She *is* Stephanie Fletcher, and she is married to the Scott Fletcher found dead in his garage at Primrose Court, that much is true.' Connie replied. 'He's her second husband and he is *a* Scott Fletcher – just not the one he was pretending to be when he met Sarah. He gave himself a new background, one partly belonging to the Scott Fletcher who went to school with Jim Holden and partly to a man with the same name who works at EDF Energy. A composite Scott Fletcher if you like. Stephanie and Scott, the ones in the photo, have no children between them. The house they live in is in both their names and there is no divorce pending. She is the Chief Operating Officer for Midshires NHS Trust and she earns a packet.'

'Which Scott Fletcher is he really then?'

'I'm working on that,' Connie replied, excitement shining in her eyes.

'Stephanie Fletcher must have had her world rocked.'

'I don't doubt it, Lao Gong.' Connie slipped her mobile phone into her handbag. 'And it would be good to know whether she found out about Scott's other life before he died or whether this little bombshell only landed after his death.'

'Wouldn't it just.' Eyebrows heading north, Peddyr pulled the zip of his jacket up to the neck. He reached out for his crash helmet. 'Keep me informed. I'll see what Dexter can shed light on. Then I'm going to risk another visit to Derwent Drive. According to Carol, the police have been and gone, taking boxes of paperwork and a couple of computers with them.'

'Then why are you going back?'

'Firstly, I'm going to return Ryan's laptop to his room, then I'm hoping to find what the police left behind.' He paused in the doorway. 'Bernie tells me that Sarah Holden bought Scott Fletcher his new truck. I'm on the hunt for vehicle registration documents that may have a receipt with them. Sarah was also buying a house for them with no assurances that he would be paying for his half. She says she didn't give him any money, but my radar says he had a plan to annex her assets.' He smiled broadly. 'Technical term for nicking what she'd got. And I want to find out how much she was worth, not just in cash terms, but in goods and chattels. If he had married her, what would the estate have been worth to him if she died...?' He left the thought hanging and blew his wife a kiss. 'Don't worry, you can soon get the paintbrushes out again. Can't do this without you, Lao Po.'

The more they found out, the more complex the possibilities became. In all likelihood, Scott Fletcher had indeed been playing a long game to swindle Sarah Holden out of her money and property. If Connie and Ryan Holden were right about Scott then he might have been doing the same thing to Stephanie Fletcher. The man had one in the bag and one about to drop in the bag. Goodness knows how many other women had fallen for his persuasive charms, Peddyr thought.

His phone rang just as he put the key in the ignition of his chosen bike for that day, his trusty tourer. It was Monica and she sounded uncharacteristically shaky. 'Pedd? Got a minute?' He stepped back into the shade of the house. In the sunshine he was already warming up to an uncomfortable level.

'I'm just on my way to meet Cousin Dexter. What's up?'

'That fucking consultant has only gone and put Ryan on a Section Three. All hell broke loose first thing, during ward round.'

'Section Three? That's detention for up to six months, isn't it?'

'Holy shit, Pedd, you actually learnt something from me. Yes, six months. What a cruel bastard that Dr Chowdhury is. How could he do that? The lad has enough to cope with.'

'Who told you this?'

'Staff Nurse Wayne Williams. He phoned me to see if I could come in and calm things down. Some fucking chance.'

'Bloody hell, you've said "fuck" twice in as many minutes,' Peddyr said, swiftly looking about to make sure he hadn't been overheard. Connie was locking the back door and came flying down the stone steps towards him, her face contorted with indignation. He covered the mouthpiece. 'It's work,' he explained hurriedly. 'It's Monica and she's upset. Ryan's fired off a wobbly by the sounds of things.' He returned to the call. 'Are you hurt?'

'No, although it was a near miss. He picked up a chair and chucked it at a window. A fruitless attempt to escape, I suspect. Anyway, it bounced off the glass and caught me on the arm. I didn't get out of the way soon enough. Must be getting old.' Her use of humour hadn't fooled Peddyr. Ryan had a quick temper and would have reacted very badly to being told the devastating news of his continued imprisonment in the mental health system. 'I'm lodging a formal complaint and getting advocacy services on board. This is every sort of wrong,' Monica continued, exasperated.

After an inauspicious start, Peddyr had redeemed himself by picking up one or two useful facts about the Mental Health Act while doing homework for his role as trainee solicitor. He was now putting them into action. 'Can Sarah remain as his Nearest Relative as it applies in law, given that she's locked up?'

There was a brief silence from Monica. All he could hear was her breathing as she endeavoured to calm herself. 'You could well have something there. A displacement... Who's next in line?'

'Maggie Holden or perhaps it's his other grandmother. I think it comes down to dates of birth.'

'I'll get back to you on that point of law. Mrs Holden Senior may be just the firepower we need. From what I know of her she doesn't suffer fools gladly.'

'And you'd be right.' Peddyr smiled to himself. 'Look, I'm tight for time. Can you let Bernie know about Ryan? When

I last spoke to him, the police were about to charge Sarah with murder. Ask the old bugger if we can all meet up tonight. At my place. In my office. We'll do food. Bring wine.'

Connie was standing next to him. When her husband ended the call, she squeezed his arm. 'You did the right thing. She shouldn't go home to an empty house after a scare like that.'

'She's had worse, Lao Po.'

'Maybe so, but between us we have more pieces of the jigsaw that need fitting together.' She gave a wicked grin adding a wink for good measure. 'And the more time Bernie and Monica spend together, the better. You know…'

He understood her thinly disguised reference but didn't think this was the best time to be playing Cupid.

\* \* \*

*D*exter Booth lived on a new housing estate in a semi that was a clone of every other house in the road. How the developers had managed to squeeze so many dwellings onto one street was remarkable. It all came at the expense of outside space, which was the reason there were no front gardens, only driveways and the occasional shrub. The back gardens would, no doubt, be the size of a handkerchief, Peddyr predicted. He was expected and Dexter answered the door, more casually dressed than he had been for work but was still presentable.

'Mr Quirk?' He held out his hand in greeting. 'Dexter Booth. Come on in, leave your bike gear in the hall. My wife is at work, so we have the place to ourselves. How can I help?' Self-assured when he spoke, there was an air of quiet maturity about Dexter Booth.

The chance to enter someone's home usually made Peddyr's life so much easier, revealing many things about the people who lived there. However, it was not the case on this occasion. None of the furniture or ornaments in the Booth household seemed to be more than a couple of years old. Neat to the point of clinical was how he would describe it to Connie later that day. The pictures on the walls were mostly of Dexter with a doe-eyed brunette; professional photographs, dreamy and posed. 'Your wife?' Peddyr asked.

'Tessa,' came the reply. 'We are about to unleash Dexter Junior on the world. He's due at Christmas. I don't suppose he'll thank us for that.'

'You know it's a boy?'

'Yes.' Dexter smiled proudly. 'We had a gender reveal party to tell everyone.'

Perplexed, Peddyr shook his head. 'You had a what?'

'I know,' the young man said with an apologetic sigh. 'It's an American thing. You have a party and tell everyone the sex of your unborn child. My mother had a complete hissy fit about the whole thing. She says it's tempting fate.' His eyes wandered to another photograph; this one in a silver frame.

Peddyr walked over and picked it up. 'Nice family shot.' It was the obligatory wedding photograph with both sets of parents. Everyone was smiling except for one. 'Is this lady your mother?' Peddyr enquired.

'That's her happy face, would you believe?'

'I'm sure she'll cheer up when her grandson arrives,' Peddyr said. 'Anyway, the reason I'm here... Ryan Holden and his grandmother could do with some help.'

'As I said in my text to you, anything I can do.' Dexter opened his palms wide. 'Let me shut down the laptop and get you a drink. Then you can point me in the right direction. I know next to nothing about psychiatric units or criminal proceedings. How's Sarah doing – do you know?' He strolled across the open plan lounge-diner and lowered the lid of the laptop on the dining table.

'Working from home? I thought you'd been given time off.'

'I asked for some annual leave, I couldn't concentrate. Once I received your message I admitted defeat and headed home. However, one or two things needed my attention. I was just checking in to see how the auction is going.' A set of sliding doors, leading to a triangular gravelled garden area, were already wide open, giving a view of geraniums and lobelia in earthenware plant pots in the far corner. Indicating a table tucked against a fence out of the sun, Dexter invited Peddyr to sit in the cool breeze. 'I'll be back in a sec. Water or squash?'

'Water will be just fine.' As Dexter disappeared through the door back into the hallway and presumably to the kitchen, Peddyr lifted the lid on the laptop. Just as he'd suspected, it hadn't shut down and he had enough time to glimpse the pages in the Google search bar before stepping through the patio doors and making a show of scraping a chair into position. Dexter had told the truth; the only page open was for Tottering's website. A good start.

Before long, the younger man returned with two tumblers containing iced water. 'Maggie Holden thinks you should delay the auction of Sarah's furniture until matters have been settled one way or the other,' Peddyr said to him.

'I think I have to take Sarah's instructions on that,' Dexter said with a questioning glance at him. His expression turned sombre. 'I can't believe she killed Scott. She's not like that, you know. Sarah is naturally gentle. This is such a shock. I didn't know anything about it until I got home from work and watched the late news. Even then I didn't realise it was Sarah until Mrs Holden phoned me, to let me know about the arrest and Ryan being taken to hospital. I can't get my head round it all.'

Silence descended for a short while as Peddyr sipped at his water. 'I've had a chat with Bez,' he said, watching Dexter's face carefully for a reaction.

'Oh, yeah. How was he smelling?'

Peddyr replied with a grin and a follow-up statement. 'He says you suspected Scott Fletcher was in some way deceiving your aunt.'

Dexter smiled, hesitantly. 'Bez said that, did he? Well, he was right. I met Scott a couple of times. Don't get me wrong, he seemed pleasant enough – if anything a bit too pleasant and full of himself. If he was as well off as he made out, then why did Sarah need to buy him a pickup truck? Why was he renting a flat and not buying one? He had no children to support from his divorce.' Dexter slowly shook his head. 'No, it didn't hang together. I spoke to Dad about it, then I mentioned it to Ryan. I wish I hadn't. Look where it got him.'

Asking about Sarah's finances might have seemed intrusive but Peddyr had to know what other information Dexter was party to. He knew about the truck, he knew about the house sale, the auction of goods… what Jim Holden had left to Ryan in his will. What else did Dexter know?

'What sort of return was Sarah expecting from the sale of her furniture? I'm only asking because perhaps it might be wiser to go ahead. The legal fees could soon mount up and Mrs Maggie Holden is funding a private investigation. She could end up out of pocket.'

The reply about profits from the sale of household items

was avoided, but Dexter did pick up on the issue of legal fees. 'What about Ryan? You said you were working for the legal team appealing against his sectioning. Won't that cost money too?'

'He gets Legal Aid, but Sarah won't qualify. I'll give you the details of her solicitor. He can take her instructions about whether or not to proceed with the sale. When do you need to know by?'

Dexter ran a finger up the condensation on the outside of his glass. His fingernails were bitten to the quick. 'The catalogue will need to be ready by the end of next week, so it could wait a few more days. I suppose it depends if the police charge her with anything.' He rubbed at his eyes and yawned. 'Sorry, haven't slept the past couple of nights. Dad keeps phoning me, asking what's happening. He's really worried about Sarah. They had a bit of a falling out recently about Scott and I think he's feeling guilty.'

'And of course he and your mum live miles away.'

Dexter seemed unfazed by Peddyr's background knowledge about his family. 'That's right. Dad took early retirement. Mum wanted to live by the sea, and in a compromise they chose Pendine so Dad can still get his petrol fix and watch the flat-track racing on the sands.' He pointed to the road outside. 'Nice bike you have there. In great nick and a decent-sized top-box.' Turning back to Peddyr he puffed out a chest full of air. 'Mine will have to go. Tessa keeps on about the risk and the expense.'

In the way of bikers, their conversation veered to the mechanical for a while as Peddyr encouraged him to stay with a two-wheel option. 'You'll regret it, that's a decent bike by the sounds of it. You could chop it in for a tourer like mine and stick the baby in one of the panniers.' They both laughed before returning to a more serious subject.

Dexter sat upright. 'Will I be able to speak with Ryan? I need his signature on the permission form to sell the items belonging to him. Or is that not possible?'

Peddyr would need Monica's expertise to answer with absolute certainty but he went with his best shot, based on what had been required for Ryan to hand over house keys and give permission to collect belongings from Derwent Drive. 'As I understand it, there would need to be a test of capacity to make certain Ryan was able to give informed consent. If you have the list of the items he's putting up for auction, and the form, I could arrange that for you.' It was a punt worth taking.

'You could? That would be great. I'll print off the list.' Dexter left the table to return to his laptop. Raising his voice, he spoke to Peddyr through the open doorway. 'I'd rather keep my relationship with Ryan on a personal basis while he's locked up. Don't want to put him under any more pressure. Know what I mean? What time are visiting hours?'

## 20

## A PAIN IN THE BACKSIDE

'Going apeshit won't help your cause,' Wayne said, staring at Ryan who lay face down on a thin mattress. 'This is how it ends in nine out of ten cases.'

His head to one side, Ryan reached behind him and hitched his trousers back into position, one eye on the staff nurse. Angry tears welled up as he felt the sting of the injection site. 'What was that shit you've given me? Explain it to me again so I can sue the lot of you for torture and assault.'

Leaning on the door frame, Wayne held a disposable kidney dish in one giant hand, an empty syringe within it. 'Count yourself lucky. You've been at the sharp end of an injection called Accuphase. It's used to knock the bejesus out of people for a week. A few years ago it would be "the ten and two": Ten milligrams of haloperidol, two milligrams of lorazepam. Then more drugs to help cope with the side effects. In the old days it was phenobarbital. Now that stuff was evil.' He tutted. 'Next time when we offer you an oral alternative, you take it. Saves the indignity.'

\* \* \*

*F*our nurses had dragged Ryan out of the morning ward round, which was held in a spacious meeting room where each patient was discussed by the clinical team who sat in conference with the consultant psychiatrist. Ryan had been invited to join the discussion of his case and soon learned that his fate had already been debated and decided upon without any input from him.

He was ushered into the room and perfunctory introductions were made, not that he took much notice of anyone other than the man in charge. Dr Chowdhury was half Ryan's height but wielded twice the power. 'I decide when you can leave this place, Ryan. That is not your privilege, it is mine. I determine your treatment for the delusions you hold so firmly.'

'I don't hold any delusions,' Ryan threw back, lurching forward in his seat.

'Then why the aggression? Why the agitation? If there is nothing wrong with you, as you so loudly insist, then why all the fuss?' Dr Chowdhury only briefly looked up from the notes he was making onto a digital pad. Uninterested in what Ryan had to say, he spoke again before his patient could answer. 'Your condition is rare and difficult to treat. However, I am an expert in this particular field of psychiatry, and I've prescribed some medication which may help.'

'No, thanks,' Ryan replied. 'After being given that pill to help me sleep, I don't want any more of your tablets. They taste like shite and make me dopey. I don't drink alcohol for the same reason.' With a forefinger, he poked the side of his head. 'I like to stay sharp.'

'Because someone is out to get you... yes, yes, we understand.'

The psychiatrist's tone was condescending, and it infuriated Ryan. 'You have no fucking idea.'

Ignoring him once again, Dr Chowdhury announced his plans for Ryan's treatment to the whole room. 'We will make life easier for ourselves and complete the paperwork for a Section Three. Ryan will commence on Risperidone at two milligrams twice a day increa—'

Ryan jumped to his feet, fists balled at his side. 'Didn't you hear me, Doc? I said, no thanks. I don't want your poxy medicines. There's nothing wrong with me. So whatever you thought, you can think again. The answer is no. I have the right to refuse. You said I was here for assessment. So by all means assess me, but don't force me to poison my body with stuff I don't need.'

Dr Chowdhury wrinkled his nose in response, smiling in disbelief at his patient's outburst. Addressing the other professionals in the room, he said, 'Oh, dear. Oh, dear. You see how well this illustrates my findings and further substantiates the diagnosis?' Resembling a priest about to confer a blessing, he raised one hand. 'Sit back down.'

Ryan was not going to be treated in such a way. 'Fuck off.' He bounced forward and stood close to Dr Chowdhury. Picking up a biro lying on the doctor's desk, he waved it in front of the consultant's face. 'I'm signing myself out. Right now,' he said, through gritted teeth.

The noise of the alarms, triggered by one of the nurses present, was deafening and brought a response from three other staff nurses and a health care assistant, who told Ryan to put the pen down and leave the room quietly. He did no such thing.

For a few tense seconds, nobody made any obvious move to intervene.

Incensed at the lack of response from the consultant, Ryan shouted over the cacophony of the bells, taking a firmer grip on the pen and raising it like a weapon in his clenched hand. 'Give me your pass, Doc. Do it now!' Frozen by panic, the psychiatrist didn't respond other than by blinking rapidly.

Before he could register what was happening to him, Ryan's head hit the desk with a loud thud as he was levered forcibly forward, his wrists locked in muscular hands and his arms twisted behind him. 'Get off!' he yelled and kicked out. 'Fucking get off me!'

Protests got him nowhere, and neither did his attempts to damage the door when he was propelled through it. He raged, he swore, he lunged and squirmed, tiring himself out.

In a Mexican stand-off within the confines of his room, he repeated himself. 'I'm not taking any tablets. I told you once. I'll tell you again. It's against my human rights. You come anywhere near me again and I'll fucking do you.'

The threats were idle ones. He had no intention of exchanging punches with the likes of Joran and Wayne. They were like cage fighters in uniform; one wiry, the other a veteran of the boxing ring with the flattened nose to prove it.

'You are your own worst enemy,' Wayne said, his tone steady. 'The more you battle, the harder things will get for you. Doctor C is already writing out papers for Section Three.' When the staff nurse explained the significance of this, Ryan erupted, picking up anything to hand that he could throw. The nurses ducked and jinked, brushing off the show of aggression with thin smiles. He wasn't making much of an impression by lobbing a pair of socks and a plastic beaker at their heads.

However, there was one thing bound to incense him beyond reason: being made a fool of. When Joran asked, 'Is that all you've got?' the last vestiges of Ryan's control evaporated. Fear tipped him towards irrationality. He lunged sideways and tipped up the mattress on his bed. It slid to the floor with a slap. When he then failed to wrench the only shelf from the wall, he changed direction and very nearly reached the window with his fist drawn back before the air whooshed from his chest as he met the floor face down. Again his captors were on him and this time there were no negotiations.

An hour later, Monica Morris appeared at the door of the aptly named "De-escalation Room" and tried to reason with him. He was hearing none of it.

'You were supposed to get me out of here, you useless fucking bitch! Now they've locked me up for longer and they jabbed me in the arse with some screw-your-brains-up shit,' he bellowed at her. Wayne was at her shoulder as they entered, asking Ryan to take a seat, which was what he did next. He took the only chair in the room, a well-padded foam affair, made mostly of polystyrene, one designed to be useless as a weapon, and launched it at the observation window only feet from where Monica was standing. It bounced awkwardly and glanced against her arm as it fell back to the ground.

'Feel better for that?' she asked, wincing.

He didn't. He felt betrayed by everyone.

## 21

# UNDONE

*B*ernard's eyes were dry and stinging from lack of sleep and although the resultant brain fug was dragging him down, he knew what was coming for his client and fought to remain alert. One look at Webster's smug expression told him Sarah Holden was going straight to jail and this was no game of Monopoly in which she would collect £200.

'Mrs Holden, you begged us to check your son's laptop computer. You said he stored information on there about Scott Fletcher, that he threatened to expose Mr Fletcher as an imposter of some sort. You claim this is evidence of how paranoid your son really was leading up to his removal to hospital.'

'That's right,' Sarah replied, hugging herself tight, anxiety etched on her features.

Acting DCI Webster tutted like a disapproving headmaster. 'This seems strange when our investigation indicates that Mr Fletcher *was* deceiving you.' He tapped his pen to the file on the desk. 'So, either your son isn't paranoid or yet again you're trying to cover up your own crime. If you had read what your son had written, you would know you had been duped.'

Sarah slowly shook her head. 'I didn't read it. Ryan told me what sounded like rubbish. It was nonsense, made up, delusional. Of course I didn't believe him. He said he'd phoned Scott at work and spoken to a man called Scott Fletcher who wasn't my Scott. The man he spoke to had never heard of Bosworth Bishops or me or Ryan. That's the raving of someone who is mentally ill.'

Allowing his subordinate to take some of the limelight, Webster sat back in his seat waving a hand at DS Helen Forstall. 'Break it to her gently,' he said.

'Actually, Mrs Holden, we did the same thing. A few hours ago we spoke to Scott Fletcher at EDF Energy, a man who was very much alive. A man who was single and therefore not married to anyone called Stephanie. A man who doesn't live in Bosworth Bishops. He remembered the phone conversation with your son, which I suppose he would.'

Bernard Kershaw stirred. 'Your line of questioning is fascinating, Inspector, but how does this implicate my client?' Disregarded once again, Webster spoke over him, staring directly at Sarah.

'How convenient then that your son's laptop computer has gone missing. It certainly wasn't found when my team entered your house. If we had it as evidence, no doubt it would give us much more information about the deceased. And because you knew what was on said laptop, I can only assume you disposed of it before you went to Primrose Court to kill Scott Fletcher, angered by learning the truth about him. Further evidence of your son's efforts to save you from the big mistake you were about to make. Further evidence that you are guilty of the murder of Scott Fletcher.' Preening, Duncan Webster drummed his fingers on the desk.

Sarah pushed a lank curl of hair away from her face. 'I never touched Ryan's laptop. If it isn't in his room or in the house somewhere, then I don't know where it is. With him at the hospital perhaps?'

As her solicitor, Bernard should have felt guilty because he knew exactly where the laptop could be found and with any luck Peddyr would shortly be returning it to Ryan's bedroom, making the police look incompetent. Unfortunately, by taking possession of the laptop, albeit temporarily, Peddyr had placed him in a difficult legal position despite this being done with Ryan's permission. But it would do his client no good to find out her solicitor was party to underhand shenanigans to beat the police at their own game, so Bernard said nothing.

Webster was unsympathetic in his summing up, once again enjoying the sound of his own voice. 'When you entered Scott Fletcher's flat on the morning he was killed, you were able to confirm his lies. Thanks to Ryan, you discovered that your lover was in fact a refrigeration engineer for air-conditioning units on industrial sites, offices and for cold storage in mortuaries. His EDF Energy ID, on a lanyard in his flat, is a fake. As was he. But you know all this.' He linked the fingers of his hands together and rolled his thumbs. 'Before we formally charge you with the murder of Scott Fletcher, can you confirm to me that you deliberately fabricated your son's mental illness, to ensure he wasn't implicated in your crime?'

Heaving himself up, Bernard interjected. 'Goodness me, Inspector. One minute you are assuming my client destroyed her son's laptop to conceal the evidence contained on it, and the next you are accusing her of lying about her son's mental state. I must object to that question most strongly,' he boomed. 'Ryan Holden was assessed by medical professionals in accordance with the Mental Health Act and as such they deemed him to be suffering from a mental illness requiring detention. My client made the request for this assessment in the belief her son was deluded. If you are attempting to generate further charges, I suggest we curtail this interview.'

The reaction from Webster was unexpected. He gave a soapy smile and apologised. 'Quite right, Mr Kershaw. I am most grateful for your direction. My team will carry out a further investigation into the actions of Ryan Holden. After all, he was at the scene, he does have motive and he is physically capable. We could indeed be looking at joint venture. No wonder your client was so protective of her son.'

There were no tears trickling from Sarah Holden's eyes, the pain too intolerable at that moment for her to produce anything but an agonised moan.

* * *

*I*t was some time later, after formal charges had been read to her, that Bernard was able to sit alone with Sarah Holden who seemed to have given up fighting for herself or for her son. Beneath her eyes lay sunken dark rings; the lids looked red against her pale face. 'My worst nightmare,' she whispered. 'It was all for nothing.'

'Please don't lose heart, Mrs Holden. I have an excellent team working hard to prove your innocence and we will do our level best to have the charges overturned as soon as possible. You have my word.' Bernard patted a document case on his knees. 'It could be some hours before a place in a remand prison is found for you and there are some important decisions for us to make in the meantime.'

'Such as?' It was hard not to pity Sarah Holden. She would most likely wither and descend into depression as the days dragged by in prison, waiting for her appearance in court. Bernard wasn't sure she had the psychological strength to make it that far, but she was to prove him wrong.

'Such as who is going to act in your interests. Mrs Maggie Holden is covering my costs, so don't fret on that count. Who do you wish to nominate to manage your personal financial affairs?'

Sarah stared into the middle distance, quivering hands resting on her knees. 'I can't ask Ryan. He may never speak to me again after this. Please help him get out of that hospital.'

Bernard rubbed the top of one ear between forefinger and thumb. The message received from Monica about Ryan hadn't been heartening. 'The work is underway. These things take time, but he will be out soon enough. And when he is, he will need somewhere to live. Should he return to the house on Derwent Drive?'

Sarah took a while before voicing her thoughts. 'Ryan's future is uncertain, Mr Kershaw. If he killed Scott, he may be taking my place in prison.'

'Quite, but let's not be too pessimistic.'

Her palms pressed together as if in prayer, Sarah rested her nose on the tips of her fingers. Strangely, having been formally charged, she appeared keen to settle as much as she could in the short time she had available. 'My first thought was Carol, my friend and neighbour, but I think finances should be dealt with by a family member. There's my brother Chris, but his wife Hilary would undermine anything he tried to do to help me and he's not the most reliable when it comes to money. Maggie is the only one I have any faith in.' She thought again. 'Or Dexter. Perhaps the two of them could manage things between them like trustees.'

'That could work. What did you have in mind?'

'Tell Dexter to go ahead with the sale of the furniture at auction. He can use Maggie's keys to access the house. He knows where everything is. I signed the forms already. Then sell the house, Mr Kershaw. I can't go back there. Maggie will need more money to pay a good barrister and, if I'm locked up for years, then the proceeds will buy Ryan a place of his own. Make sure Dexter is reimbursed for his time and give him five thousand pounds as a gift from me. Tell him he can also have everything in the workshop and adjoining garage. He has a list of the contents already. That's a present too. Ryan isn't interested in anything needing maintenance or repair.'

As she spoke, Bernard scribbled down her instructions as fast as his cramping hand would allow. 'I'll get this typed up, but for now put your signature at the end there.' He read it back to her. 'Those details correct? And you're sure you're not being too hasty in selling the house?'

'Can you imagine what it will be like for me to walk the streets of Bosworth Bishops doing my shopping after this? Innocent or not, I'll always be the woman charged with the murder of Scott Fletcher. The disgraced widow of Jim Holden. If I was freed tomorrow, I'd put the house straight on the market. I wouldn't even set foot in the door.'

Apparently resigned to imprisonment, Sarah picked up the leaflet given to her by the custody sergeant who'd read out the charges. The information from The Prison Reform Trust was for first-time female prisoners, a guide as to what to expect. 'Where will they send me?' she asked, panic rising in her voice. 'Somewhere local?'

'Eastwood Park is the nearest women's prison. Gloucestershire,' Bernard replied, gently.

'Not too far then.'

'But they could send you anywhere,' he said, preparing her for the likelihood of being miles away from friends and family. 'Maybe Bronzefield or Styal. As soon as you are transferred I'll be informed and I'll be in touch with Mrs Carol Brightman, assuming she agrees to take your personal items to you.'

'She will,' Sarah said, wiping her nose on the cotton handkerchief given to her by Bernard in the interview room. 'She'll come wherever I'm sent. And don't worry, she has my spare house keys. Although please don't tell Ryan that. She's my secret weapon and there are some things he doesn't need to know about.'

## SAY CHEESE

*T*he flats at Primrose Court were built for professionals needing a convenient place to live and were a popular choice for private landlords in search of an investment opportunity. There were twelve flats in all, and each had a garage in the block to the rear. From there it was an easy stroll into town or to the station. There was no real character to the place, which was functional but cared for. The landings were well lit, the stairs uncluttered, and a row of metal post boxes lined the secure front entrance. A code pad was used by residents, with visitors using an intercom system to gain access. The rear entrance had its own code pad. Connie took all this in as she made a circuit via the footpath that ringed the building, weaving between neat box hedges in order to avoid the police tape which still cordoned off the garage block and parking areas.

Trina McIlhenny was more than happy to tell her gripping story of the murder on their doorstep. Anything but tired of repeating herself, she had readily agreed to meet with Connie. 'I watch a lot of *Law and Order UK*,' she said, ushering her visitor through to the living room of the first-floor flat she and Colin rented through Craven & Tilbury Letting Agents. 'We've been here four years now and we love it. It's so posh and what we deserve after all the hard graft in the factory,' she added proudly. Trina was in her late forties and there was no evidence of children in the family. The photographs about the place were of Colin and her on various seaside holidays. Caravan parks seemed to feature heavily. More prevalent were pictures of pet cats. The latest, a tubby tabby, was curled up in the corner of the sofa snoring softly. 'That's Pepper,' Trina explained. 'She's a rescue. Our fourth, and the calmest one we've ever had. She's no bother.'

'What does your husband do for a living?' Connie enquired, stroking the cat gently.

'He's a supervisor at the cheese factory. Shift work, which he don't mind. I work there too but they've given me time off for the shock an' everything. I knew all about it from *Casualty* and *999 What's Your Emergency?* Watch all of them, I do.' She settled herself easily into a chair, showing no signs of nerves let alone shock. 'Like the new three-piece suite? We got it in the summer sale.' Connie nodded appreciatively. There was always a sofa sale on somewhere, and as Trina was a television addict, no doubt she would be an advertiser's dream. 'I'm dead envious,' Trina went on briskly. 'You being a private investigator an' all... must be so exciting.'

At this Connie laughed through her nose. 'Not a word I would use to describe the job. Mostly it involves lots of online research, asking endless questions, and is far from stimulating. But today is different, Trina. Today I've come to listen to your exciting story. Tell me about your neighbour. Why would anyone want to kill him?'

This opened up the verbal floodgates, forcing Connie to ask permission to record Trina using her phone. 'My shorthand isn't what it used to be,' she explained. With no objections, Connie could safely tune in and listen. She followed the near-spherical woman into the confines of a galley kitchen where two mugs of milky coffee were made with much stirring. Connie wasn't asked for her preference, it was coffee with one sugar, take it or leave it.

'Scott seemed so nice. Good job, new pickup truck an' all. When he and Sarah from the letting agents started going out it was so romantic. Like *Blind Date* but without Cilla. We all knew about it. He seemed proper happy and told Colin they were moving in together, buying a place of their own. It was sweetness and light and happy ever after. Then it went wrong all in one day.'

'One day?' Connie queried, bringing up the rear as Trina led her back into the lounge, mug in one hand, a plate of cheese and crackers in the other.

'Well, not quite in one day,' Trina corrected herself. She settled in her seat, shifting her ample bosom by pulling at a bra strap one at a time. 'There was some trouble between Scott and Sarah's boy. I heard he's been carted off to the madhouse and I'm not surprised. He was always creeping about down at the garages. Shifty. Once, Colin asked him what he was doing there, and he said he was spying on Scott because he wasn't who he said he was. He said Scott was pretending to be an old friend of his father's but was a liar and had stolen parts of other people's identities. People who were all called Scott Fletcher.' She laughed wildly, rolling her shoulders, waving her arms. 'I ask you...Mad. Absolutely off his head.'

'How did Scott react to these accusations?'

Trina smiled with a gentle hum, reaching for her mug of

coffee. 'Calm as a cucumber. Felt sorry for the lad, he said. Told us Sarah was trying to get him some help from doctors but wasn't having much luck. That's the trouble when you're mad, 'cos you don't know it. See?' She replaced the mug on the table at her side without having taken a single sip.

'And the day Scott was killed, was Ryan here?' Connie glanced at her phone to make certain it was recording the torrent of detail. The timeline was vital evidence.

'Every bugger was here that day. Like Piccadilly Circus it was. The intercom went at about eight o'clock in the morning. Some woman calling herself Mrs Fletcher was looking for her husband Scott.' Trina's eyebrows were raised so far they disappeared beneath her wispy fringe. 'Well, we told her he was our neighbour. She said it was a surprise visit, so we let her straight in of course.' She leant forward to give a stage whisper. 'And we accidentally wedged the front door open an inch or so…'

There was no need to feign animated anticipation, Connie was tingling with it. 'What happened next?'

'A blazing row. Better than telly. I said to Colin it was a blooming good job we were both on a day off otherwise we'd have missed the drama.'

'What was the row about?' Connie asked, trying to keep Trina's mind on the key facts and away from the realms of fantasy.

'About how Scott was cheating on her with another woman. He was given two days to collect his belongings and told to expect divorce papers. Wham. Just like that. We never knew he was married. Told us he was already divorced, see.'

Bearing in mind that Trina had already given a statement to the police, she was no less enthusiastic in telling the story a second time. In the relaxed surroundings of her own home she appeared to revel in entertaining her visitor. Something Connie was grateful for. 'And Mrs Fletcher then left. Did you see her drive off?'

'In her flashy Mercedes with a private plate. STEF F1. You could tell she had money, that one. Shiny teeth and lip gloss. Mulberry handbag and not one of those snide ones from the market, mind. This one was the real thing. I'm almost sure of it.'

'And where did she drive off to? Which direction?'

Trina inclined her head and gave Connie a wide grin. 'Oh, you're good. The police didn't think to ask us that one. Mrs Fletcher turned left, then left again and parked in that cul-de-sac opposite. She were still sat there when we went out to do the shopping.'

'What about Scott? What did he do next?'

'He didn't do nothing for a while. It were early. He usually goes out most days if he's here but he works away a lot.' She looked across at Connie, drawing breath. 'Oh, my God. You don't think he was having Sarah on about the divorce, do you?' Her eyes gleamed. 'The dirty bugger! He already had a wife and wanted another one. Well, I never...'

'Did you ever watch *The Jeremy Kyle Show*?' Connie asked, somewhat astounded that Trina hadn't worked this out until that very moment. To her it was obvious.

Trina laughed in response. 'Cor, well, I'm blowed. I can't wait to tell Colin. He won't believe it.'

The interview was rapidly going off track and Connie began to wish she'd paid more attention to Peddyr's techniques. This was his area of expertise and one she had yet to master. 'Trina, did you see Ryan Holden in the area that morning?'

'Sarah's boy? Yes, we did. I told the Old Bill that an' all.

Me and Colin went to get the car to do the shopping, see. About half-nine by the time we'd had breakfast and I'd tarted myself up a bit. My highlight of the week is a trip to the shops. Now, normally we'd be gone for hours, but we was expecting my mother for lunch so we cut it short, just got the necessaries.'

'I see. Where did you bump into Ryan?'

'By the garages where he normally hangs around until he sees Scott. Then he has a go at him and buggers off. He's done it before.'

Connie was flummoxed by this. Why? Why would he wait for Scott to come out, she wondered? 'When you say, "has a go at him", what do mean precisely?'

Trina frowned as if trying to conjure up the right words. 'Ryan would harass him. Say things like: "I know you're not Scott Fletcher. I will find out who you really are and when I do, I'm going to publish the truth." Something like that.'

'And that's all?'

'He took some photos of the garage once, with 'is phone, and tried to get pictures of Scott with his motorbike, but I'm not sure if he ever managed to or not because Scott never went out on it. I think it were broken, or he were doing it up.'

'What about on that day? What did Ryan do?'

'Same as usual. Scott was already walking across to his garage as we were coming out the back door, see. We'd heard his flat door go. Not that we were following him on purpose.'

Connie couldn't help but smile. She was quite sure the McIlhennys had been listening out for movement from their next door neighbour, desperate to witness the next instalment.

'The boy... I say boy but he's a nice-looking lad really...

hench, as the girls in the canteen would say. Tall, always neat and clean – not like them other nutters on the High Street. Anyway, I digest… He shouted, needled Scott a bit then wandered off again, like what he always do. Me and Colin passed him in the car when we was on the way to the shops. He were smiling to himself but apart from that you'd never know he was barking. About ten o'clock that was.'

'Did you see anyone else in the vicinity?'

'Nope. Nobody apart from Scott's mate with the motor-bike. We've seen him before. He drove in as we drove out.'

The breath seemed to catch in Connie's throat. 'And his name?'

'Not a clue, don't know what he looks like even, but his motorcycle is blue with a screen thingy on the front and he wears black everything, if that's any help.'

It wasn't, but the next part of the drama divulged by a fervent Trina was most intriguing. According to her, she and Colin had dashed back from the shops and had arrived back at their flat in time to see Sarah Holden approaching the front of the block on foot. There was no sign of Stephanie Fletcher in her Mercedes. 'We was unpacking the shopping like and we heard her come up the stairs. We didn't know where Scott was but we heard Sarah ringing his bell, knocking on the door, and then Colin stuck his head out, like you do. Sarah had let herself into Scott's flat. Nothing unusual there. They were together, a couple. It's only normal.'

'And what time was this?'

'About… just before eleven.'

Furnished with the facts from Bernie, Connie knew that the answer fitted with Sarah's account of her morning. Ryan was back at Derwent Drive having his mental health assessed by this time and Scott was in his garage, something

Colin and Trina didn't discover until they went looking for an item of shopping they'd left in the car. Evidently it took two people to search for a wayward tin of food. 'How long was it between hearing Sarah leave the flat and when you went to find your missing corned beef?'

'A few minutes. It's hard to say. Not long.'

## ONE MAN'S JUNK

$\mathcal{F}$ollowing his meeting with Dexter Booth, Peddyr received a call from Bernie. The update was not good. Sarah had been charged with the murder of Scott Fletcher. Bernie was on his way to break the news in person to Maggie Holden and asked Peddyr to join Monica in informing Ryan Holden. She would need back up.

With no option but to agree, Peddyr rearranged his plans. He rode to the Marsworth Unit with a view to returning to Derwent Drive after that. It was going to be a long hot and sweaty day.

Monica greeted him with a plastic beaker of cold water at the ready. He guzzled it down. 'How's your arm?' he enquired.

She rubbed it. 'Not too bad. I had more trouble with that obstreperous consultant who is threatening to report me to my superiors. According to charmless Dr Chowdhury, steroids have nothing to do with Ryan's presentation and I am talking out of my arse. He didn't actually say that, but it's what he meant. Nasty little knobstick. We had a showdown and I won on a legal and moral technicality. How did you get on with Dexter?'

'Better than I expected,' Peddyr replied, heading for a refill of water. 'Is there somewhere I can dump all my gear? I'm bloody sweltering.'

'Do you have to wear all that?'

'Better to be safe than sorry, Monica. ATGAT is the key to surviving on the roads, no matter what the weather. ATGAT: all the gear, all the time.'

Ruby-Rottweiler was at her post on reception. A woman of Amazonian proportions and a preference for fuchsia pink nail varnish to add the finishing touch to her lashes and luminous lipstick, she took a lot of persuading to guard Peddyr's expensive gear. 'This is not a cloakroom, Mr Quirk. Can you imagine what would happen if every Tom, Dick and Harry asked me to mind their coats?'

'I can't leave them by the bike, and I can't leave an expensive crash helmet in here it'll get nicked, Ruby. The lockers for visitors on the ward just aren't big enough, which presents a problem when we have clients to see today.'

There were certificates hung on the wall behind Ruby, one attesting to her being voted employee of the month, another for completing a health and safety course. Above these hung a corporate poster. 'I do understand. It's more than you are obliged to do, but it really would help me out. And I see you've won an award for excellent customer service. I wouldn't normally ask… only…'

When a luminescent smile appeared on Ruby's face, he knew the deal was struck. Flattery never failed. 'Don't make a habit of it. They'll think I've gone soft,' she said, pointing to the door to a built-in cupboard where she took possession of Peddyr's jacket and crash helmet. 'You can return the favour one day.'

'In need of legal advice?' he asked.

'No, I'm in need of adventure,' she replied, licking her lips in a provocative manner. 'Never been on the back of a motorbike. And you do seem like the sort of fella I could get up close and personal with, if you get me. I'll bring my own airbags,' she said, fluttering her lashes before glancing down at her considerable frontage. Unnerved, Peddyr pivoted on his heels with a loud squeak of his biker boots, only to find Monica laughing and pointing at him.

'You should see your face!'

Over his shoulder he caught Ruby chuckling away to herself and waving to Monica. 'Got him, good and proper!'

'Thanks, Ruby,' Monica replied. 'I enjoyed that.'

Peddyr smirked, appreciating the harmless banter. 'And you put all your apprentices through this, do you?'

Stripped down to tee-shirt and leather trousers, the temperature was more bearable in the air-conditioned building, but he wasn't a very credible trainee solicitor dressed like that. 'We'll say your car is in for service.' Monica handed him his visitor badge on a lanyard, which he placed over his head as he followed her to the ward. 'You'll be glad to hear that Ryan Holden is a lot calmer since the injection kicked in. I only hope he stays awake long enough to listen to what we have to say.'

The reactions from the patients to Peddyr's appearance in bike leathers was a mile away from how they had responded to him when wearing a suit. 'Alright, mate,' said a man in shorts. He touched his forehead in salute. 'What do you ride?' The suspicion Peddyr had encountered in the same man on his first visit to the ward had evaporated – all because of what he wore. The same thing happened when he met Ryan.

'Peter, my man,' the young man declared with a wide dreamy grin. 'I didn't take you for a biker. You should meet my cousin, he's into bikes. Like his dad and my old man.' The words were slurred and for a moment Peddyr wondered why, until he recalled what Monica had said about the drugs in Ryan's system. 'I use pedal power,' he continued, flexing his arms and checking his biceps. 'Have you come to get me out?'

There was no painless way to impart the news they had come to deliver. Monica stepped forward. 'I've been to see Dr Chowdhury and made a sound argument against your detention on Section Three. The papers were not completed as required and I was able to persuade your consultant to keep you on Section Two until such time as a comprehensive assessment is made to indicate the need for continued detention in hospital. I gave him a copy of my own assessment report to help him along.'

In his default position on the edge of his bed, Ryan's knees jiggled at a rapid rate. He looked up at Monica who had been advised to stay in the doorway. 'You're fucking good,' he said.

'Don't you mean: "Thank you, Mrs Morris and I'm sorry about throwing furniture at you"?' she replied.

'Yeah, sorry about that.'

'So you should be,' she admonished. 'Just don't do it again.' The room fell silent for a few drawn out seconds before she spoke once more. 'We have something to tell you concerning your mother.'

This time the show of bravado failed. Ryan's body sagged. 'Fuck it. They've charged her. She's going to prison, right?'

'I wish we had some better news for you, but please don't worry. Sarah has a very good lawyer. One of the best.' Monica looked across at Peddyr who was inside the room by a few feet; beyond him stood Joran, primed but outwardly passive.

Peddyr asked if he and Monica could sit with Ryan for a while. 'We have some things to talk about,' he explained. 'Confidential business and… I think we'll be fine.'

Joran tilted his chin. 'I'll be right outside the door. We have to be able to see Ryan at all times whether you're there with him or not. A precaution, I'm sorry.' He gave a short lift of one shoulder as he motioned to Monica to enter the room. 'He's calmer now, you know how these things work.'

Peddyr sat down opposite Ryan and explained about his visit to see Dexter and how helpful he had been. 'He's going to come and see you this evening if he can. He was worried about you.'

'Top bloke,' Ryan said. 'He and Uncle Chris put me on to Scott Fletcher.'

'So, I heard…' Peddyr replied.

Even though Monica had received an email from Bernard Kershaw detailing financial arrangements to be put in place for Sarah Holden, Ryan was not to be made party to these. It was imperative that confidentiality was maintained so far as Dexter's role went. There were, however, some other interesting issues to be explored, which Peddyr carefully outlined. 'I have a list of items belonging to you that are going to auction. Can you check through it and make sure it's correct? If you're happy, there are some forms to sign. Monica will go through the same capacity test questions as before and get your doctor's confirmation. That way you are covered and so are we.'

'Sane enough to know what I'm doing.' Ryan took the

list. 'Yeah, that's it. Ancient garden sculptures and an expensive Turkish carpet do not float my boat. They can go.'

'Is there anything in the garages belonging to you?' Peddyr asked.

Ryan blew out through his lips. He swayed slightly and yawned before giving a response. 'Apart from Mum's car they're full of old junk. Stuff that Dad hoarded. Crappy old jalopies Mum should have sold off, but Scotty-Boy said she should keep them in Dad's memory. For their sentimental value. Why would anyone want to do that?'

The niggling thought that had been plaguing Peddyr came to the fore with an electrical ping in his brain. 'Are we talking about your father's bikes?' When Ryan spoke about hoarding, a recent memory of the bikes outside number seven Derwent Drive flashed into Peddyr's mind. Bikers and collectors, even ones as eccentric as Kenny Eversholt, hated selling their bikes. Jim Holden would have had a number of motorbikes, just as Peddyr himself did. A bike for every occasion, as Connie would say. What's more, Peddyr didn't think the bikes Ryan was talking about deserved to be referred to as "old junk". The Jim Holden he knew was meticulous when it came to his rides. 'Don't you want any of the items in the garages?'

'No thanks, Peter. You can tell Uncle Chris that he can buy them if he wants. Now Scott is dead I can do what I like with them.'

'Are they yours to sell?'

'Good point. I think one or two are supposed to be family heirlooms, but the rest belong to Mum. You should ask her.'

Peddyr swivelled in his seat and raised a silent query of Monica. 'There's no mention of any bikes on this list,' he said to Ryan.

'In which case we can only assume that the bikes are in your mother's name and would be left to you in the event of her death.' Monica managed a half-smile and reassured Ryan that this would be dealt with through his mother's solicitor. 'We'll worry about that another time.'

'Do what you like. I still don't want any of that old scrap.' He rubbed at his eyes and yawned once more. 'The house will have to be cleared. She'll sell. I would. I'll stay with Granny Holden for a bit, then get another job.' He held his hand out slowly, as if it were an effort to raise his arm. 'I'm knackered. Give me the forms to sign. I need a kip.'

While he scrawled his signature on the papers, Peddyr pushed him for one more answer to something very important. He leaned in and whispered, getting closer than was safe. 'Listen, Ryan. What were you doing at Primrose Court the morning Scott Fletcher was found dead?'

Ryan lifted his heavy eyelids. 'I didn't kill him. I went there to wind him up, get him to crack and tell me what he was up to. He wasn't the real Scott Fletcher.' Pausing only to scratch at his forehead, Ryan continued in a dull monotone. 'He didn't come out to the garages for ages, so I went to the front of the building and there was a woman sitting in a big fuck-off Mercedes watching his flat, staring up at the windows. The car had a private plate spelling out her name. I was sure it was his wife, because her name is Stephanie. Everything else I know about him is on the laptop.' He rubbed his palms against his cheeks, trying to rouse himself. 'When he came out the back, I shouted to him that I knew about his wife. He strolled on pretending he hadn't seen me. Ignoring me. That's why you're asking. You know I'm telling the truth.'

'Yes, Ryan,' Peddyr confirmed. 'We believe you about Scott Fletcher not being who he says he was. The information you stored on the laptop has been really vital in helping us piece together what happened to you. It goes a long way to explain how you ended up in here. We just need to find who killed him, because it wasn't your mother and unfortunately she's heading for remand as an innocent woman.'

'Yeah, well it wasn't me either. So maybe Stephanie walloped him on the bonce. Unfaithful husband and all that.'

## 24

## SCORN IN ACTION

*S*ending a text to her husband before setting off, Connie was feeling proud of her efforts and, with help from Ryan's laptop revelations, particularly pleased at how easily she had been able to find a home address for Stephanie Fletcher. There was plenty of time for her to drive to Theale and back and still prepare supper for four people by eight o'clock that evening. It wouldn't be much of a chore to put on a simple buffet.

The motorway journey was taken up deciding what to cook, and her mind soon wandered to thoughts of the coming festive season. It was months away and most people wouldn't have given it room in their lives until November, but she was so excited to be having both her sons together at the same time that she had broken the waiting time down to weeks. It sounded so much nearer. With little Euan there for Christmas it would be magical.

'Take the next turning on the right,' Sat-Nav-Suzie directed.

'Turning right,' Connie announced, checking her

mirrors before flicking the indicator. 'Oh, this is dead posh,' she said. The street was tree-lined and tranquil. Impressive brick-built detached houses were set back from the road, many with gravel driveways and lavish entrances, some with security gates barring visitors.

'You have reached your destination.'

'Thank you, Suzie. Very good directions, as usual,' Connie said, patting the dashboard. Progress was slow as she searched for the Fletcher residence, scanning the walls and gateposts as she drove by. 'Why can't they have numbers like everyone else?' she grumbled. 'The Haven… Idlewild… Landfall.' The end of the private road was fast approaching where there was a convenient place to make a U-turn and glide past the houses on the other side of the road. Ahead of her, a silver saloon car pulled out from one of the properties and sped off towards the main road. There were two occupants in suits and ties. Connie grinned.

'I think we may have found the house,' she said, continuing to talk to Sat-Nav-Suzie as if she were a real person. 'Those were policemen. Takes being married to one to know one.' Having checked for the correct house name, she pulled over to the kerb, deciding to give Stephanie Fletcher a breather from questions before bowling in and annoying her. She stepped out of the car to stretch and take in the summer air, faltering when she heard a wild cry of anguish followed by a metallic clanging sound, followed by another, and another.

Swiftly she grabbed her handbag from inside the car, locked the vehicle and ran towards the house, taking her mobile phone from her pocket. On the driveway was a Mercedes, private number plate confirming to Connie she was indeed at the correct address. The double-garage door was wide open, and a raging woman was swinging wildly with something resembling a length of scaffolding, hitting out at what Connie assumed must be a prized car belonging to Scott Fletcher. A wild array of expletives punctuated each forehand and overarm swipe. 'You absolute fucking bastard!' The woman's face was contorted with fury, screaming and flailing at the vehicles within, she didn't hear Connie approaching.

The anger of betrayal on display was thunderous and the full force of it was being aimed, not at a car, but at three different motorbikes. 'That ought to do it...' Connie mumbled to herself. Destroying what had been precious to a deceitful husband would go some way to expressing the hurt. 'Are you alright?' she shouted, while staying well out of range should Stephanie Fletcher's wrath come her way.

'Do I look like I'm alright?' the woman replied, spitting the words from her mouth and taking another forceful swing at a headlight. 'And who the hell are you?' Stumbling to a standstill, breathing hard, she allowed the weapon to fall from her hand. It clanged onto the ground, revealing itself to be an aluminium baseball bat. 'Oh, no. Please don't tell me he had another woman on the go? I really don't think I can take much more today.'

The colour seemed to drain from Stephanie Fletcher's face. She looked past Connie and down her driveway. A couple had appeared in the gateway staring nervously in their direction. 'Come to gawp have we?' At this they soon disappeared from view. 'Nosy neighbours. If it's not them it's the bloody press. Great. I forgot to close the gate when the police left...' She gave Connie a contemptuous look. 'Well? Who are you? Wife number three?'

With a buzz, Connie's phone vibrated. She ignored it, not wishing to appear rude. 'No. My name is Connie Quirk and I'm with the defence team at Bagshot & Laker investigating your husband's murder.' She produced a business card from the front pocket of her handbag. Given the opportunity she would have taken a look at her phone but daren't because she had a horrible sinking feeling in anticipation of what it would say. Foolishly, she had gone chasing after answers from Stephanie without considering her own safety. Stephanie Fletcher, wielding a hefty bat had just smashed up several motorbikes in anger. She could easily have done the same to her husband in revenge for infidelity. Peddyr would be furious when he found out his own wife had run towards such danger.

'Then speak to the police,' Stephanie snipped, snatching the card from Connie's fingers.

'They run their own investigation; our job is to build a defence for the accused.'

'They've just told me his girlfriend, mistress... other woman... has been charged.' Stephanie tossed her head. 'I don't know what the hell to call the woman.' She took time to steady her breathing, staring again at the card Connie had handed to her. 'I shouldn't be as angry with her as I am with him, should I? She was an innocent party from what they've told me. As ignorant as I was.' With a forceful huff, she bent down and picked up the discarded bat once more. 'Sometimes there aren't enough things to bash.' Aiming a final blow to an already battered petrol tank, Stephanie swore once more, and a shiver snaked up the length of Connie's spine.

Walking deeper into the garage, Stephanie asked her inside the house. 'The press will be here again any second. I need to close the gates. So you either accept my invitation or piss off. It's up to you.'

Common sense did not prevail. Against her better judgement, Connie followed Stephanie inside the garage where she pushed a button on the wall to close the electronic gates and another to shut the garage door behind them, sealing them inside the house.

Leading the way through an internal door, Stephanie paused to prop the baseball bat against a wall. 'Security,' she said. 'Scott said I should keep it handy for when he was working away from home.' She faced Connie, angry tears forming. 'No wonder his business was in the red. He didn't have time for work, he was too busy poking his plonker elsewhere. I knew there was something fishy about buying that pickup when his books didn't balance. I bet she gave him more money for that truck than I did for those damned bikes of his. What a pair of idiots. He took us both for a ride. I'm glad she killed him.'

It would have been Connie's nature to defend Sarah Holden's innocence on hearing this statement, but she faced a dilemma which silenced her. If Stephanie was covering her own guilt and was the one who had killed Scott Fletcher then she would not take kindly to Sarah Holden being viewed as blameless. So, when Stephanie moved off, striding across a tiled floor into a vast kitchen, Connie glanced at her phone. 'Excuse me. The office needs me to check in. I'll just send a quick text back,' she said.

Stephanie filled a kettle. 'Tea or coffee?'

'Nothing for me, thanks,' Connie replied. She would have loved a drink but was too unnerved to accept one. Glancing at the text, she grimaced. Peddyr had told her not to meet Stephanie Fletcher. The text was forthright. *Turn the car around and come back right now.* She poked at the keys to formulate a reply and give the address where she could be found, wondering if he would soon be scraping her dead body from a patio. The response from a furious Peddyr breached their no swearing agreement.

'You'll be coming up with evidence for a defence based on what grounds?' Stephanie asked. Her tone was stilted. 'Self-defence?'

'It's hard to say at this point.' Which it was because Connie's mouth had completely dried up. 'There may be a case for provocation, but we have yet to build a full picture of what happened leading up to the events. I was hoping you may be of some help.'

'Look, lady. I'll be straight with you. That man has taken everything from me. My dignity, trust, love, money and probably my job. It will be all over the papers. How can I be expected to hold a responsible position when I allowed a man to dupe me so easily? So blatantly? He's a scammer.' Instead of filling her mug with boiling water Stephanie picked it up and launched it into the sink where it shattered. 'Fuck him.'

Startled, Connie jumped and backed away. 'I've chosen the worst possible time to call without making proper arrangements,' she said, her voice wobbling. 'This must have been a terrible blow for you. Perhaps I should come back another time.'

Stephanie rounded on her. 'Oh, no you don't. You waltz up to my house, uninvited. You demand to interview me. You look at me with pity in your eyes. Ask your questions. This is a one-time only deal.'

In a state of shock, Connie scrabbled around for something to write on, eventually pulling the necessary equipment from her bag. Some time earlier she had told Trina McIlhenny that an investigator's job wasn't very exciting, how wrong she was. In her text to Peddyr she had lied and told him she was fine because visions of her husband flying up the motorway to her rescue seemed like overkill. Now she wished she hadn't been so glib.

In reaction to the thought of having her head caved in at the hands of Mrs Fletcher's security adviser, and ashamed of how freely she was being intimidated, Connie gritted her teeth. She would have to manage this situation herself. 'This will go to court,' she reminded Stephanie. 'Crown Court. And you will be called as a witness. If you have any sympathy for the lady who must be feeling as aggrieved as you are, then please give me what help you can. My questions will be polite and open. A barrister will not be so kind when he cross-questions you.'

Stephanie gripped the edge of the sink, staring down at the mess she had created. 'I'm sorry, I didn't mean to be so vile. What do you need to know?'

With a tangible truce in the air, Connie hopped onto a barstool at the breakfast bar. Stephanie remained standing while, leaning against the worktop, she strangled a tea-towel. Less than fifteen minutes had elapsed before they were interrupted by the house phone, but it had been a productive time. It seemed Stephanie had told the police she was at the flats the morning Scott Fletcher had been killed. They had asked her to confirm this based on witness statements from the McIlhennys. 'And I stayed in my car, seething. Not knowing what to do because at that point I thought it was a fling. I had no idea he was planning to marry the woman.'

'Why did you leave when you did?'

'Because there was no reason to stay. He was there alone, so I hung around in case she showed up.'

'And what time did you give up and go home?'

The tea-towel twiddling stopped. 'I'm not exactly sure. I got there early, maybe eight-fifteen, and I must have been in the car for over an hour. Perhaps nine forty-five.'

There were more facts to be sought, and Connie placed

her hands together, intertwining her fingers. 'How did you find out that he was having an affair?'

Stroking her throat as if bile had risen and burned from the inside, Stephanie said, 'I took a phone call from a local undertaker the night before. One of Scott's customers. They rang home instead of his work mobile, claiming to have misplaced his business card. His wife happens to work as an administrator in my building and she unwisely gave him my number.'

'Unwisely?'

'Giving out my private details is a breach of policy, data protection, confidentiality...' Stephanie explained. 'The chap I spoke with said how nice it was to have met me, and what a small world to have bumped into me and Scott in Dovedale.' She paused, the hand sliding from her throat to rest on her upper chest. 'I strung him along for some more detail because, as lovely as it sounds, I've never been to Dovedale and I've never played Pooh-sticks, which is apparently what I was doing when he came across us.'

'And that set you on a mission.'

'Too bloody right it did. Being taken for a fool isn't something I can tolerate. It seems Scott went to a lot of places I didn't know about. Some of them involved adultery.' It felt to Connie as if she were one question away from a spectacular truth when the phone rang, and Stephanie dashed to answer it. The handset soon crashed back into place. 'The Daily Albion wanting a quote.'

'I doubt they'll be allowed to print what you said to them,' Connie replied, with a shy grin. Stephanie returned the smile and sank onto a high stool next to her.

'Anyway it's all over now. Scott is dead. He can't rip anyone else off. I'll hand in my resignation. Lick my wounds somewhere nobody knows me. I think I'll change back to my maiden name.'

Taking advantage of this calmer mood, Connie paved the way for her departure. 'You have my card. It is possible we may ask for a more detailed statement as we near a court date. I'd better go. I've taken up a lot of your valuable bike-smashing time.' She picked up her mobile from the breakfast bar. 'Better let the office know I'm on my way back. If you could open the gate for me?'

'No need. The pedestrian side gate opens from the inside. Just make certain to close it behind you.'

Encouraged by a smile from Stephanie, Connie took a leaf from Columbo's book. 'One last question, if I may. Did you drive straight home when you left Primrose Court?'

\* \* \*

Sinking into the driver's seat, Connie started the car and said a relieved hello to Sat-Nav-Suzie. 'Take me home and quick about it,' she said, before remembering to call Peddyr. He didn't answer. 'Probably on a bike,' she said, sending a text to reassure him that she was on her way. She was about to pull out from the kerb when he rang her back.

'Don't worry about cooking tonight. I'll do it.'

'What?' She stared at the screen to confirm she was correctly connected to the car Bluetooth system. 'Is that Peddyr Quirk of Bosworth Bishops or has he been abducted by aliens?'

## 25

## KENNY IN HOT WATER

*D*etermined to return Ryan's laptop, Peddyr dashed from the Marsworth Unit back to Bosworth and Derwent Drive, weaving through the traffic. Coasting in from the road he then left his motorbike on the driveway rather than at the kerbside. This would have worked as an unobtrusive means of accessing the property, but he failed to take account of Carol Brightman who sprang through the adjoining garden gate waving a pair of long tongs in the air. 'And where the hell do you think you are going?' she challenged. He finished pulling the crash helmet from his head and grinned at her.

'Very threatening,' he said. 'Do you wear pink rubber gloves to confront every would-be burglar?'

'Peedwire! It's you. Jeez, man, you gave me a fright. I didn't know you were a hell's angel.'

He laughed lightly. 'I'm not. And I never knew you were Fanny Cradock.'

Carol stared blankly back. 'Who?' She looked down at her striped apron, then at the tongs in her hand. 'Oh, these… I'm having a crap day. My freezer broke down so I'm cooking everything. Please say you'll take a honey-glazed gammon home with you?'

'If it will fit in the panniers on my bike, then I'd be glad to,' he replied. Taking off his jacket he removed his mobile from a pocket and checked for confirmation from Connie that she had done as instructed. 'Balls,' he said.

'Problem?'

Peddyr read the reply from his wife and wasn't reassured, her saying she was safe wasn't enough to quell his reservations. The fact that she had disregarded his request to call off a visit to Stephanie Fletcher's home address made him uneasy, as did the knowledge that the woman had been at the flats the day her husband had died. This was far from a sensible decision on Connie's part. Also, undertaking interviews on her own wasn't how they usually operated, but with time against them it was the only way to cover the necessary ground. It played on his mind, making him rush his text reply and his visit to Derwent Drive.

'Listen, Carol. I'm going to return Ryan's laptop to his room and have a quick rummage for anything the police may have overlooked. Do you know where Sarah keeps receipts for goods? Things that were worth worrying about. Purchases of a TV or a lawnmower for example.'

Waving the tongs about, Carol ummed and aahed several times before conceding that she hadn't a clue where such things would be found. 'Try the office. Downstairs, off the lounge. That's where I'd keep them if I were her. The police will most likely have them already, but you go for it.' She turned on her toes. 'Must dash. I've got half a cow on the barbecue. Call by when you're done.' She whirled round again before reaching the gate. 'Oh, and if you speak to her solicitor guy, give him a message to tell Sarah not to fret. I'll run a vacuum over the carpets before she gets home. When the police were here they left their grubby mark wherever they went. I think that's why they get called plod. Don't forget to reset the alarm when you've finished.'

Peddyr cringed. In his hurry to complete his list of things to do, he'd neglected to inform Carol of the news she would be dreading. He decided to break it to her once he had checked in with Bernie.

Fifteen Derwent Drive was much as he had last seen it, with one or two exceptions. There were dusty footprints on the cream carpet of the lounge and doors had been left ajar which had previously been closed. There was an unimpeded pathway from the hall to the office on the far side of the light and airy lounge and a space on the desk where a computer had recently stood.

'Bastinado,' Peddyr said, a small frown crinkling his forehead. 'They've stripped the place clean.' He could well imagine the scene; policemen carrying boxes of papers, bills, correspondence and computers out through the front door and into a waiting Transit van. He exhaled loudly through his nose. 'Nothing to see here.' He retraced his steps and mounted the stairs, following another trail of dusty footprints along the landing. 'Jeepers, Ryan won't be happy about this.' The sliding wardrobe door had been left open and some thoughtless police employee had rifled through the clothes inside, not replacing them with the precision required by the owner.

Having put Ryan's laptop back in its rightful place, he found the same slapdash approach had been taken in Sarah Holden's bedroom. 'Bastinado,' he said again. 'A proper bunch of bastinados.' Monica had given him this new expletive as a present and he was making good use of it.

In their search for evidence to back up the case against

Sarah, the police had been careless as well as inconsiderate, leaving drawers open and shoebox lids not replaced squarely. What they hadn't done was to check inside them thoroughly enough.

It was apparent from the contents of her vast, wall-to-wall wardrobe that Sarah Holden had a fine collection of shoes and boots. They filled the available space below her clothes. Peddyr wasn't an expert when it came to women's footwear and once confessed to Connie that he thought Jimmy Choo was rhyming slang, however, he knew this was not an accumulation of pricey high heels and glitter. Sarah had a more realistic take on life. Pumps, ankle boots, brogues, and tall leather boots were arranged on shoe racks with boxes stacked behind them. Some of these boxes had more fancy shoes inside and one box to the back of the wardrobe floor caught Peddyr's eye because it was more robust and larger than the others.

Removing it from the base of the wardrobe with a grunt as his injured knee protested, he placed it carefully on the bed. A box of memories, it contained old photographs, pictures of Jim Holden in uniform, Ryan as a baby. Cards and memorabilia from their wedding and Ryan's Christening were all inside. As were Jim's service medals and a small pot containing baby teeth. The lid had been askew when Peddyr spied it, so the police had obviously looked at the contents. What they hadn't realised was the significance of the items.

'Gotcha, you bugger,' Peddyr said, taking out his mobile and photographing a number of sheets of paper, some receipts, and a magazine article. He called Bernie and wedged the phone to his ear with one shoulder. 'Is it alright for me to speak to Carol Brightman about Sarah being charged?' he asked, continuing to remove items from the wooden box, placing them on the silken bedspread.

His friend sounded fatigued. He had recently left Maggie Holden and was on his way home for a soak in the bath. 'If you would, old bean. So far I've not been notified when or where she's going, but Sarah has asked if Carol will visit her and take some clothes and personal items as soon as she gets to her new temporary home.'

'How is she?'

Peddyr heard the lengthy sigh. 'Pretty good, all things considered. She still thinks Ryan killed Fletcher but, having put herself squarely in the frame through misguided loyalty, she has resigned herself to a stretch inside until we can prove her innocence. She's pleaded not guilty and given Maggie Holden and Dexter Booth joint power of attorney.'

This brought Peddyr up short. 'Interesting choice. Not her own brother?' He looked down at the pile of paperwork he had found and listened with care as Bernie explained what Sarah's instructions had been. 'So you are saying that she trusts Dexter above her son and her brother? Based on what you've just told me and what I've found out, I'm not sure if I do,' he said. 'Does Dexter know any of this yet?'

'No, I'm seeing him tomorrow.'

'Good, in which case we'll talk about it when I see you later. Don't fall asleep in the bath.'

It was time to speak to Carol, so he repacked the wooden box and returned it to the wardrobe, ensuring he tidied up the boxes and shoes as he went. A subconscious gesture. 'Poor old Sarah. How on earth is she going to cope in a women's prison.'

Carol Brightman was waiting with the door open as he walked up her path. 'A gammon, a leg of lamb, a dozen sausages, a slab of beef and a spatchcock chicken,' she said.

'I've wrapped them carefully and I'm pretty sure they'll fit in your boxes.' She directed him through to her kitchen.

When he caught sight of the food parcels he salivated like one of Pavlov's dogs. It was impossible not to, the air was thick with delicious meaty smells. 'Crikey, this is no place for a vegetarian. How much do I owe you?'

'What?' she gasped. 'You insult me by asking such a question?' Flicking wayward curls behind her shoulder, she tutted in disapproval. 'Shame on you.'

He shrugged. 'Well, if you insist. I can't really refuse such a generous offer, but I wouldn't want you to be out of pocket.'

'I'll claim it on my insurance. I won't lose out,' she replied. 'Find anything of interest next door?'

'Not really. The office was stripped out and the investigation team didn't leave much for me to find. It was worth a try.' He took in a deep breath. 'I may be back tomorrow if I can find the keys to the garages and workshop.'

'In the kitchen, inside a cupboard by the back door, but you'll need the code for the alarm,' Carol said, helpfully. She handed him a carrier bag to hold open and placed the foil-wrapped food inside. 'Running away again so soon?'

'I have to, Connie may—' His phone sounded, rescuing him from unadulterated flirtation. 'Ah, speak of the devil,' he said, juggling carrier bag and phone. 'Damn. Missed the call.' He excused himself and stepped outside to phone Connie back. He wasn't gone long, and Carol had finished loading two more bags by the time he re-entered the kitchen.

'Everything okay?' she asked.

'Yes, all good on the domestic front.' He smiled reassuringly. 'But, before it gets into the media, there's something you need to hear.'

Carol sank down at her kitchen table, shocked to discover that Sarah had been charged with murder and that her best friend was shortly heading for remand. 'Sweet Jesus,' she said, wiping her brow with a forearm. 'You know she didn't do it, right?'

'Her solicitor is certain she didn't,' Peddyr assured her.

'So, she's covering for Ryan,' Carol said, staring up at him.

'What makes you say that?'

'Because he went out that morning, and when he came back he was in a real hurry and had a look about him. Like he was pleased.' She paused to explain. 'I mean, he often looks like that because he's so full of himself, but this was different.' Searching again for a better description she tapped fingernails on the table. 'Victorious. That's the word. Like he had won a fight.'

Ryan's nosy neighbour had watched him leave and seen him return. She had also managed a few words with Sarah when she had left the house to avoid being present for Ryan's mental health assessment. 'Sarah was crapping herself. She couldn't stay chatting for long but asked me to head him off if he went out again before the men in white coats got here.' Carol flapped her hands. 'Her plan was to stop Scott from moving in and focus on Ryan's needs until he was better. There is no way she was intending to kill Scott, so logically it means Ryan killed him and Sarah was the one who found the body. Why the police can't see that beats me.' With an indignant huff she slammed one hand down onto the table. 'Jeez, I told them all this.' Looking again at Peddyr, she let out a low groan of frustration. 'That inspector has bad breath because his brains have rotted.'

'Webster.'

'Yeah, that's the guy. He should be demoted for incompetence.' Although not able to say so, Peddyr couldn't disagree, but he wasn't so certain that Ryan was guilty of murder. Stephanie Fletcher had been at the flats too and she had as good a motive as Ryan. She might have used the line from the compressor to strangle him, but using the compressed air to finish her husband off by firing it into his body until his intestines burst, was another matter. This unexpectedly gory detail had come from Bernie who, via the old boy network, had wrangled details from the forensic pathologist ahead of the obligatory disclosure from the police. The reason behind Sarah Holden withholding such detail was simple. She didn't know because she hadn't killed Fletcher.

The question remained: did Ryan know enough about the risks of compressed air to make use of the weapon at his disposal? Not being gifted with a love for mechanics did not preclude him as a possible suspect. He would have known how to use a compressor even if it was to pump up the tyres on his bicycle and therefore, reasoned Peddyr, he could easily have finished off the bash on the head with a pinch of the nose and a lungful of compressed air. Such a vengeful act.

The timeline was critical and Peddyr hoped both Bernie and Connie had details which either discounted Ryan altogether or put him firmly in the prime suspect slot. There were pieces of the puzzle still missing.

'I'd better go. Mr Kershaw will be in touch as soon as he hears something about Sarah's detention. I'll drop by again tomorrow. I need to make an inventory of everything in the outbuildings. We should know by then where she is.'

It took several attempts to arrange the bags of food in order to close the lids on his panniers. The gammon he placed in the top box; it was the size of the one Connie would buy for Boxing Day, and was dripping with sweet juices, so Carol had put it into a plastic container. Fully laden with enough food for a medieval banquet, Peddyr headed home.

He had barely changed into second gear when he was forced to brake hard. A crimson Ford Fiesta swerved across the road in front of him, no signal, no warning. It came to a halt on the driveway of number seven. Irate, Peddyr drew up to the kerb, flipped up the visor of his crash helmet and yelled at the offending driver who was squeezing himself free of his car. 'Oi, Kenny. Try bloody looking before you manoeuvre. Any sodding closer and I could have been talking to the tarmac.' Peddyr was wearing a jacket with high-vis panels, a white crash helmet and his bike had daytime running lights. He couldn't have been more visible.

The same could also be said of Kenny Eversholt, the driver of the car. He, however, didn't dress in a turquoise satin shirt and mustard coloured trousers as a precaution, he wore them because he liked the attention. As he levered himself to a standing position by hauling on the driver's door, Peddyr shook his head in wonder. There was no mistaking Kenny. His eccentric dress sense was a familiar sight on Derwent Drive although he was barely tolerated by some of his less enlightened neighbours. He raised a hand to his brow, squinting against the lowering sun. 'What's your problem, ducky?' As he spoke the material of his shirt shimmered and his satin pantaloon trousers took on a life of their own when he danced in agitation.

'My problem, Kenny, is that you nearly wiped me out. If I hadn't braked when I did you would have a motorbike in the side of your car right now.'

'How do you know my name, and what are you doing here?'

Forced into a conversation, Peddyr turned off the ignition and took his crash helmet off. 'Remember me?'

He was met with a look of recognition and disappointment. 'Oh, God. You're that private dick who was helping Gabriella, last year. Why are you here?'

With a long sigh Peddyr again pointed out to Kenny that he had very nearly caused an accident. 'Your driving is bloody awful.'

'So I keep being told. I'm sorry, ducky. I had so much on my mind. Honestly, I didn't see you.' The man was fidgety, switching his gaze from Peddyr to his house and back again.

'You should be more bike aware, given the number of the things you actually own,' Peddyr moaned, sweeping his eyes around. 'Sold a couple have you?' he enquired.

'Some bloke made me an offer on the '68 SS125A I should have refused.' He sighed, mumbling regretfully the price he had sold it for.

Peddyr groaned. 'Sounds like you were done...'

'Broke my heart to see it go, ducky, honestly it did. He asked for first refusal on the other little Honda, same year and everything but worse condition, but some bastard nicked that, so he's out of luck.' Slapping a flattened hand to his chest he screwed up his face and glanced at Peddyr. 'And, yes, it did cross my mind that it could be the same bloke. I told the police. They will investigate, if they can be bothered.' Kenny didn't have a good relationship with the law. He was on the sex offenders register, a fact well known to Peddyr but not to the general population of Bosworth Bishops who simply viewed him as the local weirdo. For his own protection he had installed security cameras.

'Nothing on CCTV?' Peddyr queried.

'Oh, yes plenty. Just nothing of any use. You can't see his

face. He knew which bike he wanted and smashed the lock. It's made me feel so vulnerable, ducky.'

Peddyr grimaced. 'You know where you went wrong. On that one there for example,' he said, pointing to the nearest bike under its cover. 'Your chain is loose and looped so the padlock is resting on the ground. Locks can be shattered easily like that. You need to rethink your safety precautions, Kenny.' Unable to leave the mystery unsolved he asked what he thought would be one last question. 'What was the name of the bloke you sold the bike to?'

Kenny seemed to shrink with humiliation as he reeled off the story of how the man had paid cash and had been so sympathetic, understanding his emotional turmoil at selling a much-loved bike. 'He even offered to post the V5 logbook form to the DVLA for me,' Kenny admitted.

'You berk,' Peddyr said, reprovingly. 'Some random bloke who knows your bikes are here, makes you a cash offer and you don't even ask his name. What possessed you?'

The reason turned out to be a case of spite. 'I did it to piss off Chris Booth, ducky.'

'Know him well, do you?'

The story from Kenny was unsurprising given that Chris Booth was a regular visitor to Derwent Drive, as was his son Dexter. Both of them had bikes and Kenny's mystery Honda collection would have piqued their interest. 'One day about three or four years ago, I was here, checking the tyres and running the engines, when the Booths both trolled up the drive. I showed them the bikes and we had a chat, like you do, ducky.' Kenny heaved a sigh. 'After that Chris never let up. Said he could restore them, his son could auction them off and we could share the profits. Whenever

I saw him it was the same thing. If he hadn't moved to the land of the Taff I probably would have given in.'

The off-the-cuff remarks were of great significance to Peddyr but didn't answer the question of who the mystery man was who had bought the bike from Kenny and possibly stolen another.

'Ever seen the bloke before? The fella that bought your bike?'

'Not that I can recall. I'm not here often these days.' Kenny had been due to move back into his bungalow the previous year but still spent most of his time these days in Kent where he had lived for years, using number seven Derwent Drive purely for hoarding all manner of items.

'What vehicle was he driving?'

It was a wasted question. Describing the pain of the hoarder relinquishing a possession, Kenny confessed to being so overwhelmed after the sale that he'd retreated indoors to cry in private rather than watch the bike's departure as the man pushed it out of the driveway and up the road away from the bungalow. 'Well, let's hope the police work it out. And as much as I'd love to stay and talk, I have to dash home to prepare dinner.'

As he left Peddyr wagged a finger at him. 'And next time you turn into your drive, look for traffic coming the other way.'

## 26

# WITHIN FOUR WALLS

*C*ut off from the outside world, Sarah Holden resorted to pacing and wracking her brains for old songs to sing, taking her mind off the interminable hours in detention. The custody officers came and went, checking up on her, bringing cardboard food and drinks at mealtimes and so far none had news of when her transport would arrive or where she would be taken. Never had she felt so adrift. Waves of nausea rolled and ebbed, palpitations rampaged, and the recriminations coursing through her mind, about whose fault this was, threatened her sanity.

Hindsight is only a wonderful thing if there is a useful outcome and lessons learnt. In Sarah's case, hindsight was akin to walking over hot coals, very slowly. On one hand she had herself to blame and on the other she also had herself to blame. She had trusted Scott and she had allowed herself to fall for his charming ways because she was lonely. Not friendless, that was something else entirely, but Sarah had been lonely for want of a loving relationship. What an easy target she had made.

Battling emotions that ranged from anger to shame, she quickened her strides back and forth across the cell. 'God, how could I have been so stupid!' she yelled.

Scott had lured her in with the promise of a future together, wooed her with old-fashioned flattery and romance, while all the time eyeing the biggest prize. Her money, her assets, her home. He was as much a leech as her brother had become after Jim's death and yet she had chosen not to see it. 'A weak and feeble woman,' she seethed. 'A bloody walk-over.'

Bernard Kershaw had seemed perplexed by her choice of Dexter when it came to power of attorney, but Sarah had made this decision with care. It wasn't fair to burden her elderly mother-in-law with the responsibility on her own, and given her frailty it was wisest to consider what would happen if Maggie were unable to undertake the task. Ryan would be furious that she had chosen Dexter over him, but then again if he was capable of killing Scott to protect his entitlement to his mother's wealth, then where would he draw the line?

'No wonder they hated each other,' she mumbled towards her feet. 'He and Scott were as bad as one another.'

Ryan had abused her kindly nature since the day he learned how, at about three years old. Scott had used her, and her brother had exploited her. 'I'm a doormat,' she concluded. 'A sad, pathetic doormat.' Since her arrest, the one small spark of rebellion came when the charge sheet was read out to her and she pleaded not guilty to murder. By then she had heard enough to realise her life-changing mistake in protecting Ryan, a mistake she had made so many times before.

Whenever life went wrong for Ryan she was there to put it right. Letters to school with excuses for unfinished homework, sweet-talking a local shop owner when he was caught stealing girlie magazines saying it was a dare, funding his gym membership when he said he didn't have enough money for the monthly fees. Once she had wired money to Thailand where he was having a lovely holiday to celebrate his twenty-first birthday and had underestimated how much he could spend on scuba diving lessons and sailing. Worst of all, she had paid for an abortion to get him off the hook with a "one-night-stand accident" which turned out to be nothing of the sort.

Sarah sat down, head in hands. 'I fed the monster,' she wailed as she admitted to herself that, to keep the peace, whatever Ryan wanted, Ryan received. Money, clothes, gadgets, cars, gym equipment, attention and praise by the lorry load. She had done the same with Scott, buying him a new truck because he said he had cashflow issues during the divorce, even though this meant delaying the purchase of a car for Ryan when he returned home with no job. Scott had even used the same empty promises of repayment Ryan always came out with. 'You are a star, I love you. I'll pay you back as soon as I can.' Kiss, kiss.

She had been as soft with her own brother until Dexter had revealed his father's wretched secret two years previously.

* * *

'Sarah, I need to ask you a special favour,' her nephew had said. She had asked him to stop calling her Aunty Sarah when he reached eighteen. It didn't sound right. Following a phone call on his way home from work, he had dropped by to see her at home. A memorable day for all the wrong reasons.

'A special favour, Dex? What's up?' She wondered if he was having worries about becoming a husband and taking on the responsibility of house ownership or wanted to talk to her about something Ryan had done. They were alone in the house; Carol had just left after a gossip session.

Putting down his mug of coffee, Dexter handed her a typed sheet. 'I made a list of the motorbikes in the garage, so you can decide which ones to send to auction. I've highlighted the ones we discussed.'

With a tight smile Sarah took the sheet of paper from her nephew. 'Thanks. Very organised. I know it's the right thing to do. I can't ask you to keep looking after so many when they are of no use to me or Ryan. And yet I feel so guilty, as if I'm being disloyal to Jim somehow.' She shook her head at him. 'Silly of me, I know. They should go to someone who will get great pleasure from owning them. We'll stick to the plan. Just the ones you've highlighted. Mind you, even if I wanted to, I can't sell the ones Jim's father owned. Can you imagine? The pair of them would turn in their graves if I did that and Maggie would be heartbroken at such a breach of trust. They should be Ryan's inheritance by rights.'

Glancing down at the list of her husband's motorbike collection, a forlorn smile reached her lips. 'What a shame he never took the slightest interest in them.' Raising her head to catch Dexter's response, she picked up on her nephew's unease. 'But this visit isn't about the auction, is it?'

'No,' he replied, drawing in breath as if stealing himself to make the next statement. 'It's about Dad. I have a simple request. Please don't lend him any more money or give him a motorbike which he won't pay you for.' He looked at her with a sadness she wasn't expecting to see. 'Dad is in debt up to his armpits.'

Allowing this to sink in, Sarah stirred her coffee unnecessarily. Her brother hadn't mentioned any problems with the business, but then again Hilary would have wanted any financial embarrassment to be kept secret. There was no real surprise when she analysed it more carefully. 'Then, let me help out,' she said. 'How much are we talking? If the business is in trouble I could be an anonymous investor.'

A short pause preceded Dexter's reply. 'The business has already gone to the wall and they may lose the house.'

Sarah threw up her hands. 'Dex! He's my brother. If I can help, I will.' She faltered, a quizzical look replacing the astonishment. 'Is this to do with another of his little indiscretions?' The subject was one of those kept out of sight, a subject hedged around and yet a well-known fact within the family. Chris Booth, local businessman, had a reputation for infidelity. With a personal investment in the family business, of both time and money, Hilary seemed to tolerate the marriage for appearance's sake and that of the children, despite the repeating pattern of her husband's sordid affairs. Some had ended badly, and some had ended when Hilary intervened. Sarah was sure it was the reason she was so indelibly unhappy.

'The latest floozy tried to top herself which hasn't helped matters, but the money he's been spending can't be accounted for quite so easily. There's only so much he can splash out on cheap hotels, dinners and drinks.'

'Has he been playing the stock markets?' Sarah asked, wracking her brains for a reasonable explanation. Chris had always flashed his cash and liked to be seen as a success, but she couldn't fathom where he had gone wrong so recently. His business sense had always been his strength in the same way that his charm had won many a contract and many a sexual conquest.

With his head lowered, Dexter finally got to the nub of the matter that was so evidently bothering him. 'I've discovered he has a massive gambling problem. One he's been hiding from all of us,' he blurted out. Head raised again, he looked across the kitchen table at his aunt who was stunned into silence. 'I say he's hidden it from all of us, but Mum knows. She's too much of a snob to admit to anyone that there's an actual problem, so she's been covering for him. Rejigging the accounts. Dipping into the savings, from what I can gather.'

It was true, Hilary had recently become more miserable than normal, and snappier, Sarah realised. Especially since Dexter's wedding plans began to take shape and the costs had begun to escalate. 'How did you find out?' she asked.

It was a relatively short story involving arguments about who was to pay for what when it came to the upcoming nuptials, but more than that, Chris had been careless in his habits. Bez was the one who spilled the beans, having seen Chris in a number of betting shops where he too would fritter away his hard-earned cash, leaving barely enough money to pay for a room in a filthy house and to fund his smoking and drinking habits.

'I made a few discreet inquiries and one of his ex-girlfriends told me he's been making use of casinos on his business trips. The more money Dad gets his hands on, the more he gambles away. He owes money everywhere. We have to cut off the supply,' Dexter said, staring hard at her. 'Tough love. That's what he needs from you. And one other thing... we have to remove the temptation of those expensive bikes.'

'The old ones? Grandpa Holden's special collection?'

Dexter nodded. 'I know this will surprise you, but to an enthusiast those old bikes are worth a bloody fortune. We must take them out of the equation before Dad gets his hands on them. Which one did you say he could have this time?'

Sarah straightened in a determined effort to concentrate on the practicalities necessary to help her brother, rather than dwell on the problem itself. 'I told him to take his pick and let me have what he believed it was worth... I never thought...' The words dried up as the awful reality filtered into her head. She stared down at the sheet of paper he had given her. 'You really think they are worth that much money?' Several thoughts arrived in a rush. 'Don't let Ryan see this. Can you imagine what his reaction would be? I have some old paperwork hidden away upstairs; do you want it?'

'No, you must hang on to it. Keep it safely, but nowhere Ryan will find it. We just need to find a place for those bikes to be stored, somewhere Dad won't think to go. And change the code on the alarm.'

Sarah was faced with the fact that her own brother had an addiction. One so serious that he needed saving from himself and a habit she had unwittingly been sustaining. 'He's not going to like it,' she said, giving a reassuring smile in an effort to ease Dexter's pain. 'But you are absolutely right.' She shook her head fiercely. 'Not a word to anyone about this. Nobody. He must never find out that you came to me. And don't worry about wedding costs. I'll help you out.'

Thinking carefully, she fell silent for a moment. 'I'll tell Chris I've had enough of his promises to pay his debts, and, as a punishment, I've changed my mind about selling him another bike, especially when he owes me for the last one and the one before that.' She put a hand to her brow. 'Oh, God... and I thought I was doing him a favour.'

The relief on Dexter's face was plain to see. He let out a long breath and thanked her as she gave his arm a squeeze. 'It will be alright, Dex, you'll see.'

Five weeks later Chris called by unannounced to see her at work, which was his way when he wanted something from her. A grey monotonous day was not improved when he caught Sarah manning the office on her own, meaning there would be no witnesses and therefore no excuse not to talk to him about personal affairs.

'Morning, Sis. Got a minute?' The phones were silent, and she was sorting rental agreements. She looked around dreading what he was about to say, fully expecting to be grilled about her decision not to let him have another bike from Jim's collection.

Keeping her voice light and airy, she said, 'It certainly seems so. What brings you here?'

'I've come to pay back some of the money I owe you.'

His reply was so unexpected that Sarah stopped what she was doing to glare at him. 'Good God, that will be a first. What's brought this on?' She then followed his gaze as he turned his head to the street outside. 'And why is Hilary sitting in the car?'

He beckoned for his wife to join him and handed Sarah a cheque for five thousand pounds. 'We've sold the house and we're moving to Wales.'

'You're doing what?' she asked as the door opened and Hilary entered the office, more sour-faced than Sarah had ever seen her. More wretched than she'd been at Dexter's wedding two weeks earlier even, although for everyone else it had been a wonderful day of celebrations.

'Have you told her everything?' Hilary demanded, standing stiff and folding her spindly arms across her chest. Sarah had never felt relaxed in her company and vice versa.

Hilary remained a distant figure, unapproachable and starchy. Her hair was always neat and cropped short, accentuating her gaunt features. She never seemed to have a good word to say about anyone and rejoiced in criticising Sarah, given the chance.

Concerned about the possibility of interruptions, Sarah rose and turned the sign on the door, dropping the catch. There was a confession coming at last, she thought. 'Best we keep this to ourselves. It's nearly lunchtime. Take a seat, why don't you, and I'll put the kettle on.'

'We're not stopping,' Hilary snapped. 'Christopher has something he wishes to say.'

Astonished, Sarah sank back into her chair. 'Go ahead.' She turned to Chris who, like a naughty child in a headmaster's office, hung his head.

'I couldn't pay you back before now because I lost the money.'

'Careless,' Sarah quipped with a laugh as she often did. Chris had made a promising start, but the confession she was hoping for never came.

'Stupid,' Hilary barked, spitting the words out with barbs attached. 'The business wasn't doing so well, and we had to borrow money.' The look of disgust on Hilary's face failed to garner sympathy with Sarah who had never bonded in any way with her sister-in-law and didn't appreciate the lies tripping from her tongue.

'Oh, Chris, why didn't you tell me?' Rounding on her sister-in-law she feigned ignorance. 'Why didn't you tell me before now? I could have helped.'

Eyes wild at the reproach, Hilary ramped up her fury and thrust out her chin. 'No, thank you. We are not beggars. We are perfectly capable of sorting this out ourselves, thank you very much. It was about time Chris and I made a fresh start somewhere else anyway.'

There was a brief hiatus as Sarah composed herself. 'If I had been told about the problem then it could have been a different matter.'

'Well, now you know.' Hilary threw a sideways glance at a shamefaced Chris. 'We've sold the house, all debts are paid, and we will be living on a mobile home park, of all places. Chris will be working in a local garage repairing motorbikes and you can tell anyone who asks that he has taken early retirement.'

'What about Celia? Is she moving with you?'

Chris shook his head. 'No, she's lodging with a girl from work. Her job is here. Dexter will keep an eye on her.'

'Do they know about your debts?'

A sharp inhalation from Hilary was enough of an answer. 'Don't be ridiculous,' she squawked. There was no mention of gambling and Sarah, always one to avoid serious family conflict, went along with the charade in the same way she did when one of Chris's extra-marital affairs came to light. Hard though it was to admit, Dexter had been right about the dire financial straits her brother was in. A mobile home park would be an unbearable comedown for Hilary, and she wondered how long the marriage could stand the strain of this final straw.

\* \* \*

Sitting up in the cell, Sarah rolled her shoulders to release the tension in her back, still thinking about her brother. Chris and Hilary, sometimes together, sometimes separately, popped back to Bosworth Bishops every other month or so to see how Dexter and Celia were getting on. Now and again Chris would stop by for a cuppa and on occasion stay for a meal. Hilary never did. All seemed to be going well in Wales, with Chris enjoying his hands-on work with bikes and engines. 'Just like the old days,' he had said. A crisis had been averted by Hilary taking decisive action and Dexter appealing to his aunt's sensible side and thus things settled down over time until the doors to the workshop were opened and Chris caught sight of Jim's motorcycle collection once again. A much-reduced collection.

* * *

*D*uring the time Sarah was clearing the house in preparation for moving to a smaller property, Chris and Hilary made a very obvious visit, at Ryan's behest, to meet Scott and sound him out. Thankfully Dexter had come with them. At the time, Sarah thought the introductions had gone well, given that the men had spent a good forty minutes in the garages where, according to Scott, Chris had reminisced about adventures with Jim on various motorbikes. It was good to see Chris so animated, pumping Scott for information on the bikes he owned and the pair of them chatting about various makes of vintage motorcycle. Not so brilliant for Sarah to be saddled with Hilary for forty whole minutes. Although she wasn't entirely left alone with her because Ryan had made use of the time to launch an anti-Scott campaign, determined to get Hilary on his side.

'Scott's too good to be true, Aunty Hilary. Mum should be more cautious. He could be anybody.'

'Ignore him, Hilary. He's just jealous because I have a boyfriend.'

'But Mum… He doesn't even work for EDF.'

'Yes, he does, Ryan.' Sarah flapped a hand and screwed up her face, apologising to Hilary who in turn raised her over-plucked eyebrows.

'If your mother has found a little happiness in her menopausal years, then you should be pleased for her. Nobody wants to be a sad and lonely old widow.'

Too insulted to rustle up a reply, Sarah swallowed down her hurt as Ryan jumped straight back in with a counter-argument. 'Yes, they do if it means keeping what belongs to them. He's a con man, Aunty Hilary. I'm telling you. She just can't see it. Watch him, he'll be selling Uncle Chris one of Dad's bikes next.'

'No, he won't, Ryan. Scott has persuaded me to keep the rest of your father's bike collection. I was going to sell all but two of them, but he won't hear of it. He says they are your inheritance, and I should keep the remaining ones. Chris can have one if he likes. He can polish it up and sell it, then pay me a percentage. That alright with you, Hilary?'

The idea was to stop Ryan carping on and to make peace with Chris while knowing that Hilary had taken control of the bank accounts; Dexter had told her as much. However, Ryan had a point to prove. 'Was that your idea? Or did it come from Scott?' A triumphant expression appeared on his face. 'I rest my case, Aunty Hilary. The con man at work.'

## 27

## THE DRUGS DO WORK

*R*yan stirred at the sound of his name when it came drifting into his conscious mind at the speed of a snail. He lifted his head from the pillow and felt the slime of saliva at the side of his mouth where he had dribbled. 'What?' he groaned, barely able to say the word without slurring, struggling to lift himself up from the bed to swing his legs to the floor.

'You've got a visitor.'

'What time is it?'

'Let's put it this way… you've missed supper.'

Ryan stared back at a blurred Joran, trying hard to bring him into focus. The news about missing another unappetising evening meal was irrelevant to him, he felt unwell, dizzy, disorientated and thick-headed. A figure in a baseball cap entered the room when instructed by Joran. By the smell Ryan knew it was Bez.

'You look like shite,' his friend said. He sat down in the only chair, within feet of the doorway, and handed Ryan a bag. 'They've searched me, like. I've brung in some of them crappy lentil crisps you like so much and grapes, 'cos that's what you have to take to people in hospital.' At this, Ryan was supposed to reply with something witty or cutting but he hadn't the words. He was forcing himself to think through the simplest of tasks; sitting upright was hard enough. 'Christ, what have they done to you?' Bez enquired, turning for an answer to Joran who sat in a chair in the corridor, taking the place of the healthcare assistant who had gone for a break.

'We gave him something to calm him down.'

'No shit. Whatever it is you gave him, don't come near me with it, I'm daft enough as it is. I don't need no chemical cosh.' He turned back to Ryan who appreciated the short interlude as he tried to gather his thoughts.

'Mum's been charged with murder,' he drawled, wondering why his mouth refused to work properly.

'So you kicked off?' Bez said, slewing the peak of his cap to the back of his head. 'Hardly surprising. No wonder you went mental, being locked up in here, like. The rozzers must be off their trolleys thinking your mum could kill a man. There's no chance.'

Ryan couldn't shake his head for fear of toppling side-ways. He clamped his hands to the edge of the mattress instead, as the frustrations of his day rose to the surface. 'No, I lost it with the little twat of a doctor who tried to lock me up in here for six months.' Getting angry seemed to help Ryan's ability to speak so he growled a few more words. 'But he didn't count on my solicitor. She put the bastard back in his box and she's going to sue him for giving me an injection I shouldn't have had. The hospital will have to pay big time for what they've done.' He scratched at his face. 'Do us a favour and ask if I can have a coffee, a strong one. I've got to shift this fucking muzzy head.'

Bez didn't get as far as carrying out this request, it had been heard by Joran who put in an order from a passing patient. 'Jesse, can you make a strong coffee for Ryan? Doreen will unlock the kitchen for you. Tell her I said it was fine as long as she stays with you.' He raised his voice slightly. 'Ryan? Any sugar or milk?'

'No, just black and strong.'

'Jesse, Ryan says thank you so much for offering to make him a drink. He really appreciates it. He would like a strong coffee, as it comes, please.'

Ryan had no idea who Jesse was until Bez whispered to him. 'Have you seen the size of that bloke? Fancy his parents calling him Jessie. He don't look like no Jessie to me, he looks more like an Indian Jabba or the Incredible Bulk.' Eyes wide, Bez craned his neck to watch Jesse shuffle past in slippers overflowing with the flesh of his swollen feet. Ryan didn't move from his precarious pose on the bed. 'So when are you getting out of 'ere?' Bez asked. The visit was destined to be a brief one because Bez had already run out of conversation, for which Ryan was grateful.

'Dunno, mate. Thanks for coming… There's nothing you can do to help, so you don't need to stay. I've got clothes and washing stuff so you can go now. Cheers.'

Looking embarrassed, Bez stood up and nodded his understanding. 'Yeah, you'd best sleep this off, like. Hope you don't get no 'angover tomorrow. I need to get out of me work clothes, like, and think about dinner and stuff, so … see ya.' He gave a half-hearted wave and left the room, saying a shy 'cheers,' to Joran as he headed for the ward exit.

In his room, Ryan fought the fatigue weighing him down and remained upright enough to accept the coffee when it arrived, carried in by Joran. 'Ryan says thank you, Jesse. He reckons it's the best cup of coffee he's had since he arrived on the ward.' Ryan gave a lopsided smirk in response. It was the *only* cup of coffee he'd had since arriving on the ward. He usually stuck to water or fruit juices.

The pillow looked inviting, but he forced himself to stand up. 'I need a shower,' he garbled.

'Sorry, Ryan but you had a shower already today and you are too sedated to be safe in the bathroom.'

'But I've been sleeping in my clothes.'

'Then have a wash at the sink and change into fresh ones. We have laundry facilities.' This wasn't what Ryan wanted to hear. Unsteadily he took several steps towards the sink, holding the rim for support with both hands, fearing a fall.

'Alright there, cousin? Need a hand?' A voice he recognised came from the doorway. Dexter. Ryan lifted his head but couldn't manage a smile.

'Come in. Welcome to the loony bin,' he slurred. 'They've given me some shit to stop me talking, walking and thinking. Seems to be working just fine.'

Dexter sat himself down and offloaded the paperback in his hand, placing it on the bedside locker. 'So I hear. I met Bez on his way out. He said you'd reared up at the consultant and got yourself an injection for your trouble. How long till it wears off?'

'Fuck knows,' Ryan replied, splashing cold water into his face in another hopeless attempt to perk himself up. 'Ask my bodyguard.'

Joran, who had overheard every word, replied. 'Everybody is different. You had a small dose but, because you're not used to it, the drugs may take a while to leave the system. A day or two you should feel less sedated.'

'A day or two!' Ryan and Dexter responded in appalled

unison. 'What the hell is that stuff?' Ryan asked, staggering back to the bed and collapsing onto it as his legs gave way.

'Zuclopenthixol. Clopixol Accuphase to be exact. You keep asking me and I tell you the same answer every time.'

Lying down on the bed, Ryan felt safer, less likely to keel over and hurt himself by crashing to the floor. He rolled his head slowly to one side to avoid increasing the dizziness as he sought to consult with Dexter. 'You heard about Mum?'

His cousin patted his knees. 'Yep. It's a really shit deal. There is no way she had it in her to kill Scott. No way.' He looked at Ryan with an apology in his eyes. 'Look, I'm sorry she thought you'd gone... you know, a bit potty. She was sure you were totally paranoid about Scott to the point of madness.' He lowered his voice. 'I said I thought he was up to something, but I never thought you'd go all out to prove it in the way you did. No wonder she thought you'd lost it. What were you thinking, following him and phoning his work?'

Closing his eyes, Ryan managed a grin. 'But I was right. A man called Scott Fletcher works for EDF, but it wasn't Mum's Scott Fletcher. A boy by that name was at school with my dad when they were about six years old, but it wasn't Mum's Scott Fletcher. He lied to her about paying her back for that fucking truck as well. He did it to fuck me off, so she couldn't buy me the car she said I could have. He lied to everyone. He even had a wife and lied to her too. I hated that slimy bastard.'

There was a firm knock at the open door from Joran, startling Dexter who flinched and sat back as if he'd been caught doing wrong. 'Sorry to interrupt so soon, Ryan, but the police are here, and they want to speak to you.'

'Tell them I already know about my mum,' he yawned. 'Good of them to call by and all that but I can't tell them anything they don't already know.' Another yawn caught him out, his eyes closed, his body felt leaden. 'No more visitors. I'm too knackered. Tell them, Dex. Tell them to come back tomorrow.' Forcing his lids to part he fleetingly opened his eyes in a silent plea.

'He does have a point. Look at him. He can barely stay awake.'

With a dismissive wave of one hand, Joran stepped into the corridor and Ryan listened in to the deep rumble of voices as he was discussed.

'Just one or two questions. Then we'll leave it at that for now. His cousin is with him, you say?' The voice became louder as a plain clothes police officer entered Ryan's room with Joran at his side and a female officer within view in the corridor beyond, at least that's who Ryan assumed she was as they were never formally introduced.

'My name is Acting Detective Chief Inspector Webster,' the man said. 'I have one or two questions to put to you, Mr Holden. Do you wish your visitor to leave?' It appeared the matter of patient choice had been removed; Ryan was expected to comply. However, he wasn't in the habit of doing anything he didn't want to, so he took an alternative approach and closed his eyes again, succumbing to the exhaustion that pulled at him.

Dexter's voice drifted across the room to where the Acting DCI was standing. 'Inspector, I really think you are wasting your time. Ryan has been given a strong sedative and he could hardly talk to me a moment ago. He knows his mother has been charged with the murder of Scott Fletcher, so you may have had a wasted journey.'

'And your name is?'

'Dexter Booth. I'm Ryan's cousin.'

Fighting to stay awake once more, Ryan clenched his

fists tight, digging his fingernails into the pads of his palms. He could hear his cousin's anxious breathing. 'Perhaps you should come back another time,' Dexter suggested.

'Or perhaps we could have a word with you instead,' the Inspector countered, triumphantly. 'The nurse tells me you were having quite a chat with young Mr Holden just now. We understand you two are quite pally and if that is the case, he's certain to have told you things of significance to our inquiries.'

'But I thought you'd charged Sarah with the murder.'

'Oh, we have, but that doesn't mean she was the only one involved in killing Scott Fletcher. It would be remiss of us not to follow up on all possible scenarios, now wouldn't it?' As he finally caved into the allure of deep sleep, Ryan smelt the faint odour of rotten eggs in the air.

## THE MEAT FEAST

When Connie reached the back door of the flat, she had resigned herself to confessing her reckless actions in meeting with Stephanie Fletcher. Peddyr wouldn't be angry with her for long, if at all, and then only out of concern. Door keys at the ready, she noticed the two plant pots just in time to avoid knocking them over with her feet. There was a note propped between them. It was from her friend Kathy, one of the florists in the shop below. 'Oh, dear, I thought she was joking.' She opened the note and read aloud. '"I've given you two chances to succeed this year. Keep them in the airing cupboard for a couple of weeks but don't forget to feed them and keep the soil moist but not wet".'

The annual amaryllis challenge was on again, much to Connie's dismay. She had yet to produce a flower from one in the past five years and had become the source of regular ribbing from Kathy who was determined to prove that anyone could develop green fingers. Connie, a renowned plant killer, was her toughest assignment to date. The only plants to survive at her hand were cacti and succulents, and then only because Peddyr occasionally watered them.

She turned at the sound of a motorbike, confirming that she had beaten her husband home by a matter of minutes. According to her watch they had an hour to pull together a supper and scrub up, and it would be a miracle if Peddyr could actually produce anything edible in such a short space of time.

Unlocking the door, she carried one plant pot at a time into the tiny utility room. 'I'll deal with you two later. Try not to die on me in the meantime,' she warned, with a fore-finger. By the time Peddyr stepped in through the door she had hurriedly set the table in the kitchen diner.

He was well laden and placed his rucksack gingerly on the floor with a clank. 'I called in at the supermarket on the way home,' he said. 'Our wine stocks are low.'

'You did buy food...'

'Don't you fret, Lao Po. I have a feast Henry the Eighth would applaud.' Puzzled, he asked why she had decided they should eat there.

'Privacy,' she replied. 'The balcony would be cold later on and didn't seem right somehow, and I know this evening will constitute working but your office is no place for a light supper. The lounge is out of bounds because it would be foolish to let Bernie and red wine near the lounge carpet after the last fiasco. What are you—?' The rest of the sentence evaporated as she gaped at the bags in Peddyr's hands. 'Good grief, what have you got there?'

He approached the work surface next to the sink and began to unwrap the joints of meat given to him by Carol Brightman. 'Ta-dah! Dinner for four hungry people.' He reached up to open a kitchen cupboard. 'Where do we keep the big plate for the Christmas turkey?'

Once the meat feast was revealed, Peddyr puffed out his chest with pride. 'There we go, all done. Now, while we have a shower you can explain to me how you got back here without breaking the speed limit. Then you can give me chapter and verse of your day. I want no nasty surprises when Monica and Bernie get here. I want to look like I knew all along what you were up to.'

Fooled into thinking she had got away with her imper-sonation of a rally driver on the way back from Theale, Connie was taken aback at her husband's rapid assessment of her misdemeanours. 'I may have driven to the speed limit and one or two miles an hour over it, on occasion,' she said, unconvincingly.

'Ro'locks,' Peddyr replied, indicating the back door and beyond it to the garages. 'The engine and tyres are still hot and there is no way you could have driven that distance in the time on a Friday without hammering down the lanes.'

'Pot, kettle, black, Lao Gong,' she replied, smiling and raising her neat eyebrows. 'And you get to use the shower first. I have salads to prepare. Even carnivores need a little greenery in their diets.' She was putting off the inevitable conversation about Stephanie Fletcher, but when she joined Peddyr in their bedroom, where he was wandering around in a pair of red underpants and nothing else, there was no escape.

'Ah, good,' he said, pulling a clean short sleeved shirt from the wardrobe. 'I like this one.' Red and white chequered, it matched his underpants and he seemed very pleased with the effect, admiring himself in the mirror. Wrapped in a bath towel, Connie grinned at the sight. 'You are putting some shorts or jeans on, I take it?'

Before she'd had time to finish dressing, Peddyr had squeezed information from her about the interviews with

Trina McIlhenny and Stephanie Fletcher. The inquisition continued as they re-entered the kitchen. 'I still can't believe you were so stupid,' Peddyr scolded. 'Now then, I want you to close your eyes and picture the contents of Stephanie Fletcher's garage. Most importantly I need to know what motorbikes she was destroying,' he added with a shiver. 'If it's the ones I suspect they are, then she may have committed the ultimate gaffe.' He seemed to hold his breath as he waited for Connie's report.

'One was red…' she began.

'Make?'

'Japanese, I think.'

'Well, that narrows it down. Look, Lao Po. This is really, really important,' Peddyr said, and she could hear the strain in his voice. 'Kenny the Perv sold a bike to someone and had another one stolen. They were worth a bob or two. In good condition we are talking four grand and Kenny let his go for a song, the idiot. I suspect Scott Fletcher was the buyer and the thief. You said just now that Stephanie had paid for the bikes he had at home. I wonder how much she gave Scott compared with what he actually spent.'

Connie could see he was trying to build evidence to suggest Stephanie had killed Scott in revenge for adultery, betrayal of her trust and for ruining her life. It was a robust motive even without the motorbikes. If the bikes from Kenny's house were in Theale in Stephanie's garage, then there was no disputing to what lengths Scott Fletcher would go in order to deceive. The question was not why he was killed but who had got to him first to carry out the deed. As far as Connie could fathom, it was a two-horse race. Ryan and Stephanie were neck and neck.

'Were any of them big old classic bikes?' Peddyr asked her, trying again to narrow down the options.

'No, not big ones at all, but I would say the red one was 1970s with a silver fuel tank, spoked wheels and had a round headlamp until Stephanie smashed it to pieces.' The kiss from Peddyr was hard and meaningful. 'You little beauty,' he exclaimed. 'Now shut your eyes again and tell me what else you noticed about any other bike in that garage.'

'There was another one similar, and a more modern one like your Triumph Speed Triple. Then there were a couple under covers that I couldn't see at all.'

'The thieving bastinado!' Peddyr announced. 'We may have to make a return visit to see Stephanie Fletcher, Lao Po. I hope you made a good impression on her.'

* * *

*M*onica arrived by taxi, bringing with her a couple of bottles of white wine and one of liquid plant food that she passed to Connie. 'I met your neighbour who asked me to give this to you,' she said, with a gentle laugh. While Peddyr set about pouring alcohol into glasses, Connie showed Monica into the utility area where they stood nattering happily, the short and the tall, not noticing the arrival of an exhausted Bernie. Connie smiled when she heard his mellow voice. She was looking forward to the evening.

'Where the hell is Monica?' he boomed. 'I thought she'd be here by now?'

'Grasshopper is with my wife discussing the size of her amaryllis.'

'Good God… Is that a euphemism for something biological I know nothing about?' Bernie enquired.

Still chatting about how easy it was to kill houseplants, Monica and Connie emerged into the kitchen bringing bowls of salad and platters of meat to the table, accompanied by a running commentary from Peddyr. 'This is a spatchcock chicken with traditional barbecue sauce,' he said, taking credit where it was not due. 'The big slab of beef is seasoned with some herbs that I can't remember the name of and is rare. Just as it should be. In fact it's so rare a good vet could probably revive the beast.'

They took their seats and raised a glass to each other. 'Here's to alcohol-induced brainwaves because we are going to need them like never before,' Peddyr announced. 'To business, my friends. What news from you, Bernie?'

Peddyr's weary friend shook his head and with it his ears gave a waggle of their own. 'No, Monica can start,' he said, forking several slices of ham onto his plate before reaching for warm, buttery, new potatoes. His piling on of food continued as she began her précis of a long day.

'Ryan Holden is currently sleeping. I predict he will wake by noon tomorrow at the earliest.' Pausing briefly to take a sip of her wine, she smiled. 'Ah, that's better... Now then, as far as Ryan is concerned, I am certain he is not, and never was, experiencing paranoid delusions. This has been borne out by information from various sources. Evidently Scott Fletcher was not who he purported to be, making Ryan correct rather than deluded. Unfortunately for Ryan Holden, sneaking about and voicing accusations only served to make him appear paranoid. The whole plan was doomed to failure from the very beginning when Ryan lied about losing his job, making out there was a conspiracy against him.'

Connie wasn't at all surprised when Peddyr stood and left the room, returning minutes later with his trusty flip chart on a stand. 'Timeline time,' she said. 'We eat, he scribbles.'

'Seems reasonable to me,' Bernie added, dabbing at meat juices on his chin with a paper napkin. Much to Connie's delight he winked at Monica. 'About time your assistant did some work, eh?'

'Piss off, Bernie.'

'Is it? In which case I'll stick to the red wine.'

With proceedings rapidly descending into farce, Connie banged on the table with the handle of a knife. 'Order! Order! No swearing at the dinner table and can we please crack on, Pedd?' Her efforts were rewarded with a look of mock offence from her husband. He saluted her and stood to attention by the flip chart, pen at the ready.

'At approximately eight in the morning Stephanie Fletcher rocks up at Primrose Court. She confronts her husband and returns to her car but does not leave the vicinity. She is still there when Ryan says he spots her some time after nine-thirty.'

Consulting her notepad, Connie ran her finger down the lines written during her interviews that day. She raised a finger. 'Can I chip in, please? When I spoke to Trina McIlhenny she placed Ryan at Primrose Court that morning, but although he allegedly taunted Fletcher there was no verbal confrontation as such, and what's more she and her husband Colin saw Ryan walking home as they drove to the shops. He had no blood on him.'

Peddyr coughed. 'We can't discount him. He had motive but would there have been enough time for him to slip into Fletcher's garage, carry out a vicious attack and be walking nonchalantly home in the time it took the McIlhennys to get their car out of the garage? It's unlikely. And surely they would have heard the racket.'

'Not if the compressor was going,' Bernie mumbled through a mouthful of food.

'But Ryan could still have turned back after the McIl-hennys drove by,' Connie added.

'Yes, Connie's right,' Monica interjected. 'He's a fit lad and could easily have run home after bashing Scott Fletcher's head in. He would have made it to Derwent Drive within the timeframe given by Sarah and by Carol Brightman. And, not forgetting the other possible suspect, what do we know about Stephanie Fletcher's movements?' Monica asked, directing the enquiry at Connie.

'Once she left the road opposite Primrose Court, she says she drove around the area, and went to the offices of Craven & Tilbury but didn't take it any further than that and never went in. It's a lame alibi.' Connie looked up at Peddyr. 'We are told Ryan is seen on his way home just after ten. But before the McIlhennys spot him, they pass a man on a blue motorbike heading into the garages at the back of Primrose Court.'

Peddyr stared at her, open-mouthed. 'What?'

## A NEW SUSPECT

*B*ernie rubbed his bloated stomach. 'Odds Bodkins. Another possible suspect, Pedd? Really?'

Almost choking, Monica chuckled. 'How very Shakespearean of you, boss.' She directed her next comment to Connie again. 'I suppose we should take Trina McIhenny's remarks with a pinch of salt. From what you've said she does love the attention and sounds like the local gossip to me.'

'Making her a clatterfart,' added Bernie, sticking to his theme.

'Clatterfart or not,' Peddyr butted in, 'she and Colin are our best witnesses to what happened that morning and if someone rocked up on a motorbike then we must follow that up.'

Not swayed by his argument, Connie threw her husband a questioning look. 'Why? You seem obsessed with bikes more than usual, Pedd. This could be a straightforward coincidence. Or is there something you haven't told us?'

Peddyr took his seat back at the table. He poked at the chicken leg on his plate. 'Yes, there is, but I can't substantiate it until I see inside the garages and workshop at Derwent Drive. The contents or lack thereof could have a vital bearing on this case.' He looked up at each of the gathered group in turn. 'The paperwork I found in Sarah Holden's wardrobe today would suggest that Jim Holden's bike collection was to die for – or kill for in this instance.'

'Balderdash!' Bernie laughed. 'With some added poppycock. You damned bikers with your romantic notions about vintage and classic cafe racers and ton-up boys. Has it ever struck you that the rest of us are not interested?'

It would have been easy to assume that, because Monica was present, the grumpy Bernie was on display, not knowing how to appear dashing and attractive to women other than by being clever with his comments. However, Peddyr had been acquainted with him too long. This was how Bernie operated. He challenged preconceptions, played devil's advocate to explore every possible scenario.

'Bear with me on this,' Peddyr said, reaching for his mobile phone. 'Scott Fletcher was into his bikes. If I'm right, he bought a Honda from Kenny Eversholt and would have pocketed two grand clear from selling it on. Jim Holden's collection contains at least six sought-after classic bikes. They appear on the list I found alongside a newspaper article from donkey's years ago. This is the star of the collection.' He passed the phone to Bernie, who leaned close to Monica to allow them to both view the pictures. 'Money is the root of all evil,' he said.

'Holy shit-balls!' Monica blurted out, followed by a rapid apology to Connie. 'Have you read this?' she asked.

Connie shook her head. 'No. Haven't had the time.' The phone was passed along and Peddyr waited for his wife's reaction, which when it came caused a ripple of laughter to shatter the tension.

'Fuffing Nora!' she said, looking at her husband and down again at the phone several times. 'Over three hundred thousand pounds at auction for a rare one... And one of these is in the garage in Derwent Drive?'

'Possibly.' Peddyr had no idea if any of Jim's valuable bikes were still in residence. He wouldn't find out until he accessed it the next day and he wanted to be there with Dexter Booth when he did. 'I searched everywhere to find out if Sarah Holden had two bikes in particular separately insured,' he said. 'She can't have the first idea how much they are worth, otherwise she would never have given the whole contents of the garage and workshop to her nephew. Never. Ever. Which may mean Scott Fletcher had already got his hands on them and what remains is relatively worthless in comparison.'

'When she gave me her instructions, Sarah Holden was explicit,' Bernie interjected. 'Her husband's bike collection was in the garage at fifteen Derwent Drive and must be given to Dexter Booth because he appreciated how best to look after it. I know very little about such machines or their intrinsic value. Models and makes were not part of our discussion. However, I will be re-acquainting myself with the last will and testament of James Holden first thing in the morning.'

Connie and Monica exchanged startled looks. 'And there is no way Ryan had the first idea of their value, otherwise he'd have worked on his mother to sell them well before now,' Monica said, her voice breathy with the enormity of Peddyr's discovery.

'And what stopped you from checking the garage for

yourself? You've been back twice,' Bernie challenged his friend.

He was right to do so because it seemed so obvious, but for one small problem. 'There's an alarm system fitted to the garages and the workshop. Carol doesn't have the codes.'

'In which case, it's a very good job I have the necessary instructions written down,' said Bernie, expanding his broad chest. 'I will be sharing them with Dexter Booth when he attends my office tomorrow. Then I shall insist he accompanies you and me to Derwent Drive to make a formal record of the items he has been gifted by his aunt. You will be my witness.'

Blowing out a lungful of air, Peddyr found it hard to imagine how Dexter was going to manage his feelings on seeing what he had been given. Not only would he appreciate the worth of the bikes, but he had already made an inventory when those bikes had been destined for auction, until Scott Fletcher stepped forward and prevented that from happening. Why hadn't Dexter informed his aunt of the value of the bikes then? Why weren't the two most precious ones insured at that address? With racing thoughts and adrenalin hitting him like a train, Peddyr silently picked at his thumbnail.

Means, motive and opportunity were on his mind. Was Dexter really at work when Fletcher was killed, or was he the man on the blue motorbike who'd arrived at Primrose Court after Ryan had left and before Sarah turned up? From what Bez and Ryan had said, Dexter Booth knew the contents of those garages intimately, perhaps making the perfect cousin a little too perfect.

An Undertones earworm arrived and Peddyr began to

hum *My Perfect Cousin* until Connie's gentle touch stopped him.

'I know what you're thinking, Lao Gong. Too good to be true.'

'Can I fiddle with your flip chart?' Monica suddenly piped up.

'Is nothing sacred?' Peddyr replied with a teasing grin. 'First you examine my wife's amaryllis in a darkened cupboard and now this? Your master has taught you well, Grasshopper. Go for your life.'

Monica turned to a fresh sheet of paper, a grin on her face. 'Suspects,' she said. 'Possibly Ryan but not Sarah. Agreed?' There were slow nods of assent from the three at the table. 'Stephanie Fletcher is also worth a look.' Once she had written the name on the flip chart, she paused to shunt her glasses higher on the bridge of her nose. 'That makes three S. Fletchers, by the way. A neat idea on Scott's part as Stephanie's middle name is Judith and Sarah's is Jane they would eventually both have been Mrs S. J. Fletcher. His middle name is…?'

'Julian,' Bernie said with a proud nod to Monica. 'It's on the charge sheet along with his address at Primrose Court. Please bear in mind that the police have yet to confirm his legal entitlement to use the name Scott Julian Fletcher and referred to him as "the man known as"…'

Peddyr could immediately see where Monica was going with her questions and so could Connie who clapped with glee. 'Brava, Monica! The man known as Scott Julian Fletcher plans to marry Sarah and then to sell the motor-bikes as the owner – S. J. Fletcher.' She hesitated for a second and grabbed at Peddyr's arm. 'Who else would have worked this out? Stephanie? Were there any other wives before her?'

Patting her hand, Peddyr wrinkled his nose at his wife. 'Over to you, Lao Po. Searches please for all S. J. Fletchers, be they alive or dead. Marriages, divorces, anything you can find.' This was her forte and without it P. Q. Investigations would be lost. 'We should have made time to do this from the off. Understand the victim and you get nearer to the culprit.'

'Name change by deed poll?' Bernie suggested, tugging at the lobe of one ear.

Connie, excited by this turn of events, began to clear the table, assisted to a lesser degree by Peddyr who conceded that as he hadn't actually done any cooking he was therefore obliged to help with the washing up. Avoiding the sink, he took it upon himself to take charge of reorganising the fridge, shuffling items around to make space for platters of cold meat. Lifting his head away from the shelf containing cheese, yoghurts and all things dairy, he made a request of Monica. 'Can you add another name to the list of suspects, Grasshopper, if you would? Dexter Booth. He must now take his place on the list.'

'Yes, he must,' Connie added.

Cross with himself, Peddyr tutted. 'I've been a bit remiss. I've more questions for young Dexter. Connie, when you've got a minute, get that thinking cap of yours on and start digging around for information on his spending habits.'

Bernie stirred in his seat and reached for the bottle of red wine to pour himself another glass. 'Oh, dear me,' he muttered. 'If my client has put her faith in the wrong person…' His thought trailed off. 'I shall have to make a prison visit and persuade Sarah to reconsider.'

'No, don't do that too soon. Our best bet is to stick to the plan. Dexter will reveal himself soon enough,' Monica suggested, accepting a refill of her own glass. Her cheeks had taken on a rosy glow and she was relaxing into the conversation in a way Peddyr took as a compliment to him and Connie. Their hosting abilities seemed to be doing the trick; even Bernie had mellowed with not a grump to be heard.

'Pudding anyone?' Peddyr asked, spying his wife balancing a pile of fresh strawberries on a large meringue filled with whipped cream. 'Apparently, once it's cut, all the calories fall out and the strawberries count as one of your five a day.'

Connie had just sat down to hers and picked up a spoon when the front doorbell rang. 'Goodness, who on earth can that be at this time?' All four of them checked their watches. 'Nearly nine-thirty, on a Friday night. We're closed,' Connie said, looking across at Peddyr with a frown.

'I'll get rid of them,' he replied, making his way through the flat and opening the interconnecting door to reception and his office. He lifted the intercom handset to converse with whoever was at the main door on Dyer Street. 'Who is it?' he barked. Part of him assumed it would be someone playing a childish prank after a few beers in the Queen's Arse down the road. The other part of him braced for a client in distress. It was neither.

'Mr Quirk? This is the police. Can we come in?'

## AN INSPECTOR CALLS

'*I*nspector Webster,' Peddyr said, dragging out the words. He opened the door at the top of the stairs to allow his visitors in. 'How may I be of service?' he asked, while wracking his brains, wondering what crime he had committed to draw this amount of attention to himself. 'Shall we go into my office?'

'It's Acting Detective Chief Inspector, actually,' Webster said, his voice a dull drone. 'Any chance of a coffee and use of your bathroom facilities? It's been a long night and me and DS Forstall here are flagging.'

This was presumptuous but Peddyr wasn't going to deny them a simple request for sustenance and use of a toilet. 'I'd be most happy to allow use of our facilities, but I dare say that isn't the sole reason for your visit,' he replied, expecting a reprimand for removing Ryan Holden's laptop or for treading on official toes by posing as a trainee solicitor. He briefly toyed with the idea of calling for Bernie. 'Do I need my solicitor present? He's in the kitchen, as it happens.'

Webster shrugged off his coat and slung it over one arm. 'Lead the way, Mr Quirk. He could be useful.'

'I was kidding.'

'I wasn't.' Again Webster indicated for Peddyr to take him through to the flat. 'And your wife may want to hear this too,' he added flatly.

Helen Forstall lagged behind, her attention caught by large photographs on the wall in the reception area. 'Is that you with Pierce Brosnan?' she asked Peddyr. She glanced from him to the wall again. 'And this one is Kevin whatshisname from *Morse*. And that one of you on the motorbike next to... No... It can't be. Can it?' Her eyes flashed in spite of her reported weariness. 'Oh, my God. They said you were some sort of consultant for films, but I thought it was a joke.'

Swivelling round to take a look for himself, Duncan Webster sneered. 'And he calls himself an expert? On what? Any old security guard with a motorbike can do that.'

There were three very bemused faces waiting for them as Peddyr led the two detectives through to the kitchen, declining to take the bait of Webster's insults. 'The police are here,' he said simply.

'So I see,' Bernie replied with a sarcastic edge. 'Thought I'd seen the last of you for a while, *Acting* DCI Webster. I'm sure you thought the same of me. To what do we owe this pleasure?' Instantly Peddyr regretted allowing Webster to dictate terms. The odious man was clearly taking pleasure from locking horns with Bernie who had consumed enough wine to make him retaliate without caution.

In a timely intervention, DS Helen Forstall stepped forward, glancing first at Connie and then at Monica. 'We're sorry to interrupt your dinner party. It's really Mr Quirk we need to speak to. Perhaps it would be better if we did meet in your office in private, Mr Quirk.' Fleetingly, she looked at her superior officer for whom she had just all but apologised.

'Here is fine,' Webster stated gruffly. 'And that coffee you offered would go down well.'

Incensed at his arrogance and rudeness, Peddyr held hard. 'As soon as you tell me why you're here and what you want with me, then I'm sure we can furnish you with a drink, Inspector.' He stared the man out. 'Well?'

Webster wiped at his nose with a thumb and forefinger, taking a sniff. 'Earlier this evening you were seen arguing with a man on Derwent Drive.'

'Was I?' Peddyr said, momentarily confused by this statement. 'Oh, you mean Kenny. We didn't argue, he nearly knocked me off my bike when he pulled onto his drive without looking. I stopped to give him a ticking off.' As he said this he realised it was hardly a good reason for two senior police officers to call at his home. 'Why do you ask?'

Webster cleared his throat loudly. 'Because Kenneth Eversholt was found dead at his home this evening. DS Forstall and I have just come from the scene. You were the last person to have seen him alive.' Having been deliberately blunt, he stood staring at Peddyr.

Lost for words for a few seconds, Peddyr shook his head and inhaled noisily through his nose. A mistake on his part, because the rancid smell of Webster's halitosis brought with it an unguarded response. 'Jesus!' Recoiling, he exhaled the word rather than speak it, mainly in protest at Webster's poor dental hygiene. Luckily for him the outburst was also a suitable reaction to the news of Kenny's death. 'What happened?'

There were a number of possibilities. Kenny had been a victim of harassment and bullying for years, he had groomed young boys in the past, he had also recently been the victim of a theft; all good reasons for taking a pasting but not necessarily enough to get him killed.

'We can't go into detail, I'm afraid. Suffice to say someone wrapped their hands around his scrawny neck and throttled him.' Smug-faced, Webster began a series of questions about why Peddyr had been on Derwent Drive, what time the incident with Kenny's car had occurred, and he checked with Connie the time Peddyr had arrived home, seeming dubious about his reported trip to the supermarket.

'And you, Mrs Quirk. You say you were at home when your husband returned on his motorbike this evening? What time was this?'

Once she had answered, Peddyr flashed a request to Connie with his eyes to say nothing else about where she had been. Webster would be furious if he knew she had visited Trina McIlhenny and Stephanie Fletcher. 'Be a love and put the coffee on, Lao Po,' he said, before turning back to Webster. 'Well, now you've put a dampener on our evening, I suppose you'll want me to make a full state-ment. Come to my office and Connie will bring you coffee and some food if you're hungry. You must have had a long day.'

Bernie smiled at him. 'Quite right, Pedd. Keep business for the office. You won't need me. I shall finish my drink and wend my merry way home across the park. See you for a swim bright and early.' He smiled across at Monica. 'How are you getting home?'

'Taxi,' she replied. 'Perhaps you could call me one, Pedd.'

Ordinarily he would have been lightning fast with his reply and said 'You're a taxi', but the invasion by Webster and DS Forstall had taken the edge off the happy gathering.

'I'll bell them from my office. I'm sure Bernie will wait with you outside until it gets here. They're usually fairly prompt.'

During this exchange, Webster sauntered over to the flip chart and had his back to Peddyr when he spoke. 'What the hell are you lot up to?'

'Building a defence for my client,' Bernie snapped. 'You and the CPS will be hearing from us shortly. You have charged the wrong person, Inspector.' Once again the wine had freed Bernie's tongue.

Tapping a finger to the chart, Webster pulled a quizzical face. 'Dexter Booth. We spoke to him earlier this evening. Nice young man. Can't see why you would be interested in him. He was nowhere near the scene of the Fletcher murder. Ryan Holden on the other hand *was* seen in the vicinity. We spoke to him too. Unfortunately he was incoherent when he answered.'

Stiffening, Monica butted in. 'You've been to the Marsworth Unit?'

'Ah, Monica Morris. What are you doing here, may I ask?' All thoughts of taxis and a tactical withdrawal to Peddyr's office seemed to have been forgotten. Webster was like a Jack Russell terrier sniffing at a hole in the ground, about to dive in headfirst and not to be distracted. When Monica explained her role regarding Ryan Holden, he smirked. 'Excellent. You can act as appropriate adult when we bring him in for formal questioning tomorrow. You know the drill.'

In response she gave a snide laugh. 'Oh, yes, and how do you propose to do that? He's in hospital under a section of the Mental Health Act, or did that fact escape your notice?' Plainly riled, she placed her hands flat on the table. 'And as you were so keen to point out, he is not fit to be questioned.'

Uninvited, Webster pulled out the chair Peddyr had

vacated and sat down opposite Monica and Bernie. 'According to his consultant, Ryan Holden is malingering, Ms Morris. Once we informed Dr Chowdhury of the facts of the case, he was quick to agree. Even said he had formulated a report which detailed that exact conclusion and agreed to remove him from section with immediate effect.' At this Monica muttered under her breath loud enough to be heard: 'My bloody report, no doubt. The crafty little f-futtock!'

Duncan Webster ignored her outburst and continued in the same boastful vein. 'When Ryan has slept off the drugs – ones he was given to reduce his violent behaviour – he will be discharged straight into our safe hands. We will question him in connection with the murder of Scott Fletcher.'

Monica slid round in her seat to catch Peddyr's eye. '*Now*, the bloody doctor decides to listen to sense.' Ryan would be going from the hospital frying pan into the police station fire and there was nothing any of them could do to prevent it, least of all Monica.

Peddyr knew that if Ryan had killed Scott then he most certainly hadn't killed Kenny Eversholt. His alibi for that particular death was watertight. So who had killed Kenny?

From what Peddyr could glean, slumped outside the front door of the bungalow, Kenny had been found by a delivery driver and was dead well before the ambulance arrived. Webster and Forstall had been called to the scene from the Marsworth Unit where they had been attempting and failing to question Ryan Holden. Dexter Booth had been visiting his cousin at the time and had confirmed Ryan's unhealthy relationship with Scott Fletcher. Given the timings, it was looking highly unlikely that Kenny's death was related in any way to Scott Fletcher's death.

However the thought was firmly wedged into Peddyr's brain and there was no shifting it.

DS Forstall sipped at her coffee and gratefully took a seat offered to her by Connie. 'You look shattered. Want some meringue to give you a bit of energy?'

'I wouldn't say no,' she replied, giving a shy smile. 'Thanks.' She pointed to the flip chart. 'Why do you have Stephanie Fletcher's name up there too?'

Peddyr took the lead, fearing his wife would disclose her unfortunate decision to interview Stephanie that day. 'You know what they say. "A woman scorned" and "hell hath no fury" like one. She was at the flats the morning of the murder. She had discovered her husband's infidelity and she didn't drive home straight after confronting him. We asked around,' he added, hoping this would serve as an answer.

Webster folded his arms. 'You've done rather too much asking around in my opinion, Mr Quirk. Ex-force you may be but riding motorbikes in Hong Kong does not cut it in the world of modern policing when it comes to murder in the UK. You are playing at being a detective by *asking around*. Don't think I don't know. First, the good people of Primrose Court and then Sarah Holden's neighbour. I suggest you keep your nose out.'

Bernie had been quiet for a while, allowing the sparring to continue. However, Webster's insults goaded him into an unreserved reaction which, owing to the high alcohol content of his wine choice, was not tempered by the use of professional language. 'Utter piffle, Inspector. My investigator has every reason to follow up on the case because my client has the right to a defence. And your understanding of his qualifications is wide of the mark, dear boy. Royal Hong Kong Police, Royal Protection Squad, a right royal shitstorm in the Middle East… Peddyr Quirk has earned his spurs ten times over. You have yet to impress.'

Connie also leapt to her husband's defence and in doing so defused a potential battle royal of egos. 'Thank you, Bernie. My husband is indeed proud of his service. His family are too. Please don't underestimate his years of duty to Queen and country, Inspector. You wouldn't like it if someone demeaned your job in such a way.' She bustled about, collecting plates and cups. 'It's getting very late. Pedd, call that taxi for Monica, please, and find coats if you would. Time to go now, everyone.' She stopped briefly to address Duncan Webster in particular. 'I take it you have what you came for?'

The dinner party had ended on a sour note, but it had at least concluded without anyone losing face. Webster and Forstall left the way they had come in, with a brief statement from Peddyr and giving no thanks for the coffee. Bernie and Monica left a few minutes later by the back door. With guests, uninvited and otherwise, on their way home, Connie continued her tidying, removing signs of a peculiar evening. Peddyr wiped the table and tried to make sense of the rapidly changing list of suspects and how Kenny's death had any bearing on the case. 'Poor old Kenny,' he mused.

'Why did they ask about your shoe size? They don't think you did it, do they?' Connie asked, concerned.

'Come off it, Lao Po. They know full well I didn't have anything to do with it. Kenny had an operational digital CCTV system over his front door. They have clear evidence of what happened and when. Unfortunately, I suspect the vicious bugger who assaulted him will have been careful not to be recognised.' He rubbed at an already clean table once more.

## THE LIDO SHUFFLE

There was a light drizzle in the air when Peddyr pushed the turnstile at the Bosworth Lido, saying a cheery good morning to Doreen Impey, who looked as if she had forgotten to put a brush through her short wiry hair that day. 'No Ted this morning? What have you done with him?' he asked. It was rare for Doreen to be at the kiosk for the early risers, usually Ted had that privilege, leaving his wife to join him later and bring a packed lunch for them to share. She was much the quieter of the two, preferring monosyllabic responses whilst giving no eye contact and rarely cracking a smile, let alone a merry quip.

'Bog's broke. Seat cracked. Caught him a nasty one last night. Gone to wake George at the builders' merchants. We can't be having that again.'

'No, indeed not,' Peddyr replied, taken aback by the length and detail of this response. This was the most he'd ever heard her say in one go. Bemused, he thanked her and moved through to seek out a locker and strip off. He had his trunks on under his tracksuit bottoms ready for a bracing dive in at the deep end, which was where he spotted Bernie, head high above the water, doing a sedate breaststroke. 'Morning, fella. Didn't expect to see you here so early. May I join you?'

'Be my guest.'

Hesitation would only prolong the agony, so Peddyr forced himself to dive in, looking as collected as he could manage. The water was chill enough to take his breath away for an instant, making speech difficult until he adapted to it and warmed up by swimming the length of the pool with added vigour. He beat Bernie by several metres. Not a difficult thing to do given the stately pace his friend maintained. They swam on for another thirty minutes before stopping to chat.

'It's a shame there wasn't a following breeze, you could have made use of those magnificent ears of yours and sailed the last few lengths.'

'Very amusing, old chap. However, you may have a point. My trunks are rather baggy. I may invest in some of those knee-length streamline ones like the Olympic swimmers wear. Don't see myself in Speedos, if I'm honest.'

'And I don't want to have to look at you in a pair of budgie-smugglers, thank you very much,' Peddyr replied, cringing at the mental image in his head.

After they had changed and packed soggy swimming togs into bags, they walked out together. 'Cheerio, Doreen. Give Ted my best and tell him to be careful in future. Those toilet seats can give a man a nasty pinch just where he wouldn't want one.'

'Righty-o, I will that,' she replied, not raising her head from the pile of loose change she was counting.

'Cheerful soul, isn't she?' Bernie commented as the two

men reached the pavement where they would head in opposite directions.

'I meant to ask…' Peddyr began. He had instructions to find out from Bernie about those moments spent outside with Monica the previous evening. Connie had woken specially early, making sure to set this task before Peddyr left for his daily swim. 'Did Monica get her taxi alright? It wasn't raining when you left, so I assume you waited with her.'

There was no fooling Bernie. 'What are you fishing for? Connie matchmaking, I suppose. I do wish she wouldn't. I remain a married man and although Deirdre has no objections to divorce, she would make my life hell if there was one whiff of another woman. Besides, Monica sees me as a friend and mentor. Nothing else.'

'In other words, you're too shit scared to kiss her in case she rejects your clumsy advances.' Peddyr tossed his head. 'You only live once. Free yourself from Dreary, sell the house, divide the spoils, buy your own less ostentatious place and have a bit of fun before it's too late. You and Grasshopper rub along great.'

Looking for all the world like an errant schoolboy caught scrumping, Bernie put hands in his pockets and shuffled his feet, staring down at the pavement. 'Well, she did ask if I'd go with her to Targets. She's signed up for a beginner's class.'

'Targets? That's the archery club isn't it?' Peddyr asked, and Bernie nodded in reply. 'Then for God's sake, say yes. Go with her. The pool will be closing at the end of the month, and you'll need another fresh-air activity to keep you busy. Try not to kill her though, there's a good fella.' Peddyr punched his friend gently on the upper arm. 'Now bugger off and I'll see you at your office later. I'll be suited and booted.'

Before his duties with Bernie and Dexter Booth were performed, he and Connie had arranged another visit to see Stephanie Fletcher who had been unexpectedly open to meeting with him when Connie had sent a speculative text the previous evening. She was in the kitchen when he returned home from the lido.

'Toast and some cereal for breakfast,' she announced. 'I'll leave you to it. I want to get on.' The table was laid for one which seemed rather pointless to Peddyr who never enjoyed eating alone.

'You can use my office for a while if you like,' he said.

'Thank you, Lao Gong. Maybe later this afternoon. As I was up and about so early this morning I thought I'd get a second coat of gloss on the windowsills in Aleyn's old room.' She smiled at him animatedly. 'He and Joe are definitely coming for Christmas too. I had a message from him yesterday. Won't it be wonderful to have the whole family together again?' A contented sigh left her lips as she stepped into the utility room where Peddyr could hear her singing while she gathered the necessary items for the task she had so willingly set herself.

'Are they staying over?'

'Of course they are.'

'In the same room?' No sooner were the words out of his mouth than he regretted saying them. 'Forget it. That was crass. They live together. It's just...' He rubbed at his wet hair and cursed his own insensitivity.

Aleyn was his younger son, the boy who looked so much like him he was often referred to as Chip by friends and family. He had the same love of sport as his father and of motorbikes. Along the lines of his parents' career choices,

Aleyn had entered the shady world of the civil servant, unable to detail exactly what he did for a living. It paid well whatever it was and occasionally he put some translation work his mother's way through a mutual contact at the Foreign Office. The Quirks were used to keeping state secrets.

Their eldest son Marshall had his mother's keen mind and Peddyr's calm nature and had chosen a career in academia. Marshall was now a professor of psycholinguistics, which Peddyr didn't really know much about, other than it made his eldest son a popular international lecturer. When younger son Aleyn declared his preference for male partners, Peddyr hadn't been expecting it; if anything he'd thought Marshall the most likely to experiment with his sexuality. Not Aleyn. Chip was supposed to be just like his father. To be a reflection of the man Peddyr was.

'It will be great to see them all again,' he said, buttering a slice of toast. He looked up to see Connie staring at him in silent disappointment, fingering a small brush in one hand.

'Is it still so hard for you to accept that Chip and Joe are getting married next year?'

'No… well… yes, sometimes. Oh, Connie, I don't mean to be old fashioned and I really like Joe, he's a good bloke, but now and again it throws me. Are they bringing the dog?' he asked, wanting to move the conversation on.

Putting the clean brush down on the table, his wife sat next to him. 'Let it go, Lao Gong. Aleyn is his own man with his own life to lead. He isn't you.'

'As I've said so often before, I do wish sometimes that you would refrain from reading my sodding mind,' Peddyr said. He leant across and kissed her cheek. 'You are right, as always. I will make a most excellent speech at the wedding and welcome Joe into the family officially like another son.'

He paused for a moment. 'Will there be two stag nights?' With the mood lightened again, Connie jumped up from her seat.

'I expect so. You can ask them on Christmas Eve and no, the dog is staying with Joe's mum for a few days while they're here. Shame really, I like Roger, such a bouncy little thing.'

Peddyr grinned. 'Roger the dog... I bet it was Chip's idea to call him that.'

'Just like his dad, a chip off the old block, no sense of decorum,' Connie replied as she disappeared up the stairs. 'I'll be ready to leave by nine,' she added, shouting over her shoulder.

With a quick glance at his watch Peddyr finished off his breakfast before heading upstairs to change into his suit. As he paused by the open door to Aleyn's old room, he cracked a smile at the sight of Connie happily brushing brilliant white gloss onto a windowsill, talking back to the local radio broadcaster for the early morning show. 'You tell them, Vic,' she warbled at the radio on the floor next to her feet. 'Bloody politicians. They can't be trusted.'

He stuck his head through the doorway. 'Oi! Was that a swearword I heard?'

* * *

The trip to Theale was uneventful, although Connie, from her position in the passenger seat, spent much of the time planning for the festive season, which put Peddyr in a sour mood. He hated the fuss and bother, and much preferred a pint in the pub without the incessant Christmas songs preventing a decent conversation. Not to mention the idiots in Christmas jumpers and silly hats who only came into the Queen's Arse once a year and took over the place.

'Are we expecting your cousin John for the usual New Year gamblers' club event?' he asked. Connie had relatives who lived a good fifty miles away but whom she saw several times a year. All mad keen Mah-jong players, New Year's Eve had become a regular fixture in the calendar for them. John Dong was Connie's biggest rival when it came to playing for money and he had passed on some of his skills to Marshall and Aleyn as they were growing up, making for a competitive match or two when they got together.

'I've been working on my strategy. There's an app I've found that—'

A raised finger was all that was required to silence his wife when news of Kenny Eversholt's death came floating from the car radio speakers. 'Local residents of Derwent Drive, here in Bosworth Bishops, are beginning to feel under siege,' the reporter said with dramatic emphasis. 'In the past week police have had reason to attend two residences in this same quiet street. At number fifteen lives local property manager Sarah Holden, currently on remand and accused of murdering her lover Scott Fletcher. I'm at number seven, where last night, the owner, Kenneth Eversholt was found on his doorstep. Strangulation was the cause, according to a witness who found the unfortunate Mr Eversholt. This begs the question: is there a killer on the loose in Bosworth Bishops?'

'Good grief,' Connie exclaimed, looking up from her ever-increasing list of things to do before Christmas. 'That will set old Whiffy-Breath off a treat.'

'That it will,' Peddyr agreed. 'Especially as he's planning to arrest Ryan Holden today. I wonder how many more people he'll drag down the nick before he finds the right one?'

Sat-Nav-Suzie had her volume turned down and, as a result, Peddyr nearly missed the turning into the private road where Stephanie Fletcher lived. He wasn't a fan of Suzie telling him where to turn and which route to take. To follow orders blindly from something computerised went against his instincts.

'I see the press are still taking an interest,' he commented at the sight of a journalist speaking into a microphone and facing a TV camera held aloft on the shoulder of its operator. Passing them by, Peddyr and Connie drove up to the gates and pressed the intercom, answered by Stephanie after a short delay.

'Come through and stop a few feet beyond the gate if you would, to make sure you're not tailgated. I had problems yesterday.'

'She's got her wits about her,' Peddyr noted. Connie packed her Christmas list inside her handbag and checked her appearance in the vanity mirror as they drew up in front of the house. 'You look just fine, "Hong Kong, darling"...' he said, making her laugh with his reference to his miss-heard lyrics of *Hong Kong Garden*.

The garage doors facing them were wide open and Stephanie was just outside leaning on the handle of a broom. 'Welcome back. Excuse the mess, I've only just calmed down enough to clear up the carnage.' Her voice was laced with regret. 'I hope I can get these fixed again. What a stupid thing to do.' She held a hand out to greet Peddyr as he was introduced by Connie. 'I'm glad you came. I seemed to get more sense out of you than the police, and there are some things I need to know.'

'Same here, Mrs Fletcher.'

'Please call me Steph. The name Fletcher makes me somewhat nauseous.' She gestured to the internal door. 'Shall we have a coffee?'

In the time it took to walk through to the back of the garages, Peddyr had scanned the motorbikes. 'Are these all of your hus... I mean, Scott's motorbikes?' he asked, disappointed by his first sight of them. There were no bikes matching the ones sold by or stolen from Kenny Eversholt. These weren't even Hondas. 'There are a couple more at the back there,' he said, aiming a finger towards two bikes under cover.

'Those are mine,' Stephanie said. 'It's how we met. Me and the duplicitous Scott Fletcher.'

'Ahhh, what do you ride?'

Lifting the covers free, Stephanie proudly showed off her two motorbikes. 'As you can see, I'm a Triumph fan. One for blatting down the lanes and this one for longer journeys. Something Scott was keen for us to do this summer. We made a couple of trips to France last year. This year we stayed in the UK and headed up to North Yorkshire, hence the heated grips.'

Disappointed, Peddyr caught Connie's eye and surreptitiously shook his head. This visit wouldn't take long. 'Which bike was he working on when he was found?' he asked out of interest.

Stephanie halted in the doorway to the house and spun around. 'Good question, Mr Quirk. I didn't know he had another bike. Mind you, I didn't know he had another woman either.'

## AN ALLY

*D*esignated as the getaway driver on the way back from seeing Stephanie Fletcher, Connie adjusted the driver's seat and galvanised Sat-Nav-Suzie into action, unmuting her. 'I'll try to avoid the Saturday shoppers,' she said, finding the route list and selecting the one she had used the day before. Peddyr was on the phone already, trying to track down DCI Webster, as she pulled out onto the busy main road heading in the direction of home. 'The press are following,' Connie said, with a momentary glance at the rear-view mirror.

The phone to his ear, Peddyr rolled his eyes at her. 'Don't be so melodramatic. They are hardly going to bother with the likes of us.' He raised his chin as his call was answered. 'Yes, I'll speak to DS Forstall instead. Gladly.' In the few seconds afforded to him while the call was being put through, Peddyr looked into the wing mirror, leaning forward. 'Coincidence,' he said.

When Helen Forstall answered she was full of apologies for the previous night. '...and thanks for the food and drink,

I was about to keel over from lack of sugar,' she said. 'Anyway, what can I do for you, Mr Quirk?' It was a straightforward request from Peddyr: what bike was in Scott Fletcher's garage at Primrose Court when his body was discovered? The marked pause from the DS was enough to let him know he was on the right track. 'Why do you ask?' she enquired, hesitating over every word.

'Because I believe it may have been either bought or stolen from a certain Kenneth Eversholt, which would mean the two killings are linked.' With the car lurching, there was a need to juggle the phone into his other hand and take hold of the handle above the passenger door. He threw his wife a disapproving look as she swung the car hard left again.

'Sorry,' she whispered. 'Trying to shake them off.'

In disbelief at her theatrics, he tutted and turned his attention back to his phone conversation. 'Just say yes or no. Is the bike a 1970s Honda 125?'

'Yes, but how the...?' There was another lengthy pause from Helen Forstall. 'Look, I'm not supposed to share this with anyone outside the team, but I think you are onto something, Mr Quirk.'

'Call me Peddyr.'

'Okay. Thanks, I will. Forensics confirmed fingerprints belonging to Kenneth Eversholt were on that bike. It looks like you were correct to link the two killings. I guess that was part of the conversation you and Kenny had yesterday.' Helen Forstall coughed, the claggy rattle of a heavy smoker, thus allowing Peddyr time to remind his wife that she was not in the world rallying championships. Fortunately she took heed and he was able to reply without being shaken sideways at every turn the car made.

'Sorry about that, Helen. My wife seems to think she's

related to Colin McRae or Carlos Sainz. Yes, Kenny told me he'd sold a bike to a bloke for cash. Then he had another one stolen, which he reported, so it will be on your records too.' He heaved a sigh. 'Did it get him killed?'

'Talking to you, or having bikes worth stealing?'

'Unless you are a druggy desperate for cash, those bikes weren't worth killing for,' Peddyr assured her. 'If it were our friendly neighbourhood scrap dealers, they would have nicked the lot. So there has to be another reason behind Kenny's death. Was there anything else that connected the two killings?'

'Blunt-force trauma to the head and strangulation in both cases. And the small matter of a size ten Vibram sole – from a boot most likely.'

'That'll do nicely. Tell me more about this boot.'

According to DS Forstall, a number of partial footprints had been found on the floor of Scott Fletcher's garage where the wearer had stepped in blood. This immediately discounted the victim who was himself a size eleven but in any event could not have trodden in his own blood having been knocked unconscious.

Colin McIlhenny had worn a size eight trainer and he was eliminated as a suspect on that basis. When Ryan Holden's clothing was examined he was found to have worn a size ten, but despite searches of number fifteen Derwent Drive, no boots were found to match those worn by the suspected perpetrator and no blood that matched the victim was found on any item of clothing or footwear belonging to Ryan Holden. A blank had been drawn on the mystery boot thus far.

One other thing occurred to Peddyr as he spoke with the DS. 'We know Kenny's death can't have involved Ryan Holden. For a start, he has no interest in motorbikes, doesn't ride one, and besides he was in hospital when Kenny was killed. His cousin Dexter on the other hand… What time did he arrive at the hospital to see Ryan yesterday?'

He heard the DS exhale loudly with a wheeze. 'Shit! We didn't think of that. He was there when we arrived. I'll find out and get back to you.'

'And while you're at it, can you check whether he really was at work the morning Scott Fletcher was killed? So far we only have his word for it. If the details held on record are anything to go by, a motorbike fitting the description of the one owned and ridden by Dexter Booth was seen at Primrose Court before Fletcher's body was discovered by Sarah Holden.'

'Where did you get that little gem from?'

'The McIlhennys. Ask and ye shall be rewarded with answers, DS Forstall.'

'I'll try to remember that… and thanks, Peddyr. Safe journey.'

He laughed as he ended the call. Safety was a matter of calculated risk and at that moment Connie's right foot had a desire to hit the floor and they were once more racing down the roads of Berkshire, making the odds of arriving home safely none too certain.

* * *

*M*onica was called to the police station shortly after twelve-thirty with a request to act as appropriate adult for Ryan, although strictly speaking he didn't need one. Obviously, Webster was covering all appeal contingencies; either that or it was a perverse punishment for their clash the evening before. Dr Chowdhury had discharged Ryan Holden from his section and from the hospital with no formal diagnosis and no follow-up arrangements or medication; not so much as a tablet or two to ease the muscle cramps in his patient's jaw, which were slow to fade. Even though Ryan was no longer deemed to have a mental illness, Monica wasn't going to argue with the request for her to accompany him while he was interviewed at the police station, but neither was she thrilled at the prospect of spending several hours in the company of the repellent Duncan Webster.

She was met by DS Helen Forstall who seemed much more alert than she had the previous evening. 'This shouldn't take too long,' she assured Monica.

'You always say that,' was the reply, delivered with a forgiving smile. 'It's a well-known fact that DI Webster keeps everyone hanging around if the clock is running down or not, and I won't be any exception after last night's disagreement.' She had resigned herself to spending the afternoon in the sweaty confines of Bosworth nick. 'I brought along a packed lunch just in case.'

If it was possible for him to do so Ryan would have been exuding steam from every orifice. He was fuming with indignant rage at the injustice of being discharged directly from hospital into a police car. Well turned out for the occasion, shaved and neatly clothed, he had clearly been planning to head elsewhere. 'Took your time,' he said, scowling at Monica. 'Now do your job and get me out of here.'

Infuriation at his manner barely in check, she managed a pseudo-smile. After all, he was only tasting freedom thanks to her efforts in the first place. 'I can sympathise but let me tell you, I'm not obliged to be here at all. So be grateful for small mercies.' She pulled out a chair and sat beside him in the interview room where they had been taken to await the arrival of Acting DCI Webster. 'And what's this nonsense about you declining a solicitor?'

He poked a finger at her. 'You are my solicitor.'

'No, Ryan. I'm a Legal Executive and I only deal with matters relating to mental health legislation. Although I'm not a lawyer, may I remind you how serious your position is? You have been arrested in relation to the killing of Scott Fletcher. You were at the scene and therefore should have a criminal lawyer present.'

Irritated, he glowered at her. 'That's what Granny Holden said on the phone. But I didn't kill him, so I don't need a fucking criminal lawyer.' It was a relief to know that Mrs Holden had been contacted. One less job for someone to do on this busiest of Saturdays, Monica thought.

Earlier, she had received a garbled message from Peddyr who, at the time, was acting as driver's mate and not enjoying the journey back from Theale where he and Connie had been to see Stephanie Fletcher. Infamous for her enthusiasm behind the wheel of a car, Monica could hear Connie in the background talking to the sat-nav, thanking the voice for a recent set of directions. After this Peddyr let fly a string of profanities as he hit his head on the side window when they caught a bump in the road.

Not only was the call highly entertaining, it was also enlightening.

If Peddyr was right, Stephanie Fletcher could still be a possible suspect for the murder of her husband. She had motive, she had opportunity, and the physical strength. However, no forensic evidence put her within the garage where the killing took place, and the police hadn't examined her car or looked to find the clothes she was wearing that day. So far, unbelievably, they hadn't even pegged her as a suspect.

Ryan also had a strong motive and there was a brief window of opportunity for him to have carried out the vicious assault on his mother's fiancé. However, yet again, forensics at this stage could not place him within the garage. The only links found which related to the killing in any way, belonged to Sarah Holden and, incredibly, to a certain Kenny Eversholt.

Somehow Peddyr had gleaned this from Helen Forstall. He had worked his magic again, Monica thought. This wouldn't necessarily prevent Ryan from being charged, but the fact he was seen with no blood on him before he assaulted the GP later that morning, could save him from joining his mother as a remand prisoner.

To make any impact, Monica knew she would have to challenge Webster and step outside her role as appropriate adult to do so. She primed Ryan. 'I want you to keep asking about Stephanie Fletcher,' she said to him. 'She hasn't been thoroughly investigated as a suspect. If you want to avoid being locked up for the night, you have to make them rethink their conclusions.'

'Why?'

There wasn't time to explain. The door opened and the interview preparations began without preamble. Webster treated Monica to a barely disguised sneer as he lamely shook her hand. 'Thank you for attending today, Ms Morris. We appreciate your time.' He went on to remind her in a patronising manner about her function that day. 'Yours is not a legal role. You are merely here to ensure the needs of the interviewee are met and that he understands what is being asked. I'm expecting you to introduce yourself accordingly for the record.'

He spoke to Ryan who shied away to reduce the impact of the invisible malodorous cloud coming his way. 'I understand you have declined a solicitor.'

'She's my solicitor,' Ryan replied, flicking a thumb in Monica's direction.

Duncan Webster let out a sarcastic laugh. 'I rest my case for having an appropriate adult present. Clearly, Mr Holden has difficulty listening and understanding what is being said to him.' He twisted to see DS Forstall who nodded and shared a look of sympathy with Monica.

'I'm not a moron,' Ryan objected.

'Then you will understand when I tell you that Ms Morris is not your legal representative while you are under questioning. Shall we begin?' Webster took out a packet of antacid tablets and popped a couple into his mouth.

'Do you suffer a lot from heartburn?' Monica asked. Her nursing brain had leapt into action and, without meaning to be rude, she was onto a possible cause for his halitosis. It occurred to her that as the man had a constipated brain, gastro-intestinal problems may be the cause of his unfortunate personal issue.

Pretending he hadn't heard her, Webster began his interrogation and Ryan answered each question with one of his own.

'Were you at Primrose Court on the morning of the fifth of September this year?'

'Yes, I was. And so was Stephanie Fletcher. Have you asked her what she did when she was there?'

They had barely started this bizarre game of question ping-pong, when the interview was interrupted. A uniformed officer entered the room with a piece of paper in his hand, which Webster snatched from him. 'This better be good,' he snapped. Perusing it, his flaccid face pinched tight.

'Interview suspended at...' He passed the report to his DS who managed to sneak a crafty wink at Monica. Something had been found. Something noteworthy.

Once Webster had scuttled from the room, his flat feet flapping against the floor like those of a circus clown, Ryan was escorted to the front desk by a uniformed officer. 'You going to give me a lift home?' he asked Monica.

'No, you can make your own arrangements, and who says you are going anywhere?' she replied with some satisfaction as the door to the interview room swung closed of its own accord.

Helen Forstall caught her by the elbow. 'Get a message to Peddyr. On the morning of the fifth, Dexter Booth's motorbike was caught by mobile ANPR which had a rear-facing camera specifically to catch speeding bikers. Looks like he wasn't at work after all.' Webster's impatient shouting reached them before she had chance to elaborate further and within seconds Monica was left standing alone in the interview room like an unnecessary understudy in a stage play.

## 33

## SKULDUGGERY

*M*rs Maggie Holden had taken two telephone calls in quick succession and neither of them brought her any cheer. The first was from Ryan. Initially she was thrilled to hear his good news; he had been discharged from the mental health unit and the doctor had said there was nothing wrong with him. Given the truth that was emerging about Scott Fletcher, she couldn't disagree. 'Why are you at the police station, dear?' she had asked. 'Helping them with their inquiries?'

It was inevitable that they would want to question him, but he was so infuriated he had taken offence. 'I'll be out of here real quick. I didn't do it. They have to let me go.'

'It doesn't quite work like that, Ryan.'

'Yes, it does.'

'I'll get on to Bernard Kershaw, see if he can send someone down.'

'I don't need anyone. I don't want anyone.'

He was so stubborn. So hot-headed. She recounted the conversation to Flora who had been sympathetic to a degree. Busily plumping up cushions on a long sofa, her companion said, 'He has made his decision. Let him deal with it, Maggie. At least we know Sarah's affairs are in good hands, so when Ryan does get home he can't squander her money in the same way as Scott Fletcher was planning to do.' She stopped in her tidying and offered a watery smile. 'Sorry, I'm only saying what we both think.'

From her position in an armchair by the French windows overlooking the garden, Maggie returned the knowing look and stared at the phone on the table by her side. It had huge press-button numbers and was a gift from Flora; a means for Maggie to maintain as much independence as she could with her arthritic fingers preventing enjoyment of so many hobbies and pastimes. 'No need to apologise. I'm part of the reason he's so incredibly self-centred. I mollycoddled the boy. At least we can rely on Dexter, who should be with Mr Kershaw right now, sorting things out. Ryan will have to make his own way in the world and realise it doesn't owe him living.'

The second phone call came shortly after this. It was Sarah ringing from HMP Bronzefield and she sounded petrified. 'Maggie? I haven't got long. Can you ask Carol to arrange a visit and bring my belongings? She'll know what I need. I wanted to let you know where I am and that I'm all right. Bernard Kershaw says he will get me out of here soon enough. Has he been in touch?'

Flora had picked up who the call was from and rushed to stand next to Maggie, holding onto her free hand, stroking it to bring comfort. Easing the mouthpiece sideways a little to enable Flora to hear the details, Maggie tried her best to reassure Sarah that everything was in hand and managed to avoid lying about Ryan. 'He's been discharged from hospital,' she told her.

'Oh, that is good news.' There was a hush before Sarah spoke again. 'The police will want to question him.'

'I expect so, dear. But not to worry, Mr Kershaw tells me his investigator is following other leads.' At this Flora grinned and Maggie made a face to acknowledge the joke that passed between them. Their afternoons and evenings were spent watching crime dramas and the pair of them often debated and guessed at "whodunnit". They saw them-selves as armchair detectives but were in fact far more accomplished at completing a cryptic crossword than they were at finding murderers.

'And I wanted to thank you for everything you've done,' Sarah went on. 'If you need to sell the old bikes to pay for a barrister you have the paperwork for proof of ownership.'

'I certainly do, dear. But there will be no need. I will never sell them.'

Maggie dabbed at her eyes with a dainty cotton hand-kerchief as she said a sad farewell to Sarah. She had no idea if and when she would see her daughter-in-law again and could only hope that the determined efforts of the Quirks and Bernard Kershaw would pay dividends sooner rather than later.

'Things are hotting up and I think we should expect a visitor later today,' she said to Flora. 'Ryan is bound to turn up when he realises there is nobody to do the cooking for him. Besides, I think Sarah would rather he wasn't left in charge of the house. He's hardly the most responsible person. He'll have that dreadful scruff Bez round and the next thing you know the place will become a den of iniquity filled with wayward girls and all manner of strays.'

A call to Bernard Kershaw was required. She needed to check where she stood legally if she made Ryan homeless by refusing to allow him to remain in the house he had grown up in. The house was to be sold in any case. 'Shall we do some baking?' she said to Flora, putting on a brave smile. 'I could do with a change of scenery and something to take my mind off matters.'

* * *

*I*n the comfortable surroundings of Bagshot & Laker's reception area, Fiona MacFarland greeted the Quirks with a ready smile. 'Good afternoon, Peddyr. My, you do look smart again today.' The smile broadened when she spotted Connie. 'How lovely to have the whole team here and early to boot. Come straight through.'

Holding back, Connie took Fiona to one side. 'Actually, I'm going to wait out here and be an observer. Do you think you can pretend I'm attending a job interview? I'll be no bother. I can work on my laptop while I sit here. Pedd has set me a couple of tasks and they can't wait.'

Her face lighting up, Fiona flapped her hands. 'How lovely. Some proper undercover skulduggery. Oh, I'd be most glad to help out. What do you want me to do?'

'Just do what you normally would,' Connie said with a grin of appreciation. 'But make sure to keep Dexter Booth detained out here for a few minutes so I can engage him in conversation. If you have time, I also need to confirm his attendance at work on the fifth of September. He's employed by Tottering's auction house.'

'Aye, that's no problem. Anything else I can help with?' Fiona enquired, her eyes sparkling.

Connie looked around at the chairs in the waiting room. 'While I'm here with Dexter, perhaps you could apologise for keeping me waiting too. Make something up about other candidates causing a hold up. You'll be great.'

The plan had to be modified slightly when Dexter arrived with his wife Tessa in tow. They took a seat and began talking to each other, politely smiling towards but largely ignoring Connie. Shortly after that a tall slender man entered through the glass doors of the main entrance and approached the couple, who appeared to be embarrassed by his arrival. Connie could see why. The man, who bore a striking resemblance to Dexter, was on edge, breathless, running hands though his hair and with sweat still glistening on his forehead. 'I'm coming in with you,' he said to them both. 'There may be legal issues for the whole family to decide on.'

'You should have stayed at home, Dad. The instructions were for me, not the whole family,' Dexter replied, throwing an uncertain look at Fiona McFarland, who helpfully guided the conversation in his favour.

'I'm afraid that is the case, sir. The appointment is for Mr Dexter Booth. And you are?'

He introduced himself as Christopher Booth. Straightening his tie, he confirmed that he was indeed Dexter's father and thus Sarah Holden's brother. Greying at the temples, he had the same thick head of dark hair as his son, but his eyes were narrower, as were his lips. 'So, Tessa will have to wait outside with me then,' Chris said, facing the couple once more.

In the confines of the peaceful wood-panelled reception, Dexter indicated a chair. 'Stay here if you want, but you are not coming in. Tess is my wife and I want her with me. I don't need you to hold my hand, and you are no good to me in this state. In fact, you're a liability.' The last statement was delivered in a low whisper.

Leaning down to retrieve a notepad from her bag, Connie heard the aside and was able to catch a glimpse of the three Booths reflected in a long mirror opposite. From what she could see of her, Tessa Booth was clearly annoyed by her father-in-law's interference, though diplomatically was saying nothing.

Ignoring his father's indignant response, Dexter kept an eye on the clock and at exactly one minute to midday the door opened and Bernard Kershaw called him and Tessa into his stately office.

Taking her task seriously, Fiona McFarland coughed sweetly. 'I'm so sorry, Connie. It won't be much longer. Can I get you a glass of water?' When this was politely declined, she offered one to Chris Booth.

'Yes, please. I forgot how far it was from the car park and I had the devil's own job finding a space to park the Transit.' He raised his eyes to the ceiling. 'I used to drive a decent car, would you believe? Bit of a come down, this retirement malarkey. A drink would be good.'

When he accepted the glass from Fiona, his hands were shaking slightly and his breathing more pronounced than it should be for a fit-looking man. 'Goodness,' Connie piped up, seeing her opening. 'You look more nervous than I feel.' She sat straighter in her chair, closing her laptop. 'Job interview. And I'm dreading it. You'd think at my age I'd be used to them.'

He didn't take the bait. 'Yeah, well, good luck. You look like you know your stuff.'

'Thanks for the vote of confidence.'

They fell into heavy silence, peppered by the sound of muffled voices from beyond the door to Bernie's office.

'Busy man,' Connie ventured, trying once more to entice Chris Booth into conversation.

'Let's hope he's as good as they say he is.' A long drawn-out sigh was followed by a rolling of his shoulders. 'My sister has been charged with a serious crime and she wants my son to manage her affairs. I found the letter this morning after they left. It came as a bit of an insult, if I'm honest.'

'Oh?' Determined to sound non-plussed, Connie held back from making judgemental comment. 'Didn't want to burden you perhaps?'

'Didn't want me to know, full stop.'

'Maybe it was easier for you to find the letter than it was to tell you to your face. It must have been difficult.'

'Maybe.'

The conversation stalled once more, but within minutes the door to the office opened and the occupants filed out. 'Peddyr will come with me and we will meet you at the house. If there are any media bods about just ignore them. Not a word to anyone about why we are at the property.' Bernie shook hands with Dexter and his wife before heading in the opposite direction towards the car park at the rear of the building, Peddyr at his side. Connie was ignored as was Chris Booth.

'Well?' he asked his son, taking to his feet and widening his stance.

'We'll talk on the way back to the car, Dad. Are you in the Church Street car park?' Dexter asked, heading for the exit, leading Tessa by the hand. She had a look of someone who had won the lottery but hadn't quite assimilated the fact. In contrast, Dexter wore a mask of grim determination, batting off further questions from his father as they pushed through the glass doors, making their way to the street.

After they had left, Connie and Fiona stared at each

other for a few seconds before exhaling. 'That was tense, Mrs McFarland.'

'It was also untrue. We never sent a letter. The arrangements were made over the phone and confirmed by email.'

'Somebody has been nosing at their son's computer then...'

## 34

## THE UNDERTAKERS

*A*t number seven Derwent Drive there were police everywhere, their number swollen by journalists and members of the public hoping to catch a grisly glimpse of the site of Kenny Eversholt's murder. Somewhat ironic, Peddyr thought, given that the bungalow looked like a CSI scene from a movie even before Kenny had been found dead there.

'We should have come in from the other end of Derwent Drive,' Bernie said, steering sedately past, the V6 engine of the black Jaguar XF thrumming.

Peddyr looked across at him. 'Yes, we should have. We look like a couple of undertakers touting for business. Keep going and when we get to number fifteen, sometime this side of Christmas if you wouldn't mind, roll gently onto the driveway. Park behind the hedge.'

The solicitor did as advised and was easing himself out of the car when Carol Brightman appeared from the front door with a suitcase in one hand, a coat slung over the other arm. As before, she was dressed in the bohemian style befitting of a creative mind, with a flowing handkerchief hem to her multi-patterned skirt and a ruffled blouse of lime green. 'Oh, my, we meet again, Peedwire,' she said on seeing who the visitor was with. 'Thank you for the lovely flowers. They arrived just now. So thoughtful.'

This was typical of Connie. A quick call to Kathy in the florist shop below the flat, and flowers had been arranged in appreciation of Carol's contribution to the tasty feast the night before. 'Don't thank me. Thank my wife. She was so astounded at not having to cook for once, she wanted to show our appreciation.' He fabricated this scene in his head, because in truth he hadn't been listening to everything Connie said when she had mentioned sending flowers. It was a vague memory drowned out by the need to find Kenny Eversholt's killer, who in Peddyr's mind was also responsible for the death of Scott Fletcher.

'Peedwire? That's a new one,' Bernie chortled.

'So, this is Mr Kershaw,' Carol said, lowering the heavy bag to the ground and holding out her hand, bangles jangling on her wrist. 'Pleased to meet you. Thanks for your call. I also had one from Maggie Holden just now, hence the packing. I have a few more things to source from the permitted list of items I can take, then I'm off to Bronzefield on Monday. They were pretty quick to book me in because Sarah's only got the clothes she's standing in. I can't imagine how awful she feels right now.'

She shrugged. 'I've done what I can. Once I found out what to do, I sent money via the portal gizmo and I'm taking her keys and jewellery from her when I get there. Jeez, I'm in such a state.' Flicking wild curls away from her face, she looked the two men up and down, humming her approval. 'A veritable feast for the eye, gentlemen. Official business?'

'It is indeed. We don't need access to the house, Carol. Just the outbuildings. Dexter should be here soon, we're making an inventory and he—'

Carol stopped him. 'No need to explain. Maggie and Dexter are taking control of affairs. And a good thing too if you ask me.' She picked up the bag at her feet. 'I'm nearly done here, and I'll speak with Dexter another time about estate agents.' Before they had chance to reply, she was slinking her way through the gate and back to her own house, leaving a fragrant cloud of expensive perfume in her wake.

It was a good few minutes before Dexter arrived during which Monica called with the breaking news that his motorbike had been caught on camera the morning of Scott Fletcher's murder. 'Well, well, we have progress at last,' Peddyr announced, tipping an abbreviated salute at Bernie with one finger. 'Some new evidence has come to light and for some reason Webster has latched on to this as the only other lead. He's released Ryan without finishing his questioning.'

He reset and concentrated on what Monica was telling him. 'Listen, Grasshopper, hang around there for as long as possible and pull in every favour you can to find out if that same bike was seen coming back out onto Bakers Lane again. There's no alternative route. Someone must have seen something; collar Helen Forstall in the toilets if you have to. She's turned into a useful ally and I've asked her to double check what time Dexter arrived at the Marsworth Unit yesterday evening and whether or not he was at work all day on the fifth. Doing a proper belt and braces job, I've asked Connie to do the same thing in case Webster sticks his oar in and messes with the line of enquiry.' He ended the call as Dexter reversed onto the driveway.

Hauling himself out of the car, the young man appeared drained. 'Sorry for keeping you waiting. I had to have a word with Dad and then drop Tessa at home.' He dragged his fringe away from his face. 'Parents... who'd have them?'

Peddyr detected a sub-plot. 'Where's your mum? She not visiting?'

An exasperated look from Dexter gave an indication of the stress he was under. 'Dad rocked up last night. Mum threw him out apparently and he landed on our doorstep shortly after I got back from visiting Ryan at the unit.' Dexter leaned against the roof of his car, arms folded, resting there in the warmth of the sunlight. 'I was home later than planned because the police decided to have a chat with me in lieu of my cousin, who was out for the count on horse tranquillisers. Anyway, the upshot is that today... Tessa is on my case about getting rid of Dad as soon as humanly possible, Ryan is now down the cop-shop answering questions, Sarah is on remand and I'm piggy in the middle.'

'Correction,' Bernie added. 'Ryan has been released with no further questions for now.'

'Has he?' Looking perturbed, Dexter glanced towards the road. 'Then we can expect him here any minute.' He exhaled slowly, shoulders drooping. 'And what do I say to him when he does turn up?'

Keen to get on with opening the workshop and garages, Peddyr walked towards the solid wooden doors. 'Worry about that as and when it happens. We're here on legal business and it doesn't include him. That's all he needs to know. Shall we?' Wasting further time discussing Ryan was of little interest in comparison to seeking the true motive behind

Scott Fletcher's death. When he prodded at his trusty notepad with a pen, taking the hint, Dexter reached into his car to collect a prepared list from the door pocket.

'Actually, I'll jot down the details, Pedd,' Bernie said, stepping forward to take possession of the notebook. 'You know what you're talking about when it comes to bikes and such like. Spell out any unusual names if you would, old chap.'

With Maggie Holden's keys now in his possession, the alarm was disarmed shortly after Dexter switched on the lights. 'This shouldn't take too long.'

Unable to help himself, Peddyr reeled at the sight so brightly illuminated. 'Love a bloody duck! This place is like an Aladdin's cave.' Everywhere was spotless, the floor painted and clean, the walls lined with tooling, shelving and spares precisely hung. A workbench took pride of place along the right-hand side, a small lathe beside it, a bench drill at one end. 'When were you last in here?' Peddyr asked.

After some careful thought, staring at the bike covers, Dexter replied somewhat warily. 'I used to come every four weeks or so until Scott took over the maintenance duties from me. So, the last time was the day Dad and Mum were invited here to meet him.'

'Scott must have been impressed to see this lot when you opened the doors. Your dad show him around, did he?'

Dexter shook his head, a slight frown appearing. 'It wasn't the first time Scott had been in here, but it was the first time Dad had seen the place in a while. It caused some friction, shall we say.'

The anticipation was becoming unbearable for Peddyr as his eyes swept the outlines of the bikes, searching for one in particular. 'I'm going to start at the back and work forward. Take all the covers off, gentlemen, and let the dog see the rabbit.' Each time a cover was lifted and put to one side, there was a pause in proceedings while Peddyr admired the machine that was revealed. A pristine Rickman Matisse was unveiled followed by a Greaves. 'Look at this Royal Enfield. The Flying Pea these were called. They used to crate them up and drop them out of planes in the war,' Peddyr said, his voice rising with the joy of each discovery.

'Run out of bombs, did we?' Even Bernie became caught up in the excitement. He put down his writing pad and lifted a cover gingerly from the bike nearest to him. 'I say… a Sunbeam. Jesus wants me for one of these.' This earned him a half-laugh from his friend and a look of bewilderment from Dexter. 'You have to be of an age to understand that one,' he explained.

There was no look of incredulity from Dexter as Peddyr had been expecting, there wasn't any such reaction showing on his face. 'All as it should be?' Peddyr asked.

'Yep. All present and correct,' came the reply.

Taking a surreptitious look at Bernie, Peddyr revealed his real reason for asking this question. 'So when your dad saw this place the last time, on that awkward visit with your mum, would he have said the same thing?'

Here was the reaction he had been waiting for. Dexter visibly froze. 'Er… Why do you ask?' he demanded, breaking eye contact to stare down at the list in his hand.

'Because I believe Sarah Holden was the owner and keeper of a Brough Superior and a Vincent Black Shadow, neither of which seem to be here even though there is plenty of room for them. To be explicit, we should be expecting to see a 1929 Brough SS100, one of only eleven built to those specifications to be exact. The Vincent isn't worth quite as much but is nevertheless one hell of a bike to own. These had been in the hands of Jim Holden's father. Sarah would not have sold them. So where are they?'

A muscle in Dexter's jaw twitched. 'I wouldn't know about that. There were a few special bikes that used to belong to Uncle Jim's father – Grandpa Holden. But only Sarah would be able to tell you what happened to them.'

'Are you saying she did sell them?' Bernie interjected before Peddyr had chance to ask the same question.

'If she did, they weren't auctioned through Tottering's.' The reply was evasive, body language defensive. Dexter Booth was hiding the truth from them and the atmosphere in the garage was becoming increasingly strained as a result.

Bernie raised a hand. 'I doubt very much Sarah would have parted with those particular machines, for one very good reason,' he volunteered. 'James Holden's last will and testament stated that certain motorcycles were to be left to Sarah on the stipulation that they should remain in the family henceforth. That was straight from the horse's mouth and it tallies with the wills we have on file for the family. My valued colleague Mr Quirk here was able to confirm the details and furnish me with an estimate of current market value.' He rested against the workbench. 'What I would like to know is whether or not Scott Fletcher was aware of the existence of these specific motorcycles. Was the family about to lose significant assets to Sarah's fiancé?'

Throwing his leg over the saddle of the nearest bike, Dexter spoke softly, absentmindedly playing with the throttle in his right hand. 'Actually, there is a possibility that Sarah moved them somewhere for safekeeping.'

To Peddyr, this sounded more plausible, but why was

Dexter throwing them this titbit? 'Oh, what makes you say that?' he asked.

Hunching forward, Dexter seemed to shrink. 'I think she did it so my dad couldn't get his hands on them. He seemed to think he had a right to at least part of the collection because of his friendship with Uncle Jim and the amount of time he'd worked on the bikes with him. To be fair, Sarah did give him at least four bikes that I know of. He was supposed to pay her for two of them but never did.'

Bernie caught Peddyr's eye and raised a query using one eyebrow. Peddyr couldn't help him with an answer. This was fresh information, and he wasn't at all certain it was valid, although some of the details fitted with what Maggie Holden had mentioned.

'Out of interest, what sort of bikes are we talking about? What was the last one given to your dad by Sarah Holden?' Peddyr enquired, probing for more accurate facts to back Dexter's most recent disclosure.

'A 1979 Kawasaki Z1000. We sold one at auction recently for twelve grand.'

Bernie blew through his lips. 'Goodness me! Why on earth would she allow her brother to help himself to such expensive items and not pay her for them?'

Peddyr was thinking along the exact same lines.

'She was easily manipulated,' Dexter said. 'And Dad didn't respect the bikes like Uncle Jim did. He tidied them up and sold them on, which wasn't the right thing to do. When Uncle Jim died, Dad just assumed he could have his share. To be fair, he may still have the bikes and be planning to pay Sarah back in instalments. You could ask him. I tend to keep out of it.'

The earworm about a perfect cousin had returned. It was becoming more obvious to Peddyr that Dexter Booth had played the good nephew so convincingly that he had outmanoeuvred Ryan and put himself in the top spot for inheriting considerable wealth. Sarah trusted him implicitly. So much so she had put her nephew and Maggie in charge of managing her financial affairs. Making himself out to be a paragon of virtue, Dexter was now painting a picture of his own father as a scoundrel and there were no records to say whether he was being truthful or not. He could be fabricating everything to discredit his own father. Only Sarah would know, and she wasn't accessible.

Unable to help himself, Peddyr glanced down at the younger man's shoes, trying to gauge the size of his feet. 'If you were Sarah, where would you have safely stored two astronomically expensive motorbikes?'

'Where they should be, I suppose…' he answered, observing Peddyr openly.

'And where would that be,' Bernie queried. 'A motor museum?'

This hadn't been Peddyr's first thought. "Where they should be" was the clue he needed. Sarah would only have allowed the bikes to remain in the security of the Holden family. There was only one family member she trusted. 'Maggie Holden has them?' he ventured. Dexter did not deny this suggestion, but neither did he confirm it as being correct. Not that he needed to. Given the unspoken reaction, a bullseye had been scored with Peddyr's first and highly educated guess.

The plan was astounding in its audacity.

The bikes had been kept in the hands of their original owner's widow, Maggie Holden who held ownership, had them insured and safely stored. The arrangement was so simple, so elegant and so easy to achieve, that Peddyr had to admire this clever strategy. There was the trigger to the killing of Scott Fletcher as plain as the ears on Bernie's head.

Dexter's course of action was clear: ingratiate himself with Sarah. Invent a reason to move the most precious bikes somewhere his own father wouldn't think to look for them and concoct a sound reason to do so, something Sarah would accept as plausible. Dexter was family, he could own the bikes without disrespecting the terms of Jim Holden's will and Ryan would willingly part with them once he knew he could pocket a decent amount of money. Not their full value, nowhere near it, because Dexter would keep the rest for himself and his pretty wife.

Peddyr positioned himself by the open door. All he had to do now was keep the young man talking while the evidence was being reviewed at the police station to prove Dexter's guilt. Peddyr could then phone Webster and hand over the perpetrator. The man who had killed Scott Fletcher.

Dexter dismounted the bike as Peddyr asked, 'Do you, by any chance, own a pair of size ten adventure bike boots with a Vibram sole?' The answer didn't arrive because it was interrupted when Dexter reached into his pocket withdrawing his mobile phone. 'It's Tessa. I have to take this.' He didn't wait for agreement. 'What…? When…? I'll be right there.' Rattled, he made for the door, phone still clutched tightly in his hand. 'The police are at my house with a warrant to search everywhere. Tessa is frantic.'

'Yes, of course you must get home straight away.' With a steely gaze Peddyr held Dexter's panicked eyes. 'Give me your keys, I'll lock this place up again. Keep it safe. You have bigger problems to deal with right now.' He grabbed the keys and moved out of the younger man's way, allowing him to head for his car.

During this brief exchange, Bernie stood with mouth agape. It had all happened so fast. Silenced by Dexter's rapid departure, he stepped outside and could only stare after the young man's car as it roared onto Derwent Drive. He rounded on Peddyr who joined him. 'You let him go?'

## CAUGHT ON CAMERA

*T*he two men stood together propped against Bernie's Jag on the driveway of number fifteen Derwent Drive. 'Of course I let him leave,' Peddyr said with a satisfied grin. 'Dexter Booth can drive home looking every inch the concerned husband and stroll neatly into the arms of the law. Save us the trouble.'

He glanced up on hearing a noise and a flustered-looking Carol waved at them as she emerged once more from the front door carrying a shoulder bag.

'I'm all done here for now. You were mighty fast. All finished?' She looked past them towards the garages. 'Was that Dex I heard leaving in a hurry? Did Ryan go with him?'

'Ryan?' Peddyr challenged, as he looked behind him for no reason other than he was following the direction of Carol's stare. 'What do you mean?'

'He was here a minute ago. I assumed he was in the workshop with all of you. I knew he'd be here soon enough. At least I think it was him… I only saw him from the rear.'

With a firm push against the gloss paintwork, Carol checked the front door was securely locked.

'Do you leave the door on the latch when you are inside?' Peddyr asked.

'Certainly not, what do you take me for, Peedwire?' Offended, Carol screwed up her nose at him. 'I'm not some rank amateur, you know. I take my obligations to Sarah very seriously. If Ryan was after his belongings he didn't try very hard,' she said, inclining her head towards the workshop then returning her attention to a puzzled-looking Peddyr.

'Maybe he went round the back, I'll take a shufti,' he said, staring up at the house.

'I didn't even realise the police had finished with him,' Carol added. The nods of confirmation from the two men resulted in a visible shudder from her. 'Well, if you find him, for God's sake don't tell him I have the spare keys. He'll pester me until I give in.'

'Your secret is safe with us,' Bernie assured her. 'In fact, we have his set of house keys in safekeeping at the office, so if he calls by, please direct him to Bagshot & Laker before close of play today, otherwise he'll have to wait until Monday.'

'Then no doubt Maggie will be expecting a visit,' Carol declared with a heartfelt sigh. 'That poor woman. What a burden she carries.' At this, Carol picked up the bag from the doorstep and asked if they would make sure to lock the workshop before they left. 'Check Ryan's not hiding in there while you're at it,' she continued, giving a saucy wink as she so often did. 'I'm off home now. You have my number if you need me for anything else.'

Without consulting each other Peddyr and Bernie

peeled away from the car and moved back inside the workshop to stand among the bikes where there was no sign of Ryan or anyone else. Determined to complete the task they had set themselves, they went about covering up the bikes and finally compiling a comprehensive list of the ones Dexter was to become proud owner of, using his list as the basis. Chassis numbers, full details, everything.

It seemed there was to be no respite from the sound of mobile phones ringing and before long Bernie was talking to Monica. Nodding, he cupped a hand over his mouth to deaden the sound of his voice. 'And he was seen arguing at the scene? Clearly identified. No? Well, keep looking. We must be sure.' By the sound of things, the news from Bosworth Bishops Police Station was encouraging.

It was all very well knowing the police were closing in on Dexter, but Peddyr's mind couldn't settle. 'Are you sure Monica said it was Dexter's bike seen in Bakers Lane on the fifth?'

When Bernie nodded his head, his jowls rippled. 'According to my able assistant, an ANPR camera caught the registration plate, but the mobile unit then moved elsewhere. The timing fits with the assault on Scott Fletcher. The size ten boots will most likely be found in Dexter Booth's garage as will a bloodstained jacket and gloves unless he's had the sense to destroy the evidence. How else would you explain the warrant?'

Peddyr stared across at his companion. 'Ah, well, that's that then,' he said. 'Connie must be wrong for once in her life. Dexter can't have been in two places at once.'

'What are you talking about?'

'That was her on the phone just now. She and Fiona have been on to Tottering's who say that Dexter was at work on the fifth. There was a valuation day. There are dozens if not hundreds of people who can place him there, for the whole day.'

'Well, he must have taken a break at some point. Although having said that… Connie is very rarely wrong, my friend.'

Peddyr was one or two moves ahead of Bernie. He reached into his pocket for his phone again and dialled the number he was looking for. He wasn't too perturbed when a woman's voice answered him. Dexter was with the police and his wife Tessa had taken the call. She sounded on the verge of tears.

'Tessa? This is Peddyr Quirk, we met earlier today at the offices of Bagshot & Laker. I'm with Mr Kershaw and we understand the police have a warrant to search your property. We are here to help but I need you to answer my questions as accurately as you can.'

'I feel a little faint, Mr Quirk. Can you call back later?' Her voice was thready, her breathing far too rapid.

'Tessa, sit down and try to breathe much slower. In through the nose, out through the mouth. Is anyone with you?' Dexter's wife was being supported by a uniformed policewoman whom Peddyr could hear in the background demanding that Tessa end the call as the phone was to be taken as evidence. 'Tell them it's your solicitor and you are seeking advice. Don't hang up. This is really important, Tessa.' Peddyr waited impatiently as this was relayed to the police officer.

'I need you to think carefully. When did your husband last use his motorbike?'

The answer was muffled, but Tessa had seemingly regained enough blood to the brain to be coherent. 'I don't really know. I would say he hasn't been anywhere on his bike for about two weeks, but I couldn't swear to it. He's been so preoccupied with Sarah and me and work and Ryan and his dad hounding him with endless calls... Why don't you ask Chris? He was here on the fifth. He went to see Dexter at work that day before going back to Wales. Ask him. I was at work too, so I don't know anything about his bloody motorbike.' Her voice was becoming more shrill with every sentence, forcing Peddyr to fire another quick question at her before the police physically removed the phone from her hands.

'Were you at home while Dexter was visiting Ryan yesterday evening?'

Peddyr could hear her begin to sob. 'No, I was at my mother's. Dex rang to say he was running late. I got back here literally seconds after him in the end and then his bloody father drew up in his van no more than ten minutes after that. Chris was in a real state, but still, he should have phoned first. It's not fair on us...'

'And I don't suppose you checked the garage to see if Dexter's bike was where he'd left it, whether the engine was warm or whether his gear had been hung up as he would normally do...'

There was a strangled cry of concern. 'What are you trying to say? Are the police going to arrest Dex?' Tessa's voice became a squeak.

Bernie came closer as Peddyr failed to console a distraught Tessa Booth when he delivered an unwelcome dose of reality. 'Most likely – but try not to panic.'

Leaning against the workbench once more, Bernie gave Peddyr a troubled look as he ended the fourth in a series of calls from Monica with the latest information from Helen Forstall. 'Without a shadow of a doubt the police will be planning to make another arrest. Dexter is heading for a cell. On the first of September a Lycra-clad cyclist presented our local police with film from his helmet cam. The recording was of an altercation with a driver. He returned on the fifth of September with further evidence and an irate demand for police to take action against the driver of the car he said had nearly driven into a motorcycle at the T-Junction of Bakers Lane and Green Lane. The cyclist was approaching the same junction and caught everything on his Go-Pro.

'Said motorcyclist, whom we know to have been riding Dexter Booth's motorcycle because the registration is clear enough, then flipped up his visor to vent his spleen at the offending driver. Frustratingly, that person can't be clearly identified from the footage as he's pictured from behind. However, the same cannot be said of the car driver. His face and identity are as plain as day.'

At this Peddyr flinched. 'Kenny Eversholt?' he asked. It had to be. And it was the reason Kenny had to die. He had seen the perpetrator leaving the scene of a murder. It was someone he knew. 'That's it then. Murder solved. It was Dexter.' He made for the door. 'Let's double check the house and the garden. If Ryan was here he will have overheard us discussing his inheritance being of value.' He looked at his watch. 'In which case he will head straight for Maggie Holden's. Give me your car keys, I'll drive. He's got no car; he'll be on Shanks's. We should catch him on his way to the bus station, if we hurry.'

'I wouldn't count on it, old bean,' Bernie replied, jangling the keys in his pocket before producing them. 'Monica says he was picked up outside Bosworth Police Station by a bloke in a white van.'

At high speed, Peddyr pieced together the information.

He was fairly certain Ryan would be with Bez and that he was heading for Maggie Holden's to claim ownership of some very expensive machinery.

'And he's got one hell of a head start.'

## 36

## RALLY DRIVER TO THE RESCUE

*H*ead in the airing cupboard, Connie poked at the soil of her amaryllis bulbs. It was barely moist in both pots. 'Blast and darn it,' she said. 'I've had the blessed things for one day and already I have to water them. I'll never remember to do this so often.' Deciding to set an alarm, she fiddled with her phone which made her jump as it rang and vibrated in her hand. 'That was quick, Lao Gong. All sorted?'

It was Peddyr's number but not his voice. 'No, it's not. How quickly can you get to Maggie Holden's address, Connie?' Bernie sounded ruffled. Not a state he was usually known to inhabit. 'We've tried ringing her but with no success. Find her and make sure she's alright. Warn her she may have an unwanted visitor and not to agree to anything.'

This was all very vague and cryptic but the urgency in Bernie's voice galvanised her into immediate action. She dashed to the kitchen, collected her keys and headed for the back door, all the while talking to Bernie. It was clear why Peddyr was driving his friend's car. Speed was required. She had no idea why Bernie was using her husband's phone. 'By a process of elimination and camera recordings... Well done, boys, you two are getting very good at this,' she said, after Bernie had given her the potted version of the evidence. 'And you think Dexter killed Scott Fletcher and Kenny too? So what does Ryan want from Maggie, other than somewhere to stay?'

Even as she spoke she ran through the computations in her head. Had Ryan and Dexter been working together all along? If Dexter needed time to carry out the murder of Scott Fletcher, Ryan would be the one to inform him of the man's whereabouts. It would have taken only minutes, and that was all the time needed for Dexter to hop on his motorbike, whiz to Primrose Court and back out again. His suit would remain spotlessly clean under lightweight motorbike gear. It was possible. An all-in-one waterproof would have been ideal for keeping blood splashes from his own clothing.

Her imagination was running away with her. Aware that she was beginning to think like her husband, she inwardly cautioned herself.

'A rare and immensely valuable motorbike and its friend called Vincent are what he's trying to get hold of, Connie. But only if Maggie is cajoled or coerced into signing them over. We think she has the bikes and the proof of ownership. Short of that, I fear they will be removed without her permission.'

It was coming together. Sarah Holden had unwittingly placed herself at the scene of a crime committed by her own nephew in collusion with her son. A son she'd thought capable of such a crime, a nephew whom she'd trusted. How very sad. The more Connie thought it through, the more obvious the conclusion became. Dexter would take the bikes to auction, he had all the contacts, and the pair of them would pocket hundreds of thousands of pounds. Means, motive and opportunity were accounted for. 'Well done, Pedd. Well done, Bernie.'

The phone logged into the Bluetooth system of the car and Connie reversed out of the garage, speeding away towards Maggie Holden's ranch-like bungalow six miles away. Peddyr's ghostly words echoed around the car as he begged her not to do anything rash if she got there before him.

'Did you hear that, Connie?' Bernie boomed. 'Just keep him talking until we get there. Pleasantries. Nothing more. He may have his scruffy chum Bez with him, but you'll see a white van on the drive if he is.'

Appreciating Bernie's ability to avoid use of profanity under pressure, Connie wasn't doing such a good job at keeping her cool. Her irritation with other drivers spilled over as she hit her hand on the centre of the steering wheel to sound the horn. 'Shift, you silly twerp!' The car in front was dawdling. Impatient, she overtook, pulling away from traffic lights not caring if she had triggered a speed camera or breached the rules of the road. If the police wanted to stop her for traffic offences then good, let them. They could follow her to Maggie's home which would save her calling them when she got there if it turned nasty. Sod's Law determined that there was not a traffic cop in sight. 'I'm nearly there,' she said to Bernie. 'I'll keep the phone on in my pocket when I get out of the car, so I'm not seen to be using one. Okay?'

'Good thinking, Lao Po,' came the distant reverberations of Peddyr's reassuring voice.

She braked hard and turned into the sweeping driveway to be immediately greeted by the sight of a rusty white box van facing her, parked on the slope some ten feet away from the double garage where Bernie said the motorbikes were housed. Pulling up as slowly as she could manage in her rush to find Maggie, she deliberately blocked off the only exit. There was no sign of anyone near the van although the rear roller was open and a metal ramp had been put in place. 'Well, the cheeky blighters,' she announced, assuming Bernie was listening in. 'I think they're about to load up the motorbikes.'

She looked about her and twisted round to scan the back seat for something she could use as a prop. On the seat was a cardboard box containing items destined for the charity shop. There was even more stuff in the boot but the box she could reach more easily from within the car contained old board games, a jigsaw puzzle or two and various other items that had found a home under the bed in Aleyn's old bedroom. She grabbed at an ancient game of Ludo, requiring only the board doubled up inside the box. From the glovebox she then grabbed a receipt and some paper-work relating to the most recent car service. These would have to do, she thought.

Unnerved, she approached the house and rang the door-bell to which there was no reply. 'There is definitely someone home,' she said loudly enough for Bernie to hear her from her pocket, at least she hoped so. 'I saw movement. I'm going round the back.' Trotting as fast as she thought reasonable for a visiting professional, she went to the side of the property, opened the garden gate and called out. 'Hello... Mrs Holden. This is Connie from Bagshot & Laker solicitors, are you at home?' Rounding the corner she was temporarily reassured by the sight of Maggie Holden, sitting with a man she knew must be Ryan Holden, drinking tea and eating cake at a table on the wide sunny terrace, a swathe of Virginia creeper on the house wall next to them waving gently in the breeze.

Her relief that she was not too late was dashed when a second man came into sight through open French windows. She stumbled slightly and the grip on her makeshift clipboard loosened when she recognised Chris Booth. In turn he was visibly ruffled by the sight of the tea party gatecrasher. She too had been recognised. What was he doing there? According to Maggie she only ever saw him at family celebrations. Something was awry.

It occurred to Connie that less than two hours had passed since she'd told Chris Booth she was waiting to be interviewed for a job. How was she to explain her presence at the home of Maggie Holden without arousing considerable suspicion? Her appearance would be way too much of a coincidence. Glancing down at her makeshift clipboard, she thanked her own ingenuity and forethought. However, a lot more quick thinking was on the cards if she was to hold the fort until the cavalry arrived.

The much younger man with Maggie Holden looked like Dexter Booth at first glance. He was, however, more muscular with a distinctly angular face and striking blue eyes. Instead of the neat haircut sported by his older cousin, Ryan had much longer hair, wavy and lustrous. A holdall was wedged under his chair. 'Oh, I'm so sorry… you have visitors,' Connie said loudly, praying that Bernie would pick up on her use of the plural. In that second, she had no way to let him know who the other man was. It certainly wasn't Bez.

'Connie, how lovely to see you again. This is my grandson Ryan who has come to stay, and this is his Uncle Christopher,' Maggie Holden said, waving a trembling hand at Chris Booth who was taking long strides across the York stone slabs towards them. 'This lovely lady works for my solicitor Bernard Kershaw.' Both men nodded but only Chris Booth made a move to shake hands with Connie.

'Got the job then,' he said, giving her a warm smile as he took a chair at the table.

'I don't find out until tomorrow,' Connie replied in a hurry, cutting off any questions or comments from Maggie that would expose her deception. 'An internal position came up, but I had to go through the motions. You know how it is.' She shifted her attention to Ryan. 'How lovely of you to visit your grandmother.'

After hearing so much about Ryan Holden from her husband, it came as no surprise to Connie that she was subjected to a winning smile that melted into a thinly disguised charm offensive. 'I've just been discharged from a short stay in hospital. Granny offered to let me stay and recuperate. And I thought she could do with my support as much as I could do with hers,' he added.

The return smile from Maggie wasn't convincing. 'Strangely enough, I predicted that he would come here as soon as the doctors gave him the all clear. I must say I wasn't expecting Christopher as well, but it's nice to have so many visitors. Flora is in the house searching for some paperwork that Ryan and Christopher need. Shall I ask her to bring you a cup and saucer?' The message was loud and clear from Maggie. Something was going on that she felt extremely uncomfortable with and she was trying to let Connie know. 'What brings you here, dear?'

Pen poised, Connie looked down at the papers she was holding against the Ludo board. 'It's a private matter.'

Ryan laughed. 'You want us to leave?'

'No, just face the other way if you wouldn't mind. It will only take a moment.' As Ryan duly shifted in his seat, crossed his legs and made a show of turning his back, Chris followed suit by looking away. Taking her only chance, Connie scribbled in large letters onto the paper.

WHATEVER THEY ARE TELLING YOU, DON'T BELIEVE THEM. AGREE TO NOTHING. KEEP SMIL- ING. HELP IS ON THE WAY.

'Just read and sign at the bottom if you would, Mrs Holden, and I'll get this back to Mr Kershaw right away,' she said, handing the pen to Maggie who read the words and glanced gratefully at Connie, nodding slowly.

'Thank you, dear. I'm glad you spotted the mistake. Please thank Mr Kershaw for his quick response.'

Without waiting for permission to do so, Chris Booth and Ryan adjusted themselves, turning to face Maggie once more. 'Okay,' said Chris, rubbing his palms together. 'Ryan, you can help me load up the bikes. It's a good job you're here… I never would have managed it on my own. Maggie, it's been a pleasure and I'm sure Ryan won't regret his deci- sion. They're going to a good home and staying in the family just as Jim wanted. Good news all round, don't you agree?'

She had been remarkably collected until this point, but on hearing this Maggie began to cry, sobbing loudly into a handkerchief.

Hunkering down beside her, Connie touched her deli- cately on the forearm and looked up into her face. It was an act, she saw. A brilliant act to delay any move from the one person who could help protect her until help arrived. 'I'll stay with Mrs Holden,' Connie announced.

Ryan agreed with her, at last showing some empathy towards his distressed grandmother.

'Oh, Maggie, please don't be sad,' Chris said, softly. 'This way, your family legacy stays in safe hands and the money will come in handy for Ryan until he's back in gainful employment. It's the least I can do to help out. Sarah wouldn't want her son left destitute because of her actions, would she?'

'That's right, Granny,' Ryan added. 'They would come to me when Mum died any way and as she's in prison...'

Chris twisted in his seat, looking back at the ivy-clad walls of the house and the open French windows. 'I wonder what's keeping the housekeeping lady with the paperwork?' he asked, glancing sympathetically at Maggie. 'The longer this drags on for, the more difficult it will be for you. I do understand.'

Connie was not sure that he was being truthful. Although there was no air of menace, there was a distinct edge of sickly-sweet insincerity, in the way Chris spoke to Maggie.

In the silent seconds that followed, a low rumbling could be heard as a car entered the front driveway. 'And I wonder who that could be now?' Chris commented, sitting up. When the doorbell rang he sprang to his feet and strode back into the house. From the same side of the garden that Connie had used to gain access, two men in sharp suits came rapidly towards them. Peddyr was limping slightly but still outrunning the more portly man plodding behind him.

'Jesus, is that you, Peter?' Ryan asked. 'Just the man. Do you have my house keys? And what are you doing here anyway?'

'He's looking after your mother's assets, which is more than I can say for you.' This reply came from Bernie as he watched Peddyr divert into the house, following Chris inside. Connie was right behind her husband.

'And where does she think she's going?' Ryan commented, folding his arms.

'To make sure Flora doesn't give your uncle any paperwork relating to those bikes,' Maggie answered, despair making her voice quaver. 'Oh, Ryan, don't you understand?'

With the grand front door wide open, Flora was on the doorstep looking about her for the person who had rung the doorbell.

'I thought I told you not to answer the phone and not to open the door to anyone while I was here,' Chris growled at her from behind.

She spun round and waved several sheets of thin paper at him. Her lips and chin quivered as she spoke. 'It took me a while, but I do believe these are the documents you asked for,' she said. Confusion appeared on her face then and she faltered, looking through him. 'What in heaven's name is—?'

'Thanks,' Peddyr said, boldly reaching out, stepping past Chris Booth and taking the papers from a bewildered Flora. He perused them rapidly. 'The bikes can't be handed over until a legal change of ownership has been completed.' He briefly caught Chris's eye. 'Peddyr Quirk, part of Mr Kershaw's legal team. Pleased to meet you, Mr Booth. Looks like we got here at a most convenient time. There's a stroke of luck.' He raised both eyebrows at Chris Booth who remained immobilised by the unexpected interruption. 'Perhaps another pot of tea if you would?' Peddyr suggested to Flora.

'And I'll help you,' Connie added, beckoning for Flora to join her out of harm's way.

With the papers folded and tucked into an inside pocket, Peddyr squared up to Chris Booth. 'Before we sort out the formalities, I have something I want to ask you,' he said.

'Go on.' Chris clenched his fists, his jaw tightened.

'Is the Brough Superior as good as I think it is?'

Confounded, Chris's mouth fell open. 'What?'

Also in a state of disbelief, Connie silently shook her head as she took hold of Flora's elbow to steer her into the kitchen. Peddyr would have a plan. What that plan was, she couldn't begin to guess but he would have one and Chris Booth would be reeled in by it.

## 37

## WINGING IT

*I*t was a simple enough concept. If it worked for Connie, then it would work for him too. Peddyr felt the weight of the phone in his pocket and prayed it was recording and that he had enough battery left for the job in hand. He would have to stay in close proximity to Chris Booth in order to get what he needed, but it was worth the risk if he could bluff out some sort of useful information to help them make sense of this turn of events. Chris Booth was not who he'd been expecting to see.

'Take me to the garage. I have to see this thing for myself,' Peddyr said, capitalising on the allure of a legendary motorbike, lulling Chris Booth into believing he was inadvertently there to help.

Sure enough, he was escorted through to an internal door and into the garage, where fluorescent lighting flickered and cast an unforgiving light. It was the smell that hit him first. 'You've had them running then?' The question was a rhetorical one. The lingering exhaust fumes were the background notes, but to the fore, hitting Peddyr's nose like a series of unforgettable memories, was the scent of Castrol. Castrol R. One of his favourite smells. 'Shall we open up the garage door and get a proper look at the beasts?'

The covers had already been removed, most likely one of the first things Chris had asked to do when he got here. Peddyr would have done the same. Chris Booth would have wanted to see the bikes he had coveted for years. Ones he thought had been lost to Scott Fletcher.

Circling the Brough, they both stared down, mesmerised by it. 'Cor, what I wouldn't give to have one of these,' Peddyr said as his opening gambit. 'And it's staying in the family, just as James Holden outlined in his will. Such a shame Ryan has no interest in anything mechanical.' He looked up to catch Chris's questioning expression. 'I visited the lad when he was in hospital. We chatted about quite a lot of things. He said you and Dexter put him onto Scott Fletcher being a money-grabbing con artist.'

A short silence followed as Chris took time to consider a reply. 'Ryan tells me that's exactly what he turned out to be. A cheap con man after my sister's money.'

'After these beauties,' Peddyr said aiming a finger at the two motorbikes in the garage, again admiring how well cared for they were. How pristine. It was highly unlikely that Maggie or Flora was responsible for this level of maintenance, so it could only be Dexter who had tended them and kept the secret of their whereabouts so tightly. 'How did you find out they were here?'

'I picked Ryan up from the police station a while ago. He phoned Dexter but he didn't have time to play chauffeur because he was meeting with you and the big man Mr Kershaw, at Sarah's place. So I offered.'

This was good news. It meant Chris was unaware of the police presence at his son's house. Ryan would also be blissfully ignorant. One advantage point Peddyr knew he could make use of.

'Ryan overheard you lot talking in the workshop. As soon as he picked up about the missing bikes he ran back to the road to stop me from driving off too far. He'd seen the bikes here while visiting his grandmother but had no idea they rightfully belonged to him. He knew I'd be interested in buying them. I thought that crafty bastard Fletcher had hidden them in his own lock up,' Chris added. 'It was a shock to find out they were here all the time. The one place I would never think to look.'

He rubbed at the back of his neck with one hand. 'Scott Fletcher must have done one hell of a job sweet-talking Maggie and it looks as if she fell for his charms. Even my stupid sister believed every word he said, and on top of that he managed to persuade her that Ryan had lost his marbles.' With this Chris jerked his head back, his eyes squeezed shut briefly. He had revealed himself to Peddyr as being more than a helpful relative. Chris Booth knew about Scott Fletcher's garage, but he had no idea that his own son Dexter was the one who had arranged for the bikes to be housed with Maggie Holden.

'Actually Ryan did that to himself. He invented a story that made him sound paranoid then started to behave like he was by following Scott Fletcher around and telling anyone who would listen that the man was an imposter.'

'The doctor says there's nothing wrong with the lad.'

'It's true, he's as sane as I am. And it's also true about Scott Fletcher being a con man. But for some reason, Dexter knows the bikes are here and you didn't have a clue. I'm amazed he didn't mention it to you.' The moment of revelation came flooding through Peddyr's mind. The information from Tessa had sealed the true culprit's fate.

Staring from one bike to the other, Chris seemed lost in a whirlpool of thoughts. 'But I thought it was Scott who hid them…'

The moment was there for the taking, so Peddyr took it. It was a massive gamble. 'And so you killed him in anger, and let your sister take the blame.'

Staggering backwards Chris turned his head towards the open garage door. 'Why would you say such a thing?'

'Because you might let Sarah rot in prison for a while, but even you wouldn't let that happen to your own son. Or would you?' Connie had been right after all. Dexter had been at work on the fifth of September, Tessa had been at her job too, but Chris Booth had been for a visit and was in Bosworth Bishops on the morning of the fifth of September. He'd had access to Dexter's motorbike because he was staying at his home.

With a sideways glance, Peddyr caught sight of Bernie in the doorway to the house, pointing to his phone and mouthing the word "police". On seeing the slight nod of response he gave a thumbs up to Peddyr as he angled away to make a vital call.

'You may also be interested to hear that the police are at Dexter's house right now. I wonder what they will find?'

The conversation had evolved into an interview, a crucial piece of evidence gathering. The interviewee was tightly coiled. If he hadn't tried to take possession of the bikes that very day, Chris Booth might never have been revealed as the killer. Greed had been his undoing. 'Scott Fletcher really messed up your plans for a happy retirement, didn't he?' Peddyr said. Expecting a series of strong denials and a list of alibis, he took the first shot before his opponent had time to raise his guard. 'Tessa tells me you were staying with them on the day Scott Fletcher was killed. Your sister was arrested that day. Strange then that you should go back to Wales in a hurry. Then, blow me, you were back here yesterday. The day a certain Kenneth Eversholt was killed.'

Bristling, Chris folded his arms tight across his chest. 'I hope for your sake, you're not accusing me of that too. Making unfounded accusations is one thing...'

The timings for when Dexter had arrived on Caister Ward had not yet been confirmed, meaning Peddyr was guessing and guessing well. Chris Booth's non-verbal reactions were telling him so. 'You thought Scott Fletcher had these bikes. You knew he was going to marry your sister and then the whole collection would be under his control. Sarah would do whatever he asked of her.'

Chris stiffened, his eyes narrowed. 'Oh, come off it! There you go again. I went back home because I had work the next day. After driving all that way, I was hardly going to turn round and drive all the way back again. And, yes, Scott bragged about marrying my sister and joining the family. And, yes, I had my worries about how controlling he was. Of course that's what I thought.'

Ramping up the pressure, Peddyr nudged him towards giving more detail. 'And Scott Fletcher managed to get Kenny Eversholt to part with a bike, which you never could. That must have hurt.'

'How did you know about that?'

'I had quite a chat with Kenny yesterday. Hours before he was murdered as it turned out. He told me you'd been sniffing around those bikes of his. Small world.'

'Why were you talking to a sicko like Kenny?' Involuntarily, Chris recoiled.

'He cut me up,' Peddyr said, continuing the conversation as if he was chatting to someone inconsequentially. 'I stopped to give him a piece of my mind and some sound advice about driving skills. I expect you did the same.' This touched the correct nerve with Chris Booth.

'You're not a solicitor, Mr...'

'Quirk. Peddyr Quirk. No, I'm a private investigator. And you have just been investigated. You may as well tell me what happened. The police will be bound to question you. They have CCTV of Dexter's motorbike taken on the fifth in near collision with Kenny Eversholt's car. They are gathering the forensics as we speak. Your son will be arrested and so will you. The rider of the motorbike can be seen on camera.' Not quite the truth, Peddyr conceded to himself, but near enough to garner an outpouring of anger.

With a snarl, Chris raised his hands aggressively. 'You don't understand. I was only here in the morning, I stopped in to see Dexter at work then went home. Scott Fletcher must have pushed my son too far.' He paused and inhaled deeply. 'I'll be honest, he pushed *me* too fucking far in the end. He phoned and asked if I wanted to buy a nice little Honda 125.' Chris jabbed one forefinger at the air. 'That was deliberately rubbing my nose in it and I won't have that. Fletcher was a fake, a lying cheating bastard. But I knew what he was from the moment I met him and saw so many bikes had gone from the workshop.'

'Your sister sold some,' Peddyr stated, not taking his eyes off Booth, waiting for the explosion of rage that was steadily building.

'Yeah, well, I didn't know that.'

'Your son did. He helped her auction them off. It seems your son is more loyal to your sister than he is to you. Again, I wonder why that would be?'

Chris Booth maintained his distance and began to pace. He side-stepped the question about his son and returned to the subject of Scott Fletcher. 'When he offered me that Honda, he actually thought I would buy the bike from him. Arrogant twat.'

Stalking back and forth in the doorway, Chris seemed almost to have forgotten Peddyr was there. He was exuding anger while telling his tale, and Peddyr was forced to inch closer, not to miss recording the finer points.

Seeing an opportunity while Chris had his back turned, he slipped his hand into his pocket and withdrew the phone, placing it carefully on the saddle of the Vincent Black Shadow without Chris noticing the move.

'I knew where he lived,' Chris went on, becoming louder and more animated. 'All I had to do was ask Ryan. Scott invited me to look at the Honda, which he said was in the garage block at the back of his flats.'

Chris stopped and pivoted around to glare at Peddyr. 'The bastard had two 125s. There was a tatty one he had robbed parts from to restore the one he was trying to flog to me.'

'And when was this?'

'The day before he was killed.'

Peddyr doubted this was accurate; he could sense that Chris Booth was lying, winging it, mixing part-truths with untruths. 'Were you wearing gloves? Only… I was under the impression that you had driven to Bosworth in that big old van of yours. I ask about gloves because none of your fingerprints were found on the Honda and I wouldn't buy a bike without giving it the once over. So, what happened?'

With each question, the atmosphere became thicker with tension and Peddyr had to plan his moves as if in a game of chess. For every action there would be a consequence. 'Let's start again shall we, Mr Booth? I would hazard a guess that you were at the garages to meet with Scott Fletcher on the fifth. Not in a van, but on your son's motorbike and wearing full bike gear. Over the phone Scott Fletcher taunted you and provoked you and you went to see him with every intention of putting an end to his scams. You went to the garage where Ryan said Fletcher would be, and there he was, sure enough. He was putting air in a bike's tyres. How did you kill him?'

A dark thunderous expression welled up into Chris Booth's eyes. This was the tipping point. The checkmate moment. 'Come on now, Mr Booth. The police know all this, otherwise how can I tell you these facts with such accuracy? This is a chance for you to get your story straight before they pick you up.' Peddyr forced himself to relax his shoulders. Would Chris Booth claim self-defence? Would he continue to deny any part in the killings? Or would he concede. There were excruciating seconds ticking by as the reply was ruminated over.

'Say what you like, I was on my way back to Wales when Scott Fletcher was killed. Anyway, he deserved it,' Chris said. Unexpectedly he made a deep throaty sound. 'Dexter did a good job on the bloke though. A fire extinguisher, throttling him with the air line, and finished him off by blasting his guts through his own arse. Compressed air, not to be underestimated.'

'And how would you know that?' Peddyr challenged, forcing himself not to look towards where his mobile phone lay, its battery life ebbing away. 'Details of how Scott Fletcher died have not been publicly disclosed. Are you telling me Dexter revealed this to you in a cosy father and son chat over a butter croissant and a cup of coffee? Come off it, Mr Booth, I know as well as you do that your son was at work at the time of the murder. There were dozens of witnesses. He can't have killed Scott Fletcher.'

The sand in the interrogation hourglass was running out, heralded by the arrival of a police car that rolled through the entrance gates and up the drive, blue lights flashing but thankfully no sirens on to alert Chris Booth to his fate before it was too late to escape.

'They can question me if they like. It's Dexter's word against mine,' Chris said.

'Is it?'

To his left Peddyr had become aware of Bernie Kershaw again, watching from the wings, ready to bundle in if he was needed. Fortunately things had remained unexpectedly calm; a relief all round, because for either of them it would have been a shame to ruin a good suit. Besides, Peddyr wasn't so sure Bernie had retained any level of fitness let alone an ability to put in a solid tackle if he was required to help, and the last thing he wanted was for Bernie to land on him and bugger up his other knee, so he herded Chris Booth outside, palming his mobile as he passed by the Vincent.

* * *

'I can't understand why he went so quietly,' Connie remarked as she poured the hot tea, passing a cup to a grateful Maggie Holden who was chatting in a comforting manner to her friend and companion. With Connie there to help in reassuring Flora that she'd done the right thing, the two elderly ladies soon regained their composure. 'You had no option,' Connie said. 'What you did was brilliant, Flora, and you delayed him for as long as you dared.'

'Oh, that wasn't deliberate,' she confessed. 'I couldn't

recall which secret place we had used to hide the documents in. We have several.'

'I can't understand any of it,' Ryan said as if talking to himself. 'He gave me a bloody cheque to pay for the bikes. Twenty grand seemed like a generous offer.'

'The cheque will bounce, and in any case they weren't yours to sell,' his grandmother reminded him. 'They will remain in the family without the need to sell them... ever.'

'But, Granny I thought it was what you wanted. I was trying to help.'

She threw him a stern look. 'Please credit me with some intelligence. You came here because you didn't have any keys to get into your mother's house and you knew I would provide free board and lodging.'

'And because your uncle used your love of money to get his hands on those motorcycles,' Flora chipped in.

The guilty look on Ryan's face didn't last long and neither did his attempts to win Maggie round with a sycophantic plea for sympathy; something Connie referred to as cupboard love, which she had resorted to as a child when she wanted a treat from her own grandmother.

'Don't give me your "Sorry, Granny, I do love you" nonsense,' Maggie snapped back. 'Your mother is in prison and yet you were more interested in making money than you were in what was happening to her. You arrived here uninvited and spent the whole time listening to your uncle's assertions that he was entitled to acquire your grandfather's pride and joy, as if they had no meaning to this family. And not once... not once did you ask me what I thought or whether I approved.' Incensed, Maggie was shaking with anger and setting the cups rattling in their saucers as she banged her fist on the table. 'You let him pressurise me and you allowed two old ladies to remain terrified for far longer than is recommended for people our age. Shame on you.'

Ignoring her grandson's protests, she asked Connie to find her handbag and they all fell quiet until she returned with it and handed it to Maggie. 'Here,' the elderly lady said, her face impassive. She handed Ryan a wad of notes. 'Take what I have in my purse. Book yourself into a B&B. You are no longer welcome in my home. Find yourself a job and somewhere to live. Come back to me when you've done so and not before. Your mother may fall for your nonsense, but I've had enough. She can deal with you when she's released.'

This shift in affections was so startling that Connie gasped, and gasped again when she caught sight of Flora giving a silent round of applause with a big smile on her face.

Ryan kicked out at the metal chair as he stood, before picking up his holdall and swearing under his breath as he marched out of the garden. The bad-tempered exit reminded Connie of Marshall when he was about thirteen years old; "Mr Sulkypants" had become her son's nickname for those early years of adolescence and for very good reason. The way Ryan had just behaved was not the attitude of an adult. Maggie had done the right thing.

'Where's he off to?' Peddyr asked as he and Bernie joined the ladies at the table.

'Checking the tail between his legs,' Connie replied with a wry smile. 'You two need a drink?'

Shaking his head, Bernie placed his hand on Maggie's shoulder and patted it. 'Actually, I have rather a lot of work to do,' he said. 'I must attend the blasted police station again and ensure that Dexter Booth is released without charge. And talking of charges – the ones against Sarah will be dropped, which will require me to chase up the authorities to facilitate her release. I shall send the very colourful Carol Brightman to collect her and bring her home.'

This perked up Maggie Holden no end. 'Oh, I do like Carol and she never let on to Ryan that she had a spare set of keys to Sarah's house. Good for her. Could you ask Carol to bring my daughter-in-law straight here, please? I have a spare room and Ryan won't be needing it.'

'I will indeed,' replied Bernie, looking very satisfied at the outcome of the afternoon's work, as was Connie. She had missed most of the tense interview her husband had held in the garage, but she and Flora had watched from the kitchen window as the police led Chris Booth to their vehicle in handcuffs. The debrief would happen later when she and Peddyr were alone. It always did.

'That won't take the rest of the day,' Peddyr announced. 'A swim and a pint in the Queens Ar... ms are called for later. Want to join me, Mr Kershaw? We could meet up with Connie and Monica for a celebratory drink and a well-deserved dinner this evening? Someone else can do the cooking for a change.'

Connie laughed at this remark. 'I second your proposal. You must be exhausted after hours slaving over a hot stove last night. I'll gladly take you up on your offer of dinner out.'

'You don't need to ask me twice,' Bernie replied. Time arranged, he excused himself, accepting grateful thanks from Maggie Holden for his unstinting and professional attention to the legal needs of her family. After waving him off, Peddyr took hold of Maggie's hand as if it were a tiny bird at risk of damage if he held it too firmly.

'We will tidy the garage, cover the bikes and lock everything up securely. The police will collect Chris's Transit van, so we'll leave that alone.' He paused briefly. 'And could I make a suggestion?'

'Please do, Mr Quirk.'

'When you and Sarah and Dexter finally get together to discuss house moves, have a serious think about loaning Jim's bike collection to a motor museum. That way you keep ownership, but enthusiasts have the chance to share them. To see them and smell them.'

In the emotion-laden stillness that followed, Maggie Holden began to cry, real tears this time. 'Oh, that is such a wonderful idea…'

## 38

## JUST KEEP SWIMMING

*P*eddyr led the way back into Maggie Holden's spacious garage. 'You can still smell the Castrol,' he said to Connie who had halted in the doorway at the sight of the two gleaming motorcycles.

'Oh, I can see what all the fuss was about now,' she said, full of wonder. 'They are truly beautiful machines. Why would anyone want to part with them?'

'For money, Lao Po. Simple as that.' He could no longer resist and, ignoring an inconvenient protest from his knee, he swung a leg over the saddle, letting out a satisfied sigh. 'One off the bucket list. Shame I can't take it for a spin,' he added. Reverently, he held the grips on the handlebars and looked at an imaginary road ahead. 'Help me out with something, if you would,' he asked. 'I can't fathom how Dexter has turned out so well when his father is an unfeeling manipulative bastard.'

Connie stood next to the Vincent Black Shadow openly admiring it, not pulling her husband up on his swearing. 'Get on,' Peddyr suggested. 'Go on, the stand is safe enough and you only weigh the same as one of Bernie's legs. Maggie won't mind.'

She did as he said, being extremely careful not to touch the paintwork. 'How fast does this go?'

'Top speed of 125 miles per hour. Not bad for a machine built in 1949. Anyway, stick to your specialist subject if you would. I asked about Dexter Booth. How come he turns out to be a top bloke and yet his father is riddled with envy, his mother is a miserable old cow and his sister as sour as lemons. How is that possible?'

With a smile, Connie answered him. 'Because when he was younger, while his father was zipping in and out of the country on business, Dexter spent as much time as possible with a man he deeply admired, a man who taught him how to look after engines, to service bikes and to appreciate their value and beauty. His Uncle Jim.' She smiled at Peddyr. 'I was wondering the same thing, so I asked Maggie about it.'

'That makes perfect sense,' he replied. 'A good job really, when you think what influence his own father could have had. Nurture wins out over nature.'

Young and easily brainwashed, after his father died Ryan Holden had spent a lot of time with Dexter and in doing so had looked to smooth-talking, man-about-town Chris Booth to set an example. He had picked the wrong man.

Peddyr's thoughts drifted back to Jim Holden's untimely death. 'I shall have to avoid mirrors for a day or two, Lao Po. I'm not sure I'm ready to look at myself.'

'What are you on about?' his wife asked, shaking her head at the odd statement.

'Guilt,' he replied. 'I'm riddled with it. I failed Jim because I didn't pursue what I knew to be right at the time and now I don't seem to be helping his wife either.' He sighed, looking across at Connie. 'Fifteen years ago I took the official reprimand and walked away when I should have insisted justice was done for Jim Holden.' At the time Peddyr knew that decision would haunt him for the rest of his life, but he didn't have the wherewithal to take on the establishment. 'Now, I'm furious with myself for labelling an innocent and honest man a killer when he's nothing of the sort. I'm losing all perspective on this case.'

The more he thought about the chain of recent events, the more certain he was there was another story behind Chris Booth's extreme actions and the man's unerring belief that he wouldn't be charged with killing Scott Fletcher. 'I'm stunned by how easily Chris Booth laid the blame at his son's feet. Despicable.'

Connie had fallen silent, allowing him a few minutes to share his feelings. She simply nodded her understanding. Deep in his gut, Peddyr could feel something was badly out of kilter when it came to Chris Booth but was having the devil's own job determining what it was.

'I hope Dexter is going to cope with all this,' Connie said. 'That young man has held the Holden family together and he's about to have a child of his own. You don't think Webster has gone in all guns blazing and upset that pretty wife of his, do you?' she asked, her voice full of concern.

It was the reminder Peddyr needed. 'Probably, but we can't do anything about that. Don't let it get to you. Now Chris is under caution, Dexter will be out of the police station and home again in no time. Bernie will see to that.' He motioned for her to dismount the Vincent. 'Covers on, secure doors, time to trot along to the cop shop and collect my phone. They should have taken what they need from it by now. If I have to give another bloody statement so be it, then it's time to clock off.'

Something was bothering Connie; he could tell by the way she moved rather more slowly than usual. 'What's up, Lao Po?'

'Shouldn't one of us see if Dexter's wife is alright?'

'Bernie was way ahead of you on that one. He's given Monica the job.'

* * *

*A*s it turned out, Peddyr and Connie were waylaid rather longer than anticipated at the police station, meaning that he had to resort to begging for the key to the lido from Ted Impey in order to indulge in a much-needed evening swim for him and Bernie. The old gentleman, on seeing the well-dressed pair standing on his doorstep, reluctantly relented with the same proviso as always. 'So long as if one of you drowns the other one pulls him out and resuscitates him. Do I make myself clear on that point, Peddyr?'

'You do indeed, Ted.'

'No drowning,' his wife added with her usual dry delivery and wrinkled brow.

Such generosity of spirit allowed Peddyr and Bernie to bathe in the cool waters and refresh their addled brains. It had been a long few days. They swam a dozen or so lengths of the pool, both lost in personal contemplation. Only when they sat at the side of the pool, towels wrapped around shoulders, making use of the last of the amber sunshine to warm them, did they speak.

'Don't beat yourself up too much, old bean,' Bernie said, swishing his feet in the water. 'Dexter made a vow to his aunt not to tell a soul where those motorcycles were being kept and what the arrangements were.'

Grateful for his concern, Peddyr rocked sideways to give a gentle shoulder barge. 'Thanks.'

'And it's not all bad. Chris Booth may have done the world a favour by ridding it of Scott Fletcher.' At this Peddyr eased the grip on his towel and it fell behind him onto the concrete slabs. Bernie had been privy to the details of Dexter's interview and thus had been at the police station to pick up the gossip about Chris Booth's arrest.

'Go on... what's the skeet?'

In her efforts to bring the detective sergeant on side, Monica had shared with Helen Forstall the theory about Scott Fletcher marrying women with his initials, and the DS went at it like a blacksmith with a hammer. 'CID's data base access is far superior to anything we could hope to get our hands on,' Bernie said. 'According to DS Forstall, Scott Fletcher is only his most recent incarnation. He had evaded the law for some years. Bigamy, fraud, broken hearts; they were his stock in trade under two previous guises.'

'So... Scott Fletcher was as bad as Chris Booth suspected,' Peddyr said, shaking droplets from his hair by rubbing his hand over his head several times. 'A case of "takes one to know one", I would say.' He glanced across at Bernie. 'I feel we've missed a few chapters somewhere. Any light to shed on why Dexter was forced into protecting his aunt from his own father? I mean, keeping things back from parents isn't unusual for anyone, but this wasn't an inconsequential secret.'

With a twist of his towel, Bernie Kershaw set about drying his ears. He made a thorough job of it, rubbing behind and within. 'For once in his illustrious career,' he began, 'Webster asked some pertinent questions during his interview of young Dexter. Your inside informer – DS

Helen Forstall – had some incredibly useful knowledge of Christopher Booth.'

'In the biblical sense?' Watching in fascination as his friend completed his ear ritual, Peddyr waited for a reply.

'Not her. Her sister. DS Forstall couldn't take part in the interview because of a conflict of interest but she had primed dear old Duncan Webster. He readily painted a picture of a man who freely indulged in extra-marital affairs and who in recent years squandered his money at casinos where he entertained said women. Including, one can only assume, Helen Forstall's sister.'

'That's what you get for shitting on your own doorstep,' Peddyr declared. 'The man has a serious lack of morals. Can't believe he and Jim were friends for so long.' He fell silent for a while, mesmerised by the sunlight as it played on the surface of the pool. 'Was Booth still in the import-export business before he trotted off to Wales?'

'I believe so. How did you know that?'

It had been a long time since Peddyr had talked about the police inquiry into Jim Holden's death and the feelings of frustration it had ignited in him. 'Chris Booth was included in the original investigation into Jim Holden's death. There were rumours about Jim wanting to distance himself from anything involving his brother-in-law, as far as business dealings went. Chris used to deal in machinery parts, shipping stuff in from Europe and China. Booth Imports was the name of the company and it had been set up with a helping hand from...'

'Jim Holden,' Bernie said, shaking his head slowly. 'A generous gesture he would come to regret, I take it.'

Bernie had assumed rightly. Chris Booth had crossed over some legal lines, ones that could have compromised Jim's career. Evasion of import duty, irregularities in paperwork were found, and formal proceedings put in motion to prosecute Chris and Hilary as company directors.

'Jim Holden was the one who instigated the investigation. He had no choice when it was brought to his attention by a friend in Customs and Excise,' Peddyr explained. 'When Jim died, Chris was considered as a possible suspect but discounted straight away. He was in hospital with suspected appendicitis and had been there for a whole day before Jim's death.'

There was no evidence to say that Chris had been tipped off about his brother-in-law's part in the subsequent prosecution, which became a moot point anyway when Jim died in what appeared to be a tragic road accident. 'Booth Imports paid the fines and reinvented themselves with a new name and carried on trading, apparently squeaky clean for the next fifteen years.'

'And they never found the hit-and-run driver who killed James Holden?'

'Never, but it wasn't Chris Booth. I've seen a copy of the hospital records.' Regret stirred in Peddyr's chest once more. 'It's a case I never solved. I can't tell you how that rankles.'

When it came to the killing of Scott Fletcher, Peddyr berated himself for not taking note of Chris Booth in more depth during the preliminary investigation. With the best of intentions, P. Q. Investigations had rushed in an attempt to free Sarah Holden, and in doing so had missed out on vital information-gathering and background checks. Poor standards, poor planning, poor execution. No wonder he had leapt to the wrong conclusion about Dexter Booth. When he had time to reflect on the type of man Chris Booth had become, he saw that Scott Fletcher was straight out of the same mould. Both were manipulative, both charming, the sort of men mud doesn't stick to.

The self-recriminations only added to his gloomy mood as did his undignified efforts to stand up. His painful knee was not cooperating, forcing him to roll in an ungainly fashion before struggling onto all fours and standing slowly as he retrieved his towel.

'You could join a circus as a performing seal,' Bernie commented, grinning.

'Go on then. You show me how it's done, O blubbery one,' Peddyr replied, folding his arms. Bernie's efforts were to be commended but as he lay on his back, belly-laughing and unable to move, he conceded graciously.

'The seal wins. The beached whale didn't stand a chance. Give me your hand and pull, you bugger.'

## 39

# CLARET

*T*he restaurant at the Queen's Arms was a rustic affair with wooden beams and a red Axminster carpet. It had looked the same for years. Monica was on her second glass of wine by the time the two damp but much enlivened men arrived. Connie rarely drank alcohol, claiming that it killed off too many brain cells, although on this occasion she had treated herself to a Rock Shandy, which contained a dash of angostura bitters.

'Enough alcohol to make me feel like a rebel,' she said with an impish grin.

'Cheers, ladies,' Peddyr said, raising his pint in their honour. 'Been here before, Grasshopper?'

'Once or twice, many moons ago... a pub crawl on both occasions. Never eaten here, although it might have been a sensible idea given the state I was in on those particular nights.' Peddyr remained amazed at how he had missed the obvious compatibility between Monica and Bernie, but then again he hadn't considered it. Dreary Kershaw had always been a barrier to Bernie's enjoyment of life until now, and her husband's compliance with their marriage vows had ensured his loveless captivity in her world of twin-sets and pearls, golf club lunches, and drinkie-poos with the "Phwa-Phwas". Monica would set him free – if only Bernie would let her.

'We usually avoid being in here too late on a Saturday. It can get a little boisterous. You're in for a treat though,' Connie chirruped, smiling across at Monica. 'The steaks they serve are legendary for their size and tenderness.'

'Just like old Jug Ears here,' Peddyr added with a nod to Bernie who had arrived at his shoulder in time to hear the backhanded compliment.

'All the better to hear you with and to take note of hurtful comments,' came the reply, tinged with amusement. With a tuneful groan, he lowered himself into a chair next to Connie. 'You may now officially recommence decorating bedrooms in time for Christmas, Mrs Q. Once again I am most grateful for your brains and application of same.' He raised his glass to hers with a clink. 'And to Monica, I would like to say a special thank you for sterling work, for battering a consultant psychiatrist into submission – metaphorically speaking, you understand – and for providing much-needed mental health expertise. And, most importantly, for putting up with Peddyr's childish behaviour.'

'She started it,' Peddyr put in quickly.

'I rest my case. Now where is the menu?'

The events of the day were discussed in hushed tones so as not to be overheard. Try as he might, Peddyr could not shake off a sense of dissatisfaction at the outcome of their investigation. He was still deeply ashamed of the way he had attributed two murders to someone who was not only innocent, but one of life's good blokes. 'Pleased to hear that

Dexter was returned to his wife unharmed,' he said, resting his knife against the side of his plate in order to take a slurp of beer.

'Only because that cream-faced loon Webster was confronted by the recorded lies from the lad's father as well as evidence from Dexter's workplace. Without your quick thinking, Dexter Booth would be talking to the walls of a cell right now,' Bernie replied.

'The man really is an ar… ticle.' Somehow Peddyr had swerved swearing at the dinner table and was duly rewarded with a grateful smile from Connie, which quickly faded as normal service was resumed. 'What a bloody mess though,' he continued, to laughter from Monica who quite clearly appreciated the fact that he couldn't possibly be expected to reduce his use of Angle-Saxon to zero. 'Sarah Holden's life has gone right down the khazi because of Webster's inability to see the wood for the trees – because of her own brother, because of Scott friggin' Fletcher, and because her selfish son will probably never forgive her for the indignity of being carted off to the nuthouse. She won't be able to show her face in Bosworth again.'

'Succinctly put, Pedd old man.'

'Not as succinctly as Chris Booth snuffed out Kenny Eversholt's perverted life.' Peddyr raised his glass again. 'To Kenny: a bad driver, a nonce, a weirdo, but a human being with a heart somewhere.'

'And then there's Dexter.' Connie was joining in the post-mortem and the repercussions of recent events for those involved. 'He now has a murderer for a father as well as a miserable mother.'

'In compensation, he does have a pretty and very loving wife,' Monica said. 'He's incredibly resilient, considering. All thanks to Jim Holden according to Tessa. We should make a toast to him as well.' This idea was received with a round of applause and suitable words once more from Peddyr who also declared Maggie Holden to be one of the savviest octogenarians he'd ever met. 'Cheers to them all.'

After this, the evening passed by in general good humour and joshing, somehow compensating for the unpleasant interruption of their meal the night before. By the time dessert arrived the conversation had reverted to the mundane. 'I had a bit of trouble with a dry amaryllis today,' Connie announced during a brief respite in the chatter at the table.

'Must be your age.' This comment earned Peddyr a firm whack on the bicep and an admonishment from Monica who did the honours because Connie couldn't stretch her arm that far. There was no apology. None was required.

Replete, Peddyr was soon ready to go home, and he shared the bill with Bernie.

Coats on, they made their way to leave through the bar and strolled directly into the path of a kerfuffle. Stuart "Gibbo" Gibbs, the landlord of the Queen's Arms, was herding a couple of vocal young men towards the exit. They were protesting with some extremely fruity language.

'Barred from one, barred from all,' Gibbo told the rowdy pair. 'I don't want to see you back in here again, ever. Do I make myself clear?'

Mid-rant, Peddyr was recognised. 'Oi, Peter. I want a fucking word with you.' It was Ryan Holden who unsurprisingly was with an inebriated and swaying Bez, holding him roughly by one shirtsleeve to prevent himself from toppling onto a table full of tightly clad women. 'Where are my keys? I don't see why I should have to kip on his stinking filthy floor when there's a decent house at my disposal. Return them right now.'

Through glazed and unfocussed eyes, Bez slowly recognised Peddyr but couldn't say the word "solicitor", giving up after a couple of attempts. 'Go around in a pack, do you?' Ryan asked, spying Monica from over Peddyr's shoulder. 'What sort of security consultant needs his mates to back him up?'

With a swift nod from the landlord, Peddyr demonstrated what sort of security he could advise on and the rest of the conversation was held outside on the pavement where Ryan ended up splayed face down. When things took a turn for the physical, Bez had wobbled his way after them with a helpful shove from Gibbo and he staggered towards Peddyr shortly after Ryan's nose began bleeding profusely. 'Best get up and go home, like,' Bez slurred to Ryan, holding his friend's shoulder to prevent a fall. It certainly wasn't out of sympathy. ''E's not used to alcohol, Mr Quirk. Can't hold it, like. 'E only 'ad one or two.'

'No need to apologise for him, Bez. He's old enough to account for his own actions.' Peddyr stood over Ryan who had managed to sit himself up and was pinching his nostrils in an attempt to staunch the flow of blood. 'There you go, sunshine. That's how you break someone's nose. Now, if you want your keys, you must contact the offices of Bagshot & Laker on Monday morning, assuming you have sobered up by then,' Peddyr announced, dusting his palms. 'Meantime, if I were you, I'd be nice to Bez. He's pretty much the only friend you have left, and beggars can't be choosers. Oh, and my name is Peddyr, not Peter. Pedd-er.'

A black saloon car drew up to the kerb, braking harshly. The driver then lowered his window to its fullest extent. 'Inspector Webster,' Peddyr said, rubbing absentmindedly at his right wrist. 'At least you had the decency not to gatecrash another dinner party. What are you doing here?'

Duncan Webster poked a finger at the pavement. 'Looking for him,' he barked, nodding at Ryan. 'Spilled claret by accident, did he? Or is this your doing?'

Peddyr shrugged. 'Couldn't possibly say, on the grounds that I may incriminate myself.'

Webster merely sneered at him, distracted by the sight of Ryan who was getting to his feet, blood making its way from both nostrils onto the front of his shirt in steady drips. 'Ryan Holden, I'm arresting you on suspicion of conspiracy to murder. We have reason to believe you assisted, aided and abetted the perpetrator in the killing of Scott Fletcher. The number and content of the calls on your mobile phone have provided indisputable evidence. Get in.' Stepping from the car, Webster continued giving the official caution to Ryan while placing him in handcuffs.

'What excellent timing, Ryan was looking for somewhere clean to spend the night,' Peddyr said, turning at the sound of footsteps behind him. It was his wife with Bernie and Monica. 'Oh, and I suggest you make use of the duty solicitor, Mr Kershaw is retiring from criminal law permanently.' The last words of the sentence were aimed at Ryan's back as it disappeared inside Webster's vehicle. 'And no need to thank us, Inspector Webster. You take all the credit and give P. Q. Investigations a shout when you need to solve your next murder.'

Connie was at his shoulder, sliding her dainty hand into his. When he squeezed it he winced with the pain such a simple action induced. 'I wouldn't want Sarah Holden to hear this, but if I'm honest, Lao Po, I've been itching to plant a fist in that little bastinado's face ever since I first met him. It's not professional to say so, it's not right what I did, but by crikey, I enjoyed every second of my little tête-à-tête with Ryan Holden just now.'

'I'm off,' Bernie said. 'I'm tired, full to the brim, and I wish to avoid consorting with the likes of you. Peddyr Quirk, you're nothing but a common scrapper. Behaving in such a way, you'll do my reputation no good whatsoever. Come along, Monica, I shall see you to a taxi and away from the lawless rabble.'

'Suit yourself. Personally, I love a bit of rough,' Connie replied, much to Peddyr's astonishment. 'I'm taking him straight to bed.' Even over the sound of passing traffic, the street resounded with Bernie's deep throaty laughter and a series of goodbyes from him and from Monica as he led her to the taxi rank.

'See you for a swim on Monday. Must dash, sounds like I'm on a promise,' Peddyr shouted out to him, striding towards home before Connie changed her mind.

As they walked along the busy pavement she rubbed at his arm. 'You don't think you're getting a wee bit old for brawling in the streets?'

He smiled down at her. 'Because you are usually right about such things, I am willing to accept that my boxing days are over for now, but only because my hand hurts like hell and my wrist is aching.' With a short laugh he added, 'At least I forgot about my gammy knee for a while, but as for the occasional bit of argy-bargy... I can't say that it won't happen again, if the need arises.'

'Whatever would the grandchildren think?' Connie replied with a chuckle.

'Grandchild,' he corrected her, but as she skipped along, bouncing beside him like a thing possessed, he had an inkling he was in for a surprise and the reason for her recent late-night excitability came spilling out at top speed.

'Next year is going to be something else, what with Aleyn and Joe getting married, and you'll never guess what?

They want to come for a visit soon, which is good because I can have a natter with Joe about arrangements for their big day… but better than that, Marshall and Hannah called earlier. I didn't want to tell you until we were alone.'

'Then spit it out, for God's sake, woman.'

'Another Quirk is being hatched, which is why you must stop fighting and swearing so much because as grandparents we must set a good example, don't you think?' Her exuberance was a delight to behold and he stopped walking to accept the tight hug she demanded.

'That's mighty news, Lao Po,' he said, sweeping her up until her legs dangled freely. 'Now, take me home at once. We must celebrate'

## 40

## PENDINE

*I*t was seven o'clock when Connie knocked on his office door and entered with a mug of coffee. 'You'll need this. What time did you get out of bed? You weren't there an hour ago, I know that much, Lao Gong. You do know it's Sunday today, right?'

Waking in the early hours, Peddyr hadn't been able to settle. Finally giving in, he escaped to his office and began a trip down Memory Lane. Not one with sunshine and laughter lining the route, but one filled with unanswered questions and frustration at every turn. As far as he could see, his most recent dealings with the Holden family had resulted in nothing short of an unhappy ending. Punching Ryan had only worsened his feelings of inadequacy, not assuaged them. Not in the slightest.

It was true enough that Sarah Holden would be released from prison and she would gain her freedom, which was the goal in the first place. He had taken up the challenge in order to make amends in some way for police failures fifteen years previously. With the knowledge that Sarah's considerable assets had been protected and the real culprit had been arrested, he knew he should feel a level of satisfaction, but he didn't.

The weight of disappointment he'd felt at the outcome had played on his subconscious mind. During the few hours of restless sleep he managed that night, he was haunted by visions of Jim Holden: the smiling family man, the determined honest officer, the crumpled victim of a callous hit and run. These video vignettes flashed by repeated on a loop until Peddyr awoke. 'Why did Chris Booth accept his arrest so calmly?' he said to a picture on the wall. Morse looked back at him but had nothing to add.

'There are no forensics to place him at either murder scene, unless they find the boots or the rest of the motor-biking gear. Does he really believe he can get away with murder?' At the time it was made, Chris Booth was unaware of the recording on Peddyr's phone. He would not have witnessed this being passed to the uniformed officer who had attended Maggie Holden's property. That recording could help see him convicted of two unlawful killings, but without it he had seemed rock solid convinced he would not be found guilty.

Determined to address this strange over-confidence in Chris Booth's attitude to arrest, Peddyr went to his filing cabinet and pulled out a set of three dog-eared folders. Records and statements that he shouldn't have copies of. 'Right. We start again.'

If he was to look Sarah Holden in the eye, he must give her answers. And he must even apologise to Ryan whom he was now certain had been used by Chris Booth in the same way Sarah had been.

Peddyr had asked himself an important question the day before: why had Chris and Jim remained friends? One answer was obvious; they were linked by marriage. Secondly, they were linked by their common love of motorbikes, and the younger Jim had taken to the lovable rogue Chris Booth who was fun to be with and confident around girls. Thirdly, Jim had business links to Chris and Hilary Booth's fledgling import–export business, Booth Imports. A business that, according to Connie, had been dissolved after the death of Jim Holden and been resurrected as CDB Imports.

'I'm going to Pendine,' Peddyr said to Connie as she placed the mug on a coaster beside him.

'Of course you are, Lao Gong,' she replied. 'Breakfast and a shower first. I'll find the contact details through Dexter and set up a visit, shall I?'

The pros and cons were rapidly computed. 'Yes... And could you ask him not to tell his mother anything about me? Just say to Hilary an investigator is being dispatched to take a statement from her about her husband. Nothing else. I need to be sure she'll be at home when I get there. Then I want you to do something else for me.' He glanced down at the files on his desk. 'Go through this lot and see whether all the commercial vehicle repair businesses in the area were accounted for when the investigation into Jim's hit and run was carried out. Check Hilary Booth's employment record. She can't have spent her life as a company director and I need to understand that woman better. Also I've written out some questions I'd like to ask Dexter. Can you handle that while I ride to Pendine? I'll phone you when I get there.'

'Hypothesis?'

'I have one...' He held on tightly to Connie's hand. 'The trouble is proving it, and in the end it won't make Sarah Holden's pain any less.'

'But it will give her the closure she's never had,' Connie replied, rubbing Peddyr's back with her free hand. When he was tortured by self-doubt she was there to smooth it out and make sense of it. 'It's time to put an end to this,' she said emphatically. 'It's eating you up and that's not fair on anyone who loves you.'

This last statement shocked him. 'What do you mean?'

Gathering up the folders and placing the list of questions for Dexter on top of them, Connie considered him as she replied. 'I know you've been avoiding mirrors, but honestly, you look like an aged Bruce Willis who's died too hard again. Stubble on your face, bruised and swollen knuckles, not to mention the furrow on your brow that's taken up permanent residence ever since we took on this case. I want my husband back, please. The funny one, not the one who has been putting on a brave face.'

Stunned, he stared back into her gentle eyes, fighting down unexpected emotions that threatened to put in an appearance. He didn't know how to respond other than to make her a solemn pledge. 'Today, I will finish this,' he croaked. 'Now do your thing in the kitchen and make me the best cheese omelette you can manage.'

\* \* \*

The fastest route wasn't the most scenic, so Peddyr opted for cutting across to the A40 through to Ross-on-Wye then on to West Wales from there. His wrist was of concern, dictating which bike he chose for the journey. Comfort and reliability over speed was the order of the day, thus his tourer was back in action and the weather was so far playing ball with only a light drizzle greeting him as he headed onto the A477. Once in Pendine he followed signs to the car park for the Museum of Speed. It was under threat of closure, or replacement with something more modern, and he didn't want to miss staring through the window while he had the chance. Besides which there were public toilets nearby and beyond was the slipway to the infamous Pendine Sands, the setting of land speed records since the 1920s.

He grabbed an unhealthy sausage roll and a refreshing cup of tea from a small kiosk and sat outside, breathing in the sea air, taking time out to phone Connie. 'I'm here, I'm in one piece, and yes, I got drizzled on, but the big old fat rain is holding off.' She was bound to ask him these things, so he saved her the trouble. 'Any luck with Dexter?'

Hand Connie a list and nothing gave her greater pleasure than working through it to provide answers. 'Question two: the answer was yes, before he and Celia were born and then at reduced hours until they started at school. Therefore the answer to question one is also yes. She was working there before and after Jim was killed. Question three: Dexter visited his dad in hospital. He recalls the hospital and the name of the ward. It checks out. The dates are on the letter from the hospital to the GP but do not tally with the hospital's own database. They're twenty-four hours out.' At this there was a short intermission while she allowed the magnitude of this discovery to sink in.

'How the hell was that overlooked?' Peddyr exhaled. 'One whole bloody day. A howling omission.'

Increasing her speed of delivery, his wife continued with her findings. 'I've put everything in an email to you. Read it in full before you go anywhere near Hilary Booth. Forewarned is forearmed, Lao Gong. The answer to question four is, Sarah Holden. I know where you are going with these, Pedd, and I think you may have cracked it. Regarding the vehicle and local garages, these were all accounted for.'

'Bugger, I could really do wi—'

'I haven't finished. Be quiet and keep your investigator's ears wide open.' Connie was brusque, meaning something else of importance had come to light. At such times Peddyr had learnt to hold his tongue and pay close attention. He slipped a hand into an inside pocket of his jacket to remove his ever-present notebook and pen, an old habit. A good habit.

'Go ahead,' he instructed.

'At the time of Jim's death there were three one-man-bands doing repairs out of barns on farms or at home addresses. I've made myself very unpopular by phoning on a Sunday, but I had a hot favourite. Jason Reid runs the Ford dealership in Bosworth. Fifteen years ago he supplemented his junior salesman's income by helping his father carrying out repairs and resprays. He was easier to locate than his father. It was a stroke of luck.'

Making a note of the address where Jason Reid's father had run his business from, Peddyr found it hard to stay on top of rising anticipation.

'Where is the connection?' he tapped the pad with the pen.

'Mr Reid Senior is still very much alive and kicking. He is also an obsessive when it comes to record keeping. It took two hours, but Jason has just come back to me. With the date and description I gave, he identified a possible, which then became a definite. The VIN is a match for one of the Booth Imports vans. Dented wing, total respray. Urgent job. A whole week before the police came a-calling at Booth Imports.' There was silence from both of them for several seconds. 'Pedd, I think it's time you interviewed Hilary.'

It was unlikely that what he had to say to Hilary Booth would improve her disposition, but it would explain why her life was empty of joy. It also explained why she had stayed with Chris for so many years, infidelity notwithstanding. She couldn't leave. Evidently he needed her to manage the finances because he couldn't be trusted, but this wouldn't prevent her from walking out on an unfaithful husband. No, something altogether darker tethered her in place.

## 41

## THE ALIBI

*M*rs Hilary Booth?' Peddyr asked, standing on the doorstep of a park home which turned out to be some miles away from Pendine. It was nearer to Saundersfoot. However, he could live with the inconvenience, the additional ride had allowed him some time to refocus.

As the door opened, he was regarded with disdain by the puffy eyes of Hilary Booth. Short of the posh frock and wide-brimmed hat, she looked much as she had in the photograph Peddyr had seen at Dexter's house. Verging on emaciated, a little too much makeup, manicured, severe: she wasn't his idea of an attractive woman.

'You'd better come in. The neighbours are nosy. I understand you have come to take a statement about Christopher.' She stood back from the doorway allowing him to enter and pointed the way through the kitchen and into a beige lounge. Once again the white crash helmet, black biker attire and high-vis stripes had led to an assumption that Peddyr was a police officer. The notebook he produced only served to back this up.

Hilary Booth was as contained as the place in which she lived. She gave nothing away, either in what she said or the way she said it. Devoid of emotion, she bade him sit, scowling as he took time to remove his jacket and place his helmet on the carpet beside the armchair he was instructed to make use of. 'You'll want to know what time my husband arrived home from Bosworth Bishops on the fifth of September.'

She was straight to the point and eager to complete the task. However, Peddyr wasn't so easily manoeuvred. His approach was far more subtle.

'Thank you for seeing me at such short notice, Mrs Booth. It must have come as a shock to hear about the arrest of your son and subsequently that of your husband.' There was no indication Hilary Booth felt anything; she was the coldest fish Peddyr had come across since removing a rainbow trout from the freezer the previous month.

Humouring him, she made a show of raising her hands to her mouth. 'Quite staggering,' she said. The prepared speech that followed was as unconvincing as she was. She trotted out dates and times, swearing that these were correct. 'He was back here by one o'clock. Perhaps a few minutes before.'

'Very helpful, Mrs Booth. I'm sure these will tally nicely with the numberplate recognition on the toll bridge.' This had been anticipated and Hilary was quick to tell Peddyr that her husband preferred to make use of the A40 route.

'The van isn't the fastest vehicle,' she went on. 'Chris can get from here to Bosworth in a little over three hours.' Predictably there were no witnesses to his return. 'He parks the van at the garage workshop where he has a part-time job and walks from there. One of the mechanics might have seen him, but I doubt it.'

'And what do you do with yourself these days, Mrs Booth? It must be a slower pace of life since you both retired. I'm told you used to be a first-class administrator. You worked at Holberry General on the main reception, I hear.' What he really wanted to do was to interrogate the woman in the way he had done her husband, but she wasn't so easy to read. 'I took the time to check your reliability as a witness. Many a case has unravelled because of an invalid witness statement.'

Perched rigid on the upholstered settee, Hilary Booth had her hands gripped tightly in her lap, scatter cushions strategically placed behind her. She barely moved. 'If it's any help, I'm not an alcoholic, I have no mental health problems, I'm compos mentis and have an excellent memory. My integrity is not in question.'

Hilary Booth had just gifted Peddyr the way to undermine her steel-plated façade. 'Oh, but I'm afraid it is, Mrs Booth. You see, giving a false alibi on behalf of your husband is something you've done before.'

There was no reply from Hilary Booth. Her cold stare remained in place as Peddyr continued.

'When your brother-in-law James Holden was killed, you assured police that your husband was in hospital at the time. Your family GP provided written proof.'

'That's correct.'

Consulting his notebook, Peddyr read out the date that Christopher Booth had been admitted for acute abdominal pain to the general hospital. He was kept in for observation and discharged two days later. 'These are the dates and details you gave.' He waited for an answer which came in the form of a curt nod.

'But you omitted to tell police one important fact. Not only did you work on reception at that hospital, but you also provided administrative assistance as far as admissions and discharges went, including sending out letters to GP practices confirming details of their patients' hospital stay. It wouldn't take much to change the letter about your own husband's treatment there. What was it, a fictional case of appendicitis or suspected gallstones?'

Swallowing hard, Hilary Booth lowered her gaze, and remained determinedly mute.

'On the day when you say your husband was in hospital, he was actually on the road, in his van. Your husband and Jim Holden reportedly had a serious falling out, but Jim agreed to meet Chris to discuss this. Why? Well, I'm guessing here... perhaps it was to find a diplomatic way forward without a permanent rift occurring in the family. Jim Holden lied to his wife Sarah, telling her he was going to a meeting of senior officers when in fact he was meeting her brother, your husband Chris.' Peddyr waited for a response. When eventually a hollow shrug was forthcoming, he went on.

'The report into Jim's death said he was parked up on his motorbike when a van drove at him from behind. The glancing blow sent him sprawling into a brick wall, damaged the bike beyond repair and killed him because, as he was parked up, he wasn't wearing his helmet. So the question is, why was he stationary in that particular one-way street if he was on his way to an important meeting at police headquarters? It makes no sense unless that was where he had arranged to meet Chris...'

No skid marks, no stopping, Jim had no chance against the vehicle that struck him.

The unresponsive Hilary remained impassive.

'Were you there at the time, Mrs Booth? In the van with your husband. Or were you the woman who took the damaged company vehicle for repair by a certain Mr Frank Reid at White Horse Farm the following day?'

The reaction when it came was swift. One moment Hilary Booth was starchy and statue-like, the next she dissolved. Her head lolled onto her chest and she sank into the wing of the settee, bringing her knees up and tucking her feet beneath her like a child, holding a scatter cushion to her face to hide it from view.

'It's all over, Mrs Booth,' Peddyr said. 'It's time to tell the truth and face the consequences, for the sake of yourself, your children and your first grandchild. What you did was wrong, and you've paid for your poor judgement ever since. Your crime has held you captive in an unhappy marriage. It has been used to manipulate you and ensure your silence.' His eyes bored into her. 'Don't compound your crime with another one. Be as honest as your son. He's a credit to you. Be a credit to him.'

It was several long minutes before Hilary unfolded. Dark smudges of mascara gave her gaunt features a haunted look and gone was the harsh exterior of an emotionless woman. Her vulnerability was painfully exposed. 'I was in the van,' she admitted, sobs wracking her body, catching in her chest. 'I didn't know he was going to do it. I'm not even sure if he planned it or whether he saw Jim and suddenly saw red. Chris said he did it to protect us, to save the business from bankruptcy, and that if I ever let on what he had done then I would never see the children again because we would both go to prison. And because I was the one who took the van for repair, I knew I was implicated.

'Chris made up a story about stomach pains and rail-roaded me into changing the hospital treatment dates in the letter to Dr Prasad. I can't explain how controlling he can be.' Unable to regain her composure momentarily, Hilary hugged herself for a minute until she could finish what she had to say. 'I wanted to go to the police so many times... I made Sarah dislike me, so I didn't have to be around her. I can't bear to look at her. I can't bear to look at myself and I hate my own husband.'

Eyeing her from across the functional room, Peddyr could appreciate her self-loathing. He'd had a taste of that himself. 'Your husband told Dexter and Tessa that you had thrown him out, which is why he arrived on their doorstep the day before yesterday. I take it that's not correct.'

Hilary grabbed at a box of tissues and pulled several free with which to wipe her nose. 'He said he was worried about how Dexter was coping with all the trauma of Sarah being arrested. I assumed he was off chasing another woman again and needed an excuse. He left here at about lunchtime on Friday and I didn't speak to him after that until he rang from the police station.' She dabbed under her eyes with a fresh tissue and glanced at Peddyr. 'If only I did have the guts to throw him out.' Her words reverberated around Peddyr's head; Chris Booth had given himself plenty of time in which to kill Kenny Eversholt, once again using Dexter's motorbike.

Peddyr accepted that, on the face of it, Hilary Booth had been exploited by her husband. He stood up and reached out his hand to her. 'My name is Peddyr Quirk, an old colleague of Jim Holden's. How about we go to the nearest police station and make a statement?'

*H*ours later, Peddyr returned to where he had parked the bike. He called Connie. When he said he would book into a hotel for the night, the relief in her voice was plain for him to hear. 'I'm knackered but satisfied,' he admitted. Happy wasn't the right word to use, although he most definitely felt brighter since leaving Hilary, who was now under investigation. Chris Booth was in for a further set of charges relating to a total of three deaths, all murders, which made him a serial killer. Quite a count. The outcome of the whole fraught last few days was that Jim Holden could now rest in peace, safe in the knowledge that Sarah was protected from her own brother's murderous scheming.

The importance of having a loving and honest family had featured heavily over the past week, something that hadn't escaped Peddyr's notice. 'Can you invite Chip and Joe over for Sunday lunch next weekend, if they can make it?' he requested of Connie. 'I have an apology to make and some bridges to build before they stay at Christmas. Just one more thing, Lao Po...' Astride the bike, phone wedged to one ear, he began to sing as passers-by stared on in disbelief: *"Hong Kong, darling... oh, oh... oh, oh, oh, oh!"*

# AFTERWORD

In 2014 a rare 1929 Brough Superior SS100 was sold at auction for £315,000.

https://www.bbc.co.uk/news/uk-england-nottinghamshire-30195048

## ABOUT THE AUTHOR

Alison Morgan lives in rural Bedfordshire UK with her engineer husband and bonkers dog. She spent several decades working on the front line of NHS Mental Health Services and latterly as a specialist nurse and clinical manager for a dedicated psychosis service across her home county. However, when a heart problem brought her career to a juddering halt, Alison needed to find a way of managing her own sanity. She took up writing. Her intention was to produce a set of clinical guidelines for student nurses but instead a story that had been lurking in her mind for some years came spewing forth onto the pages of what became her first novel.

Since then she has become an established crime writer, unable to stem the flow of ideas. From a writing shack at the top of her garden she creates stories with memorable characters, always with a sprinkling of humour, often drawing on years of experience in the world of psychiatry where the truth can be much stranger than fiction. To find out more about Alison please check her website **www. abmorgan.co.uk**.

# ACKNOWLEDGMENTS

My thanks heartfelt thanks go to all the team at Hobeck Books, including my fellow authors, for their support: the bloggers, reviewers and dedicated subscribers. Special thanks also go to Jayne Mapp for the cover design which happened like magic, and to Lynn the miracle editor who shaped this story by filing the rough edges and guiding me sensibly but firmly toward my goal.

My unerring gratitude also goes to Rebecca and Adrian, who *are* Hobeck Books, for their cheerful encouragement and positivity. Thanks for giving life to the Quirks!

# THE QUIRK FILES BY A B MORGAN

## OLD DOGS, OLD TRICKS

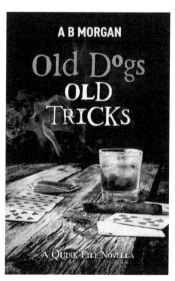

David Corcoran is dead. Did he die of natural causes, or was he murdered? His daughter seems to think there is more to his sudden death at the sleepy Blackthorne Lakes Retirement Village than a case of another day, another resident meets their maker. Enter Peddyr and Connie Quirk, newly formed PI husband-and-wife team, to 'act' as residents to see if they can sniff out the truth. Can they pull it off? Will Connie convince the Blackthorne golfing set that she's a real resident? Is there more to this story than simply old man dies happy?

To download your free copy of the prequel to the Quirk Files series, please go to the Hobeck Books website **www. hobeck.net**.

OVER HER DEAD BODY

**A B MORGAN**

# OVER HER DEAD BODY

THE QUIRK FILES BOOK ONE

CAN GABBY'S
DEATH CHANGE
HER LIFE?

**Gabby Dixon is dead. That's news to her...**
Recently divorced and bereaved, Gabby Dixon is trying to start a new chapter in her life.

**As her new life begins, it ends. On paper at least.**
But Gabby is still very much alive. As a woman who likes to be in control, this situation is deeply unsettling.

**She has two crucial questions: who would want her dead, and why?**
Enter Peddyr and Connie Quirk. husband-and-wife private investigators. Gabby needs their help to find out who is behind her sudden death.

**The truth is a lot more sinister than a simple case of stolen identity.**

*Over Her Dead Body* **is a 'what if' tale full of brilliantly drawn characters, quirky humour and dark plot twists**

PRAISE FOR OVER HER DEAD BODY

'OMG WHAT A PAGE TURNER!! … I finally turned the last page at 2am.' Peggy

'This really is one of the best books I have ever read!' Pat

'A clever, clever read.' Livia

'A hope there are plans for this to be a series.' Dee

'…brilliant. Totally different to anything I've read before.' Donna

'…full of charm, mystery, humour and great characters.' Linda

'A wonderful page tuner that captivated me right from the start. A treasure to read.' Misfits Farm

'excellent.' Billy

'A compelling read.' Kes

'Just couldn't put it down.' Lynn

'Couldn't put this down.' Janet

Available to purchase from Amazon.

ALSO BY A B MORGAN

*A Justifiable Madness*
*Divine Poison*
*The Camera Lies*
*Stench*
*Death by Indulgence*
*The Bloodline Will*

# HOBECK BOOKS – THE HOME OF GREAT STORIES

We hope you've enjoyed reading this novel by the brilliant Alison Morgan. To find out more about Alison and her work please visit her website: **www.abmorgan.co.uk**.

Please visit the Hobeck Books website for details of our other superb authors and their books, and if you would like to get in touch, we would love to hear from you.

Hobeck Books also presents a weekly podcast, the Hobcast, where founders Adrian Hobart and Rebecca Collins discuss all things book related, key issues from each week, including the ups and downs of running a creative business. Each episode includes an interview with one of the people who make Hobeck possible: the editors, the authors, the cover designers. These are the people who help Hobeck bring great stories to life. Without them, Hobeck wouldn't exist. The Hobcast can be listened to from all the usual platforms but it can also be found on the Hobeck website: **www.hobeck.net/hobcast**. Listen to Episode One to hear A B Morgan discuss her life as a writer, this book and her leap into the world of narration.

Finally, if you enjoyed this book, please also leave a review on the site you bought it from and spread the word. Reviews are hugely important to writers and they help other readers also.

Lightning Source UK Ltd.
Milton Keynes UK
UKHW021044051221
395029UK00005B/168